A Timely Affair

JANICE BENNETT

ZEBRA BOOKS
KENSINGTON PUBLISHING CORP.

P9-AQX-596

ZEBRA BOOKS

are published by

Kensington Publishing Corp.
475 Park Avenue South
New York, NY 10016

First printing: March, 1990

Printed in the United States of America

For Courtney, Curtis, Ida, Karen, Margaret, Ronnie and Terry. Here's looking at us.

Chapter 1

Belinda paused in the doorway, too awed to do more than stare. So this was Almack's! Her large brown eyes widened with excitement as her eager gaze swept the room. Never had she seen so many leaders of the ton gathered together, so many notables, so many people who had been pointed out to her with an air of hushed reverence by her godmama. There was the Countess Lieven with Mrs. Drummond-Burrell and Princess Esterhazy. And Beau Brummell himself! And just beyond him . . .

She swallowed hard, fighting down sudden nerves. Beyond him stood the tall, Corinthian figure of the Marquis of Allbury. In spite of her resolve to keep her wayward heart under control, that unruly organ beat faster. Abruptly, she turned away. With so many beautiful, important ladies in the room, what chance did she have that he would even notice her?

"Miss Layton?" Lady Jersey swept up to her.

Belinda looked back at her in amazement, then stared past the club's patroness to the elegant figure of the marquis who came up behind her. Belinda opened her mouth but was unable to speak.

"May I present the Marquis of Allbury as a suitable partner for the waltz?"

7

As if in a dream, Belinda accepted his offered hand. He was so tall . . . If only she could flirt with him, as she knew any other lady would do without hesitation. Allbury was the biggest prize on the Matrimonial Mart! And she was nothing but a country mouse who would bore him.

"Well, my little mouse?" he asked, unconsciously echoing her thoughts. "Did you think I would forget you?"

A deep rumble penetrated Andrea Wells's consciousness, jarring her out of the delightful world of the novelist's weaving. The noise grew steadily to deafening pitch and the approaching underground train rounded the bend, bursting out of the darkness of the tunnel into the artificial light of Green Park Station. It slowed and screeched to a halt only a few feet away from her.

Back to reality. With a wistful sigh, Andrea closed the book and placed it with loving hands into her giant shoulder bag. The fictional Regency era, with its enjoyable characters and elegance of manners, would wait for her.

The doors of the train cars slid wide with a mechanical hiss and the London commuters crowded out onto the cold cement platform, one line-change nearer to reaching home. Andrea huddled deeper into her down-filled jacket, inched closer with the impatient crowd, then climbed aboard. She barely managed to find a seat before the doors snapped shut behind the last passengers and the train lurched forward and plunged into blackness. In only minutes the subway would reach Charing Cross Station, the next stop on the Jubilee Line. A fun and fast way to get about, but it lacked the charm of a curricle-and-four or even a hackney carriage.

Resolutely, Andrea thrust such nonsense from her mind and concentrated on the advertisements plastered along the interior of the car. She had come to England to see *all* the sights, not just the ones mentioned in the

8

Regency novels she loved. And she'd made a good start on it today. She was exhausted.

At least she hadn't had to walk all over London. But by the time she reached the sanctuary of her luxurious hotel just off Trafalgar Square, she'd have been grateful if she never had to take another step. The combination of jet lag and all-day sightseeing had done her in. Hiding in her room, ordering from room service, and spending the evening curled up in bed with the fictional Belinda and the Marquis of Allbury to keep her company suited her mood to perfection. She couldn't think of a better way to complete her first full day in London.

While she waited for the elevator, she glanced into the lobby newspaper stand and scanned the headlines. A scandal rag, with two-inch-high letters proclaiming that the next royal baby would be fathered by an alien, caught her eye and she grinned, unable to resist. She bought it, then stepped into the lift for the ride to the nineteenth floor.

Idly, she opened the paper and glanced over the entertaining sheets. The header about a two thousand-year-old mummy found in a peat bog and clutching a Sony Walkman appealed to her. Then a surprisingly clear photograph which showed a painting of a gentleman in Regency-era dress caught her eye.

And held it. She drew a slow breath to steady herself, but it didn't work. Bemused, she stared at the arresting face, her mind in an unaccustomed whirl. Here was a man—a real man, rugged and masculine—and strong-willed if his jutting chin was anything to go by. He could serve as the model for a romantic hero in any novel—and one about whom she would want to read, over and over. With difficulty, she dragged her gaze from the enigmatic face and looked instead at the caption, which promised the details of a two hundred-year-old family curse

9

returning to haunt the present occupant of what appeared, from a second photo, to be a sinister old mansion.

The elevator door opened, startling Andrea. Back to reality, she reminded herself somewhat ruefully. Stifling a yawn, she tucked the paper under her arm and told herself she could wait until dinner to read his story.

Right now, all she wanted was to get off her feet. Her room, which stood only halfway along the plush, carpeted hall, seemed miles away. But she made it and let herself in with the key. Quiet comfort greeted her.

She tossed the newspaper onto the bed, then sent her heavy purse after it. On the whole, it had been a day well spent. The two different tours of London helped her get her bearings, and her free time acquainted her with the ins and outs of the Underground system. Tomorrow she could begin to satisfy her longings. She would visit every locale ever mentioned in a Regency novel, and love every moment of it.

Exhausted, she sank into a chair, kicked off her shoes, and put her feet in their heavy wool knee socks onto a low table. Jet lag was the pits. Dinner would just have to wait for a bit. As if of its own volition, her hand reached across the bed and snagged the novel that had fallen out of the top of her bag. Opening it with a contented sigh, she allowed herself to submerge into the delights of a long-ago Wednesday evening at Almack's and a waltz in the arms of a handsome marquis.

When the phone rang, her heart skipped a beat, then settled. The modern device intruded, having no business in the historic world of the novel that enveloped her. She tried to ignore the offensive instrument but it didn't do any good. It rang again, insistent.

Andrea marked her place in the book and laid it aside with deliberation, allowing the phone to make its third demand for her attention. She'd expected this call, though part of her hoped it wouldn't come. Jim must have found her letter on his desk that morning.

On the fourth ring, she rose from her chair and crossed to the bedside table where the instrument sat. It might be the desk clerk calling about the tour brochures she requested. But she doubted it. On the fifth ring, she picked up the receiver.

"Hello?" Keep it calm, Andrea ordered herself. Don't let him get to you.

"Andrea?" Jim Borman's voice reached her, clipped and angry. "Where the hell have you been? This is the fourth time I've called today! I was beginning to think your sister gave me the wrong hotel. Didn't they give you my messages? Or aren't you returning any calls?"

"Not while I'm on vacation. And yes, thank you, Jim. I'm having a lovely time. London is terrific. The weather is cold and overcast, but it hasn't snowed yet. I hope it will by Christmas." She finished on a note of false brightness.

Over the line, across the vast ocean that separated them, she could hear his teeth grind. The sound afforded her immense satisfaction.

"Don't be flippant." He didn't bother to hide his exasperation. "I found your letter of resignation on my desk this morning. What the hell do you mean by quitting?"

"I told you before I left I was going to." She sat down on the bed and smoothed a few strands of long blond hair toward the braid that hung down her back. Her hand only shook a little.

"Andrea—!" He broke off, then rallied. "Look, honey, just because we had a fight, that doesn't mean you had to leave the firm. Nettle and I have been talking about offering you a partnership, you know."

Was he dangling a carrot in front of her nose? The analogy insulted her. She straightened up. "Nettle,

11

Borman and Wells, Accountants?" Her tone took on a deceptive sweetness. "Oh, I'm sorry. You'd planned on Nettle, Borman and Borman, hadn't you?"

His voice changed, making him sound colder than usual. "You know I want to marry you."

"Yes, then you could own two thirds of the business instead of just half. Controlling interest."

"Well, why not? Come on, Andy, even you've said old Nettle isn't going after the right kind of clients. If I— we—could make the decisions, we could take on a couple of really major accounts. I need your support."

"All you need is a yes man to agree with you."

"Just someone to back me up with Nettle. I lost a big bonus because of him. If you'd been a partner, I could have pushed that deal through."

"I'm not interested in a business merger with you, Jim."

He drew an audible breath. "Look, Andy, maybe I said a few things I shouldn't the other night, but we were both pretty mad, remember. And rushed, with you leaving for England the next day."

"Oh, I do remember, believe me. But I meant every word of it."

The unmistakable grinding sounded again, and she grinned. At last, after two years, she had finally succeeded in turning the tables, putting him on the defensive instead of herself. A triumph, but a disturbingly hollow one. For most of those two years, she had honestly thought she loved him.

He broke the silence that stretched between them. "When you get back next week—"

"I bought an open-ended ticket, so I can stay in England up to a month. And I don't think I'm going home one minute before I have to."

"Why don't I fly over for a few days so we can talk? I can take some time, I don't have to begin Taylor's year-

12

end closings till after Christmas."

"No." The syllable came out sharp and uncompromising. "Didn't you listen to a thing I said the other night? I don't want to marry you. We . . ." She groped for the words to express how she felt, then fell back on a term that appeared often in the Regency novels she read. "We shouldn't suit."

"We get along fine."

"As long as everything goes your way, you mean. But you don't like me to have ideas that don't agree with yours."

"What . . . ? Oh, that nonsense again, is it? Are you still upset because I said romance novels are trash? Now, really, Andy, you're an intelligent, well-educated woman. You're not going to let something that silly come between us, are you?"

Her hand clenched on the phone. "No. But it has nothing to do with our respective tastes in reading material. It *has* to do with your making judgments and decisions without knowing the facts. *And* with your not listening when I tell you something."

"All right, I'm listening now. *Why* do you read those . . . what did you call them?"

"Regency novels." She spoke the words through gritted teeth, then explained, with exaggerated patience, for at least the fifth time. "Books that take place in England around the time of the Napoleonic War, when George III was declared mad and his son was made regent. And I read them to escape from the pressures of work—exactly the same reason you read."

"But I choose good—"

"These books are every damn bit as good as the stuff you like!" With difficulty, she controlled her temper. "I don't happen to like reading about drugs and Vietnam and underworld shoot-ups and extramarital affairs. I prefer a world where etiquette, manners, and a sense of

13

personal honor mattered!"

"This is ridiculous! We're arguing over a bunch of stupid books. Look, Andy, I know you need a vacation. Things have been pretty hectic around here, with the Petite Cafe chain having fiscal year-end last month. Go ahead, take a couple of extra weeks and relax. Your job will be waiting when you get back."

She closed her eyes, counted to ten, then glared at the receiver. She could picture Jim sitting in his leather and chrome office, looking out over the mid-December snow that covered the Minneapolis streets. And she could picture herself married to him, trapped by his ruthless and occasionally unethical business standards. The thought was enough to give her hives.

"I don't want the job." She snuggled into the comforting softness of her Icelandic wool sweater, purchased that afternoon during her tour's free hour at Harrods.

"You're throwing away your career?" Apparently, he found that prospect more incomprehensible than her not wanting to be his wife.

"Not in the least. I'm only twenty-seven, I have an MBA, I'm a damn good CPA, I know computers, and I've got over two years of experience in a respected accountancy firm. I can find another job easily."

"Andrea—" For the first time, he sounded worried.

"Good-bye Jim. And Merry Christmas." She hung up the phone. This time, she counted out a full minute. After all, he had to go through overseas lines and the hotel operator.

When she reached fifty-nine, the phone rang.

Resolutely, she turned her back on it.

Dinnertime, she decided. It might be early, only just after six, but it was dark outside with all the chill of a December night. Under the circumstances, she would eat downstairs, in that rather posh-looking restaurant she

14

had spotted just off the lobby. The peremptory rings of the phone followed her into the luxurious bathroom where she drowned them out by the simple expedient of slamming the door and turning on the water full force.

When she emerged ten minutes later, a reassuring silence greeted her. She changed her socks and tight jeans for stockings and a midcalf camel skirt, and pulled the soft sweater low over her slender hips. Grabbing up her purse and newspaper, she hurried out of the room. As she locked the door behind her, the phone rang again.

She never could explain anything to Jim. Once he had an idea fixed in his mind, nothing short of dynamite would dislodge it. She jabbed at the elevator button with undue force, then tapped the folded paper with an impatient finger while she waited.

The elegant interior of the restaurant in which she presently found herself did much to soothe her nerves. A hostess guided her to a table in a far corner where the subdued lighting provided an intimate atmosphere. If only she had someone with whom to share it. When a waiter appeared, she ordered sherry and accepted his recommendation of sirloin tips with a burgundy and mushroom sauce. Settling back to wait, Andrea regarded her fellow diners.

It took only minutes for her to realize she was the only person eating alone. Well, not quite alone, perhaps. Jim's unsettling presence hovered about her, as possessive and irritating as if he were there in person. She'd replace him. There was another man—or at least the portrait of one— awaiting her attention. And she would very much like to learn something about him.

After glancing at the fanciful headers for the unbelievable stories on the first few pages, she found the photo again. Irrationally, her heart lifted. By the dim light of the restaurant's chandeliers, she studied the full-length portrait. She wished she could see it more clearly,

15

for the gentleman's features fascinated her.

She couldn't quite define his expression. Sardonic, perhaps, in true heroic fashion? Were his eyes wicked, gleaming with devilish amusement, or were they world-weary and bored? And the tragedy was that she would never know. She thrust a pang of yearning aside. It was ridiculous to fall for a man dead nearly two hundred years.

Resolutely, she turned to the story. But between the small print and the insufficient light, she failed to make out more than a few words, and most of those capitalized names. "Greythorne Court" must be the crumbling mansion, but the gentleman most certainly was not Catherine the Great. Nor did the reference to the "Imperial Star" make any sense, though that name struck a chord in her memory. A diamond, she thought. It might well be the jewel that glittered in his neckcloth. A careful scrutiny of the caption beneath the photo revealed him to be Richard Westmont, first and only Viscount Grantham.

That was certainly intriguing. She could only regret not being able to decipher the story. Instead, she contemplated the probably sinister character of a man who had brought down a curse upon his family; he must have been a villain rather than a hero. With a sigh, she folded the paper once more, shoved it inside her already full purse, and turned her attention to the dinner presented to her by an effacing waiter.

By the time she finished her sirloin tips she had succeeded in banishing Jim from her thoughts. She ended the meal with chocolate mousse and brandy-laced coffee and felt much more at peace with the world. Rummaging through her bag, she found her wallet and paid her check.

According to her watch, it wasn't even seven-thirty yet. For once, though, time didn't seem to matter; she

16

was dead tired. She returned to her room, got ready for bed, and reached for the scandal sheet.

It wasn't in her purse. Andrea sat down on the edge of her mattress, a frown creasing her brow. She must have taken it out during her search for the money. Disappointment, surprising in its intensity, filled her. She would have to wait until tomorrow, when she could buy another copy, to read about Viscount Grantham.

At least she still had Belinda and Allbury to keep her company. Armed with the book, she crawled under the comforter and slipped contentedly back into the elegant, if fictional, world of Almack's and London at the height of the Season. When the phone rang, she rolled over and gritted her teeth until, some fifteen rings later, silence returned.

She spent the remainder of the evening engrossed in the pages of her novel, grateful for the writer's recreation of the Regency era. It must have been a marvelous time of elegance, manners and etiquette, of beautiful gowns and waltzes, of noble titles and influential men. Right along with the country-bred Miss Belinda Layton, Andrea enjoyed solving the protocol of seating a difficult dinner party. To her delight, they struggled with the tricky problems of who outranked whom, who possessed political significance, and whose title was the oldest and most important.

At last, with a sigh, Andrea laid the book aside, her eyes too tired to continue reading. She removed her contacts and placed them on the bedside table where even her blind gropings in the morning couldn't miss them. As she settled down, she couldn't help but wonder if that glorious, glittering world of the novels possessed any reality beyond the imagination of a few writers.

Wouldn't it be wonderful to know for certain! It would be such fun to see London as it appeared then, unchanged, the way the people of the Regency era knew

17

it . . . She drifted off to sleep with that tantalizing thought playing about the corners of her mind.

She did not stir again until the pale but determined wintry sunlight seeped through the curtains into her hotel room. For several minutes she remained lost in a pleasant daze in which fantasy interwove with reality, and the Regency period, not the present, was real. She waltzed at Almack's in the arms of a dark-haired, glinting-eyed Corinthian hero who put the fictional Allbury to shame. Her flowing gown swirled about her as they danced to the lilting strains of a chamber orchestra. Overhead, hundreds of candles flickered in crystal chandeliers.

The light intensified, and Andrea closed her eyes tightly, trying to deny the intrusion of morning. Her dream slipped away and she reached out, trying to follow her hero, but he was gone. She rolled over, filled with a vast longing to follow him. She knew him somehow, recognized him from somewhere. Perhaps, if she tried, she could capture him once more . . . She curled into the soft, unfamiliar bed, surrounded by the warmth of the down comforter.

The ringing of the phone, loud and urgent, roused her. Groaning, she groped for her watch and held it away from her face as she peered farsightedly at the dial. It remained a blur.

The phone rang again, persistent. After a moment's hesitation, she picked up the receiver. Somehow, she must convince Jim she was fed up.

"Andrea?" He sounded relieved to have reached her. "Look, honey, we've got to talk."

She gave up the struggle with her watch and set it down on the covers. "What time is it, Jim?"

"It's just after midnight—no, twelve-thirty—here. That would make it about six-thirty, your time."

"You woke me up."

18

"I haven't been to bed yet. I called an airline and I can get a flight tomorrow afternoon. Will you meet me?"

"No." She struggled up to a sitting position, drew her knees up to her chest, and hugged herself with her free arm. "We don't have anything to talk about."

"Because I don't measure up to those damned heroes you're always reading about? Andy, no man could! They only exist in the warped imagination of female writers."

She let that pass. "I don't expect a man to be 'perfect.' Just to have some sense of honor."

Silence answered her. Then, at his stuffiest, Jim began: "If you're referring to the Stapleman-Edgemont account . . ."

"Yes, I am, among others."

"If a man wants to get ahead in business he has to bend a few rules. You know that." Now he merely sounded conciliatory. "Listen, Andy, I'll wait a few days before I fly over. You're probably right, you need some time alone. I'll call you later, okay, honey?"

"Don't bother, Jim." But as she hung up the phone, she knew it was hopeless. He'd keep calling. If she hadn't paid the exorbitant hotel rates in advance, she'd be tempted to move.

And that thought reminded her of where she was—and the sights waiting for her today. Not even Jim could depress her for long when Bond Street, Grosvenor Square, and Hyde Park all beckoned. And she would walk down St. James's Street, in honor of every Regency miss who had been barred from that gentlemen's haunt.

She wiped long, loose hairs from her face and reached for her contacts. With these in place, she was not only able to find her watch where she had dropped it in the soft folds of blanket but also to read the dial. Six-forty. A bit early, but she had so much ground to cover today!

She ordered breakfast from room service and hurried into the bathroom to wash her face and dress. By the time

19

her meal arrived, she had put on her makeup, jeans, and a bulky cowl-necked sweater. Sitting at the small table, she lifted the lid from her plate of scrambled eggs, toast, and grilled tomatoes and studied the "Regency novel tour of London" list she had created for herself.

What a day awaited her! With the "Official Tourist Information" map spread before her, complete with its listings of the Underground stations, she went to work planning her morning. Her practical, businesslike mind chided her for taking so much pleasure in so fanciful a pursuit, but a deep, inner voice answered back "why not?" She deserved to indulge in a little escapism after Jim's manipulations of the past few months.

Having settled that argument with herself, she collected her jacket and purse. A quick check in a mirror assured her that her hopelessly straight blond hair remained neatly in the braid that reached almost to her waist. She hurried out to the elevator.

Five minutes later, she emerged into the damp, overcast morning and shivered. There might well be rain before afternoon. But that wouldn't slow her down. Nothing would stop her from enjoying the Regency-era sights that filled the books she loved.

Her "go-as-you-please" pass, permitting her unrestricted use of the subway trains, proved invaluable. The Jubliee Line carried her straight to Bond Street station, from which point she strolled to her heart's delight through fashionable Mayfair.

Her first goal, by way of Brook Street, had to be Grosvenor Square so she could see for herself the rows of stately mansions. The American Embassy might now occupy one side, but if she concentrated, very hard, she could banish the cars and modern intrusions that crept in and envision the square as it might once have looked.

She walked on through the increasing drizzle, happy just to know that the streets she traversed had existed in

Regency times. She could almost see the characters about whom she read walking or driving right along with her. There could be no denying the age of the stately homes that lined the roads, and she steadfastly ignored the traffic.

Mount Street led her to Berkeley Square and Bruton Street, which she followed to New Bond Street. Here she was in her element. Stores might have changed hands, some had not been founded until the late 1800's, but many still stood exactly where they had since Regency times. She slowed her steps, not wanting to miss a single storefront or any of the signs and plaques that dated the fascinating shops.

Then at last, before her, stood Piccadilly. Fortnum & Mason, Hatchard's. . . . She checked her notes for the addresses, then walked faster, eager to enter these famous shops that had been open since the 1700's.

Just entering, however, was not quite enough. Nor was browsing. But the shops proved quite willing to send her purchases to her hotel, so no worries of weight or bulk raised their ugly heads. She soon lost herself in selecting suitable gifts for her family and friends back home.

Not until almost two o'clock did her energy give out. She emerged from a haberdasher's, whose sign proclaimed that it had been in business since 1783, into a steady rain. Ahead of her stood a pub with a sign in a window announcing luncheon specials. Shelter, food, and rest—at this moment, she couldn't possibly want anything more.

Fortified by a steak-and-kidney pie and a half pint of ale, she felt ready to continue her pilgrimage. The icy breeze still whipped loose strands of hair into her eyes, but at least the rain had let up. Andrea consulted her map, ignored the weather, and started briskly down the busy road past the Ritz Hotel. Another block and she reached St. James's Street.

At the corner, she paused and looked about, trying to envision elegant gentlemen "on the toddle" to their clubs. But the sidewalks were deserted except for two middle aged women in polyester pantsuits. At least there would be no one to gossip about her shocking conduct in walking down this street where once no female with any claims to gentility would dare to have been seen!

On that whimsical thought, she started slowly forward in search of White's, Number 37. She looked about, eager, then spotted the building just across from her.

Fairness forced her to admit it wasn't anything out of the ordinary—but it hadn't been famous for its architecture. Only its Bow Window. And that, she was thrilled to note, was very much in evidence. With a sigh of pure contentment, she examined every line. If only she could enter those sanctified portals, what memories they must hold, what stirring events must have occurred within those walls!

Perhaps if she really studied it, she could imagine a "tulip of the ton" or perhaps a "buck of the first head" strolling up the street and entering the club. Allowing the suppressed romantic within her full rein at last, she closed her eyes tightly, concentrated, then opened them again. The sounds of Piccadilly traffic reached her.

Only she wasn't alone anymore. A man, dressed in yellow pantaloons, a cutaway coat, Hessian boots, and a tall beaver hat, sauntered down the road, swinging an ebony cane in one gloved hand. How perfectly marvelous—and right on cue, as if she really had conjured him up from the past! He must be attending some fancy-dress function at one of the clubs that still lined St. James's.

He didn't so much as glance at her. But to her surprise, there was something familiar about him. Andrea stared hard, trying to place it. The dark, thickly curling hair that protruded from beneath his high-crowned beaver, the jutting chin . . . It hit her, suddenly. If she didn't know better, she would swear he was Viscount Grantham, the man whose portrait had appeared in the scandal rag!

He reached the entrance of White's, went right past it, then turned toward the Bow Window. As Andrea watched in disbelief, the famous window faded. In its place—or rather, superimposed right over the top— appeared stairs and a doorway. The man walked up those nonexistent steps, the hazy door in the center of the equally hazy bow window opened, and he entered the club. The door and stairs vanished behind him.

Chapter 2

Andrea blinked in an attempt to clear her obviously fuzzed contacts. White's stood before her, the door and window just where they ought to be. Well, her imagination really *did* gain the upper hand for once—and with a vengeance!

Was this what all that novel-reading did to her? Made her long so much for a bygone era that she began to see things? She gave herself a mental shake, then looked searchingly about. Much to her relief, the street remained empty except for the puddles that formed in the steady drizzle.

Still, she hurried away, unsettled. She had come to St. James's Street to see the sights mentioned in Regency novels, not indulge in romantic visions. With resolution, she strode down the block to Boodle's, number 28, her next destination.

By the time she reached it, she felt a measure better. She never realized she possessed such vivid daydreams—or that the picture of Viscount Grantham haunted her! Forcing the uncanny incident from her mind, she returned her attention to the club before her.

Boodle's was really quite an attractive structure. The blackened brick and stucco lent it character, but she knew little about it. Heroes in the novels were often members, but seldom actually visited the place. Scenes in gentlemen's clubs were usually restricted to White's, Watiers or the occasional—and unspecific—gambling hell.

Brooks's stood almost directly across the street, but it did not hold her interest for long. Heroes invariably were Tory in their politics and did not visit this haunt of the Whigs.

She turned and looked back up the street toward White's. No mysterious figures prowled the sidewalk, everything appeared normal. That's what jet lag and indulging in ale in the middle of the day got her. From now on, her fantasies could just remain in the back of her mind.

She glanced at her watch and her good intentions fled. It was almost four o'clock. How could any real Regency novel lover *not* stroll through Hyde Park at this hour? She consulted her map, then hurried along Cleveland Row, which bordered St. James's Palace at the end of the street. At the corner, she turned down the Stable Yard.

Heading along the Mall brought her to the Queen Victoria Memorial. She spared this only the briefest of glances, for although she knew she should admire it, it hadn't been there in the early 1800's, and at the moment all her thoughts focused on that era. Knowing full well she was being silly, her pace quickened as she followed Constitution Hill between Green Park and Buckingham Palace Gardens.

And there, across Piccadilly, was her goal. Traffic roared about her. She waited until it was clear, then ran to the safety of Hyde Park Corner. Opposite her stood Apsley House, Wellington's home, which had been converted into a museum in his honor. But that could wait for a later visit; it was three fifty-five . . .

Her heartbeat quickened in anticipation, refusing to be

stilled. It might be ridiculous, but it was almost four o'clock, the hour of the Fashionable Promenade! And here she was, just entering Hyde Park. If only she might be a passenger in a racing curricle—or better, driving her own high-perch phaeton, perhaps with a pair of perfectly matched grays harnessed to the shafts! Well, barring that, she would stroll along the walkways and try to decide whether or not the vehicles would have followed the current Carriage Drive. And Rotten Row, the tanbark, even the Serpentine all waited to be discovered.

In a state of near bliss, she wandered along paths between dormant hedges and tried to envision these with spring foliage. She had no idea when the fashionable afternoon ramble through the park had faded in popularity, but today she would make it in memory of all those great ladies, Tulips and Pinks of the Regency.

When a horse pulling a carriage trotted toward her, her heart almost stopped. This was no imaginary or ghostly vehicle, however, but a very modern one, and one for hire, at that. Delighted, she stepped forward and hailed it.

The driver pulled up, and Andrea climbed up to the seat. Closing her eyes, she swayed with the movement of the vehicle and wondered if it were "well-sprung." She had no idea, nothing with which to compare it.

For a brief moment, her impulse to dream again won out. What fun it would be if she could open her eyes and find herself in a barouche, the park filled with Exquisites, and leaders of Society! But to her mingled relief and regret, only joggers, not Park Saunterers, met her searching gaze. Not so much as a single Buck or Blade could she see. Considering her experience before White's, she was rather glad.

As they neared the end of their circuit, another carriage came toward them, pulled by four magnificent black horses. Not a modern vehicle, but an antique curricle—or perhaps a reproduction! Andrea leaned forward, eager to catch a glimpse of the driver's elegant costume.

And she froze. A man whose features almost exactly resembled the portrait of Viscount Grantham drove past as if he didn't even see her carriage. Recovering, Andrea swiveled about in her seat to catch one more glimpse of him.

The road behind her lay empty.

Andrea blinked, then started as a rider emerged from a side path in the bushes and fell in behind. But it was a girl dressed in breeches and a fisherman knit sweater, with a raincoat covering her forward seat saddle and velvet hard hat. A very modern rider.

The carriage jolted to a stop. Andrea stood up slowly, almost afraid the vehicle would disappear out from under her. A chill breeze whipped loose tendrils of blond hair about her face, but it helped steady her reeling senses. She jumped to the ground, handed the driver several pound notes, and waved aside his offer of change. She felt shattered, as if every known convention of logic had just betrayed her.

Why was she seeing things? Had her years of reading Regency novels affected her mind? If so, she was likely to wind up in the modern equivalent of Bedlam. But both incidents seemed so *real!* And both times she saw the same man.

The same man. Richard something, Viscount Grantham. He of the two-hundred-year-old curse. She checked the direction those thoughts took her—it was impossible. He couldn't be haunting *her!* There was no reason for it. She had never even heard of him before the previous day, when she had seen his picture in that newspaper.

Thought of that portrait conjured him up so vividly in her mind that for one horrible moment he actually seemed to stand before her again. No, not horrible. Fascinating, intriguing. She would give a great deal to actually meet him.

And that, it dawned on her, explained these unsettling occurrences. Her breakup with Jim had upset her more than she realized. Viscount Grantham's portrait intrigued her, and subconsciously she cast him in the role of her personal hero. And after her wanderings through the Regency-era sights of London, it followed naturally that her tired, depressed brain projected images of her romantic yearnings. She was more of a fool than she realized.

A gust of icy wind set the park shrubs rustling. Andrea huddled deeper into her warm down jacket and wished she'd brought a woolen scarf. She felt cold, all the way through her being, with an emptiness that engulfed more than the merely physical.

But she couldn't just stand here shivering. She straightened up and started walking, quickly though without direction. It was all well and good to enjoy a light romantic fantasy, but this carried it to extremes.

Her best course would be to learn something about this Viscount Grantham. Perhaps then he would lose his tantalizing appeal. Now he was nebulous; she could make of him what she would. But knowing the details of his life would prevent her from molding him to her desires. She would buy another paper and read about his curse.

Darkness gathered about her, forcing her to slow. A quick check to orient herself revealed the location of the Curzon Gate and she struck out quickly for the Hyde Park Corner Underground station. She would ask at the hotel newsstand, then take the account up to her warm room to read.

In a surprisingly short time, she entered the comfortable, heated lobby. At the desk, a young clerk handed over her key, along with four messages. Three, she saw at

28

a glance, were from Jim. These she crumpled up without reading. The fourth was from her sister Cathy, saying—typically—to call only if she were in trouble and otherwise to enjoy her vacation.

Smiling at Cathy's casual orders, Andrea headed for the little stall near the elevators which displayed neat stacks of newspapers. But to her dismay, the one she sought was no longer there. A new edition stood in its place. Viscount Grantham would keep his secrets from her for another night.

More disturbed than seemed reasonable, she made her way up to her room. Her disappointment was all out of proportion! What did she care, anyway? She had allowed her romantic fantasies to run riot over her, but that wouldn't happen again. In a few days, Viscount Grantham would be the merest memory. And she would set about providing herself with a new heroic image right now.

With that intention, she ordered dinner from room service and retired with her novel to a steaming bath delicately scented with perfume. Within minutes, all problems fled before Allbury's frantic drive into the depths of the Hertfordshire countryside in search of his beloved Belinda who had fled from scandal in London. But all too soon, the story ended. Andrea closed the book, dried herself off, and headed to bed with another tale.

This time the hero was blond and blue-eyed and so classically handsome as to make maidens swoon at the sight of him. Not at all her type, Andrea conceded, but still a Corinthian who could "drive to an inch" and had more than once "popped in a hit over Jackson's guard." And he displayed a devilish sense of humor, much to the discomfiture of his heroine.

At last, her tired eyes scratchy from the lenses, the print began to dance on the page before her. Andrea laid the book aside, took out her contacts, and turned off the light. But almost as soon as her eyes closed, the image of her own dark and rugged hero rose in her mind. Waking recognition blended with the unreal quality of approaching sleep and her dream of the night before returned to enfold her. Grantham stood before her, tall, laughing, holding out his hand to her, beckoning her to come to him. Giving herself over to her longings, she slipped into the only world they could ever share.

This time they waltzed on a summer night in a ballroom filled with candles and flowers. A soft breeze brought the scent of roses through open French windows. He led her outside, where they danced on a terrace lit by tiny fairy lights. The quarter moon glowed softly and the night was so warm she had no need of her shawl. Gray eyes smiled down into hers as he released her slowly, lingeringly. He backed away, beckoning as he went . . .

"Come back!" She sat up, suddenly awake. Disorientation washed over her, then retreated. It was morning. Another dream. And again, it had been *him*.

She groped for her lenses and fitted them into her eyes. If only she could have followed him into the Regency era! But almost two hundred years separated them. Reality and fantasy just couldn't mix. It would be far better for her to forget him rather than learn more about him. She would get on with her sightseeing and relegate Viscount Grantham to the realm of dreams, where he belonged.

She pulled on her slippers and padded to the bathroom to throw cold water on her face. Drying vigorously with a soft towel helped shake off the last vestiges of sleep, though a lingering depression and regret remained. A taste of romance, no matter how insubstantial, left her everyday world that much emptier.

Determined to fill it, she concentrated on her morning. Her first destination would be King Street—all four of them listed on her map, if necessary—while she tried to locate Almack's. And then—well, the maze at Hampton Court might provide an enjoyable afternoon.

Her search for the famous Marriage Mart proved elusive, for not one tangible clue remained as to its actual location. Somewhere, of course, there must be a record, but she had no idea where to look. Like many earlier young ladies of insufficient birth or connections, entry was denied her.

> If once to Almack's you belong
> Like monarchs you can do no wrong.
> But banished thence, on Wednesday night
> By Jove, you can do nothing right.

The couplets from Pierce Egan's account of the ramblings of Tom and Jerry ran through her mind, making her smile. The holiest of holies, the social club that held the making—or breaking—of damsels bent on taking the town by storm and contracting brilliant alliances, was beyond her touch. By Jove, she did nothing right.

Since her attempt to storm the sacred portals of Almack's had failed, she turned her attention instead to finding Gentleman Jackson's Saloon. That meant Bond Street again, and possibly as fruitless a search as she had just undertaken. But she wouldn't give up without trying.

Nowhere could she remember reading if the famous boxing school were located on New or Old Bond Street. Not taking any chances, she began her search at the Piccadilly end, determined to walk slowly, reading signs, until she found her goal. It proved a pleasant stroll, if somewhat cold, passing before the aging buildings of brick and multi-paned glass.

At least her fantasies of the day before no longer intruded on her. Three hours had gone by without so much as a glimpse of a ghostly figure. Her practical mind was once again in control. With that comforting knowledge, the last lingerings of uneasiness faded away.

They returned in an unsettling rush the next moment. There, strolling toward her near the corner of Bruton Street, dressed much as she had seen him on St. James's Street the day before, came Viscount Grantham. Andrea shook her head to clear her mind, but he remained where he was, now looking into a window that displayed leather luggage so old fashioned as to belong in a museum.

A thrill danced up and down her skin, elusive, barely there. Not of fear, but of something she couldn't name. In a moment it vanished—along with the man and the display.

Not a trace remained. China dinner plates now filled the window and a girl in tight jeans with an obscene legend on the back of her leather jacket walked up and stared in.

Andrea looked about, frantic. Crowds of people filled the street, but not one of them seemed to have noticed anything strange. It was only she he haunted! But why? Who was Viscount Grantham and why did she keep seeing him?

This might all be nothing more than her fanciful yearnings, as she had decided the day before. But once she realized that, he shouldn't keep cropping up except in her dreams. Yet here he was again, in a different place and on a different day.

She shivered, and knew it was more than cold. The experience left her panicky, her pulse pounding, as if she had been touched by a breath of air from another era. Yet not fear, but desire, filled her. She longed to go to him, speak to him, cross the boundaries of time that separated them. But that was impossible.

She drew an unsteady breath, recognizing the truth. She had no choice. She *had* to learn something about

32

him, and as quickly as possible. That scandal rag, which reported his story—and his curse—was her best bet.

At the first newsstand, she found a current edition of the paper and obtained the address of the publisher. They would be bound to have back copies—and possibly even more information on file than had been included in the story. But if she ever revealed the reason for her questions, she would very likely appear in the next edition herself.

Thirty minutes later, though, as she stood outside the locked door of the paper's office on Fleet Street, her heart sank. Sunday? She hadn't even realized! Now what was she to do?

Pull herself together, for one thing. And then try thinking. Where could she get information about Viscount Grantham? The only thing she knew about him was the name of his home, Greythorne Court.

She could go to Somerset House, where all records of births, marriages, deaths, and wills were kept. But that would only give her the bare facts, just dates, names, and little else. She wanted to know so very much more. And besides, it would be closed on Sunday, too.

A guide book, perhaps? Even from that blurred picture, it had been obvious that Greythorne Court was a house of considerable size and antiquity. Perhaps she could find a history of the house. Or better yet, it might be one of the many stately British homes that opened their doors to tourists.

The idea—and determination—took root. She would visit Viscount Grantham's home. Just the thought set her spirits soaring. There was nothing she would rather do.

The first step would be to check her "Open-To-View" ticket, which gave her access to dozens and dozens of such homes. She set off back to her hotel at a brisk walk, driven on by a strange urgency.

The list stuck out from a pocket of her garment bag.

Eagerly, Andrea scanned the many names, only to set it aside at last in disappointment. Greythorne Court was not among them.

But even if the present owner didn't open the house to the general public, he might permit select tours to go through. And that she could find out easily enough. Andrea picked up her phone, dialed the desk operator, and asked to be connected with a travel adviser. Moments later, a woman's crisp voice answered her.

"I want to visit one of the stately homes, but I'm not certain which—if any—tour goes there. Can you help me?"

"Certainly. We have an alphabetical listing. Which one is it?"

"Greythorne Court."

"Just a moment, ma'am. Yes, here it is." She named a tour line.

Her heart beat rapidly with her excitement. "Can you book me a place?"

"If you will give me your room number, I'll call you back with more information."

Andrea complied, then hung up. Restless, she stood and paced about the room, unable to believe her luck. A guided tour of Greythorne Court! Surely, once inside, someone would be able to tell her all she longed to know.

The phone rang and she dove for it, completely forgetting her reluctance of only the day before to answer. The capable voice of the travel advisor greeted her ears. "There is a tour leaving every other Monday—one tomorrow and another in two weeks. They last six days and visit a total of seven stately homes in southern England, then finish off with a day in Bath. Greythorne Court is the sixth stop, just before Woburn Abbey. The accommodations are at either first-class hotels or country homes. There is even an Elizabethan coaching inn that has been remodeled." She named a staggering

34

price, then asked, "Are you still interested?"

"Yes!" For the opportunity of getting inside Grey-thorne Court, she would pay anything. "Is there room on tomorrow's tour?"

The arrangements made, Andrea hung up the phone and found that her hands trembled.

She sank down onto the bed and closed her eyes. Was it fate that a tour visited his home? She felt strangely as if he beckoned her. With every ounce of her will, she summoned up the image of Viscount Grantham in her mind.

"All right, you've issued your challenge," she whispered. "And I'm calling you on it. I'll meet you on your own territory."

Tiny goose bumps rose on her arms and set her skin tingling. Almost, the fanciful thought occurred to her, he answered for the echoes of a deep laugh sounded in her head. For one tantalizing, frightening moment, it seemed as if she stood at the brink of time and dared to look over the edge.

Chapter 3

Drizzling rain seeped down Andrea's neck and chilled her face where it was exposed between woolen scarf and hat. The tour driver loaded her garment bag and overnighter into the luggage compartment of the motorcoach, then turned to grab the next stack of cases. Andrea blinked the trickling drops from her eyes, shifted the strap of the tote provided by the tour, and climbed onto the bus.

On first impression, it was large and luxurious, just as the brochure had promised, complete down to the reclining seats. The insufficient leg room was an added bonus, she decided with mild sarcasm as she settled down by a window. She tucked the tote under the seat before her as if she were on an airplane. The brochure had also promised air-conditioning, but that wasn't one of her high priorities at the moment. A heater would be more appreciated.

The other passengers piled on, laughing and noisy. Children squabbled over seats and a couple of disgruntled preteen punks with green and pink brushes for hair and safety pins in their ears slouched down across the aisle from her.

Andrea turned away and pulled out the travel

36

brochure from her purse. It remained folded open to the page that gave a brief paragraph description of the last two estates they would visit. She reread the bit about Greythorne Court for perhaps the fiftieth time.

"Preserved as it appeared during the lifetime of Viscount Grantham, a perfect example of Regency-era living." The phrase ran over and over in her mind. A perfect example of Regency-era living. Wasn't that exactly what she had always longed to see? Secretly, she always felt she belonged in that bygone era. Now, finally, she could see all the details she had read about so often— the wall hangings, the furniture, the paintings and knicknacks.

Her reverie was interrupted by the guide for the coming week, who picked up the microphone and welcomed them all to the tour. The doors swung closed and the bus pulled away from the curb.

A thrill of anticipation raced through Andrea. In only a few short days, she would at last learn something of Viscount Grantham.

By dusk of the fifth day, as they left Blackfriars Abbey twenty miles outside of Salisbury, Andrea couldn't face the prospect of one more richly decorated, sprawling house. The image of Grantham no longer haunted her. She settled into her padded seat on the motorcoach, leaned her forehead against the window with her eyes closed, and gave way to a depressing fit of melancholy.

That wasn't getting her anywhere. To shake off her despondency, she pulled out her current novel and sought escape in the long-vanished era she loved.

Over an hour later, the motorcoach slowed and she glanced out the window into the darkness of the December evening. They had reached their hotel for the night, it seemed. The luxurious bus turned off the road into the gravel yard of a low, rambling Elizabethan inn. Andrea closed the book and stowed it into her huge purse.

"Oh! Now, *this* is beautiful!" The petite, elderly lady who occupied the seat next to Andrea leaned across her to get a better look at their accommodations for the night.

"It certainly is," Andrea agreed, managing a smile for the woman's enthusiasm. She couldn't see much by the motorcoach's large headlights as they pulled into what must once have been the coaching yard. As little as a century before it must have bustled with carriages and postilions calling for changes, with ostlers running up with fresh horses. Now, only cars parked there while their owners dined within.

It took nearly half an hour for the members of the tour to receive their room assignments and be escorted up the creaking old stair and along the rambling wings. Andrea found herself allotted a small rear bedchamber with a view of a kitchen garden drenched in moonlight. It proved strangely soothing.

She turned back into the room and unearthed her toiletries case from the bottom of her carryall. The shared bathroom, she had been assured, stood only three doors down the narrow hall. It was only a mild inconvenience, considering the age and beauty of the inn.

She had only just picked up a towel when the phone beside the quilt-covered bed rang. Surprised, she answered it.

"Andrea?" Jim's voice came across the line, sounding even more annoyed than usual.

Her stomach tightened and she forced herself to relax. "Yes, Jim? How are you?" Inane, she knew, but what could he expect?

"Damn it, why didn't you call or leave a message for me that you were going on some idiotic tour? Do you

38

have any idea what I had to go through to find you?"

"Didn't it occur to you that I might not want to be found?" She drew a long breath to steady herself. "Look, Jim, there really isn't anything to be said."

"Look, Andy—"

"I don't want to marry you, Jim."

"But . . ." He broke off, then: "Have you met someone else over there?" he demanded, suspicion rife in his voice.

An odd grin quirked up the corners of her mouth. "In a manner of speaking, yes."

The line went dead. Andrea replaced the receiver, a wistful smile just touching her lips. Jim was incapable of understanding her aversion to his questionable ethics, but another man was something to which he could relate. She wondered, with a touch of humor, how he would react if he discovered the "other man" had been dead nearly two hundred years.

Down the hall in the tiny bathroom, she rinsed her face and hands, then touched up her makeup. She returned the case to her room, then contemplated the prospect of finding her way downstairs without a map. It would be a challenge. As the door closed behind her, the phone rang once more.

She turned the skeleton key firmly in the lock and faced the dark corridor. Dim-wattage light bulbs hung at irregular intervals, their wires stapled to the ceiling to keep them from dangling in the guests' faces. It must have appeared delightfully eerie by candlelight. And dangerous, she realized, as she stumbled over a sunken section of flooring. Age might have charm, but it also contained a few pitfalls.

With renewed care, she traversed the uneven passage, down two steps, around a corner, up another step, along a cheerfully crimson-papered hall, down three stairs, around another corner where at last she found herself in the main corridor, facing the ancient, rough-hewn staircase. She descended to the lobby below, and the proprietor himself bowed her into the dining hall which must, until very recent times, have been the common room.

She paused just over the threshold and scanned the comfortably filled room. A trestle table near a mutli-paned window stood empty, and Andrea wended her way between the diners to it. When a waiter garbed in Elizabethan costume approached, she ordered a dry sherry and the specialty of the house, duck à l'orange.

Sipping her drink, she leaned against the wooden back of the bench and looked about. The inn's remodelers had done an admirable job of blending modern conveniences and necessities without destroying the atmosphere. Still, she would have given a great deal to have seen the place as it looked when it was first built. Or better—as it had appeared during the Regency, bustling with coaches and activity.

A sigh escaped her. She had visited a great number of sights, but London was now a modern city and the Regency era had vanished forever, buried beneath layer upon layer of everyday living. She might dream of seeing Hyde Park and Grosvenor Square exactly as they had appeared nearly two hundred years ago—and not just with the eye of her imagination—but it was a hopeless dream, and she knew it. Greythorne Court would be as close as she could ever come.

Her enthusiasm rose for the first time in days, banishing the unsettled feeling that lingered after Jim's call. She could hardly wait until the morrow. She probably should bring film and flash batteries for her camera, but somehow that thought seemed a sacrilege, out of character for the period. To do it properly, she really ought to provide herself with a sketching pad, as the young ladies in the novels always did. Unfortunately,

40

she couldn't draw anything recognizable by anyone—including herself.

As soon as she finished eating, she made her way through the wandering halls back to her room. In record time she prepared for bed, then curled up in a chair with her Regency novel. Unless she wanted Viscount Grantham to start haunting her dreams again, she had better replace him in her thoughts. Resolutely, she opened the book, found her place, and slipped happily into the novelist's world.

Lady Juliana stooped to cut the rosebud, then laid it with care amongst the others in her long basket. A shadow fell across her and she looked up into the dissolute face of the Duke of Arundel. He raised his quizzing glass to better examine her flowers.

"Delightful," he drawled. "But the blossom in your cheeks puts these to shame."

Those particular blossoms of which he spoke took on an even rosier hue. "La, your grace, what fustian you talk!"

"La," indeed! Andrea glared at the book; it was perhaps not the best choice to divert her mind this night. Did ladies really talk like that? And surely any female as gently bred as the sickeningly sweet Lady Juliana would never use a term like fustian! Flummery, maybe, but certainly nothing stronger.

Andrea shook her head in disgust. This Juliana was a simpering miss if she'd ever seen one! In real life, she would never be able to deal with a dissolute rake like Arundel. Though if one were to talk about reality, it wasn't likely that Regency-period men were really as "dissolute" as this writer professed. During the course of the story, the Duke of Arundel had already had three successive mistresses in keeping, described, in turn, as "a bit o' muslin," "a Cyprian," and "a high flier," and this was only Chapter Four! And Lady Juliana, orphaned at the tender age of three, had been raised by her vicar uncle

41

in the depths of the country and had never before met a rake. The girl simply didn't have what it took to deal with a Corinthian of Arundel's stamp!

Andrea closed her eyes. Now, if *she* were in Juliana's place . . . She had the advantage over a character in a novel. She was a modern female, not raised to believe herself inferior to a man. She had earned her own living for years. A "woman of experience," she could be called. She swallowed, shaken by a sudden realization. If she had lived during the Regency era, she would be on the shelf, a positive ape leader!

Well, it was a good thing not to be a schoolroom miss, she told herself firmly. It would be more fun to be an older heroine, one well versed in the arts of flirtation and at home to a peg in society. It really would be too uncomfortable to find herself at Almack's and have no notion how to go on!

She thrust the wistfulness of that last thought aside. Almack's had been closed for a very long time. Instead, since she dealt solely in the world of make-believe, she turned her thoughts to a perfect hero of her own.

Banishing the image of Viscount Grantham, she tried to conjure up another in her mind. He would have to be a rake, one past praying for and hardened against feminine wiles. But then he would meet her and her unusual qualities would intrigue him. He would try to forget her in a series of meaningless affairs, of course, but her image would haunt him until, drunk and furious, he would burst into her bedchamber in the dead of night, waving a special license and demanding that she upon the instant become his wife.

The corniness of the scenario thus created sent her off to bed giggling. Once huddled beneath the quilts, though, her errant mind returned to the fictional Duke of Arundel. She herself would be a much better heroine for him than that pathetic Lady Juliana with her countless baskets of flowers! No gently nurtured female had what it took to deal with dark, brooding eyes that smoldered with passion. They would frighten the proverbial socks off the shrinking violet!

Andrea snuggled down under the comforter, dismissed Juliana and her Arundel from her mind, and turned her attention back to her own unknown hero. He would have broad shoulders and his coats would fit as if they were molded to his form. He would need the assistance of his valet—or more loving hands—to help him into these exquisite creations. And he would patronize Weston, not Schultz, who catered to more dandified tastes. He would be every inch a Corinthian.

She indulged in a luxurious stretch and gave herself over to imagining every detail of this perfect creation of hers. He bore a striking resemblance to Viscount Grantham, she realized in dismay—a man who now had existence only in her dreams.

And there, she supposed, would be the only place she could ever find such a hero.

That thought still depressed her the following morning as the motorcoach tour set forth once more. She was a reasonable, capable woman, she chided herself. She did just fine on her own. Yet part of her still wanted a handsome, honorable, romantic hero to carry her off, ignoring her objections and kissing her until she was unable to protest any longer.

She stared out the window at the narrow country lane lined with high hedges. Over the tops she glimpsed fields, mostly dormant in the winter gloom. Puddles of water bordered the road, a remnant of last night's rain.

It wasn't like her to give in to such a maudlin mood. She closed her eyes, then opened them to stare bleakly up at a sky as dark as if it were approaching night.

The rounded roof of a stone tower caught at the corner of her vision. Through the hedges, she glimpsed an

Elizabethan manor in the distance. Greythorne Court? Her spirits lifted as she craned her neck, eager for any sight of it. A little farther along the road, the motorcoach slowed and made the precarious turn onto a gravel drive and passed through an iron-work gate.

Andrea sat up, alert, unable to drag her gaze from the house they slowly approached. This was not at all the decaying, sinister mansion she had envisioned from that hazy photograph in the scandal rag. If she had created a home for a hero in a Regency novel, it would have looked like this. Ivy covered the walls of the low, rambling building and framed the numerous mullioned windows. Chimneys rose from the strangest locations and a gray stone tower stood regally on the east side. On the west, a pile of broken stones poked out from a grass-covered knoll, separated by a crumbling wall from the timbered house—another tower, one that had fallen.

The bus pulled around the fountain at the center of the circular drive and Andrea rose to her feet, unable to sit still as they came to a stop. She climbed down to the gravel and looked about, spellbound, as the others pushed past. The expansive lawns, the formal gardens— everything was perfect! Beyond the broken tower there was even an ornamental lake, on which several graceful swans floated. Not even the threatening rain could dim the beauty of this estate. Every bit of it was exactly as she could want.

To her dismay, the tour group started ahead. Andrea wanted to stay where she was, gazing at the beautiful house. But it was was so perfect on the exterior, what must it be like inside? She hurried after the others, suddenly anxious to enter through the huge, arched wooden door held open by an elderly and very proper butler in period costume. Holding her breath in anticipation, she stepped into the hall where their tour guide gathered them together.

44

"This is the most perfect example of Regency-era living you are likely to see anywhere," the woman announced in her perfect expository tones. "The home has been kept exactly as it appeared in 1810, when its owner, Richard Westmont, first Viscount Grantham, was killed in the collapse of the West Tower."

The oddest tingling sensation ran across Andrea's skin, as if a breath of air just brushed her. Here, in his house, it was almost—almost!—as if she had stepped back in time. The surroundings bespoke a bygone era, the atmosphere held nothing of the modern world. A feeling of hushed expectancy hung about her, as if everything waited . . .

She moved away from the others, seeking to separate herself from these present-day intruders. Her gaze roamed about the hall, resting on the tapestries, the cavernous hearth that looked as if it could—and probably had—roasted an ox whole. Beneath her feet, the floor had been worked in green-and-white marble tiles, creating a bold geometric pattern. She found her throat strangely dry and tried to swallow.

"Richard was created Viscount Grantham for services performed while a member of the army fighting Napoleon," the guide continued. "He sold out after the death of his father, which followed closely on Richard's being severely injured in Spain. After Richard's death, the house passed into the hands of the earls of Malverne. Their ancestral home, Malverne Castle, adjoins this estate. But the earls never took possession of Greythorne Court. A rather unusual sales document, made up by Lord Grantham's father, William Westmont, specifically stated that his direct descendants must be permitted to live in the house for two hundred years.

"Now, if you will examine these hangings on the oak-paneled walls . . ."

The tour moved off and Andrea lost the thread of the

speech. Everything appeared exactly as she imagined. And the details! In awe, she looked about at the drapes, the gilt-framed paintings, the locked glass cabinets filled with snuff boxes, miniatures, and other small but exquisite antiques. The guide's voice droned on, but Andrea paid it little heed. At any moment, she almost expected to come face-to-face with Viscount Grantham. And this time, she wasn't so sure that he wouldn't see her.

They entered the book room and Andrea drew up short, her spirit soaring. It was as if she had walked into the past—literally, not just figuratively! She looked about, her eyes wide. Shelves lined the walls, filled with leather-bound volumes. A massive cherrywood desk stood to one side, and in the center of the room were placed several glass stands, one holding a jeweled knife, the others snuff boxes of every description.

"Here you see part of Lord Grantham's collection," the guide explained. "It began as a hobby when he was a very young man and, as you can see, he added extensively to it during his travels."

The guide turned and led the way through a number of connecting saloons to a music room decorated in tones of blue, creamy white, and gold. A harp, a pianoforte, and a harpsichord were carefully spaced about the chamber. She continued her prepared speech, but a pulsing buzz filled Andrea's ears, blocking out other sound.

As the others moved off once more, Andrea lagged behind, fighting an almost uncontrollable trembling. She turned about slowly in the middle of the room, bewildered, bemused, knowing only that she belonged here, in this house, in the period of time it represented.

With an effort, she marshaled her fanciful sensations and forced them back in line. She ran after the others, who had already returned to the Great Hall. They started up the Grand Staircase and Andrea trailed her fingers along the banister of polished mahogany. This was better than any novel come to life.

"And now we come to the Picture Gallery," the guide announced. "There are several exquisite paintings here. The one of the second Westmont is believed to be a Holbein. The one of Aurelia, mother of Richard, is definitely by Gainsborough. The painting of Isabella Westmont, on the eve of her marriage to Mr. George Brixton, is next, and is of inferior quality to another portrait of her in later life, with her five children from her second marriage to Mr. Giles Kendall. And over here we have one of Lord Grantham."

Andrea glanced at the sweet-featured face of the raven-haired woman, then turned to the other wall, where high, mullioned windows overlooked the drive. The tour group had paused before a portrait there, and Andrea's gaze came to rest on the epitome of her dreams.

Viscount Grantham. It was him, all right, the man whose image haunted her. She had conjured up surprisingly accurate glimpses of him, based solely on that black-and-white photograph of his portrait.

She studied him with care. Here was a face more resolute, more ruggedly handsome, more dashing and rakish than ever she could have imagined on her own. Black hair curled thickly about his head and a lock fell artlessly forward over his high brow. He looked directly at her, the piercingly gray eyes compelling her to move closer, to come to him, to reach out and take the painted hand held out to her.

Her insubstantial dreams and thoughts of her Regency novel tour slipped away, unnoticed. When the others moved on, she paid them no heed. Nothing mattered but this painted likeness, this man who had lived—and died—so very long ago. The Regency details of his costume, which should have enthralled her, faded into insignificance beside the man himself. Her gaze moved from his strong, tanned hand which held a riding whip, across his broad shoulders in their exquisitely fitting mulberry riding coat, to his square chin, the high cheekbones.

And those eyes, those magnificent eyes that held her entranced, that called to her as if across the years, drawing her closer, ever closer . . .

A rustle of skirts startled her. Andrea blinked, then turned to stare at a housemaid in Regency-style costume. It must have been copied from an original, for it looked perfect to Andrea. A white muslin apron and mobcap topped the high-waisted gown of gray fabric. The girl regarded Andrea with curious eyes, then bobbed her a curtsy, smiled shyly, and hurried past.

As Andrea's gaze followed her, the maid's figure blurred, then faded. In moments she became transparent, then simply vanished.

Chapter 4

Andrea backed slowly away, her eyes riveted to the spot where the maid had disappeared. It was impossible! Was the house haunted or was her mind again playing tricks on her? Just like it had done to her in London, when Viscount Grantham kept popping in and out of nowhere . . .

She turned to look back up at the portrait, but his enigmatic smile gave nothing away. What was it about that man that made her brain abandon its grip on reality and fabricate images? Only this time it had not been him that she saw. And also, she realized suddenly, her vision had seen *her!* Viscount Grantham had passed her each time as if she hadn't been there.

This wasn't real—this *couldn't* be real! But that maid had seemed so alive, no mere conjuration of a brain too deeply steeped in Regency novels. There had to be a logical explanation.

She had heard before about ghostly figures being seen in ancient manor houses. Was that it? An image projected across time of someone actually walking down the hall almost two hundred years ago? But that didn't explain the curtsy or smile!

She wouldn't entirely rule out ghosts, but that

explanation didn't satisfy her. Nor did the possibility that she had muddled her mind with romantic slush, as Jim darkly prophesied. She was quite sane—except for this tendency to see Regency-era people wandering about.

No, not Regency-era people, just Viscount Grantham, and now a servant in his home. The whole thing revolved around *him*. She walked up to his portrait and stood just far enough away so that she could gaze up into his face.

"What do you want from me?" she whispered.

His painted eyes stared back, unseeing yet compelling. They almost mocked her as they once again drew her into the mysteries of their steely-gray depths. She fell under their spell, losing herself in them, and time ceased to hold any meaning as the minutes slipped away.

"Are you all right, my dear?" A gentle, cultured voice broke in on her absorption.

Andrea jumped and turned to stare wide-eyed at a slender woman with silver hair arranged becomingly about her fine-boned face. Searching gray eyes met hers and Andrea swallowed convulsively. No visitor from the past, this time. The woman wore a very modern tweed skirt and silk blouse.

"Do you like Richard? That picture has always been a favorite of mine." The woman looked up at it, a fond smile warming her gentle expression. "He is my great-—I forget just how many greats—uncle."

"I . . . I'm sorry." Andrea looked about, confused. She felt disoriented, as if she had just emerged from some world isolated from the one in which she now found herself.

"Were you with the motorcoach tour? I'm afraid they left well over an hour ago."

"An hour?" Could she have been lost in that portrait for so long? "I . . . I'm terribly sorry! I had no idea. But—didn't they miss me?"

"I told them to go."

"You . . ." Andrea stared at her blankly.

The woman smiled. "I saw you looking at Richard, my dear, and thought you'd rather not be disturbed. I feel that way myself, sometimes. My butler will drive you to your hotel whenever you're ready."

"That's very kind of you." And the oddest part of it, Andrea realized, was that those words were no mere politeness. "I would have thought you'd be anxious to throw out intruders like me."

A strange smile just touched the woman's lips. A prickling sensation danced along the back of Andrea's neck—not of fear, but of nerves, as if something momentous had occurred but she was unable to quite put a finger on it. Andrea's gaze strayed back up to the portrait and she was unable to drag it away.

The woman's smile broadened as if she were pleased by Andrea's absorption with her distant relative. "Richard was a remarkable man, though somewhat bored, I fear, by civilian life. There were very few records of what he did while in the Army, but when he sold out he was a colonel, and he never purchased his promotions."

Andrea nodded slowly. The man in this portrait would be capable of taking on anything. "What happened to him? The guide said something about the West Tower?"

"Yes, a tragedy. And just when he had finally settled down, too."

Andrea hesitated only a moment. It behooved her to apologize again, thank the woman for her forbearance, and take her leave. But here was someone who knew all about Viscount Grantham—and was more than willing to talk about him. How could she resist the temptation? "Tell me, please!"

"Well, he was apparently very restless after selling out," the woman said. "He engaged in every dangerous sporting pursuit of his time, and I imagine he must have been rather free with what was known as the 'muslin

51

company.' You must understand, my information comes from letters kept by his sister Isabella, and I am quite certain she would not have been aware of the more—shall we say rakish?—details of his career."

"Probably not." Andrea's agreement was no more than a whisper. She was prepared to believe anything of this remarkable-looking man.

"Would you care for some tea?"

With reluctance, Andrea turned from the painting to look at the woman. She found she was being studied intently by those lovely gray eyes. Yet the scrutiny didn't make her feel uneasy; if anything, excitement filled her . . . At the prospect of learning more about Richard, Andrea told herself. With a last, backward glance over her shoulder at his portrait, she followed her hostess from the Long Gallery.

"Allow me to introduce myself," the woman said as they started down the curved Grand Stair. "I am Catherine Kendall, a descendent of Richard's sister Isabella and her second husband, Giles Kendall."

"Andrea Wells. I . . . I'm an American."

"Andrea." Miss Kendall breathed the name in satisfaction. "And an American. Such a lovely name," she added.

Andrea looked at her, curious. It was almost as if the woman had guessed her name and was pleased to discover herself correct. Was she a psychic?

"Oh, Jane!" Miss Kendall paused in the Great Hall and called to a maid in a costume almost identical to the one worn by the apparition Andrea had seen upstairs. But there was nothing otherworldly—or othertimely—about the girl who hurried up to her mistress. "Please bring tea to the Gold Saloon, will you?" With a nod to dismiss the maid, Catherine Kendall ushered Andrea into an apartment not visited by the tour.

Andrea crossed the threshold and stood transfixed as

her gaze drifted over the room. Even the private living quarters mirrored Regency times. She would have expected Miss Kendall's rooms, at least, to show signs of modernization, yet not even a telephone was in evidence.

She turned to see Catherine Kendall peering at her closely through delicate gold-rimmed spectacles. The impression of a searching scrutiny vanished in a moment, and Miss Kendall came forward, smiling.

"It is a beautiful house!" Andrea looked away, embarrassed. "It is very kind of you to put up with me like this."

"Not at all, my dear. I'll enjoy talking about Richard—with you."

Andrea met the earnest gray eyes and thought she understood. They shared a fascination with Grantham. Or was it more than that? The entire Regency-era atmosphere of the house, so carefully preserved by its occupant . . . "You would have liked to live back then!" Andrea blurted out, recognizing in that instant a kindred spirit.

A telltale flush crept into Miss Kendall's cheeks. "For me it's impossible. But it's what you've wanted, also." She made the words a statement of fact.

Andrea nodded. Her trembling started again and she turned away, then impulsively, back to the woman. "Tell me more about Richard. You said he was bored after selling out?"

Miss Kendall seated herself in a wing-back chair upholstered in cream and gold and gestured for Andrea to take the matching one opposite. "He committed almost every crazy indiscretion and extravagant folly out of restlessness, until his cousin came to live with them. If only he had lived—" She broke off, shaking her head, as the maid Jane wheeled in a tea cart, complete with milk jug and sugar bowl.

She poured out, urged Andrea to try a scone, and

proceeded to converse about the weather, the delights of having a Scottish cook, and other unexceptionable topics. Andrea made polite rejoinders, but sensed the withdrawal on the part of the other woman. Miss Kendall's thoughts seemed elsewhere, as though her mind busily weighed possibilities while she mouthed polite nothings. Disclosures about Viscount Grantham appeared to be at an end.

Andrea finished her tea and rose to her feet. "I've intruded on your time long enough."

"Not in the least, my dear. Would you like to know more about Richard?"

"Very much so!"

"Then would you care to come back tomorrow? I should be delighted to show you about the rest of the house, the parts not normally open to a tour." She held out her hand. "Until tomorrow, then."

Catherine Kendall's butler drove Andrea to the hotel on the outskirts of Bath where the tour intended to put up for the night. An early dusk darkened the sky as she sought out the tour guide, made her excuses, and took formal leave of her escort for the past few days. This taken care of, she went straight to her assigned room where she remained, staring blindly into space, her mind in total confusion.

Why was Miss Kendall being so hospitable to a stranger? There was that bond between them, their fascination with the Regency era—with Richard. Miss Kendall must have sensed it before they even spoke, while Andrea stood before Richard's portrait, or she never would have permitted her to remain when the tour left. Or was there more to it than that? The way Miss Kendall looked at her—almost as if she recognized her and was trying to place where they had met before.

Andrea lay back on her bed and closed her eyes.

Unbidden, the painted image of Richard Westmont, Viscount Grantham, rose in her mind. He was the key; all questions and answers revolved about him. Well, perhaps tomorrow she would learn what she needed to know. For once, she did not seek solace from a novel when she at last climbed into bed.

The butler called for her the next day. Filled with an anticipation for she knew not quite what, Andrea went out to the ancient Rolls-Royce.

As soon as the car turned through the wrought-iron gate, a sense of timelessness reached out and wove its spell about her. The house—the entire estate—seemed to welcome her. That thrilling sensation swept over her again, prickling her skin until she trembled all over. She stepped out onto the gravel walk and turned back to look at the Rolls-Royce. To her relief—and barely acknowledged regret—it remained an automobile and did not turn into a barouche. Andrea turned away, stifling an irrational pang of disappointment.

Inside the house, the sensation of past blending into present became so strong that Andrea almost began to believe in the reality of the visions that had haunted her. Here, she wouldn't be at all surprised to see Viscount Grantham's entire family and staff of servants moving about the rooms. And more than she could have believed possible, she wanted to wander among them, be a part of their world.

Wide-eyed, tinglingly attuned to the charged atmosphere that surrounded and permeated her, she followed Catherine Kendall from chamber to chamber in the private portion of the rambling mansion. Each room seemed more perfect than the last, each seemed to hold some lingering presence of past occupants. And more and more, Andrea felt that she belonged. When they at last paused in a bedchamber, she had no need to ask whose

55

this had been.

"It has been occupied by the masters of the house over the years, but I had no need of it." Miss Kendall advanced into the center of the apartment, then turned back to face Andrea. "I have had it restored to its Regency-era appearance—or at least as close as I could come to it. I would like to think this is the way he had it. Richard, I mean. And do you know, sometimes I can almost feel him here. Does that sound too fanciful to you?"

"No, it doesn't. I—" Andrea broke off, unable to express the feelings that rampaged through her. She had been shivering ever since she entered this room. He must have stood where she was now, must have seen the great four-poster bed with its mulberry velvet hangings, must have used the silver comb and brush set that stood on the cherry wood dresser. If she closed her eyes, she could almost feel him here, beside her. But somewhat to her surprise, he did not appear.

"He fascinates me," Miss Kendall said.

She led the way from the room, back along the Long Gallery. Unable to prevent herself, Andrea stopped before the portrait of the long-dead man who obsessed her. She was drawn to the painting, helplessly, like a tiny boat caught in a powerful undertow, dragged inexorably toward him. The key to her mystery lay in this, in his painted image, she knew, but *what was it?* What hold did he and his home have over her?

No matter where she wandered about the house and gardens that day, his portrait lured her back. No visions rose up to haunt her, yet at every moment she sensed the presence of unseen people from ages gone by. Or were they all from a particular age—*his* age? Once more, she returned to gaze up into the painted face with the gray eyes that both teased and enticed her.

Toward late afternoon, Catherine Kendall found her there. Gently, the woman said, "I think it's time you and I had a talk, my dear."

"About Richard?" Andrea turned to her, uncertain.

"Him. And why you are here. Over tea, I think."

Her hostess led the way to the Gold Saloon once again. After the maid left them and they sipped the hot liquid from delicate china cups, Miss Kendall settled back in her chair. "Did you come to Greythorne Court by chance?"

"No." Andrea set down her cup and took a deep breath. "It's not very easy to explain. It . . . I suppose it all stems from my reading Regency novels. I came to England to see all the places they mention."

Miss Kendall nodded encouragingly. "And did you?"

Andrea shook her head. "The first day I was in London I . . . oh, this just doesn't make sense! I saw a photograph of Viscount Grantham's portrait in a scandal rag."

"So, *he* brought you." The words, the merest breath of sound, escaped Catherine Kendall.

Andrea nodded. "I never got to read the article. I only saw his picture. And then I . . . I began to actually see *him!*"

The other woman set down her cup with a sharp clink. "Please explain."

"I know it sounds crazy. The first time I saw him was on St. James's Street. He wasn't dressed the same as he is in the portrait, but I recognized his face. He went into White's Club—only he didn't use the front door. As he approached, some hazy steps and a new entrance appeared in the middle of the Bow Window."

Miss Kendall picked up the teapot, started to pour herself another cup, then set it down. "Did you know that that's where the door used to be—in his time?"

Andrea's eyes widened. "It was?"

"It was moved in 1811 when the Bow Window was put

57

in. After Richard's death. Where else did you see him?"

"On Bond Street and in Hyde Park. And upstairs, here, I saw a maid—and she saw me, I'd swear it!"

Miss Kendall nodded slowly and raised large, troubled eyes from her cup to Andrea's face. "Do you believe in the possibility of time travel, Miss Wells?"

A shaky laugh escaped Andrea. "Intellectually I would have to say it's impossible." She recruited her forces with an unsteady sip of her tea. "But there are times, here in this house, I could almost believe in it."

"I have often felt it. I thought at first it was just because I have always lived here. There's a certain timelessness about the place. But recently I've begun to wonder if there wasn't more to it than just that, if there might not be some physical way to actually travel back through time. Please don't think me a crazy old woman!" Her voice took on a note of anxiety. "I have never actually met any people walking about as you have. But sometimes I've *felt* their presence."

A faint clattering caught Andrea's attention and she looked down to see her hands shaking so badly that her tea threatened to spill out of the cup into its saucer. She set it down on the table. "I . . . I feel them, too. Almost as if they want me to join them."

Miss Kendall nodded once more as if she had come to a difficult decision. She rose and walked over to a delicate Queen Anne desk. From the top drawer, she drew out a miniature portrait, looked at it for a moment, then held it out to Andrea.

With a hand that trembled so that she could barely control it, Andrea took the miniature and stared down at a delicate rendition of what might have been her own face. The features were exact, even to the prominent cheekbones and the straight nose a shade too long. Yet the blond hair was cut and curled into a lovely halo effect, and the expression in the wide-set brown eyes held more happiness than Andrea had ever dreamed possible. At the bottom, in delicate pen strokes, was the date of May 1810.

"I looked for this after you left yesterday." Miss Kendall's voice sounded as if from a great distance. "This is Andrea, Richard's cousin from America."

Chapter 5

Andrea stared at the tiny portrait, and her throat constricted with an emotion too intense to express. "It . . . it's me!" The words tore from her, hoarse and barely audible. "But that's impossible!"

Shock blended with panic and breathless excitement. The likeness was so exact—too exact to be coincidence, even though the picture showed her hair cropped in becoming ringlets rather than the long braid she always wore. And the expression of pure happiness in the portrayed face . . . Andrea had never experienced such joy.

She spun about to face Miss Kendall. "You really think I posed for this, don't you? That I was there, in 1810. All that talk about time travel . . ."

Catherine Kendall kept her voice calm. "When I saw you looking at Richard's portrait yesterday, I recognized you, but I could hardly believe it at first. Your name . . . your being an American . . . the way you reacted to the house—even your showing up here now, when I need your help! Yes, I am very sure it's you."

Andrea's knees weakened and she sat down abruptly. "It isn't possible," she repeated.

"You've only been in this house a very short time. If

you'd lived here all your life, as I have, the idea wouldn't seem all that absurd."

Andrea looked down at the miniature she held, shaken. "Why has he brought me here?" she whispered.

"I think I know."

Andrea glanced up quickly. "Do you? You said you needed my help. What is this all about? Why is he haunting me?"

"I can't say why it's you, as opposed to anyone else. Perhaps because of your love for his time. But *someone* must find the Imperial Star and save the Court."

"What do you mean?" She found it difficult to breathe.

"You are aware that I do not own Greythorne Court?"

Andrea nodded, then swallowed. Her throat felt uncomfortably dry. "The tour guide said something about the earls of Malverne."

Miss Kendall rose as if unable to sit still a moment longer and took several pacing steps about the room. "Richard's father, William Westmont— Oh, it is the most upsetting story! There was some rivalry between William and the third earl, Sylvester. I don't know much about it. Some wager, I fear, for William was the most shocking gamester. It doesn't really matter. Sylvester came into possession of an icon, a beautiful thing, and William swore to have it from him. It was supposed to have belonged to Catherine the Great of Russia—a picture of the Madonna and Baby Jesus, who held a star in His hands, above their heads. Its light illuminated the picture, giving it its name, the Imperial Star."

So that explained the scandal rag's reference to Catherine the Great, at least. But still, Andrea frowned. "When I saw the Imperial Star mentioned in that paper, I thought it was a diamond."

"There was a diamond by the same name, which also belonged to Catherine the Great. In fact, she was said to have named the stone after the icon because both had the reputation of bringing good fortune. But the icon was said to be even more valuable than the necklace."

"It's odd to think of a diamond being lucky, isn't it?" Andrea mused. "They usually have histories of murders and curses."

Miss Kendall smiled. "Not this one. It was supposed to bring love and wealth to its owners—at least until it was lost."

Andrea, whose gaze had returned to the miniature, looked at her. "Was it cut up?"

"I have no idea what became of it. I believe it remained in the possession of the tsars until the 1850's, then simply vanished. But the diamond doesn't concern us. It is only the icon that matters."

Catherine clasped her hands tightly. "The icon was stolen in 1803 from the Empress Mother of Tsar Alexander—the one who fought against Napoleon. There was apparently some shocking scandal, with a French bride being selected for one of the tsar's cousins. She ran away with a French lover, taking the Imperial Star icon with her to pay for their escape to America. It disappeared, then turned up in 1808 in the possession of Sylvester, Earl of Malverne." She broke off and gazed into the fire.

"What happened then?" A nervous, creeping sensation danced across Andrea's flesh, akin to premonition. They were all tied up together somehow: the Imperial Star, the fate of Greythorne Court, Richard—and her own destiny.

"William Westmont bought the icon and nearly beggared himself—and the family—to do so." Catherine kept her gaze on the flames. "Sylvester accepted his offer—much more than William could possibly afford— and William used the Court as security. He gambled, did I tell you that? Anyway, I think he hoped the icon would bring him luck and he would be able to win enough to pay his debt. But before he could, he was killed by a stray bullet while out shooting."

"It certainly didn't bring *him* good fortune." Andrea found her cup and took an unsteady sip of her tea. "I suppose that's where the paper got its story about a curse. What happened to the icon?"

Catherine shook her head. "I don't know. It simply vanished. It's possible William gambled it away before his death, but—"

"But you don't think so?"

"No, not really. There are no records of it anywhere. If someone either won it or purchased it from him, there should be some evidence of it. It's almost as if it ceased to exist."

"And you have a theory?" Andrea watched the woman through narrowed eyes.

"I think that William gave the icon to Richard." Catherine turned to look directly into Andrea's frowning eyes. "He was home on leave just before his father's death. And William does not seem to be one to leave things to chance. He gave it to Richard, I am certain, and Richard hid it somewhere."

"I wonder where?" Andrea's gaze wandered about the room as if she expected to see the icon protruding from some secret panel.

"I have no idea, but finding it is my only hope! Oh, if only that fire had not broken out in the West Tower! If Richard had lived . . ." With an effort, Catherine collected herself. "But he wasn't able to redeem the Court. At least our family has been permitted to continue living here."

"Why?" Andrea fingered the miniature in growing agitation.

"Sylvester didn't produce the sales document until well after William's death. But it stipulated that any direct descendants from either Richard or Isabella must be permitted to live in the house. I don't know how Sylvester ever extracted such an agreement from William! But the solicitors said it was genuine, and so the house passed to the earl. We Kendalls have always lived here, but now, Miss Wells, I am the last direct descendant." Catherine Kendall strode up to Andrea, her expression distraught. "The current earl is in distressed circumstances and plans to sell Greythorne this coming spring."

"The curse, again." Andrea drew a deep breath, then let it out slowly. "Could you not buy the Court yourself?"

Miss Kendall shook her head. "We have had very little money since the death of William. Giles Kendall, Isabella's husband, was a younger son, you must know." She broke off and stared at her clasped hands. "No, we have proved an improvident lot."

"But the two hundred years aren't up yet," Andrea pointed out, having done some rapid mental arithmetic.

"Do you really think I would stand a chance in a court of law? My only claim to living here lies in a very peculiar document nearly two centuries old. I cannot afford to hire solicitors—and I have no heir to live here after me. Edward—the current earl—is a friend, but he needs the money this estate would bring to save his ancestral castle. I can't blame him—but neither do I want to lose my home."

She raised beseeching eyes to Andrea once more. "That really is you in the miniature, I am certain of it. Please, will you travel back through time? Find the Imperial Star and place it where I can find it, so I can purchase my home!"

"Will I . . ." Andrea's voice trailed off. She rose abruptly to her feet and took several agitated steps, clutching the miniature in her hand so tightly that the sharp corners of the silver frame dug into her palm. "The . . . the possibility of traveling through time is only a theory, and a pretty iffy one at that!"

"I know." Catherine Kendall did not seem the least bit ruffled by Andrea's assertion.

"It's impossible!"

"It's never been proven, you mean."

Andrea blinked. "It's never been proven," she repeated, her voice the merest thread of a whisper. She turned away, then back to Miss Kendall. "I . . . I think I want to go back to my hotel."

"Of course, my dear. This has been a rather unsettling experience for you. But look again at the miniature."

Andrea did. It was of herself, she would swear to it. But that was impossible . . . or just not yet proven? Confused, frightened, and more than a little intrigued by the possibilities, she went out to the Rolls-Royce.

Back in her room, the evening stretched before her, long and empty except for her whirling thoughts. Could she really travel through time? If she did, she would actually be able to see life during the time of the Regency for herself! The idea left her shivering and excited. Almack's, the Promenade in Hyde Park, the Season—she would actually be able to see what everything had really looked like! She could discover for herself if the world really had been as glittering and elegant as the novels claimed.

And she would meet Richard Westmont, Viscount Grantham. She sank down on the edge of her bed and closed her eyes. His image rose up in her mind, as clear and enticing as if she stared once more at his portrait. How she would like to know this man . . . That was one thing she couldn't deny. She wanted to know him, more than she had wanted anything in her life.

She bit her lip as the truth dawned on her at last. She wanted to go back in time. For more than fifteen years she had read novels set in the Regency period, absorbed every bit of information and every cant phrase within their pages. She had waltzed at Almack's a thousand times in her mind. But it had never been enough. She had longed for more—to actually live during the Regency era, not just pretend.

Restless, she stood and pulled off her warm sweater and tossed it over the back of a chair. Her jeans followed. But as she drew her silky nightdress out of her overnighter, she stopped.

Was it impossible? The memory of that shivering touch she felt in his house returned to haunt her. That had been tangible, real. If she wanted, badly enough, to physically transport herself into the past, could she make it happen?

Mind over matter. Was that the answer? The human brain possessed hidden powers that no one had yet tapped. If she wanted this, more than anything, and concentrated every fiber of her being on achieving her goal, could she defy all known scientific logic and succeed?

Well, why not? To anyone living at the time of the Regency, the idea of a television set would be ludicrous. Just because the means of time-travel had not yet been discovered, that didn't mean it was impossible! After all, if Benjamin Franklin, Thomas Edison, the Wright Brothers, and so many other inventors and adventurers hadn't stuck their necks out and tried some pretty crazy ideas, where would modern technology be today?

Arguments jostled each other in her mind, but she knew the decision had been made in her heart the moment she saw that miniature. Or had it been even before then, when she first saw the photograph of Richard's portrait?

This was what she wanted—though a flicker of fear raced through her. If she succeeded in this impossible quest, she would never again see her sister, her parents, or friends, or anything familiar, for that matter. She headed into the unknown and unguessed, walking away from everything she knew. For one long, terrible moment, she wondered if she had the nerve for such an adventure.

But if she didn't make the attempt—and succeed!—Greythorne Court would be sold and the perfection of the old house destroyed. The elderly Miss Kendall would have to leave her home. And worse, she would know herself a coward, afraid to try for the one thing she wanted more than anything else.

As she sat there, the image of Richard rose up in her mind, beckoning, drawing her inexorably like a moth to a flame. She shivered at the analogy but couldn't deny it. Richard Westmont, Viscount Grantham, held her fate, and she was compelled to seek it out, no matter the cost to herself.

Andrea went down to the waiting Rolls-Royce the next morning, nervous, breathless, desperately aware of the enormity of what she intended. But not for one single moment did she consider abandoning her new purpose. Everything for which she had longed during the past fifteen years of novel reading lay ahead, hers to be experienced, hers to be grasped. She had to succeed! She had a purpose, a reason, someone to help . . . and Viscount Grantham to meet.

Miss Kendall awaited her in the Gold Saloon. As soon as Andrea entered, the woman rose from her chair and hurried forward. Fine lines etched deeply about her eyes, betraying her concern.

"Have you thought about—what we spoke of?" she asked as soon as the butler had departed.

Andrea met her beseeching gaze. "It won't be easy."

Miss Kendall gripped her hands. "There must be a way! I've felt things in this house sometimes . . ." Her voice trailed off in a whisper.

Andrea nodded, then closed her eyes, summoning up the sensations she experienced before. They came to her, tantalizing, teasing, but no more than the merest hint. "It's here, but not tangible enough. But upstairs . . . Richard's portrait!"

She hurried out of the drawing room, up the curving mahogany stair, and ran along the Long Gallery until she reached the picture. Viscount Grantham's painted image stood before her, his eyes mocking, his lips curved into that intriguing, beckoning smile. It was here, all right, strong and compelling.

She opened herself to the peculiar tingling sensation that danced over her flesh, but it wasn't enough. Gazing into the painted face, she walked up to the portrait and reached out a tentative hand, just touching the canvas. Somewhat to her surprise, it remained solid, cool, and rough from the paint. She lowered her hand, bemused. For one moment, she almost thought she could walk right through it.

"It . . . it may take time." Catherine came up behind her and looked uncertainly into Richard's gray eyes.

"Time," Andrea repeated.

Catherine shook her head as if trying to break a spell. "We must make this as plausible as possible! You must absorb the feeling of the period, become part of it. Find a room in the Court where the sensation of blending with the past is strongest, then stay there. We'll move in anything that might help you."

Andrea's gaze remained on Richard's painted features. "His room. His room and his picture."

"We'll fix it up at once." Catherine stepped back, all bristling efficiency now that the decision had been made. "You'll need something to wear. It would never do for

68

you to arrive in 1810 in *that*." She gestured toward Andrea's calf-length wool skirt and cowl-neck angora sweater.

Andrea blinked and moved away from the portrait. It was difficult to think, to concentrate on details, in its presence. It overwhelmed her. "I'll have to make a traveling gown. And a pelisse." She started back down the stairs, trying to escape the benumbing effect of Richard.

Catherine caught up with her. "And money. You cannot go penniless, and you cannot take your own baggage. You will have to buy things!"

"Money." An odd smile twisted Andrea's lips. "If I succeed in going back, I don't think I can take anything with me that already existed then. After all, something can't be in two places at one time. That lets out cash of the period."

"So it does!" Catherine stared at her blankly.

"Jewelry!" Andrea decided. "I can buy something here that was made after the Regency and sell it back then. A diamond . . . No, pearls. All the strands of pearls I can afford."

"That makes it so much easier." Catherine squeezed her arm. "But will it be enough?"

Andrea hesitated at the base of the staircase. "I don't know. I doubt it. I'm not exactly rich. I have no idea what it will be like or what I'll need."

"It will take money, and vast amounts of it, if you plan to enter the fashionable world."

Andrea turned to stare at the woman, her eyes wide. "Would I be accepted or shunned?" For the first time, the realities of the situation dawned on her. "Society— Richard's world—was one of birth and breeding! I won't have any family, any connections! I could never be anything more than a—"

She broke off, not able to speak the words. She would

be treated not as a lady, not as a heroine in a romantic novel, but as a member of the demimonde, a "charming little barque of frailty"—if the description could be applied to any female pushing five foot eight! That was not what she wanted! She longed to be a member of the haut ton, accepted by the fashionable world. She wanted to go to Almack's and be granted permission to waltz, to live out all her favorite novels. She didn't want to hang about the fringes of society, unrecognized by ladies of quality!

This was terrible! She wouldn't fit into Richard's world. She wasn't destined to see the alluring glamour of the Season but the seamier side of life, the world of gaming hells, opera dancers, and courtesans. It might be exciting—but not what she had in mind, not the Regency era of her dreams.

"It would take them at least six months to receive any confirmation of your existence."

Catherine's voice jarred Andrea out of her unhappy reverie. "What would?" She stared at the woman blankly.

"Why, to discover that you really aren't a relation, of course." Catherine smiled at her.

"I . . . I was woolgathering. Whose relation am I?"

"Why, Richard and Isabella's, of course. They accept you as their cousin from America, remember? You will have come to London to meet the right sort of people. I will write you a letter of introduction, pretending to be an aunt or some such thing. We did have family there, you must know, so they won't think it the least bit odd that you came to visit them."

"But I'll need to purchase baggage and hire an abigail!"

Catherine frowned at Andrea's protests. "I wonder where—and when—you'll arrive. It will probably be here, in this house. Well, then, we must make up a story to account for your lost baggage and maid. Your ship sank?"

Andrea shivered. This was all becoming real! She was actually going back to Regency times, actually going to live out this fantasy Catherine and she had created. Her excitement grew.

"The ship—" She broke off, then shook her head. "No, everyone would be bound to know that no ship sank, not where I could have been rescued at least."

Catherine's face brightened as a sudden thought struck her. "How about highwaymen? They could steal your trunk, because it would be crammed full of things from America, brought for presents. If you say you landed in Portsmouth, and the theft occurred near there . . ."

"No!" Andrea cried, warming to the theme. "The theft will occur on the dock, by men I believe to be porters. Only they vanish with my trunk! And I wouldn't have brought much with me, because I'd be planning on purchasing new gowns in London!"

Catherine beamed her approval of this story. "And the abigail?"

"Oh, she broke her leg getting off the ship." Andrea supplied the excuse of every heroine she had ever encountered who needed to explain the absence of a maid. "And I had no notion how to go about hiring a new one!"

They returned to the Gold Saloon and Catherine poured out tea. Andrea trembled so badly she couldn't sit still.

"It all seems so possible now!"

"Your story of theft will also explain your lack of money."

"No!" Andrea shook her head. "I won't have Richard and Isabella franking me. From everything you've said, things were tight enough for them already. I want to pay

71

my own way."

"But how?" Catherine regarded her in concern. "Unless you can purchase a fortune in pearls."

Andrea leaned back in her chair and stirred milk and sugar into her tea. "No. And since I cannot earn any money, I shall have to win it."

Catherine looked dubious. "Games of chance are so uncertain! You might well lose what little you have!"

"Games of chance, yes." Andrea looked up, her eyes sparkling, and met Catherine's uncertain gaze. "But what of the outcome of a horse race? The results are published in papers. I have only to copy down any number of winners from various races and have someone place my bets."

Catherine was lost in admiration for this scheme. "But what a great deal of research we must do! We have no idea in what year you'll arrive!" She broke off, her expression arrested. "How odd, to think of it as a reality that you may really find the Imperial Star for me. But it must be true!"

Leaving Catherine to compose a letter of introduction from a supposed American relation, Andrea returned to her hotel to pack her bags. She would move into Richard's room at once. A dancing, tingling sensation raced through her. To be in his room, among his things . . .

She could barely believe she was actually doing this! But she must believe. If she were to succeed, there could be not the least doubt in her mind. Nothing must hinder her! She had to go back in time to the Regency era—to Richard.

By the time she returned to Greythorne Court, Catherine had rung up Malverne Castle. She greeted Andrea with the news that Edward, current Earl of Malverne, had been somewhat amused by her peculiar request but had promised to send over a number of the antique form books that his ancestors had collected zealously and stored in their massive library. These, Catherine assured Andrea, contained the names and histories of many horses running in the races, along with their prior wins.

"We must be able to find the information in these. If you handle it carefully, you'll be able to win enough money to keep you in comfort." Catherine led the way up the Grand Staircase.

"Oh, nothing will do for me but to be able to command the elegancies of life!" Andrea felt as if she floated up the steps. A giddy sense of unreality surrounded her.

"You must win a substantial fortune, you know." Catherine regarded her in concern. "Enough to keep you for the rest of your life. We have no idea what happens to you after Richard's death. It is possible, of course, that you may marry a rich man."

"A man of substance," Andrea corrected. "Perhaps I shall meet a nabob who has made his fortune in India."

They reached the Long Gallery and Andrea paused to look once more at Richard's portrait. His gray eyes seemed to return her regard, mocking, tantalizing, almost challenging her to dare the impossible and come to him from across nearly two hundred years.

"Soon." She made the whispered word a vow to him. Soon she would meet him in person and discover for herself if those full lips always held that enticing, quirking smile.

"Andrea!" Catherine's soft voice dragged her out of her absorption. "Come along and look at his room. Tell me if there is anything that doesn't seem right to you."

Andrea followed her to the next wing and they entered the Master Bedchamber, the room that had been Richard's and now would be hers until she made the transition into the past. She closed her eyes, reaching out with her mind, seeking a sense of his presence, a sense of a time long gone. Her skin felt burning hot and tingled with a prickling, dancing sensation as if a chilling breeze had just brushed across it.

She drew a deep, ragged breath and shivered convulsively. She had to stay here—she had no choice! For one panicky moment, she felt captured, trapped by some unseen force within these four walls of the bedchamber. But whether it was the room itself or her own desires that held her prisoner, she couldn't tell.

Fear overwhelmed her and she forced her eyes open. Her surroundings spun dizzily about her, then settled, retreating harmlessly back to where they belonged. Nothing threatened her, nothing reached out with cloying hands to hold her captive. Yet the atmosphere remained heavy, stifling, as if the ages converged together here, in this chamber, blending time into a oneness.

"Andrea?" Catherine laid her hand on her shoulder and Andrea jumped. "Does anything need to be changed?"

Andrea shivered again. "I . . . I don't know." Forcing her mind to concentrate on details, she studied the room. "My bags must go. And that." She crossed to the dresser and picked up a hand-held mirror, not understanding how she knew, only that she did. "This wasn't his. Nor the clock." She pointed to the mantel, where an elaborate ormolu timepiece stood.

Wandering about the apartment, she touched things, knowing somehow that many did not belong but that it didn't matter. Only those two items intruded into the setting that conjured Richard vividly to her mind.

"And I'll have his portrait brought here this afternoon. Where should we hang it? Over here?"

"No. There." Andrea pointed to the wall opposite the massive four-poster. When she went to bed at night, she would be able to lie there and stare at him, and he would be the first thing she would see upon awakening in the morning. He—his portrait—would be the focus she needed for her transition through time. *He* would make it possible.

They were interrupted by the butler, who announced that a large box had arrived from the Earl of Malverne and had been placed in the Gold Saloon. Catherine and Andrea went downstairs at once and unpacked the crumbling volumes of the turf. These delighted Andrea, not only for their potential monetary significance but also for their age and the sporting spirit they represented.

After placing them in chronological order, Catherine regarded them dubiously. "When should we begin?"

"It's Richard I'm concentrating on, so I suppose I'll arrive while he is master here." Andrea bit the tip of a nail. "How about the date of the portrait? That's my image of him. When was it finished?"

"In June of 1808." Catherine smiled suddenly. "I looked it up in the records this morning. It was commissioned shortly after Richard was created Viscount Grantham."

"And when did he die?"

"May 16, 1810, when the West Tower caught fire and collapsed on him."

"Then that's our ending date." Andrea swallowed hard, not liking to think about it.

What will become of me then? Frantic, panicky questions filled her mind. What would her life be like in that period of history? She rose abruptly and strode to the long French windows that let out onto a paved terrace and garden beyond.

Dear God, what was she doing? There was absolutely nothing wrong with her current life. She had—until she quit—a very good job, a comfortable condo, a man in her life whose only real faults were a certain ruthlessness in business and not being a fictional hero out of the pages of

75

a romance novel. But she had turned her back on everything to chase a dream, and all because of a man with whom she could never have a life because he would die so very young.

She drew a deep, steadying breath and turned back into the room. She had made her decision and she would follow it to its conclusion. Straightening her shoulders, she returned to the table.

"Let's get started." She picked up a copy of the *Turf Remembrancer* and started scanning the pages.

Only two other projects took them away from this occupation. They made one trip into the nearby town to convert every penny Andrea possessed into five strands of the most perfect pearls they could find. And she purchased twelve yards of light-brown wool. A search of the library at the Court produced antique fashion plates and Andrea, with Catherine's assistance, set to work copying one of these without recourse to a sewing machine. In only four evenings, they fashioned a very becoming traveling gown with a low, scooped neckline filled with a lace insert and a single deep flounce decorating the hemline. A matching pelisse took another two nights.

Every other minute they spent poring over the oddly assorted collection of form books. They noted down any wins that occurred during their allotted time limit and, on Catherine's insistence, they added a few winners from later races.

"Just to make certain you'll have enough money to live on after Richard's death," she explained. "We don't know if you will be able—or even want!—to return to the present."

The finished list covered just over seven tightly handwritten pages. Her financial future was secure, Andrea reflected as she tucked the sheets safely away into the reticule she had fashioned from the wool remnants. All she had to do was sell her pearls and get a gentleman to place the bets at Tattersall's for her.

With this much of their preparations complete, they turned their attention to Richard's bedchamber. Andrea needed every detail exact; the atmosphere had to be perfect, conjuring up images not only of the Regency era but of Richard as well. She knew, unquestioningly, that it would be Richard himself, and the strength of her desire to go to him, that would draw her back through time.

After an exhaustive search of the other rooms, Andrea selected several snuff boxes and a framed hunting print, the latter discovered in the bookroom, to keep with her. She arranged everything to her satisfaction, sewed the pearls into the seam of her pelisse, and placed the letter of introduction in her reticule along with her list of race winners. With hands that shook with suppressed excitement, she donned her traveling gown and pelisse, to which she tied the reticule.

She came out of the combined dressing room-bathroom to find Catherine waiting for her.

"Are you ready, my dear?" The woman came forward, uncertain, holding out her hands.

Andrea took them in a warm, trembling clasp and nodded.

"We won't disturb you. I'll bring your food myself and place it just inside the door. And towels and . . . and anything else you need. I suppose I'll know that you've made it when you're no longer here." Standing on tiptoe, she kissed Andrea's cheek. "Good luck, my dear. And remember to hide the Imperial Star where I can find it."

"I—" Andrea broke off and looked about the room, seeking a likely spot. "I'll conceal it in the platform of Richard's bed."

Catherine started to draw back, but Andrea gripped her fingers a moment longer. Now that it came right down to it, she admitted freely—to herself—that she was scared

stiff. But she wasn't going to let that—or anything else—
stop her.

"You'll be just fine." Catherine blinked back emotional tears from her own eyes and managed a tremulous
smile. "Farewell, my dear. Be happy." She pulled her
hands free and hurried out the door. It closed softly
behind her, shutting Andrea into her Regency-era
shrine.

Andrea swallowed, nervous, and for one terrible
moment the finality of sealing her fate oppressed her.
She shook it off. Whatever came to her now, she had
made her decision and she would not abandon her quest.

Her gaze roamed the chamber, resting on the snuff
boxes, his combs, a single candlestick, always returning
to the portrait of Richard. She walked up to it and stared
into the ruggedly handsome face.

"Now." She whispered the word, making it half an
order, half a plea. "Bring me to you, Richard. I'm ready."

But a physical passage across almost two hundred
years of time was not going to be easy. She acknowledged
that fact, then dismissed it firmly from her thoughts. She
was ready to go through anything to reach this man. She
lay down on the bed, made herself comfortable so she
would have no distractions, and focused every part of her
conscious being on his painted face. Squarely, she met
the gray eyes that seemed to mock her.

"You'll look at me very differently before long." She
made the soft words a vow.

She concentrated on him, on an enameled snuff box,
on a hunting print she somehow knew he loved.
Constantly, she willed herself to join him. And minute by
minute, hour by hour, her sense of self slipped away,
replaced by the urgency of her desire to shift through
time. The present, her surroundings, even her conscious
thoughts all became a haze and she lost track of the
passage of hours—or was it days? She could remember

eating several times, bathing, even washing her hair, but the clock lost all meaning and she had no idea whether she slept or not.

Always, Richard dominated her being. Nothing mattered but him, his eyes, his firm, cynical mouth that haunted her through that peculiar blending of half-waking, half-sleeping. Always, his image hovered before her. She could even see him with her eyes closed!

Day after day, even as she performed such mundane tasks as dressing or eating, he filled her mind until nothing else existed for her. As she lay in bed at night in the darkened room, almost—almost!—she could hear his voice. She existed in a limbo of half-waking, half-dreams until reality lost all meaning. Had she indeed gone insane, as she had once wondered? But nothing mattered anymore, nothing but Richard's compelling eyes, the strength of character in his face, the soft voice that tantalized, calling her, laughing as she strove to reach him across the ages . . .

"Andrea . . . Andrea . . . where are you?" His voice, soft and hazy, played about the fringes of her mind.

"Richard?" She mouthed his name, but no sound came out.

"Andrea . . ." It was louder this time, more urgent, stronger than before.

"Damn it, Bailey, where are you?"

Chapter 6

Andrea turned her head on the soft smoothness of the pillow. It was hot—or was it her cheeks that flamed as if they were smoldering coals? She had no idea how long she had been there. Richard's painted image burned into her mind, floated before her eyes. His voice echoed through her brain, from deep within her longings.

Or did it come from the doorway this time? His words sounded crisp and commanding, not soft and alluring. And it was not her name he called.

"Bailey!" The name was repeated. "Lay out my shooting coat—the ground is too hard for riding!"

She sat up and opened her eyes. She couldn't see clearly. Everything about her blurred as if she looked through a fog—or without her contact lenses. She blinked and felt the familiar scratch that meant the lenses had slipped out of position. She straightened them but the details of the room remained hazy.

The door to the antechamber opened and in strode a man; tall, dark, ruggedly handsome with eyes of a piercing, unyielding gray. Richard, more dynamically alive than he had ever appeared to her before!

Instinctively, Andrea shifted to her hands and knees on the bed and crept behind the mulberry hangings that bordered the great four-poster. The heavy velvet felt cool in her tingling hand. The musty smell of age had vanished. The fabric crushed beneath her fingers; the texture became her focal point of reality—or of sanity—the only one of her senses that did not play deceitful tricks on her.

Fear, panic, exultation, and disorientation mixed within her for one horrifying moment. She had succeeded! He was there—but had she brought him forward or herself backward through time?

He did not wear the familiar riding dress of the portrait. Instead, an exquisitely fitting morning coat of blue velvet appeared to be molded to his broad shoulders. Andrea drew in her breath, her head still dizzy, her muscles weak and trembling. Here was the epitome of her every fantasy . . .

He moved his head, unknowingly giving her a clearer view of his face. His features appeared more dissolute than she remembered, his eyes bloodshot. He must have made a pretty batch of it last night, she guessed, and had to restrain an almost hysterical giggle. None of this seemed real. The desperate suspicion flickered through her mind that perhaps she had not managed to cross nearly two hundred years but merely lost her sanity.

"Bailey?" Richard turned his back on her.

She eased herself out of the dark, concealing folds of his bed curtains. If this were real, if she were actually in the past, she had to be careful. She couldn't be found here or she would be thought a thief! And then they would never believe her letter of introduction and she would wind up at Newgate or be transported or . . . She fought down an almost hysterical desire to giggle. She had one last hurdle before she was safe. She had to get out of the house, then arrive properly by way of the front door.

Keeping worried eyes on Richard, she inched her

soundless way across the deep carpet and slipped behind the long window drapes of matching mulberry velvet. *He must like the color,* the vague thought drifted across her mind. It was brighter than she remembered. Was it her befuddled mind that created these details, or were they really unfaded by the passage of so much time? If so, that could only mean she had succeeded!

The thought was cut off by the entrance of a sharp-featured man of slight build, garbed in somber black. The "correct attire for a gentleman's gentleman"! A wavering elation filled Andrea at this discovery, briefly banishing her confusion. She would finally learn what all those Regency terms meant, and at first hand!

Fascinated, Andrea watched as the newcomer sailed majestically up to Richard and helped to ease his muscled arms from the sleeves of the coat that did not allow so much as a spare centimeter of material. The shirt beneath was immaculate, of fine linen, she supposed. She was wholly unfamiliar with what the fabrics of the time ought to look like. Weaves and textures undoubtedly changed over so many years.

With the coat neatly laid aside, the valet knelt before him and removed the slippers from his feet. Richard set about taking off the pantaloons of buff stockinette and Andrea hastily looked away. She had no idea what sort of undergarments men wore at this time—she had only wondered about women's!

But as intriguing as Richard might be, this was a flagrant invasion of his privacy. She leaned back against the window and closed her eyes, too disoriented to think clearly. A wave of panic swept over her, leaving her shivering. Her heart pounded so hard that she felt it in her ears.

"If your lordship would care for a scarf? It is quite cold outside, I believe." A tenor voice startled her.

"Devil a bit." Richard's deep, cheerful baritone

response sent a quivering thrill through Andrea. "Just a pleasant nip in the air."

She peeped out, around the heavy edge of the drapes, and caught her breath. Richard, in his "shooting dress," was even more ruggedly, devastatingly masculine than she could have imagined. His buckskin breeches set off an excellent leg to advantage and the olive-green coat, while not fitting as tightly as the one he had worn earlier, was no less perfect in cut and set. Broad of shoulder, slender of waist and hip, muscled of thigh . . . Andrea swallowed.

With difficulty, she lowered her gaze to the shining black boots that encased his lower legs and feet. They didn't look like the Hessians of her imagination! Disappointment shot through her, only to be replaced at once by reason. He would never wear anything so elegant for tramping about the muddy countryside. She had so much to learn—but how she would enjoy lessons from him.

Richard examined his reflection in the cheval glass mirror, adjusted his neckcloth, thanked Bailey, and left the room. Andrea drew back within her curtain, praying the valet wouldn't see her. He moved with deliberation as he collected his master's discarded garments and brushed them off. The blue velvet coat he carried to a huge wardrobe and hung with care. Next he brushed the stockinette pantaloons, folded them with loving hands, and placed them on a shelf in an armoire.

He took forever, and with every dawdling moment, Andrea's nervousness grew. Would he never leave? The trembling that had almost ceased began all over again until she was positive the valet would see the shaking curtain.

She grasped her lower lip between even white teeth and bit until she tasted blood. She had to control herself! It was just shock—shock from seeing Richard, from shifting through time, from being so damnably afraid of what she had done that she couldn't think! She wanted to be alone, to lie down, to recover. Right now, she honestly didn't know whether this was all a dream or if she was really there. Her longings to actually see the time of the Regency—and Richard—might very well have created these images, leaving her to confuse them with reality.

At last, Bailey appeared to have straightened the room to his satisfaction. He went out through the antechamber and Andrea breathed a sigh of relief. She leaned weakly against the wall, waiting, hoping against hope that the valet would not return. After about five minutes, she marshaled every ounce of courage she possessed and emerged from her hiding place.

A quick check assured her that her reticule still hung from the sleeve of her pelisse. She unfastened it and slipped it over her wrist. The bulky weight of her pearls along the lower front hem bumped into her ankles, comforting and reassuring.

But only for a moment. She must still get outside, and without being seen! She had no idea how many servants there would be in the house. Nor, for that matter, when she had arrived! Was it 1808? Bailey called Richard "my lord," which indicated it was after he had been created a viscount . . . and after the death of his father, as Richard plainly occupied the master's bedchamber.

She closed her eyes and ordered her muscles to stop quivering like gelatin. She had better get outside. Never had she felt so devastatingly unsettled, so lost, so out of control. It wasn't like her in the least, and she was determined not to succumb to it.

Crossing to the door, she put her ear against it in her best imitation of a heroine from a Regency novel. The panel was so thick, there was no hope of her hearing anything. She stooped farther and put her eye to the keyhole. Darkness shrouded the antechamber beyond.

No windows opened onto it and no doors were open.

Taking this as a hopeful sign, Andrea went in. She repeated the same dramatic process at the next door, and was rewarded with a better view. Light flooded the hall from the high, arching windows at either end, though her limited field of vision did not permit her to see them. No servants, no members of the household passed through the few feet she could see.

Ordering her rapidly retreating courage back into line, she stepped into the corridor. This was familiar, yet strangely not the same. Different ornaments stood on the occasional tables, different wallpaper hung above the wainscoting. But the direction of the secondary staircase wouldn't have changed, and she hurried to it.

She peered cautiously over the banister but saw no one below. Richard's suite of rooms were on the second floor—what the British called the first. Below her stood a selection of state drawing rooms that opened off a corridor which led to the Great Hall. In the other direction, the same corridor led to the servants' hall and their stairway.

Andrea crept down the steps, holding her breath, afraid to make a noise. Her luck held. She saw no one, though the sounds of muffled voices came from the direction of the Great Hall. She looked about, went to the third of the connecting drawing rooms, listened at the door, then slipped inside.

Her escape route had been carefully planned, for it had seemed likely she would find herself in Richard's room—if she succeeded. The thought wrenched an involuntary gasp of laughter from her throat. Dear God, just what *had* she succeeded in doing? Hallucinating? Losing her mind? That seemed more likely than that she was really roaming about Greythorne Court a good hundred and fifty years before she was even born!

She forced her mind back to the task at hand. Whether

this was real or just a deluded dream, she might as well carry on with it.

A long, mullioned French window let out onto the terrace. Andrea unbolted it and slipped outside, shivering now from the icy breeze as well as from nervous reaction. She had only to make it to the shrubs, which backed up against the wood. Through this and she would emerge onto a distant lane and to safety. Without looking back, she ran for cover.

The spinney in which she shortly found herself proved more difficult than she had anticipated. Not knowing anything about Regency footwear, she had removed the manmade soles from her flat shoes, leaving them soft, pliable, and unfortunately thin. Twigs and sharp rocks jabbed at the bottom of her tender feet. She huddled into her woolen pelisse, wished it could have been her down jacket, and trudged doggedly on.

At last, several bruises and a stubbed toe the richer, she emerged from between thinning trees to find herself facing a hawthorn hedge. This was straggly, still growing and filling in, and she was able to slip through without damaging her pelisse.

On the verge of the lane, she looked up at the sky. It was late morning, guessing from the weak sun that peeked through the heavy cloud covering. She glanced at her wristwatch—or rather, at the white strip on her slightly tanned wrist where that indispensable item had always been until she removed it. Well, if anyone remarked on it she could blame it on a bracelet. And she would obtain a new watch—or was that an antique one?—as soon as possible. She was a modern slave to the clock.

Safe for the moment, her spirits lifted. What an adventure this was! Whatever might come of it, she was here, and she was going to enjoy it to the fullest. She turned and began the long trudge along the lane, back to

Greythorne Court.

Her route followed the distant perimeter of the estate. She remembered it as a very pretty lane in her own time, but in the Regency it was nothing more than a dirt cart track. A half mile was enough to convince her that her savaged shoes were not up to this sort of travel.

She should have visited museums and done some serious studying on things like footwear. But it had never occurred to her! For her, "the Regency" meant the world as it existed within the pages of a novel where precise details were never mentioned and never concerned the characters. Reality never came into it.

Fear tugged at her once more, but she refused to give in to it. All right, she didn't know exactly what life would be like; she was terribly ignorant about any number of very important facts. But she would learn. And surely she knew some things from the novels she'd read. She would get along very well.

Wide puddles of mud blocked her way and the passage of many wooden- and iron-wheeled vehicles had left deep ruts. The verge boasted prickly, thorny weeds. Unerringly, she stepped on every rock and branch that blocked her path.

With relief, she spotted the crossroad, where she turned onto a wider, well-tended lane. Walking became easier, for while it might not be paved, there were fewer holes—would they be called potholes?—and the footing smoother, despite the mud. And then, her heart filling her throat, she saw the beginning of the redbrick wall to her right. Not much farther now . . .

The entrance to the Court was still—or did she mean already?—marked by a curving wrought-iron gate. Andrea continued slowly, sidestepping the puddles left from an overnight rain. The walk had done much to settle her agitated spirits. She might still be wrapped in a sense of unreality, but at least she no longer trembled.

It had been a longer walk than she had expected and her feet hurt from stumbling over rocks as she at last turned onto the gravel drive. She emerged from the lining row of yew trees and stopped short, staring. The difference in the house was amazing! It was familiar, yet . . .

Beauty and serenity surrounded her, filling her with a sense of peace. If it looked like this now, in the dead of winter, she could only imagine what the riot of spring would be like. The house, even shrouded in the grayish, wintry light, was gorgeous, all stone and ivy. The West Tower, a fallen ruin in her own time, stood tall though somewhat broken. When it collapsed . . . She looked away, not wanting to think about that.

On the far side of the drive, a lad knelt on the scythed lawn and pulled a few straggling weeds from a damp flowerbed. Andrea went up to him.

"Excuse me, is this Greythorne Court?"

"Aye." The boy eyed her with lively interest.

"Thank you." Andrea swallowed hard and continued up the winding drive to the fountain that stood before the house, then beyond to the two shallow steps that led to the massive oaken front door. Without giving herself a chance to think or lose her nerve, she raised the brass knocker and let it fall. Her adventure was about to begin.

Chapter 7

Minutes passed and nothing happened. Licking suddenly dry lips, Andrea let the knocker fall once again. Had she done something wrong? Had she not been heard? Did people knock a number of times and loudly, not just once? Her stringently restrained panic broke free, flooding over her.

The door was pulled wide and a portly, stern-featured man stared directly across at her. A muscle twitched at the corner of his mouth, but that was the only emotion he betrayed.

A discreet, wooden-faced butler! Recognition of this specimen, so prevalent in the novels she loved, helped to steady her reeling world. He was familiar, a real man who fitted the bill to perfection. Everything might not be so strange after all.

"Yes, miss?" His tone, coolly polite and not overly encouraging, commanded respect from unworthy personages like herself.

Andrea's fighting spirit emerged. She was not going to be intimidated by a butler! She faced him squarely, her shoulders straightening as she drew herself up to her full, impressive height.

"I . . . I have come to see Mrs. Isabella Brixton." In

spite of herself, she stammered. "My name is Andrea Wells. I am a relative from America."

The butler glanced at the drive, very much aware that no carriage had pulled up. His assessing gaze brushed across her, registering contempt, before he bestowed a shallow bow upon her and stepped aside to permit her to enter.

Was her appearance that bad? She and Catherine had copied that fashion plate with extreme care! Andrea cast a frantic eye over her apparel. Mud splattered across the hems of her pelisse and gown, and twigs and particles of weeds and brush clung to the woolen fabric. She must look as if she had been crawling through the bushes— which was exactly the truth.

"If you will come this way, miss?" The butler led the way across the Great Hall.

Andrea followed slowly, looking about in awe. In Catherine Kendall's day, the house had a deserted feel, perhaps carefully cultivated so the tourists who viewed the place would not upset its occupant. But now, Greythorne Court was a home. She could feel warmth here, and she desperately wanted to stay, to be part of it.

To her relief, the butler led her to the Gold Saloon. This was reassuring, for she had visited the room frequently with Catherine. Yet it, too, was different. The chairs were still Sheridan, but the display cases holding Richard's snuff boxes and other tiny treasures had not yet been built. A beautiful Aubusson carpet in tones of gold and muted blue spread across the floor. A fire crackled merrily in the hearth, and Andrea went to it at once to warm her chilled hands.

"If you will wait in here?" The butler bowed once more and closed the door with a firm click.

Andrea bit her lip. She was here! She stood in Richard's home, and he was outside somewhere, on the grounds. She would actually meet him soon, not just see a projection of his image or stare at a painted rendition of his haunting features.

The door opened and a dark, vibrant little creature stepped into the room, instantly recognizable from her portraits. Glossy ringlets clustered about her piquant face and a flounced morning gown of yellow gauze, decorated with white embroidered flowers, fluttered about her.

"Miss Wells?" Her lovely, musical voice sounded uncertain.

Andrea found herself tongue-tied with nerves, unable to do more than nod like a marionette on a string.

"Do sit down. Though to be sure, you must be chilled! Prindle—our butler—tells me you did not come in a carriage."

"No, I—" Andrea broke off, floundering. Reaction caught up with her and, to her disgust, tears slipped down her cheeks.

"Come!" Isabella Brixton hurried up to her and a warm little hand grasped Andrea's cold one. "Sit down, my dear, and you must tell me what brings you." She pressed Andrea onto the sofa and went to pull the bell rope. "So very cold this morning, is it not? Yet my brother would go out shooting! There is no accounting for the tastes of gentlemen, is there?"

Andrea managed a wavering smile as she retrieved a handkerchief from her reticule. At least she had remembered not to bring paper facial tissues.

The butler, who must have been hovering just beyond the door, swept inside. "Yes, madame?"

"Some warm negus, if you please, Prindle." She glanced at Andrea, who huddled on the edge of a wing-back chair. "And perhaps some cakes?"

The butler's impassive features relaxed. "At once, madame."

Andrea caught the note of fondness in his voice; he

must be devoted to his young mistress. That would make him suspicious of a stranger who thrust herself into their midst. She would have to be very cautious.

"Now, then." Isabella sat opposite her in a comfortable chair. "I am Isabella Brixton, Lord Grantham's sister. And Prindle tells me you are a relative from America?" The soft voice held a questioning note.

"Yes. That is . . . I have a letter," Andrea stammered. She drew it from her reticule and handed it over. "What a mull I am making of this!" she exclaimed suddenly. "Behaving like a watering pot! I do beg your pardon, Is— Mrs. Brixton."

Isabella smiled. "Not in the least; you must have had a tiring journey." She fell silent as she scanned the sheet. "Aunt Elmiria," she murmured. "Why, she must be Mama's cousin! Oh, how delightful, for I remember Mama saying how much she liked Elmiria! And you are her niece."

"I'm not related to you, actually, except by marriage," Andrea hastened to say. "And ever since I have arrived I have been thinking what a shocking thing this is to have done, to just descend on you in so ramshackle a fashion, hoping you would be so kind as to sponsor me for a Season! So . . . so dreadfully forward of me!" To her relief, the Regency phrases came easily to her tongue. They ought to, for she had read them often enough.

A gentle, merry laugh escaped Isabella. "Why, I confess I am delighted! We shall not let either you or Aunt Elmiria down, I assure you. Nothing would please me more than to introduce you into Society! And to think I have been so very bored. You will stay with us, of course, will you not? Where have you left your luggage?"

"I . . . it was stolen."

"Stolen! How dreadful! But how? No, wait, you are shivering! How thoughtless of me." The letter fluttered into her lap as she leaned impulsively forward and grasped Andrea's hands. "Wait until you have had some refreshment. I shall help you set about procuring new things at once, my dear Miss Wells. I do not know what shops are like in America, but one may find everything that one could possibly desire in Bath. I am sure you will enjoy it of all things. I know *I* shall."

She broke off as the door opened to admit Prindle bearing his ladened tray. Isabella poured a glass of the steaming liquid from a tall carafe, and the delicious aromas of nutmeg, lemon, and wine filled the room.

Andrea sipped it, surprised to find how very sweet it tasted. Isabella offered her a tray of "biscuits," which appeared to range from a variety of cookies to slices of heavy cake.

"Which are the macaroons?" Andrea could not keep the hope out of her voice. Isabella went off in another trill of laughter and pointed them out. Andrea bit into one, savoring the rough texture and the almond flavor. So *that* was a macaroon. "And a ratafia biscuit?"

Isabella looked over the tray, then shook her head in apology. "I am afraid there aren't any. But do try a slice of poppy-seed cake. It's our cook's own recipe, and she prizes it highly."

Andrea did try it, for, to her surprise, she was ravenous. She had no memory of the last meal she had eaten. It might have been no more than hours ago, or as much as days! She finished the cake, ate two more macaroons, and began to feel somewhat better.

Isabella watched her indulgently. "Now, if you are feeling more the thing, please tell me what happened. I am agog with curiosity. So very vulgar of me, I know, but there it is." She accompanied the words with a smile so charming that Andrea warmed to her.

"I should never have arrived on your doorstep like this, unannounced!" Andrea flushed, assailed by guilt.

But it was for the sake of Isabella's own descendant that she had done it!

"When you did not have any luggage or even a maid? Of course you did right to come to us at once. I am so glad you did!" There could be no doubting Isabella's sincerity.

"Well, I could hardly put up at a hotel."

Isabella giggled. "I should say not! But tell me, how did it happen?"

"It was the stupidest thing, I assure you," Andrea lied glibly. Now that she had eaten something, she felt more up to the ticklish explanations. "My maid, who is the silliest creature imaginable, fell and broke her ankle as she left the ship at Portsmouth. And then nothing could induce her to remain in England. She is the most dreadfully superstitious soul, and now is convinced she should never have come at all. For you must know," Andrea went on, ad-libbing freely, "that she fell on the dock in New York before we set off, and has been gloomily foretelling disaster at every turn of the journey. According to her, it is the greatest miracle that the ship did not sink. She vowed she would take the next boat home and not remain a moment longer than necessary on this wretched shore."

"My poor Miss Wells!" Isabella exclaimed, half laughing. "You are most certainly well rid of her. Have you not yet hired another?"

"Indeed, I did not know how! And then there was my trunk. You must know that while I was sending sailors to fetch a doctor to my maid, two men came up and asked where I wished my baggage taken. I never thought! But when I arrived at the inn they had suggested, the landlord told me that my things were not there. He sent a tap boy back with me to search, but those dreadful men were nowhere to be found."

"It's disgraceful!" Isabella bristled with indignation.

"Such a terrible time as you have had! I'm surprised you didn't turn about and return with that horrid maid. But never mind, we'll do our best to make up for this unpromising start to your visit. And we'll begin right now. You must be exhausted. You have come directly from Portsmouth?"

"Yes, I . . . I took a stage." She hoped that was correct. "And I walked from the village."

"Walked!" Isabella was aghast. "My poor Miss Wells! Your room will be prepared in a trice, I promise! How tired you must be!" She rose to ring the bell once more.

When the butler entered, she sent him for the housekeeper. This lady, a comfortable-looking soul, arrived shortly and Isabella gave orders for the Rose Room to be prepared.

"For you will like it excessively, I make no doubt," Isabella assured her as the housekeeper left. "It has the loveliest view of the formal gardens. Now, do have some more negus and tell me how Great-aunt Elmiria goes on."

"She . . . she is doing remarkably well." Frantically, Andrea wondered if any hidden pitfalls lurked for her unwary tongue. "She . . . she is . . ."

The door opened, saving her. Two ladies were ushered in, though Andrea barely noticed them. Her gaze came to rest on the gentleman who followed and she could not tear it away. Richard, First Viscount Grantham. She had seen him before, but now . . . She swallowed convulsively.

This was a man to have drawn her back through the ages—and the thought was not the least bit fanciful. His presence filled the room, making her vividly aware of him. Never before had a man caused her to react like this. And if just looking at him could turn her bones to water . . .

She halted her thoughts with difficulty. In this century, she could not allow her impulses and desires to take charge. If she met him at a party at home in Minneapolis, she might well be in his bed before the night was over, and reveling in the experience. But here—and now—she must behave with decorum.

Damn the sexual mores of the Regency. Only a wanton, a courtesan—or a married woman—could get away with what she longed for at this moment!

"Lettie! And Miss Moreland! What a delightful surprise!" Isabella rose at once to greet the two ladies.

"I . . . I didn't realize you had a visitor." The delicately dark young lady addressed as Lettie shrank back timidly.

"This is Miss Wells, a cousin from America, who has come to stay with us. Richard, come do the pretty."

"Yes, Prindle told me we have a guest." The affected drawl in his deep voice did not disguise the temper he barely held in check.

Andrea stiffened. He was being quite rude!

Isabella gave an uneasy laugh. "Really, Richard, what a way to greet her! My dear Miss Wells, allow me to introduce my brother, Lord Grantham."

Andrea held out a tentative hand, hoping he would kiss her fingers. He took it in a warm clasp, sending a shiver of pleasure through her at the touch, but he merely awarded her the slightest bow.

"Delighted." He forced a note of politeness into his voice.

"Now, that's a rapper," Andrea murmured, to herself rather than to him.

A startled expression lit those piercing, disconcerting gray eyes. She met their sudden stare with a bland expression of her own. A slow smile of appreciation lit his whole face.

"Perhaps not as much of a rapper as either of us might have thought." His words were for her ears alone.

"And this is Miss Moreland and her niece, Miss Letitia Moreland."

Andrea extended her hand to the older woman, who barely pressed it with a cool, limp touch. Every plane and angle of her narrow face beneath the high-poke bonnet held a reserve hardened by disapproval. She straightened herself up to her meager inches and regarded Andrea through sharp, pale eyes. Not a hint of a smile softened the severity of her narrow lips.

"A pleasure." Before Andrea could respond, Miss Moreland turned back to Isabella Brixton with an imposing rustle of purple satin.

"What a terribly long way to travel, all the way from America!" Miss Letitia Moreland regarded Andrea with round, wondering blue eyes, rather as if she believed Andrea to have swum the whole way. The truth would really knock her for a loop, Andrea reflected, and prudently kept it to herself.

Isabella cast a frantic, beseeching glance at her brother, whose scowl deepened at Lettie's inane comment. Was he like to give the poor chit a set-down? Andrea wondered, allowing her thoughts free rein with the Regency expressions she loved. He looked to be churlish enough.

"Have you been spending Christmas at the Castle?" Isabella rushed into speech without waiting for Grantham's biting tongue to go to work. "So delightful a place, even in the depths of winter."

"Yes, it is." Lettie's face fell as if the words recalled her to some unpleasant memory. She managed a brittle smile for her hostess. "Wilfred is down, but then I suppose you must know that."

"Is he?" Richard's voice sounded sharp. "We haven't seen him—at least he has not come to pay a *regular* call."

"Really, Richard, you are being most disagreeable! It is

no wonder he does not visit me more often." Isabella frowned at him.

Andrea stepped back, away from the other four people. She was nothing but an intruder—and an unwelcome one, to judge from the deep, frowning lines that marred Richard's high brow. She had no right to barge into the lives of these people! Yet that was precisely what she had done and, whatever second thoughts she might have now, she had committed herself. There was no turning back.

Lettie stared hard at the pale-blue gloves that matched her muslin morning gown. "I . . . I have come to wish you very happy on your engagement. I am sure you and Wilfred will deal famously together."

Wilfred? Andrea looked up, startled out of her guilt, and racked her memory. Isabella's second husband had been named Giles! Her eyes widened in alarm. She must have arrived before her first marriage . . . But no, she couldn't have, for Richard was already Viscount Grantham and Isabella was Mrs. Brixton. So who was this Wilfred?

A wave of dizziness washed over her, leaving her with a sense of floundering disorientation. Her presence might affect history—just by being here, she might be altering the course of events!

"Perhaps I should explain." Isabella's gentle voice broke across Andrea's tumbled thoughts. "Wilfred is the son of our neighbor, the Earl of Malverne. We have just become engaged. Lettie—Miss Moreland—is the earl's ward. We have all known each other forever."

"Longer." Richard's muttered word was clearly audible.

Isabella cast him a reproving glance. "Now, whatever has gone wrong, Richard, you must not take it out upon our guests. Miss Wells has been having the most dreadful time!"

The furrows in Richard's brow deepened and his enigmatic gray eyes clouded over as if with an impending storm. He listened to Isabella's recital of Andrea's fictional woes and some of the harshness left his expression.

"A terrible beginning to your stay, indeed, Miss Wells. We shall do our best to ensure that nothing more occurs to distress you." An elusive charm lurked in his smile, as if he set himself out to do the polite for his sister's visitor.

He made it too obvious. He must wish her at the devil, Andrea guessed. Something must have occurred to put him out of temper.

Inwardly, she sighed. This was proving to be quite a letdown to her expectations, not to mention a blow to her ego. From his reputation, she expected a delightful rake who would instantly set up an enjoyable flirtation with her. Perhaps he did not admire tall, fair females. The thought was lowering.

"Was the ocean rough on your journey from America, Miss Wells?" Miss Moreland couched her question in measured accents. Her piercing gaze rested on Andrea. "Such a strange place as that must be. Not civilized, in the true sense of the word."

"No, it isn't." Goaded by the contempt in the woman's voice, Andrea directed a smile of false sweetness at her. "Why, there are red Indians roaming the streets—if you can call those cart tracks streets!"

"Indeed?" Miss Moreland seemed pleased to have her poor opinion of America confirmed. "How very dreadful! And so you have come to England? A very sensible thing to have done, to be sure."

At the moment, Andrea wasn't so very sure about that. She glanced at Richard and found him looking daggers at

Isabella, obviously trying for a word alone with her.

"And such a shocking beginning to your stay." Lettie shook her pretty head, setting the dusky ringlets dancing about her delicately featured face.

"How very odd to think of Mrs Brixton as a chaperone, to be sure." Miss Moreland's tone held only disapproval.

"A widow of two years standing, and engaged to Malverne's heir? I doubt Isabella has ever been so respectable in her life!" Richard drawled in defense of his sister. "She might be somewhat lacking in decorum, but I assure you I am working on that."

Isabella hunched a pretty shoulder. "You are being odiously disobliging. Miss Wells, I beg you will pay him no heed."

"You are quite right, my dear." Richard directed a slight bow to the assembled company. "If you will excuse us for a moment, there is a matter I must discuss with my sister. Miss Wells? Miss Moreland?"

He held out a peremptory hand to Isabella. She hesitated, then shrugged and stood to accompany him to the fireplace, where they stood slightly withdrawn.

"So many exciting things have happened to you!" Lettie heaved the sigh of inexperienced youth. "Oh, I do so envy you! I have always felt it would be of all things the most delightful to have a truly wonderful adventure!"

"I have just seen someone lurking in the bushes." Richard's voice, though soft, drifted across to them, plainly audible.

Andrea stiffened. He must have seen her! But no, it had been more than an hour since she had been near the house. It must have been someone else.

"What a singularly foolish thing to say!" Miss Moreland's voice made her jump but effectively recalled her to the conversation at hand. "A wonderful adventure? To have all one's possessions taken from one? To endure weeks on a tossing ship? Really, Lettie, where do you get your nonsensical notions?"

Lettie shrank, and Andrea took pity on her.

"It has been somewhat uncomfortable, but you are quite right. I cannot think of anything more dull than to never take even the littlest risk."

Lettie bestowed a warm smile on her and risked a defiant glance at her chaperone.

Richard's raised voice made them all glance toward where brother and sister stood. "I won't have him calling in this ramshackle manner! Damn it, Bella, his intentions are honorable, he's asked you to marry him. Why can't he call at the house like a man? I won't have him lurking in the bushes or arranging trysts with you in the shrubbery!"

"It is no such thing!" Bella made feeble attempts to hush him. "I have not seen him since Christmas."

Miss Moreland stiffened. "A dreadful welcome for you, I fear, Miss Wells."

"It is quite my own fault!" Andrea clenched her hands together. "It was unforgivable of me to have arrived this way, without warning!"

"Oh, no, pray do not think so!" Lettie looked earnestly up at her. "They will both of them enjoy your visit immensely, I promise you."

"I won't have my sister's name bandied about by loose tongues, which is what will happen if you keep on like this. I wouldn't be the least bit surprised to discover it was you who arranged these assignations!"

"I may have flirted a bit before my marriage, and I might have drawn down censure from a few straight-laced dowagers, but I am *not* a hoyden! I know where to draw the line!"

Richard snorted.

Andrea flushed, angered by his conduct. How dare he rake down his sister, and before visitors, at that! And if it

101

was loose behavior they talked about, he was no paragon of virtue. She had few doubts he currently had a mistress in keeping, somewhere. She could only be glad she herself had grown up in a generation that had begun to do away with the double standard. For men to feel they must "protect" their sisters and daughters from enjoyable encounters was the outside of enough!

"I understand it is not uncommon for the most shocking rakes to be overly strict with the females of their own families." Andrea addressed the too loud comment to Miss Moreland.

That lady stiffened in disapproval of such reprehensible outspokenness.

Richard directed a penetrating gaze at Andrea. Sudden amusement replaced his scowl. "Just so, ma'am."

She held that gaze, challenging. For the first time, he seemed to really look at her. His wide-set eyes opened a bit more and he fumbled at the breast of his shooting coat for the quizzing glass that hung about his neck by a black riband. He raised it and subjected her to a thorough inspection.

She watched, fascinated, as he permitted his gaze to roam over her face, taking in every feature, measuring, appreciating. His scrutiny wandered down to her white shoulders that were partly exposed by the scoop neck of her light wool traveling gown. Her breath came more quickly as his regard came to rest on her breast as it rose and fell. Never had she considered herself to be generously endowed in that department, but there was nothing in Richard's manner to make her suppose he was not pleased with what he saw. Her figure was trim, if somewhat on the tall side.

He allowed his glass to drop, and a slow smile lit those remarkable eyes and twitched up the corners of his mouth.

"Enchanting." He made the word a pronouncement.

"You speak from experience, of course?" A slight bite lent an edge to her words. He had regarded her like an object!

"Vast experience, I assure you. I am accounted quite a connoisseur."

"Really, Richard!" Isabella objected.

The lousy male chauvinist pig! The term night not have been invented yet but it certainly applied to Richard, Viscount Grantham. She felt betrayed by her favorite writers. None of them had portrayed their heroes as they really had been, with hateful prejudices and only one place for women—in their beds.

She encountered his enticing smile and had no doubts that that particular thought currently occupied his mind. Another realization followed hard on the heels of the first. A rake need not be flirtatious to be effective. What was she getting into with him? If it was his bed, it was going to be on her terms—with him accepting her as an equal—or not at all.

Chapter 8

Andrea looked about her bedroom, delighted by each
and every Regency-era detail. It was decorated in shades
of soft pink with rose-patterned silk drapes at the
window and about the canopied four-poster bed. A small
oil lamp stood on the bedside table. A pair of matched
triple-branched candelabra stood on the dresser and four
candlesticks rested on delicate cherrywood tabletops
about the spacious chamber. A fire burned industriously
in the huge hearth that stood opposite the bed, dispelling
the chill and damp that lingered in the air. Only a
minimal amount of smoke wafted into the room.

She crossed to the multi-paned bow window and
peeped out at the dormant garden below. Even in the icy
depths of winter, the leafless shrubs held a certain formal
beauty. Not a single weed dared to stick its head through
the frosty ground.

A knock sounded on her door and Isabella burst in,
followed by a comfortably proportioned woman in a
dove-gray round dress and mobcap. She was not in the
least the "dour-faced" abigail of the novels, but Andrea
liked her on sight. Gowns of the most shockingly
diaphanous material filled her plump arms.

"This is Jervis." Isabella introduced her woman. "I

told her what happened to you, and we have ransacked my dressing gowns and night things. She tells me they are not the least bit suitable for an unmarried lady, and that is quite true, but you must have something to wear, after all!"

Jervis set the delicate muslin, gauze, and lace robes on the bed and Andrea picked one up. What had happened to the severe, high-necked sacks she had imagined ladies of the period wore to bed? Or were these just Isabella's fluttery—and downright provocative—preference?

"Jervis is the dearest creature." Bella smiled fondly at her abigail, who directed an admonitory cluck at her young mistress. "But she does not approve of my choice of nightthings. Only imagine! Nothing can convince her I am not still in the nursery!"

Andrea held a sheer muslin gown up to her shoulders and looked dubiously at the good four inches of her blue skirt that showed beneath. "I fear I am somewhat taller than you."

"Jervis is a positive genius with a needle! She shall add a long flounce, though no one is likely to see you in this, anyway. And tomorrow we shall go to Bath and order new gowns for you!" Bella's eyes sparkled at the prospect. "Here, Jervis, use one of the others. This one," she decided at random, picking up another almost transparent gown. "You may cut this up for flounces."

"Thank you, Jervis." Andrea looked shyly at the woman.

Jervis gave her a long, measuring look, then smiled in a motherly manner. "A nasty business, having your trunk stolen, miss. Now, don't you worry none. I'll have this ready for you by evening."

Bella tugged on Andrea's arm. "Do come downstairs. I have had Prindle lay out a nuncheon in the breakfast room, for you cannot tell me you are not ravenous. And as for Richard, it never ceases to amaze me how much a gentleman can eat."

They went downstairs together and entered the breakfast parlor. Richard was there before them, standing at the sideboard with plate in hand. He had changed out of his mud-splattered buckskins and coat into riding dress, which set off his rugged masculinity to unsettling advantage. Andrea drew in her breath, overpowered by this perfect image of a Corinthian.

"You are certainly setting an elaborate table today." Richard gestured at the variety of dishes that lay before him.

"Of course. You are quite fortunate you have me here to keep house for you. And do not try to tell me you eat better at your club, for I know that would be a . . . a whisker!"

"Oh, a regular bouncer." He allowed her the point. "Certainly this is better than at my lodgings."

"Such civility!" Bella fluttered long lashes at him in feigned astonishment. "Are you trying to make amends for your earlier surliness?"

Richard smiled, and to Andrea it seemed the entire room brightened.

"It seems I must apologize." A touch of humor added a new dimension to his already intriguing voice. "Blame it on my recollections of your somewhat adventurous youth. You cannot deny you had the local lads positively haunting the place."

"I did, didn't I?" Bella preened herself.

"Do you remember that moonling who wrote execrable verse to your eyes, then stood under your window at night to read his ghastly offerings."

Bella giggled. "They were awful, were they not? Yet you must admit, it was quite flattering?"

"Good God! Are you hoping to inspire your Wilfred to so endanger his health and clothing as to venture out at night in the depths of winter for you?" He shook his head in amusement, robbing the words of insult. "You'll be doomed to disappointment!" He returned his attention to the all-important consideration of his nuncheon.

Emboldened by his lighter mood, Andrea joined him at the sideboard and touched his sleeve. He looked down at her from what seemed to her a great height; he must be about six foot three, she decided. A perfect height for a lady of five foot eight. She stifled the thought as a speculative gleam lit eyes that were now a smoky blue.

"May I speak to you for a moment—in private?" she whispered.

His brows went up in surprise. "As soon as you have eaten?" he suggested.

She nodded and took a slice of beef and another of chicken. She was tempted to tear open one of the freshly baked rolls and make a sandwich and wondered with a sense of longing whether or not it would be proper for a lady to call for mustard. She decided to behave with caution. Much could be forgiven an American, for they would expect her manners to be odd and rustically provincial, but she didn't want to shock them unduly, either.

As she finished eating, she felt herself under scrutiny and looked up to find Richard watching her. He stood at once. "If you would come with me for a moment, Miss Wells? Perhaps I can answer some questions for you."

Andrea excused herself to Isabella and went through the door which Richard held. She followed him up the corridor, across the Great Hall, and down a side passage to the book room. Stepping inside, she felt instantly at home.

Not much had changed over the years. Even several of the glass cases were already here. She went to them at once and looked at the beautiful and unique snuff boxes within. Richard's hobby, she remembered. Perhaps he would show them to her someday, tell her a little bit about their histories.

"Now, what may I do for you?"

She turned to see him half sitting on the edge of the huge cherrywood desk that gleamed from constant polishing. She cleared her throat, nervous in his dynamic presence.

"As . . . as you know, everything I brought with me has been stolen." She dove right in.

"And you find yourself somewhat at a stand?"

There was a note of cynicism in his voice! He must think she begged for money.

"You are quite wrong. At least—well, I'm not at a stand, precisely. Certainly not at point non-plus." His lip twitched and she looked at him with an assumed wide-eyed innocence. "Have I said something amiss?"

"Not in the least. I find it refreshing not to be faced with a mealy-mouthed miss. You were saying that you are not scorched?"

"No, but I am without the ready."

His grin broadened at her serious tone. "But you have the means of rectifying this, I presume."

"I do, but I shall need your help. I have brought with me some pearls that . . . that my great-aunt felt would bring a better price on this side of the Atlantic. Only I have no idea how to go about selling them."

His brow snapped down and all trace of amusement faded from his face. "I will not have you selling your jewels while beneath my roof!"

She would have been more delighted by his coming the masterful, autocratic male over her if it did not create difficulties. She straightened up. "Pray, do not be absurd! They were purchased expressly for this purpose. If you will not help me, then I shall do it myself."

"Do not be ridiculous!" He glared at her, momentarily at a loss.

"I'm not. I'm merely being practical. *Someone* must do

it, and at the moment you are the only gentleman of my acquaintance in England. I can hardly ask a stranger. So if you will not, it must be me."

"You wouldn't know how to go about it!"

"No, but I can always find out."

"I will not have any guest of mine wandering about Bath trying to pawn her jewels!"

She nodded. "Quite right. I mean to sell them. But I've never done this sort of thing before. I really think you could negotiate a better price than I could."

His jaw clenched and several seconds passed before he spoke. "All right, I'll dispose of them for you. But I can't say that I like it."

She gave him a mischievous smile. "You do not have to like it, you know. Just as long as you do it."

He stared, dumbfounded, at her for a moment, knocked off balance by her unexpected comeback, then burst out laughing. "My dear Miss Wells, I can see that our acquaintance is not destined to be dull."

"No, that it most certainly will not be!" She broke off, uncertain how to go on.

"Well, Miss Wells? Why do I have the feeling that you have another, and probably far more outrageous, request to make of me?"

"Because you are perfectly right. I do." She peeped up at him through her lashes and was surprised to see the startled expression that flashed across his face.

He had it under control in a moment. "Tell me the worst," he invited.

"I . . . I will need you to place a considerable portion of the proceeds on a horse race for me."

"Good God! Of all the hare-brained, ramshackle . . .!" His eyes took on the color of cold steel as his features hardened in uncompromising lines. "No! A lady may enjoy a quiet flutter, but I will not, under any circumstances, aid you on any ruinous course!"

She flushed. "Is it not permitted in England for a female to bet on the turf?"

"It is not ladylike."

"But I have very little money, even considering the pearls. There is certainly not enough to frank my entry into society." She adopted a coaxing tone. "So I really have no choice."

"Are you quite certain you did not lose your trunk in a bet?" Exasperation filled his voice.

A choke of honest laughter broke from her. "I assure you, I am not addicted to gaming in any form. This bet will be a certainty."

He came away from the desk, strode over to one of the display cases, and stared at it in silence. When he spoke again, his words were stiff, heavy with disapproval. "You have no need of large sums while you enjoy the protection of my roof."

"It would hardly be proper to permit you to purchase my gowns," she pointed out. "And at this moment I have nothing but what I stand up in! Under no conditions will I permit Isa—Mrs. Brixton to pay my bills."

He drew a deep breath. "Which horse and which race? And how, may I ask, can you be sure it is a certainty? Unless I am much mistaken, you only arrived on these shores two days ago. Did some Captain Sharp give you a tip?" He almost sneered the word.

"No, feminine intuition, that's all." She gave him an enigmatic smile and wondered if the phrase was yet in use. "But you will never know how I make out if you do not place the bet, will you?"

In spite of his irritation, he began to be amused. "Miss Wells, you are the most unusual and shocking female it has ever been my dubious honor to meet. Very well, I shall sell your necklace and bet—half, shall we say? of the proceeds on the horse of your choice."

"Thank you, my lord. I am much obliged."

"There is to be a meet at Newmarket tomorrow. Will that do for you?"

She hesitated. "May I let you know?"

"As you wish." He bowed her out of the library.

She walked down the passage, oddly disturbed by their encounter. She had gotten her way, but something bothered her . . . He had not acted as she had expected. Richard was a real person with thoughts and actions of his own, not ones she laid out for him. He argued rather than flirted with her. She might be no more than a few hours into the past, but already it had ceased to follow the plot on which she had decided for her adventure.

She swallowed hard, recognizing the truth. This wasn't a novel written where she could rework the scenes the way she wanted in her mind. This, as crazy as it seemed, was *real!* She had to concentrate on what she was given and make the best of it. And the first thing was to place that bet so she could obtain that root of all evil, a few rolls of softs!

She had to discover the date—or better yet, the year!—without arousing curiosity. Thoughtful, she nibbled at the tip of one delicate finger. What she needed was a newspaper. She headed back across the Great Hall and saw Prindle, the butler, emerging from the Gold Saloon.

"Excuse me!" She hurried up to him. He bowed with a stiff, oppressive formality, which she tried to ignore. "Is there a copy of . . . of the *London Times*?"

"In the Red Drawing Room, miss."

He gave her directions to the other wing and she thanked him, then pursued her quest. After a quick survey of the apartment, she found the paper lying on a small round table. She picked it up, looked at the date, and her heart filled her throat. January 3, 1810! It must have taken her nearly two weeks to make the passage through time!

111

Then the year sank into her bemused brain. It was 1810, already, and Richard would die in only five and a half more months. She dropped the sheets.

Of course she had always known he was going to die. She just hadn't realized it would be so soon. She forced her mind into a practical vein. What mattered was helping Catherine by finding the Imperial Star. Richard was merely the means to bring her back in time to accomplish her goals. And right now, she needed money.

Focusing on that thought, she hurried up the stairs to her room, where she jerked open her reticule and dragged out the bulky list of race winners. If Richard was going to die shortly, she could not let herself fall in love with him. She had best concentrate on the business at hand, of establishing herself financially—and enjoyably—in this time.

And if she were going to take Society by storm, she needed a wardrobe of considerable value. She folded up the pages listing races prior to the current date and threw them onto the fire. That still left a number from which to choose. But there was nothing for Newmarket on the following day. She frowned. She would have to find out where the various race tracks were located.

Her next entry was for Cheltenham on January 7. Now, if Richard went to London, it wouldn't matter where the race meets were held. He could place her bets at Tattersall's. In the meantime, she would order whatever she needed and have the bills sent to the Court. She could settle them as soon as she had her winnings from the races. Perhaps Richard would help her set up a bank account for herself so that she could write checks—or were they called drafts? She had so much to learn!

They dined that evening with Isabella not changing her gown so that Andrea would not feel out of place. Richard came to the table in riding dress, though Andrea

112

could tell he was not best pleased. A stickler for proprieties, she decided, and wondered if he preferred satin knee breeches, even in the country.

Prindle and the two footmen brought in the first dishes, and for Andrea, all other thoughts fled. There were so many different things from which to choose! She ate with delight, sampling a pigeon roasted and stuffed in what Bella told her was the Flemish style. Next she tried white collops which proved to be sliced chicken in a sauce. The vegetables she recognized, but not the intriguing but elusive aromas of their seasonings.

"If I eat everything, I'll gain the most shocking amount of weight," she sighed as the third course was brought in. "Will there be a syllabub?"

Isabella laughed. "No, but I shall have the cook prepare one especially for you tomorrow night."

When Andrea at last laid aside her fork, unable to eat so much as another bite, Isabella rose and led the way into the drawing room. Andrea would much rather have stayed to watch Richard take snuff and drink wine. It occurred to her that she had no idea whether or not Beau Brummell had yet laid down the dictum that port was only suitable for the lower orders to drink.

She swayed and caught herself on the wall as a wave of disorientation swept over her. This was 1810, an actual date, not that mythical, amalgamated, unnamed year in which novels always take place. For that matter, Prinny wouldn't even be made Regent until the following year. If she wanted to be technical about this, she was in the Georgian period, not the Regency era at all.

"We must plan your wardrobe." Isabella's delighted voice broke across Andrea's flying thoughts. Apparently not noticing anything amiss with her guest, she ushered Andrea into the drawing room and closed the door behind them. "You will need so many things! Oh, what fun this will be." She rang the bell and sent the footman who came in response for her collection of *La Belle Assemble* and the *Ladies Home Journal*.

The young man shortly carried in a hefty pile of fashion magazines. Andrea and her hostess were soon lost in the dazzling world of cottage and sontag sleeves, letting-in lace, lutestring, and Athenian braces. They were interrupted from this nearly an hour later by the entry of Richard, a scowl marring his rough-hewn features.

"I just glimpsed someone slipping through the shrubbery again," he informed his sister. "Damn it, Bella, I know Wilfred doesn't like me, but this is carrying things too far! I'm going to let the dogs loose, and you may warn him or not, as it pleases you. How did you ever come to be engaged to so hen-hearted a creature?"

"It could not be Wilfred!" She bristled in defense of her betrothed. "Just because you were used to . . . to make his nose bleed—"

"Draw his cork," Richard supplied.

"—whenever you boxed as children," Bella went on, ignoring the interruption, "does not mean he is afraid of you or your . . . your cutting tongue!"

Richard snorted. "You can't tell me he has ever shown a preference for my company!"

Bella shrugged. "He does not share your sporting tastes, that is all."

"No, he is far more concerned with setting the ton on its collective ear with some outrageous quirk of fashion. Good God, Bella, what on earth do you see in him?"

"A husband who won't break his neck on the hunting field!" She looked away abruptly.

Andrea reached out, her gentle heart torn by the pain in Bella's voice. Richard gave the slightest shake of his head, restraining her. Andrea drew back, surprised, but in a moment she saw there had been no need. The face Bella turned to them showed only the veriest trace of

114

remembered sorrow and mourning.

"Now, do stop being so provoking, Richard. Wilfred is not one to behave in so shocking a manner, and you know it. Besides, we have a matter of far more concern on our hands. We must take Miss Wells to Bath in the morning so that she may replenish her stolen wardrobe."

"But . . ." Andrea looked from one to the other, uncertain. "If you really did see someone, Lord Grantham, should we not alert the . . . the watch or . . . or something?"

Richard drew his frowning gaze from his sister. "It was probably naught but the wind, rustling a bush."

"Pay him no heed, Miss Wells." Bella was once again her teasing, merry self. "He's just put out tonight and looking for an excuse to rip up at someone." She eyed him with true sisterly spirit.

"By my arrival?" Andrea could not prevent herself from asking the question.

"Oh no, Richard is merely cursed with the devil's own temper. Aren't you, my dear?"

"It's nothing to worry yourself over, Miss Wells." Curtly, Richard dismissed the subject.

Andrea glared at him, feeling as if she had just been patted on the head and told to run along and play like a good little girl. It was irritating not to be treated like an intelligent adult. Surely, not all men of this time regarded women as inferiors. Heroines were always such strong-willed ladies who defied convention, and that was what their heroes liked in them. Unless, of course, such heroes only existed in fantasy. Reality, as she was rediscovering every moment, could be very different. An unsettling pang of dismay shot through her.

"I'm off in the morning to the races, so you ladies may do as you please." Richard perched on the arm of Bella's chair and raised his quizzing glass to regard a fashion plate depicting an elaborate evening toilette.

"With that Giles Kendall?" Bella looked up at him, her disapproval patent.

Andrea stifled a gasp. Did Bella not like her future husband? And she was engaged to the wrong man! What a muddle affairs were in.

"What of Giles?" Richard directed the glass at his sister's lace cap. "Very fetching, love."

Bella shrugged. "Oh, do put that thing away. You always seem to be at your wildest when you're with Mr. Kendall."

"You haven't even met him." Richard's eyes mocked her. "Well, perhaps that is just as well."

"Horrid man." Pointedly, Bella returned her attention to the magazine.

After the tea tray had been removed, Andrea followed her hostess out into the Great Hall, where candles had been left on a table at the foot of the staircase. Andrea lit a taper from the burning branch and, carefully shielding the flame with her hand, mounted the steps. The furniture, the walls, everything receded into deep shadows, giving the old house an eerie feel. No wonder ghosts walked the halls of so many English manors! The ceiling seemed miles above her head and she could not see clearly beyond the circle of meager, wavering light.

Isabella escorted her to her room, rang for Lily, the housemaid she had assigned to Andrea, and waited until the girl arrived. Together, they assisted Andrea into the night dress that had been altered for her by the competent hands of Jervis. Isabella wished her good night, she and the maid went out, and Andrea found herself alone.

She removed her hard contacts, wrapped them in a handkerchief, and set this within easy reach on the table beside the bed, then stifled a yawn. She was too tired to think clearly. Tomorrow or the next day, when she was rested, she would set about discovering the fate of the

116

Imperial Star. It probably hung innocently on a wall somewhere, just waiting for her to locate it—and secrete it in the frame of Richard's bed. That was probably why no one saw it for the next hundred and seventy-five odd years. *She* was the one to hide it so mysteriously.

Dismissing the matter from her mind, she snuggled into her bed, through which a warming pan had been passed. A hot brick, wrapped in a towel, nestled at her feet. For an age that had never heard of electric blankets or even the good old-fashioned hot water bottle, they seemed to manage quite nicely. Exhausted, she fell into the first real sleep she had experienced in she had no idea how long—almost two weeks, she was sure!

It seemed only minutes later when something clicked, disturbing her. She stirred, yawning, and the clicking repeated.

Andrea sat bolt upright, blinking at the morning sunlight, and found herself staring not at the wall of a hotel room but at a rose silk curtain hanging about a great four-poster bed. She sank back against the pillows, dizzy and cold from the shock. She was at Greythorne Court—and still in the past. It hadn't all been a dream; she was really here.

A small hand pulled back the curtains, and Lily smiled shyly at her. It must have been the opening and closing of the door that awakened her, Andrea realized.

On the bedside table, beside her handkerchief, rested a tray bearing rolls and a cup of steaming hot chocolate. Andrea sat up again, allowed Lily to arrange the pillows for her, then leaned back against the stack, luxuriating in the whole experience. This was all every bit as wonderful and pampering as she had dreamed. What a way to start a morning!

And what a morning it would be! They would go to Bath, she would see the Pump Room and Assembly Rooms and shop on Milsom Street. There were so many things she wanted to do, like visit the Abbey and Sydney Gardens. But first she would go shopping, and before the day was over, no matter what, she would possess her very own bandbox!

She rose and, with the inexpert help of the fumbling Lily, donned her sole dress, which had been brushed and cleaned to admiration.

She hurried downstairs and found Isabella and Richard already in the breakfast parlor where they had partaken of their nuncheon the day before. She stopped just over the threshold and swallowed hard. Richard turned toward her and the frown vanished from his rugged countenance, replaced by an easy smile. It didn't seem possible that any flesh-and-blood man could so perfectly fit her dreams. Yet there he stood, his lips twisting in amusement while she remained dumbstruck in the doorway.

She pulled herself together. His perfection, as far as she was concerned, was only physical, after all. He left a great deal to be desired in his attitude toward women. She wouldn't mind trying to educate him—but she had so little time. He would die in just a few short months . . . Forcing the unwelcome thought from her mind, she went to the sideboard and lifted lids at random, selecting items for a breakfast she no longer wanted.

The carriage drew up at the door almost as soon as she finished the light meal. Jumping up at once, Andrea announced herself ready.

A soft trill of laughter escaped Isabella. "Have you not forgotten your reticule?"

Thus reminded, Andrea ran upstairs, grabbed it up, and hurried back down.

Richard stood alone in the Great Hall, holding the morning's post. He looked up as she came lightly down the steps and smiled. "Enjoy yourself, but don't draw the bustle with a vengeance."

"Oh! That reminds me!" She bestowed on him one of the pearl necklaces and a slip of paper with the information for her bet.

His pleasant expression vanished beneath a grim scowl. He took the items and subjected the pearls to a rapid examination. Still holding them, he directed a searching look at Andrea.

Goaded, she glared right back at him. "I haven't stolen them, if that's what you're thinking. And unless I'm much mistaken, that strand will fetch a pretty price."

"Undoubtedly. And you stand to lose a great deal on this ramshackle venture of yours!"

"Females are not wholly ignorant of the sporting world," she informed him in lofty tones. "Or can you not bear the thought of sharing it with them?"

He didn't speak, but the glare he directed at her was clearly intended to quell such pert forwardness.

She met it with a look of wide-eyed interest. "Are you trying to stare me out of countenance?" The prospect delighted her—though more than she cared to admit, his coldness did not.

This evaporated in one of his lightning changes of mood. "I can see it would not be an easy task." He chuckled softly.

"No," she agreed. "I don't think it would be. And I would much rather see you 'depress pretension' with your quizzing glass, anyway. I am certain you would do it so very well."

"What an odd female you are!" He regarded her in an exasperation not unmixed with enjoyment.

She inclined her head as if acknowledging a compliment of no mean order and, as Isabella joined them, took her leave. At the door, Andrea glanced back to find Richard watching her, an intrigued expression in the depths of his marvelous, stormy eyes.

Chapter 9

The cumbersome berline, designed for carrying its passengers in stately comfort rather than style, entered the cobbled streets on the outskirts of Bath. Andrea leaned forward, unable to contain her excitement. So this was Regency England! She was really here, where she had longed to be for so many years.

Over Isabella's laughing protests, she let down the vehicle's window, allowing in a blast of icy air, so she could look unimpeded about into the gray, overcast street. She didn't want to miss a single detail.

Chill wind whipped color into her cheeks as she leaned out. Her excited gaze scanned the four-story buildings of gray and yellowed-white stone that lined their way. January might not be the best time to go sightseeing, but it would do. Oh, how it would do!

"Well?" Bella's gentle, teasing voice called her. "Does it live up to your expectations?"

"Oh, yes! It's absolutely—" Andrea broke off. "That poor little boy!"

A scrawny, raggedly dressed urchin darted across the street, deftly avoiding being run down by the carriages that did not so much as slow for him. He disappeared down the area steps of one of the many connected houses.

120

"Did you see that poor creature?" Andrea spun to face Bella.

"Probably a climbing boy. Pay him no heed, my dear." Bella smiled. "We shall be in Milsom Street in just a moment."

Andrea nodded, but when she returned her attention to the window, she barely glanced at the fashionably dressed members of the ton who huddled into their elegant wraps as they signaled sedan chairs or strolled the short distance to the Pump Room. There were other people on the street, not well dressed—not even adequately garbed, considering the iciness of the weather. Children who shivered, old people, bent and crippled, who were pushed aside to permit the wealthy and influential to pass undisturbed—or perhaps worse, simply ignored by their "betters."

"Is . . . can nothing be done for these unfortunate people?" Andrea demanded.

"My dear Miss Wells! Pray, do not let the sight of them disturb you! Are there no poor in America? They are cared for, I assure you."

"How?" Any care they received appeared patently inadequate.

"Why, there is the parish and any number of orphanages and charitable societies, I am sure. Now, do not trouble yourself over them. We are here for a very different purpose, and I promise, you shall enjoy it of all things!"

Andrea sank back against the squabs, much of her delight in the expedition fading. How could she revel in the purchasing of new gowns when there were so many people about her shabbily clothed? If only she had a purse full of coins. But at the moment, she had nothing. That would change, as soon as Richard—Grantham, she meant—returned with her winnings. She would set a portion of them aside to help these people.

Being reasonable, she recognized there was little she could do single-handedly to change the plight of the homeless and hungry when she had no money herself. But later, when she knew more about the time and the political situation, she would make some waves. She made it a vow and felt somewhat better.

Suddenly the shining image of her Regency heroes and heroines began to dim. It didn't seem possible they could live their lives of frivolity, spending hundreds of pounds on a single gown or jewel, when even half that amount would feed all the poor of the city for a week or more!

As they turned down Stall Street and passed the Grand Pump Room, her indignation at social injustice faded. Here, where the Polite World gathered, the outcasts and eyesores of society were not permitted to intrude themselves. And in their absence, Andrea realized to her dismay, it was all too easy to forget their existence in the delights that now met her bemused gaze.

The carriage pulled up in Milsom Street and they stepped down to the pavement. Perhaps the thrill of shopping, the aura of elegance that permeated the atmosphere, kept the beau monde blind. In moments, she herself had eyes for nothing but the shopfronts and signs that hung above the doors. She needed so many things and at last she could browse through real Regency-era items to her heart's content.

"We will get more in London." Isabella, laughing at her undisguised awe, caught up to where Andrea hurried ahead, looking at everything with wide, eager eyes. "Just purchase enough to cover your current needs."

"Where shall we begin?" Andrea didn't care. Everything—anything—would be wonderful.

"A mantua maker," Isabella pronounced. "If we find something you like, perhaps they can make alterations to it while we visit the milliners and haberdashers." She linked her arm through Andrea's and led her down two more doors, to where a sign announced the establishment of Madame Celestine, modiste.

An elegant ruched walking dress of mahogany-brown wool hung in the window. It looked to be, in modern terms, approximately a size three. And with all the ruffles and bunches of ribands, Andrea knew she would look a positive fright in such a creation. She swallowed, nervous, knowing full well that her unusual height would probably send the unsuspecting modiste into a spasm.

Gathering her courage, she followed Bella inside. Much to her pleasure, the shop matched the innumerable descriptions she had read, resembling nothing so much as a small salon. Gilt-framed mirrors lined the walls and delicate spindle-legged chairs and settees were set about the room. A curtain of deep-blue velvet hung across an opening through which a gaunt woman of indeterminate years emerged. Her prim mouth parted in a welcoming smile at sight of her visitors.

"Madame Brixton! What a pleasant surprise." She came forward with an imposing rustle of silk to take the hand of one of her most valued clients.

"Madame Celestine, we have urgent need of your services." Bella brought the tentative Andrea forward.

The modiste regarded her with the critical eye of the professional. "Indeed you do. But never fear, we shall have her looking more the thing in a trice."

"You are not French!" Andrea stared at the woman in surprise.

Both Bella and Madame Celestine laughed. "It is the name that brings the patrons in," the modiste explained. "Not even the dreadful revolution, or the shocking behavior of that upstart Bonaparte, can convince the ladies of society that any but a French dressmaker will do for them. And for me, this is not a problem of great difficulty." For the last words, she adopted a heavy

123

French accent. "What is it that you require, mademoiselle?"

"She has had her trunks stolen, Madame Celestine. Only imagine, she has naught but what she stands up in."

"*Voyons!*" The French exclamation came easily to the woman's lips. "But you will need so much! There must be two morning dresses, a riding habit, a carriage dress, a pelisse, and two . . . She glanced at Isabella Brixton, who nodded her approval. "Yes, two evening gowns."

"And two more nightdresses, shoes, stockings, chemises, handkerchiefs, gloves, and hats!" Isabella ticked the items off on her fingers. "You will purchase more in London, of course, but we will not go up for the Season for another two months. No, don't look so shocked, my love. You can hardly wear the same gown for so long."

The next several hours flew by in a whirl of muslins, laces, pattern cards, and fittings. The elaborate creations of frills and ruffles were no sooner glanced at than discarded as unsuitable. With a statuesque figure like Miss Wells's, the efficient and knowledgeable Madame Celestine pronounced with aplomb, quiet elegance must be the rule. Cambrics and wools, suitable for country attire in the dead of winter, replaced the sarsnets and silks.

Madame Celestine and two shop assistants hovered over Andrea just as if she were at one of the more expensive stores back home. While one woman fitted her into a morning gown, another brought forward a walking dress to hold up for her inspection. Andrea relaxed, feeling more secure with this familiar routine, and entered into the spirit with relish. Only she must remember not to request to see something in a different size.

At last, Andrea stood up in a round gown of rose crepe scooped low at the neck and filled in with a white muslin inset fastened by tiny seed pearl buttons. Little puffed sleeves perched precariously on the points of her shoulders. Her dubious gaze ran down the length of skirt to the unadorned hem and at least ten inches of the light muslin shift she had made for herself that showed beneath. The modiste clucked her tongue.

"A single flounce at the hem," the woman decided. "Not too full, but enough to give an attractive swing as you walk."

"And the sleeves? Could you also add something at the bottom to make them a little longer?"

"But, my love, they are the height of fashion!" Bella protested.

"Possibly, but on me they look ridiculous."

Her point was unanswerable. Madame Celestine sent for scraps of fabric, and together they decided on a second puff, below the first, that covered her arm almost to her elbow. Bella nodded, pleased by the result.

Andrea glanced at the pile of garments lying across the settee in the workroom. A rather beautiful riding habit of royal-blue merino lay on top, the last thing she had tried on—and known she could not leave the shop without. And beside the habit lay two evening gowns and another morning dress. This was more incredibly fun than anything she had imagined!

Leaving these garments for the seamstresses to alter, Isabella led her out of the shop into the wintry air. Andrea shivered. She would have to buy a shawl, and while she was at it, a muff wouldn't be unwelcome. She glanced at the one of silver fox in which Bella stuffed her hands. It was beautiful, but Andrea drew the line at real fur. The fox needed it more than she. Perhaps she could set a new fashion by having one made up out of wool.

"Slippers next?"

Bella's voice recalled her wandering thoughts. They stood before the window of a cobbler's shop, in which a selection of boots and slippers could be seen. Andrea cast an appraising eye over her own size eight and a half D's and grinned. This wasn't going to be easy.

Nor was it. The salesman, who greeted them enthusiastically, no sooner glanced at her feet than his fatuous smile faded. He took her own shoe, from which she had removed the manmade sole, and shook his head.

"I can't say as I've seen anything the like of this before."

"They were made in America." Well, Hong Kong, actually, but Andrea could see no reason to complicate matters further.

"Ah, that explains it." It was obvious that it did not, but no one wanted to pursue the point, least of all Andrea.

"Can you make her something?" Bella turned from her examination of a pair of leather half-boots dyed a deep blue.

"Aye, I'll have to," came the man's rueful response.

Andrea flushed. She was well aware that her feet were larger than the shops would be prepared for, but he needn't make it so clear that delicate little feet were expected of a lady.

To alleviate her own embarrassment—as well as her pressing needs—she placed a considerable order, covering everything from evening slippers to riding boots. The shopkeeper's aloofness vanished and he became all obsequious desire to please. After taking patterns and noting down her preferences in colors, he bowed them out the door.

"Odious little man!" Bella tucked her arm through Andrea's. "If he were not the best bootmaker in Bath, I vow I would never enter his door again."

"It is quite all right. As long as he can fill that order quickly. My own shoes are quite shockingly uncomfortable." In fact, if a Regency-era equivalent of Reeboks or Nikes had only existed—and in her size—she would have

126

unhesitatingly bought a pair to wear home.

Their next stop was a milliner's and Andrea looked around at the selection of bonnets and caps with lively interest. She loved hats, but preferred wide, sweeping brims to the upright pokes that added unnecessary inches to her already formidable height.

Bella swept up to the shopkeeper and handed over the swatches of fabric obtained at the modiste's to line the selection of bonnets she assured Andrea were indispensable. Andrea, shocked by the extravagant prices quoted to her, insisted she would need no more than two, at least for the moment. Bella finally let her have her way—on the condition that she not turn down a close-fitting riding headdress with a deep-blue plume that curled down to brush her cheek.

A nightcap and rather pretty confection of lace and feathers finished their purchases there. With the milliner's assurances that the hats would be delivered to their carriage within two hours, they were satisfied.

By the time they reached the haberdashery at the end of the street, Andrea was exhausted. Yet there were still any number of essentials to procure. She paused just inside the doorway and looked about, wondering where to start—and how quickly she could get it over with.

It seemed oddly familiar. An uncomfortable wrenching gripped her stomach as the thought drifted through her mind. This haberdasher's was very much like the dime store two blocks from her condo. There were the same vast array of goods, everything from tooth powder to stockings to the Regency-era equivalent of a curling iron!

She swallowed hard and fought the sudden rush of panic. Dear God, was she homesick? But *this* was now her home. She was no longer reading a novel which she could close at any time and find herself safely back in her own home in her own era.

With a determination and single-mindedness that startled the gentle Bella, Andrea set about making her purchases. In a very short time, she found herself in possession of a back-laced dimity corset with shoulder straps, a new reticule, soap, a comb and brush, stockings, a shawl of Norwich silk, and an array of undergarments.

Dizzy from so much shopping and from trying to block out intruding memories of her former life and the family she would never see again, Andrea accompanied Bella back to Madame Celestine's. They entered the elegant salon to be greeted with the news that the rose crepe gown already had been altered to fit. Fatigue and depression gave way. Andrea put it on and spun about before the long mirror, delighted by the swirling skirt and the sleeves that covered her arms comfortably. Yes, these were the clothes she longed to wear. She was in her element. She would make herself very happy in 1810 England.

To her further pleasure, her brown pelisse blended well enough with her new gown to wear over it. Andrea might think it a shame to cover so beautiful a creation, but practicality ruled the day; the temperature outside had dipped perilously close to freezing. They left the shop with her old dress done up in a bandbox, to Andrea's unending delight. She owned one at last!

Unable to restrain herself, she hurried back down the street to the milliner's where the first bonnet of chip straw she had ordered had just been finished. Rose silk now lined the high poke, and matching rose ribands clustered in knots about the crown and hung down from the sides. Andrea promptly tied these in a flirtatious bow beneath one ear.

"Why, you look much more the thing!" Isabella nodded her approval at the transformation of her protégée.

Andrea peered in the mirror, gratified by the results.

She looked a real Regency miss! The subtle rose of the bonnet lining warmed the brown of her eyes and set reddish highlights in the smooth blond hair that she had braided and wound about her head in a crown.

"Nothing could look more delightful!" Isabella assured her.

They went out to the street and Andrea's desire to stroll about the town died aborning. The sun, which gave off a faint but determined light, rode very low in the sky, casting a golden glow over the black, threatening clouds that hovered over the city. It would be dark in a little less than an hour. Somehow, they had shopped the entire day without so much as stopping for lunch or a cup of tea. No wonder her head ached! She could use a sugar lift, she thought.

"Let us return to the Court." Bella headed her dragging steps toward the waiting berline. "I vow I have not been so exhausted this age!"

The carriage, when they reached it, was comfortably full of parcels arranged on the forward seat. The rest would be sent out to Greythorne Court over the next couple of days. Andrea settled into the backseat beside her hostess and sighed.

"Can we return to Bath soon?" She peered out the window as they retraced their route over the cobbled streets. "We did not get to see any of the sights. And I so want to visit the Pump Room and sample the famous waters."

Isabella, in spite of her tiredness, went off in a merry peal of laughter. "Certainly we shall, if you are determined, but I give you fair warning that the waters are quite horrid. Why, the only time I tried them I felt ill for a week."

"And I want to see the Assembly Rooms and Sydney Gardens, also." Determined, Andrea reminded herself of all the wonderful treats in store. She *wanted* to be exactly where she was. And there was no need to hurry, to cram everything into one brief vacation. She had all the time in the world—the rest of her life, in fact. She was here, in her beloved Regency era, to stay.

She closed her eyes as the enormity of what she had accomplished washed over her again. She had a whole new world of manners and mores to assimilate and make her own. She was in an alien environment—but at least it was a friendly one. And Richard, who had drawn her back. . . . She forced her thoughts from him.

The interior of the carriage grew darker by the moment. Beside her, Isabella, worn out by the day's shopping spree, dozed peacefully to the swaying of the well-sprung vehicle. She might as well rest herself, Andrea reflected. The next few days would be quiet, though. Richard would not be there. She could devote her time to finding—and hiding—the Imperial Star.

When at last they drew up before the Court, a break in the clouds permitted the rising quarter moon to bathe the lovely old house in a soft, silvery glow. Andrea caught her breath in awe—and held it as fear welled up instead. At the corner of the East Tower, a dark figure, clearly illuminated by the unexpected light, slipped through the shrubbery.

"Isabella!" She shook her companion. "There! Do you see someone?"

Bella sat up, blinked sleepy eyes, and looked. The shrubbery gave one last rustle and subsided as a cloud blocked the moonlight once again.

"Probably nothing more than a groom." Bella evinced very little interest.

Something white fluttered near the tower wall and a shocked exclamation escaped Isabella as another figure disappeared in the opposite direction toward the house.

"Trysting with a chambermaid, I make no doubt. The low, vulgar creature! I wonder which one? You may be sure I shall have Prindle lecture them about this sort of thing."

Andrea shivered. Servants trysting in the shrubbery in the icy chill of a January evening? It didn't seem likely. But if not, who could it have been, and what could they have been doing? As far as she knew, there was nothing remarkable about the East Tower. The West Tower was a different story.

She hugged herself as the cold of the night penetrated to her heart. She was imagining things! Yet Richard had seen someone skulking about the grounds, too. There couldn't be a connection between these incidents and his impending death! It didn't make sense. Still, she was filled with a sense of foreboding that she could not banish.

Chapter 10

Richard Westmont, Viscount Grantham, flicked the whip with an expert crack between the near horse's ears. The pair of matched blacks broke into a canter and the curricle surged forward around the lumbering farm cart that blocked most of the road. Once away from this obstacle, though, Richard did not slow their pace.

Giles Kendall folded his arms and leaned back against the seat. Cold wind ruffled his sandy-brown locks and whipped bright color into his face. "Temper, temper," he murmured.

Richard spared him a scathing glance. "I do not like to be used."

"I'd hardly call it that. My own sister has an occasional flutter on the turf."

"She doesn't go at it like she's a damned Captain Sharp!"

"You are creating in me the liveliest desire to meet this unconventional American cousin of yours."

"Unconventional!" Richard snorted. "Ramshackle, you mean. She's like to set the town by its ears if we're not careful to keep an eye on her."

He relapsed into the stormy silence that had characterized their journey since they set out from Cheltenham

132

that morning. He shouldn't have gone to the meets—either of them. Newmarket had been boring, from beginning to end. And as for Cheltenham! The best horses had been hampered by the muddy condition of the track and outsiders, who normally would not even have been placed, sailed across the finish line lengths ahead of their betters. How had that exasperating female known?

His hands, in their skintight leather gloves, clenched on the reins. He was taking after his father, gambling away what little money remained to him. Damn these so-called gentlemen's pastimes! And damn Miss Andrea Wells for sending him to a second disastrous meet!

He still seethed inwardly as he slowed the curricle to make the turning onto the gravel drive at Greythorne Court. He'd been away for almost two weeks, twice as long as he'd intended. What had the little minx been up to in his absence? Suddenly, despite his irritation with her, he wanted to know. He could only hope she had not seriously disturbed Bella.

He drew the pair up before the fountain in the circular drive and sprang down. The front door opened and a footman hurried out to take charge of their baggage.

Samuel, Richard's groom, ran around from his perch at the back of the carriage and took the reins. "Can't remember when we made the trip in better time, m'lord."

Richard caught the accusing note in his longtime servitor's tone and a twinge of guilt struck him. He didn't usually let his anger get the better of him. "Were you bounced about? You should have given me a shout."

"Criticize your driving, m'lord?" Samuel gave an excellent imitation of appearing horrified. "It would be more than me position was worth!"

In spite of himself, Richard grinned. "Damn your impudence! Get off to the stables and warm yourself up."

The footman, joined now by his assistant and Prindle, carried valises indoors. Giles and Richard followed. As

133

they entered the Great Hall, Bella hurried down the stairs.

"Richard! You've been an age!" She subjected him to an enthusiastic embrace. "How was Newmarket?"

"Cold and wet." He kissed her cheek and set her aside. "This, my dear, is Giles Kendall. He's come to stay with us for a couple of days."

"Oh." Bella turned to her brother's striking companion and managed a false smile. "How . . . how charming to meet you at last."

Giles took her hand and raised it fleetingly to his lips. "Charming, indeed. I have long looked forward to making your acquaintance."

"Has everything been all right?" Richard looked about the hall. He had been mentally preparing a rousing rakedown on the impropriety of behavior that characterized a certain young lady, and it only added fuel to the smoldering coals that he could not deliver it without delay.

"We have been having the most delightful time. Oh, Richard, Andrea is the most wonderful houseguest, for you must know she is thrilled with even the most commonplace entertainment. I vow I have not enjoyed myself so much this age!"

"I am glad she has not been a burden on you." At this moment, he didn't want to hear her praised, either. "What have you been up to?"

"Teaching her to ride. And don't look like *that!* I am a very accomplished equestrienne, and well able to help her. She has made such remarkable progress, you will be quite proud of us both. And I've been showing her over the house." Here, she frowned prettily. "I fear you would be the better guide for her. She is so very interested in paintings, and you know more about them than I."

"Where is she?"

"In the Gold Saloon, I believe. When I left her, she was embroidering handkerchiefs."

"Then I shall leave you to become acquainted with Giles. I wish a word with Miss Wells."

He strode across the tiled hall, down the corridor, and flung open the door. Andrea looked up from the handkerchief over which she labored, startled. Vivid color flooded her cheeks and her eyes widened with pleasure as she saw him.

She abandoned her attempts to thread the royal-blue silk into her resistant needle at once. In spite of her strict orders, her heart lifted. Richard was back. She looked up at him, finding it disconcertingly hard to breathe.

He stopped just over the threshold, staring at her, a gleam in his steely blue-gray eyes. Tension pulsed from him, tangible and unnerving.

"I have brought you your winnings." He remained where he was, his scowl setting deep lines in his brow.

"Thank you." She rose, not able to sit still under that piercing regard. "Did you have an enjoyable time?"

"Except for worrying—needlessly, as it turns out— that you were taking a rash step." He drew out a soft leather pouch from his coat pocket and handed it to her. "Your pearls brought four hundred pounds. I placed your bet for two hundred, as you requested, and received excellent odds. Your winnings have come to fourteen hundred pounds."

Andrea let out a deep sigh. "I am so very glad! That should cover my most immediate needs. Thank you so much for your assistance."

He strode over to the fire that burned high in the hearth, glared at it for a long moment, then turned back to Andrea. "Being an American, you may not be aware of this, but it is improper in the highest degree for a female to be as familiar with the turf as you appear to be. I suggest, for my sister's sake, that you not display your knowledge too freely."

"Is this one of those fields that only gentlemen are permitted to enjoy?" A challenge lit her sparkling brown eyes.

"It is. A lady may indulge in an occasional flutter, but she is not expected to make her fortune on the nags."

The savage note that underlay his voice startled her.

"I don't see why it should upset you, so," she said, weighing her words with care. "I shall take care to be most discreet, I promise, and only place my bets through you."

"I have no desire to be used as a go-between for your vices, madam!"

She tilted her head to one side, refusing to cower before him as he seemed to expect. "I would hardly call it a vice. I merely need to frank myself for the Season. And as I have lost everything I brought with me, I must take the only course open to me."

"While you are beneath my roof, you will have no need for large sums of money!"

Had they not already had this argument? He must be very angry, indeed, to bring it up once again.

"What? You would offer to pay for my gowns?" She tried teasing. "Now that *would* be most improper!"

His hands clenched. "Your funning humor is betraying you into utterances that would best be held in check, madam. While you are in my sister's charge, I will thank you to behave with a measure of decorum." In two long, restless strides, he stood before her. "I realize that as an American you may have trouble in knowing how to go on, but Isabella, for all her flightiness, is excellent ton and can hint you into the accepted mode."

Andrea flushed, her own anger welling up. "I have not the least desire to be either missish or biddable, I assure you! I shall be an Original."

"I am pleased you have made such definite plans for

your future." His tone could have dripped icicles. "But I repeat—"

Andrea did not have the privilege of learning what he would repeat. The door burst open once more and Isabella entered the room with a man only slightly shorter than Richard, whom Andrea did not recognize.

"This is an old friend of Richard's." Isabella stood back, stiff, making her dislike of this intrusion very clear. "Mr Giles Kendall."

Andrea stared from one to the other of them. This was the man Bella would marry. Yet neither one of them showed any signs of planning such an event in the foreseeable future. Gathering herself together, Andrea stammered a greeting.

If the Corinthian before her noticed her discomfiture, he gave no sign. His hazel eyes held a twinkling smile as he made her a magnificent leg.

"I must congratulate you, Miss Wells." He bestowed a singularly charming smile on her. "Next time, you must recommend something for me! Has Richard been asking you for a tip? Beggared, both of us. Our damned screws weren't even placed!" He gave his tousled head a rueful shake. "Told him we should have followed your lead."

Richard turned and stalked from the room. So that was what lay behind his ill temper, Andrea realized. Not only did she have the unfeminine folly to bet on the horses, but she committed the even worse sin of winning while he lost.

Prindle entered the room and bowed to Giles. "Your curricle has arrived, sir. I have requested your groom to drive it on to the stables. Would you wish to speak to him?"

"Yes, thank you." Giles bowed to both ladies and took his leave.

Andrea sank back down in her chair, dismayed. Richard was no creation of hers but a living breathing man—

as aggravating as the rest of his sex, in any time. This was no fairy tale where Prince Charming was forever perfect. She had committed the folly of falling for a portrait, and now she had the dubious privilege of meeting the chauvinistic, disagreeable reality behind that rakish, enticing smile.

Giles Kendall departed for his hunting box in Melton Mowbray the following morning, amid Richard's assurances that he would join him at the end of the week. Isabella made no secret of her delight at the brevity of his stay, but Andrea watched his curricle disappear around the bend in the drive with mixed feelings. How, she wondered, were Giles and Bella to marry if they did not get to know each other?

She had the opportunity that evening to meet the primary obstacle in the way of the union. Wilfred, son and heir of Sylvester, third earl of Malverne, came to dinner, along with Miss Moreland, Miss Letitia Moreland, and his sire. Andrea had met the two ladies previously, but she had not yet encountered the gentlemen.

Nor was she prepared. The portly, comfortable figure of the Earl of Malverne faded into insignificance when compared with his flamboyant son. Andrea had read descriptions of dandies many times, but nothing could have led her to expect the reality of Wilfred. From the top of his preposterous, tapering tall hat to the soles of his slippered feet with their giant emerald-studded buckles, a "vision" was the only term that could apply.

He made a magnificent leg, sweeping the lime-green atrocity from his pomaded sandy-red locks as he did so. Rising, he possessed himself of Andrea's hand and just brushed his lips across her fingers.

"Enchanted, Miss Wells." He drawled the words, his voice as affected as his grandiose mannerisms.

138

Andrea took her lower lip firmly between her teeth and ordered her quivering chin to stop betraying her amusement. This was really too good to be believed! A Tulip of the Ton, no less. Oh, she wouldn't miss him for the world. And he had not the least notion how ridiculous he appeared.

He turned from her to the gilt-edged mirror that hung above the hearth in the Gold Saloon where they had gathered before dinner. Standing on tiptoe, for his inches were adequate rather than generous, he assured himself that the voluminous folds of his neckcloth remained in place and the points of his shirt collar, which rose stiffly to the corners of his eyes, had not relaxed their rigid precision.

"Well, glad to see our little Isabella has some female companionship." The Earl of Malverne addressed himself to Andrea and nodded in the manner of one who had made up his mind on the subject and would not be easily dissuaded. "Not right for her to live here alone, with only Grantham to pay her fleeting visits."

"It's not only Grantham, Pater." Wilfred shook out the old-fashioned ruffles of Mechlin lace, which he seemed bent on bringing back into à la modality, about his wrists. Dissatisfied with the result, he pulled them farther from the confining sleeve of his emerald velvet coat and tried again. "Lettie and the Dragoness toddle over to pay their respects. And so do I." He smiled in a fatuous manner as he looked across to where his betrothed sat in conversation with the two ladies.

"Well, now, my boy, you mustn't go calling her that. Dragoness, indeed!" Malverne cast an uneasy eye to assure himself that the formidable woman under discussion had not overheard. He fussed with the lapels of his coat of blue superfine. "What a strange idea you'll be giving Miss Wells."

"I am sure it is no such thing. Is it, Miss Wells?"

Wilfred fumbled among the numerous fobs and chains that crisscrossed the wide lime-and-white stripes of his satin waistcoat, found the quizzing glass that hung from an emerald riband, and leveled it at her bemused but delighted face. He allowed the glass to drop. "See, Pater. She smiles, and the entire room brightens."

"Rattlepate!" Malverne shook his head, not quite sure what to make of his heir's affectations. "Pay him no heed, Miss Wells."

"Indeed, I shall not. How shocking if I were to listen to the blandishments of so accomplished a flirt."

"That's the girl." The earl beamed up at her in approval. "Sensible little thing, ain't you?" He folded his pudgy hands across the ample expanse of his subdued floral waistcoat. "Though not so little. A fine figure of a woman, my dear, a fine figure of a woman." He nodded, several times, and his rosy cheeks took on a darker hue. "Fine figure." Still nodding to himself, he strolled off to join his ward and her chaperone.

"You must forgive his odd manner, my dear Miss Wells." Wilfred arranged himself in a delicate Sheridan chair and stretched his stockinged legs out before him. He examined the delicate clocking through his quizzing glass, then allowed the eyepiece to fall with a contented sigh. "I was afraid—quite afraid, I assure you—that they had become splattered with mud, despite my cloak. I am most relieved."

Andrea pondered the permissibility of a lady commenting on the pristine nature of a gentleman's hose and decided not to risk it. She would have to discover what subjects were considered proper for predinner conversation. Playing it safe, she asked. "Do you make a long stay in the country?"

"But there is nowhere else!" He raised delicately fine brows. "The village is dreadfully thin of company just now and Brighton is dreary beyond words at this time of year. But there is always Bath! One is not quite sunk into boredom."

Before Andrea could ascertain whether "the village" did indeed signify London, Prindle entered to announce dinner. Malverne came up to them and offered Andrea his arm, leaving his son to take in Bella and Richard to escort both Miss Moreland and Lettie.

They took their seats at table and Andrea glanced toward Isabella, who sat mercifully near. Andrea's uncertain manners had served for quiet family gatherings. She could only hope she would not disgrace herself in the presence of guests.

"You must write to your man of affairs at once, Richard." Isabella served herself from the soup tureen held by the second footman. "I will not be fobbed off with some tiny house in an unfashionable quarter of town this year."

"Planning great events, my dear?" Richard slid a piece of poached salmon onto his plate and replaced the fish slice on the serving dish.

"Do not be obtuse. We must hold a ball to introduce Andrea into Society. And then there must be another, in honor of my engagement."

"An unending round of delights, I apprehend." He sounded resigned rather than pleased.

"There is no need for you to stay the entire time." Bella pouted prettily. "But you must at least be present for the balls."

"Why do you not combine them into one?"

Andrea saw in this suggestion Richard's natural aversion to the fuss, bother, and expense surrounding lavish entertainment. Bella, though, perceived it as a splendid excuse to make the event the social highlight of the season. Her blue-gray eyes lit with eager delight.

"The beau monde will talk of nothing else for months!" She breathed a sigh of pure ecstasy.

"By Jove, I should think not!" Wilfred nodded as vigorous an approval as his prodigious neckcloth permitted. "'Twill set them all by their ears! Ah, and it will give you a chance to try out all those dancing lessons, Lettie." He threw a smiling glance across the table to his father's ward.

Lettie nodded but kept her attention focused on her plate. "It . . . it will be of all things the most delightful. I'm to be brought out this Season, you must know."

"Are you?" Bella blinked, momentarily startled out of her absorption. "But to be sure, you have turned seventeen! Yet it seems only yesterday you were still in the schoolroom." She reached across with impulsive warmth and clasped Lettie's little hand. "I shall take you about, my love, never fear. You and my dear Miss Wells make the perfect foil for one another. What attention you will attract!"

Miss Moreland did not appear to approve of the suggestion. "I am sure we shall manage quite well, Mrs. Brixton."

"But you are unacquainted with the patronesses of Almack's. If she is known to be under my wing, there will be no problem in obtaining vouchers for her."

Miss Moreland stiffened. "I am sure it is very kind of you, but Malverne's ward needs no one to lend her countenance."

"Will you be in town for the entire Season?" Richard addressed the remark to Malverne, neatly cutting off his sister's heated rejoinder and calming the brewing storm clouds.

The earl shook his head. "Don't seem to go in for that sort of thing anymore. I'll come up for the ball, of course. Wouldn't look right if I didn't. But I don't travel much these days."

"It's becoming impossible even to get him into Bath, except to drink the waters." Wilfred gave an exquisite

142

shudder. "While I, on the other hand, can scarcely wait to return to a more civilized way of life."

"Tired of the hardships of winter?" Richard's eyes narrowed. "The chill nights make evening calls so uncomfortable, do they not? Or do you like trudging through shrubberies in the wet and cold?"

Wilfred met the steely gaze with an appalled stare. "Trudge through shrubberies? Good God, why should anyone want to do that? And as for chill nights! No! A pleasant stroll on a summer's day, perhaps. But you'd have to be touched in your upper works to do it on a winter's eve!" He shook his head. "All those sporting events you watch, Grantham. You take my advice and give them the go-by. Your're beginning to take queer notions into your cockloft, dear fellow, very queer notions."

Richard's lip curled in a sneer, but a slight frown creased his brow. Andrea watched these signs in concern. Apparently, he no longer suspected Wilfred of being the shrub-lurker. In that estimate, she inclined to agree with him. Wilfred appeared to be a gentleman too obviously concerned with his own comfort and appearance ever to do anything so unconventional—and so certainly ruinous to his outer garments.

Lettie looked from one to the other, perplexed. "Why would anyone wish to walk in a shrubbery at this time of year? I am sure the ground must be much too muddy! I would not venture beyond the terrace—unless perhaps we followed the lane."

Andrea, who had had experience with the local lanes, opened her mouth to assure Lettie she would not find such a walk in the least agreeable, but stopped herself. Her gaze brushed across each of their visitors. Not one of them seemed the sort to conceal themselves in bushes and peer in at the house. Nor did Wilfred appear in the least bit afraid of Richard. Confused by his quicker

143

intelligence, perhaps, possibly intimidated by his larger and more musclar frame, but nothing more. He displayed no hesitation in coming to the house. Whoever it might be, Wilfred could not be the shrub-lurker.

Bella threw her brother a beseeching glance, anxious to get him off this topic. "We must go up to town early, Richard, but we—Andrea and I—can stay at a hotel until you can arrange for a suitable house."

"Early?" He dragged his frowning gaze from Wilfred. "Why?"

"To go shopping, of course, silly! What else? Andrea will need any number of new gowns, and while what she has purchased in Bath does quite well enough for the country, we must visit only the most fashionable modistes in London from now on."

Richard's gaze came to rest on the yellow gauze half-dress with the lace puffed sleeves that Andrea wore. The white gauze of the undergown foamed about the chair legs. "I see nothing amiss with her appearance."

A trill of laughter escaped Bella. "My brother, the master of the elegant compliment. Of course there is nothing amiss! She looks delightful! But she must always appear in the first style of elegance. With Wilfred's advice, and her elegant carriage, she will lead fashion, mark my words."

Andrea started. "Lead fashion! Pray, do not be nonsensical. I am far too tall and will more likely be shunned. But I do wish to be properly gowned."

"Do not fear being an American, Miss Wells." Richard caught her gaze and held it. An approval lurked in his gray eyes that left her disturbingly breathless. "Society may be shallow, but did you not tell me you intend to be an Original? You will take them by storm!"

The term "acid rain" sprang to her mind, but she stifled it. "I will be thought shockingly provincial." She shook off the unsettling spell of his compelling eyes and forced a bright smile to her lips. "I promise you, I intend to procure a guide book and visit all the sights, no matter what anyone says. I will go to the Tower and the British Museum and St. Paul's and Bartholomew's Fair." Her eyes gleamed with growing enthusiasm. "And I am dying to see the Peerless Pool!"

Miss Moreland gasped, and both Letttie and Bella giggled. Wilfred stared at her, sincerely shocked, while Malverne gave a guffaw of laughter. Richard's eyes kindled with appreciation.

"Hoyden," he murmured. His expression held a challenge not unmixed with amusement.

"Is that not better than being stupidly missish?" Her face a mask of innocent inquiry, she met his gaze squarely.

A gleam flashed in the depths of his eyes. "Infinitely."

Bella laughed, delighted, breaking the spell that held Andrea captive, yet eager to meet any challenge offered by Grantham. "Only rustics do such things. You will cut the oddest figure!"

"A positive April-gawk!" Wilfred agreed.

"I thought you all eagerness to show Miss Wells about." Grantham regarded his sister in mock surprise.

Bella ignored it. "If I took her everywhere she wants to visit, I would be quite worn down."

"Very true. We should warn you, Miss Wells, it is quite unfashionable to enjoy yourself." Yet Richard did not sound displeased with her.

"That's as may be, but I refuse to waste so much as a single moment of my time. I want to see everything. And I do not care a . . . a fig if I am thought unusual or eccentric."

"One must have money to get away with being an eccentric." Wilfred nodded wisely. "You mustn't— simply mustn't—do anything that might embarrass Bella."

"I'm sure she couldn't." In spite of her words, Bella cast an uneasy glance at Andrea.

"There's no question of any such thing." Richard eyed Wilfred in distaste. "I will escort her myself, if necessary, to preserve the propriety."

Andrea blinked. He would do what? She met his gaze, with its open invitation to an enjoyable battle of wits, and her heart jumped in the most disconcerting manner. He was bored! And apparently he thought that keeping her in line might entertain him. It would certainly entertain her.

But she didn't want to become involved with him, not any more than was strictly necessary, at least. As intriguing as the prospect might be, she knew it would only lead to heartbreak. Of course, she could always— no, she couldn't change history. She could not lure him away so that he was not at Greythorne Court on May 16. It might have disastrous unforeseeable consequences.

Sobered, Andrea concentrated on her plate. The footmen presented course after course to her, but she found she no longer had much interest in either food or the novelty of her first Regency-era dinner party. She didn't want Richard to die. And there wasn't a thing she could do to prevent it from happening. With relief, she welcomed Bella's rising to her feet, the signal for the ladies to withdraw to the music room.

At Miss Moreland's suggestion, Bella seated herself at the pianoforte and embarked on a lovely old ballad. This, to Andrea's surprise, proved highly stylized, not the simpler tune of the American version she had heard before. She sat in silence, listening, until Lettie moved to her side.

"Have you been enjoying your visit, Miss Wells?" Lettie kept her voice soft so as not to interrupt Bella's playing.

"Indeed, it has been quite delightful. But please call

146

me Andrea."

Lettie smiled shyly at her. "Will it not be wonderful to go to London? I have not been there since I was a child!"

"I have not been there at all." Well, it *was* true. Her visit had not yet taken place—and would not, for about another one hundred and eighty odd years!

"Oh, what fun we shall have! I . . . I do so hope you will let me see all the sights with you!" Lettie's large blue eyes glowed at the prospect.

"Why, of course. If we can but get someone to act as our guide."

Lettie sighed in relief. "I am glad. You can have no notion how frightened I have been at the prospect of going to London. Don't laugh, I beg of you. It is quite silly, I know, but I am not in the least brave, and the thought of being among so many strangers terrifies me. But now I shall have you, my dear Miss Wells, and we will face our first Season together."

"Indeed we shall." Andrea blinked. Somehow, she could not feel that the gentle, timorous Lettie would share many of her tastes. Yet the girl had adopted her as a friend—or mentor, more like—she realized. The silly chit had elevated her to near heroine status for her bravery in supposedly crossing the Atlantic. If she only knew the truth!

The gentlemen joined them, and shortly afterward Prindle wheeled in the tea tray. After only one cup, the visitors rose to take their leave, pleading the inclement weather as their excuse for departing so early. Bella protested, but Richard, his expression one of scarcely veiled boredom, sent for their carriage.

As he turned back from seeing their guests off, Bella planted herself firmly in his path.

"Well, Richard? I believe you owe me—and Wilfred—an apology."

"I believe I do." His tone held little interest in the

subject. "It is certainly not he who has been lurking under the windows."

His sister stood on tiptoe and planted a kiss on his cheek. "There's a dear. Now, do stop being disagreeable about it and promise to come to Bath with us in the morning." She regarded him without much real hope.

"What? And watch you spend money? No, I thank you!" He ruffled her raven curls in an affectionate manner. "You know I have no taste for women's fashion."

"Now, that's a . . . a plumper!" Bella borrowed one of his phrases. "No, I promise, not another word, but do not think I don't know what you get up to! Now, say you will help me show Andrea about. She has not yet seen any of the sights."

His gaze strayed to where Andrea stood on the third step, her candle holder clutched in her hand. The flickering light bathed her in a warm glow. His eyes narrowed, an odd expression lurking in their depths.

"I suppose I must go just to ensure you do not set Bath on its ears with some outrageous prank." Abruptly, he sketched a bow and strode down the hall toward his bookroom, leaving the two ladies to stare at one another in astonishment at his good-natured acquiescence.

Chapter 11

Andrea descended the stairs slowly the following morning, lost in thought. So far her tours of Greythorne Court under the guidence of her hostess had turned up no sign of any painting that might conceivably be the Imperial Star. From the description given her by Catherine Kendall, it should be easy to spot, very distinctive—and very valuable. It might well be hidden for that reason.

Grantham was a collector at heart, and every collector loved to show off his treasures. She would start dropping hints about how much she loved religious art—or perhaps Russian art. Or better yet, both. She needed results.

Much to her relief, she found she could begin at once; Grantham had not changed his mind about accompanying them to Bath. She more than half expected he would, for she could think of few things more boring to a gentleman than to be obliged to escort a lady bent on seeing the sights. But he was in the breakfast parlor before her, dressed in an elegant riding coat and buckskins.

He looked up from his tankard of ale as she entered. On the plate before him lay the remnants of a rare sirloin of beef. A hearty eater, she decided, yet there didn't seem

149

to be an ounce of fat on him. He must keep physically active to prevent gaining weight. His body, under his tight-fitting clothing, appeared lean and well-muscled. She looked away, confused by the rush of sensations caused by her wayward thoughts.

"So, you are ready betimes. I've never yet known a female to be late when she intended to spend money."

"But I do not go to the shops this day, my lord." She recovered her composure and charged right in. "I go simply to see the sights. I thought we might visit the Abbey. I find religious art so . . . so very beautiful, do not you?"

To her disappointment, he merely said, "If you intend to walk about, you might have picked a better day for your expedition."

She discovered he was right as soon as they went outside. An icy breeze whipped the skirts of her wool pelisse about her ankles and dark, heavy clouds hung low, threatening snow. Reluctantly, Richard sent his mount back to the stable and entered the berline behind the ladies. A footman hurried from the house with hot bricks for their feet and Richard draped the robe over Andrea's and Bella's knees. Assuring himself they were comfortable, he signaled for the coachman to set forth.

Andrea stared out the window, wondering how to bring the conversation around to priceless icons without appearing to pry. She had thought Richard and Bella would brag over the possession of such a piece of art. But neither of them had so much as mentioned it, despite her comments. She would have to make her questions more pointed in the future.

Large white flakes began to fall, drifting slowly at first, then faster and harder, covering the landscape in a delicate blanket that melted almost at once. The coachman slowed his pair as the footing became damp and treacherous.

"Oh, dear." Bella turned to her brother as if she expected him to do something about the disagreeable weather. "Richard, this is too awful."

"Poor planning, my dear. The clouds have been gathering for days." A hint of laughter lurked in his voice, as if he enjoyed seeing their scheme for sightseeing brought to naught. "Shall I have them turn about and go home?"

"Of course not." Andrea drew her gaze from the muddy road.

"You can hardly walk about the town in a blizzard," he pointed out.

Andrea considered. "Will not the Abbey or the Pump Room be open?"

An appreciative gleam lit Richard's eyes. "Determined," he murmured. "Now, why does that not surprise me? The Abbey will be cold and deserted, but the Pump Room it shall be." He settled back against the squabs, half closing his eyes, but his thoughtful gaze rested on her eager face.

Andrea leaned forward again, her spirits lifting in spite of the gloom outside. It was the Pump Room she really wanted to see, mentioned in so many novels. She would find other opportunities to talk about paintings.

Very few people could be glimpsed on the almost deserted streets as they passed through the outskirts of Bath. The flakes of snow became smaller and fell more heavily, leaving a fragile layer covering the cobbles and muffling the sounds of the horses' shod hoofs. They wound their way through the town, and in a few minutes pulled up before the Pump Room.

Richard jumped down and turned to hand out first Bella, then Andrea. His hand lingered on hers and a smile glinted in his eyes. "I hope this will not be a disappointment."

"It couldn't be." Her fingers tightened about his for a

moment, then she hurried toward the shelter of the porch, disturbed. Even the most casual contact between them set her unruly senses soaring. She could not, no matter how great her desire, yield to this purely physical attraction.

Thrusting his intrusive presence from her mind, she followed Bella into the building. Just inside the door, she stopped, eyes shining, her worries evaporating. She was here—really here, not just imagining it. Slowly, she turned about, her gaze sweeping the room in a full circle as she tried to memorize every detail.

Almost a hundred people crowded the building, from the very elderly to members of the nursery. Apparently, Bath society had little else to do on a snowy day. A sigh of pure ecstasy escaped her. She could look her fill—or better, she could join the throng, for she was one of them now, as she had longed to be.

Richard touched her elbow and she jumped, startled by the tangible, physical proof this was no fantasy. She laughed in a mixture of nerves and excitement and allowed him to guide her to a chair. Bella drifted with them, exchanging greetings with a large number of acquaintances.

Richard leaned close to Andrea as he seated her. "There is one of the sights of Bath." He murmured the words in her ear, careful not to let anyone else overhear.

Andrea choked back her gasp of delight. The woman he indicated was perfect, from her outmoded gown in lavender satin brocade with its natural waist to the patches on her painted, wrinkled cheek to the curling ostrich plumes that topped off an elaborate coiffure of silvered locks.

Bella directed an admonitory glare at them and, drawing Andrea back to her feet, went to greet the lady warmly. With a great show of deference, she begged to introduce her protégée to Lady Eddington. The name meant nothing to Andrea, much to her regret, but she responded politely to the brusque questions about the rigors of life in America. Satisfied, Lady Eddington dismissed her abruptly, waved her away, and turned her attention to another helpless young lady. Andrea stepped back, uncertain whether to be affronted or amused.

"Don't worry, she takes everyone that way." Richard offered his arm to Andrea and led her off. "She is famous for her rudeness, but she can ruin a newcomer to Society by merely expressing disapproval."

"How very odd that such a creature should be permitted to have such power."

"You do not approve?" Richard raised a quizzical eyebrow.

"Do you?" she shot back.

"No, but one indulges her. She is far too old to change her ways, now. Over there is General Cathcart, who has lost a leg, but, as you can see, his crutches in no way impede his captivation of the fairer sex."

She looked across at the erect, white-haired gentleman who held court at a table amid a bevy of his contemporaries, mostly female. "And who else is here?"

Richard looked about. "There is Lady Bevis." He pointed out a stocky woman in an elaborate bonnet. "And young Chartley, Addison's heir. If you want to see a Bath Quiz you have only to direct your attention to the left and see Mrs. Witherspoon."

The lady he pointed out wore a fashionable gown in the Grecian style, all filmy drapery cut excessively low at the bosom. Her figure, to Andrea's critical eye, most closely resembled an army tank, a thought she could not share with Richard, for he would be unfamiliar with the concept.

A pang of regret shot through her. They came from such different backgrounds, almost as if they spoke different languages. She was forced to grope through a limited vocabulary to express her feelings and ideas.

"Tired?" His voice sounded soft near her ear. "Perhaps a glass of the famous waters?"

"Oh, yes!" Her momentary depression vanished at the prospect. "How I have longed for a taste!"

Smiling at her enthusiasm, Richard obtained a glass for her. "Here, you may now achieve another of your ambitions." She accepted it, eager, and he watched with a devilish gleam in his eyes as she took a tentative sip.

"Why, it is not half as horrid as everyone makes out!"

He chuckled and took the glass from her. "There's no need for you to drink it all, you know."

"No, perhaps I won't." She allowed him to place it on a convenient table, then accompanied him along the Promenade, avidly staring at the gowns, mannerisms, and jewels of the Fashionable World.

About halfway through their first circuit of the room, she became aware of a very lovely young lady looking pointedly in their direction. Andrea's fingers tightened on her escort's arm. "Who is that?"

Richard followed her gaze and the lady waved, then lowered her face in a combination of come-hither look and pretended shyness.

"Is she one of your flirts?"

He stiffened. "And what, may I ask, do you know of that?"

Andrea considered, not the least abashed. "Well, she is quite pretty. And so is the brunette over there, who seems bent on catching your eye. I must say, you do not seem to be particular as to coloring, do you? But they are both quite lovely."

"Yes, all my flirts are." His tone was that of one goaded. Still, a reluctant humor forced its way up into his dancing eyes. "I do have my reputation to consider, you know."

"Heavens, then I had best take my leave of you! It

would never do for anyone to think you had set up a 'long Meg' as your latest. Have I that right, by the way?"

A muscle twitched at the corner of his mouth. "You have, if you mean a tall female, but I would rather describe you as a Juno." An enticing gleam invited her to stay with him—and to something more, if she were willing.

She was not. She averted her warm face and forced a teasing note into her voice. "Now, why does 'Juno' make me think of female spaniels or terriers?"

He laughed. "A goddess, then."

Startled, she looked up into his face and saw the fascinating light in those misty gray eyes that must have been the undoing of any number of unsuspecting damsels. But she was very suspecting and he was far too intriguing. Instinctively, she withdrew, an act of self-preservation.

His expression closed and she realized, to her utter amazement, that she had hurt him.

"And here we have another Bath Quiz," Richard said acidly.

She turned to see Wilfred seating himself beside Bella, who laughed gaily at something he said. He tittered in a manner that made Richard grind his teeth in irritation.

"Would you care to join them?" Without waiting for her answer, Richard took her over and left her at their table.

Whether he meant her to be a chaperone for them or just wanted to get rid of her, Andrea could not be sure. When she glanced over her shoulder to find him, she saw he had made his way to the enticing brunette, who welcomed him with flirtatious pleasure. Andrea felt an irrational disappointment.

She was distracted by a portly gentleman of advancing years who strolled over, greeted Wilfred who did not seem overly pleased by his intrusion, then cast an obvious and appraising glance toward Andrea. Wilfred supplied the expected introduction, and Lord Brompton made an elegant bow, hampered only by the creaking of his Cumberland corset.

"Forgive me if I thrust myself upon you, but how could I help but be drawn by so beautiful a visitor? Your presence drives away the dreariness of the day." He seated himself at the table, bent upon making himself agreeable. "Do you stay in Bath, Miss Wells?"

"No, with Mrs. Brixton, at Greythorne Court."

"She has come to us for the Season," Bella put in, her tone cool.

"A beautiful place, I believe. I have not visited it—yet. But it is not so very distant from Bath as to make a morning visit ineligible."

"But the weather!" Andrea demurred, uncomfortable under his steady, admiring eyes. She might need to enlarge her very small circle of acquaintances, but she drew the line at Lord Brompton.

"The weather is as nothing." Brompton made an expansive gesture and beamed at her. "My horses and I delight in snow."

Andrea managed a polite smile at his nonsense. Brompton obviously considered himself something of a ladies' man. Now she had him pegged—the elderly roué of the novels who terrorized innocent, silly chits and drew derisive sneers from others. She found it amusing that such a person really existed.

If only others fell into neat pigeonholes. She glanced at Richard, who was promenading with his brunette, his attention completely absorbed by the vivacious beauty hanging on his arm. In a fit of not-fully-understood pique, Andrea returned her attention to her companion. "Do you live in Bath?" She had absolutely no interest in his answer, but could think of nothing else to say.

"I have only come on a visit, fair Hera."

"Not Juno?" she asked before she could stop herself.

Wilfred snorted, then turned the sound into an unconvincing cough.

"Lord Brompton's estates lie in the north, near Leeds." Bella frowned in disapproval at Brompton's familiarity.

"Indeed they are." Brompton smiled on her, apparently unaware of Bella's politely disguised dislike. "And how glad I am that I came to spend the dreary winter months with my sister, for it gives me the opportunity of meeting such a charming new acquaintance."

He continued with his ponderous flirtation until Andrea became vividly aware of a presence hovering just behind her. Brompton broke off in mid sentence and rose to acknowledge Richard. That gentleman nodded coolly and turned to address Andrea.

"Would you care to take a stroll about the room with me?"

Her teasing rejoinder died on her lips. Tension radiated from him, unsettling her. With nerves fluttering, she rose, and for several minutes they walked without speaking. Unconsciously, she braced herself for the storm that was about to break.

"It is not the thing for you to be setting up flirts." He broke the silence, his tone reproving.

"Was that what I was doing?" She bristled at his censure. "How silly of me. I thought I was successfully keeping an aging Lothario at bay."

"Don't play off your tricks on me, my girl. I cut my eye teeth long ago! You were deliberately flirting with him!"

"I was doing no such thing!" She faced him, defiant. "Do you really think I could find him in the least bit appealing? And for that matter, look who's talking! Flirting seems to be a rather common occupation around here."

157

"Common, indeed. Brompton is a shameless rake and you should not be in his company."

"I wonder what a shame*ful* one would be like," she mused, momentarily diverted.

Richard stiffened. "I will thank you to behave with some measure of propriety while you are in my sister's charge!"

"Considering she was sitting right beside me, I think that's coming it a bit strong." Her large eyes flashed. "Do you actually dare to condemn *my* behavior?"

"I most certainly do."

"But it is no different from your own!"

"It is—simply because you are a lady. A man doesn't earn the reputation of being fast."

"No, merely of being a rake, and that seems to be a compliment." The light of battle shone in every line of her countenance. "But it is *not* a compliment to be labeled a loose fish or a libertine."

His face darkened. "You are a shocking baggage," he snapped.

"Because I do not mince words and I'm not afraid to stand up to you?" She responded angrily. "What pitifully poor creatures you must be accustomed to!"

Bella joined them, effectively cutting off his reply. Detecting nothing untoward in their combative stance, she slipped her hand through her brother's free arm and gave it a gentle tug.

"I am quite done-up with the cold and am ready to go home. We can show Andrea nothing more until the snow stops."

"It *has* become rather chilly in here." Andrea glared at Richard, not sure whether she was glad or sorry the argument had been broken off. "But we can return later, can we not? In better weather? I have not yet seen any of the sights, and I do so wish to see the Upper and Lower Assembly Rooms. And the Abbey," she added, remembering the interest she must cultivate in religious art.

"Of course we shall," Bella assured her.

Grantham led them out to the waiting carriage without a word. Once inside, though, he let down the window and called to the driver, "Take us past the Lower Rooms, and go slowly, if you please. I wish Miss Wells to be able to look her fill." He put the window back up against the blast of freezing air.

"Impudent." Andrea hunched her shoulder and ignored him. When the berline slowed, though, she did look at the rather commonplace building and a deep sigh escaped her. "Oh, if only there were an assembly!"

Richard laughed suddenly, his foul temper evaporating. "She is like to exhaust you, Bella. You are brave indeed to agree to take her to London! I suppose I shall have to go along to make sure she does not wear you to a thread or get herself into trouble."

Bella blinked, profoundly shocked by such an offer. "But did you not pledge yourself to stay with Mr. Kendall in Melton Mowbray until late March?"

Richard shrugged. "Perhaps I will. Though I do not think I'll go to him until after you are settled in town. This is no weather for traveling into the north."

The Assembly Room passed, Andrea sank back against the carriage seat and fell silent for the remainder of the journey home. It would be best for her peace of mind if Richard *would* leave the Court, but oh, how she was glad he would stay. She felt so alive when he was near, even if they did fight.

She stared out the window, watching the swirling flakes blur the landscape. A soft, white covering hid the ground and clung to bare tree limbs and the fresh, clean, icy scent filled her nostrils. At last, the berline turned through the wrought-iron gate and proceeded up the raked gravel drive of the Court.

159

Andrea sat up straight. "Lord Grantham! There's something moving over there. Do you see? A dark shape, near the East Tower?"

Richard stiffened. "I do. And I'm going to settle this nonsense here and now."

The grim note in his voice frightened Andrea, but she held her tongue. The carriage pulled up before the house. Before it came to a complete halt, Richard jumped to the ground and took off at a run.

Chapter 12

Andrea gripped the door of the berline, her heart beating hard and rapid as she stared through the swirling snow after Richard's disappearing figure. It couldn't be any real danger for him. It couldn't—it was still a long time before May! But she had to know.

Before she realized she had moved, she was running toward the bushes. Behind her, Bella called her name, but Andrea paid no heed. Richard might be heading into trouble, and she had to help! Breathless, she drew up at the corner of the house and peered about, unable to make out anything but the roughest of shapes through the grayness of the storm. An icy wind swept through the yew trees, moaning eerily and sending a shiver through her as it whipped long tendrils of escaping golden hair into her eyes.

"Richard? Lord Grantham?" She hugged her pelisse closer about herself as she shouted.

He did not respond, and for a moment terror filled her. The thought of his vitality and energy being brutally extinguished was too much for her to bear. She started forward once more, determined that he should not face this nameless danger alone.

At a dividing of the path, she stopped again and her

anguished gaze searched down each shrub-lined way. "Lord Grantham!" she called, but the wind whipped her words away. All sound seemed muffled by the falling snow.

Then steady footsteps answered her. "Miss Wells?" In another moment, Richard's tall, broad-shouldered figure rounded a corner and approached from down the path closest to the gray stone walls of the Court. "You shouldn't have followed me."

She ran to meet him and barely stopped from throwing herself into his arms. "Did you see anyone?"

"No. There was no one there." He looked down at her and frowned. "You're shaking! Come, let's take you into the house. It's freezing out here."

Andrea clung to the arm he offered and he led her through the maze of paths. She was being foolish! This was only late January. If she were going to lose her head and fly off in an unreasoning panic every time she thought he might be in the least bit of danger, she'd be a basket case long before May.

In minutes they reached the shelter of the front door. Bella stood just inside the Great Hall, waiting.

"The servants again?" she asked as they came in.

Richard paused, and a crease formed in his brow. "Again?" He took the shoulders of the pelisse that Andrea unfastened and helped her out of it. "What do you mean?"

"Why, that the servants have been trysting in the bushes." She eyed Prindle in indignation as he closed the door against the storm. "Andrea and I saw them while you were away at the races."

Richard removed his greatcoat and tossed it over the butler's waiting arm. "Is this true?" He directed the question at Prindle.

The man stiffened visibly. "I am sure it is no such thing, my lord. No one on the staff would behave in so improper a manner."

"Bella?" Richard raised a questioning eyebrow at his sister.

"Well, I saw a flutter of white, like an apron . . . No, really, Richard. This is ridiculous! Who else could it have been? There is not the least reason for any strangers to be about here."

"No." He seemed on the verge of saying more, then abruptly turned on his heel and left them. He crossed the hall and headed down the passage to his bookroom.

Andrea stared after him, resisting the impulse to follow. He had put more inflection in that one syllable than she had thought possible. He had sounded so odd, as if he suspected something, and something about which he had no intention of telling them. Her worries for his immediate safety flooded back with a vengeance. Just because he wouldn't die for several months didn't mean nothing would happen to him. He still could be hurt, even maimed . . . Uneasy, she went to her room to put off her bonnet and remove her dampened half-boots.

Throughout the remainder of the afternoon, she kept a surreptitious watch out the windows. Snow drifted down with unrelenting persistence, leaving a virgin carpet several inches thick on the icy ground.

Richard, entering the Gold Saloon where Andrea had been sitting with Bella over their needlework, joined her at the mullioned panes.

"That should cause our unknown friend some difficulty." His satisfaction sounded in his voice.

"Do you think so?" Bella looked up. "I thought it had begun to let up a little."

"It has. Which means anyone skulking about will leave clear tracks which can be followed."

Andrea shivered. "Bella must be right and it is only the servants." But somehow, she didn't really believe that. She remained where she sat, staring out into the growing darkness through brooding eyes.

The following morning dawned clear and bright, banishing both the swirling flakes and Andrea's depressed spirits. Unable to remain indoors on such a beautiful day, she set off on a brisk walk about the grounds. Snow crunched beneath her booted feet and crisp air filled her lungs, bringing with it the clean, sweet smell of wet leaves.

As she rounded the brick wall that surrounded the stable yard, she saw Richard swing up into his curricle, gather his whip and reins into one hand, and give his horses the office. He drew in at sight of her, stopping his pair as they came abreast of the gateway.

"Are you thinking of riding? The sun is like to leave a film of ice on the snow and make the ground treacherous."

She shook her head. "I just wanted to walk. Do you drive far?"

"Only to one of the farms. I set workmen to repair a roof two days ago, and I want to make sure the work has been done properly." He raised the whip in salute and allowed his fidgeting horses their heads.

Andrea watched him drive off, a slight frown creasing her delicate brow. She should have known he'd be an excellent landlord. If only he didn't possess so damnably many admirable traits! Then perhaps she wouldn't like him so much.

She crossed the cobbled yard, let herself out by a narrow gate, and emerged into a hedged path on the other side. The tall line of yew trees kept the sun from melting the top layer of snow, which made her footing relatively secure. She continued her walk, enjoying the simple pleasure of undisturbed nature.

A bit over an hour later, as she trudged along the muddy lane relishing the smog-free air and watching her breath form clouds, she heard a light carriage approach.

She turned to look, then stepped quickly to the side of the rutted lane to allow the curricle to sweep past. Instead, Richard drew in rein and brought his team to a stand.

"Would you care for a ride back?"

She needed no second invitation. Quickly she climbed up beside him, eager for her first ride in a real curricle. As soon as she seated herself, they started forward and Andrea gripped the edge of the swaying seat. His hands remained so steady, so smooth, as he kept the animals to an even trot.

"Are you in the habit of driving yourself?" His sharp eyes did not miss the intentness of her scrutiny.

"I have never had the opportunity."

His mobile brows flew up in mock amazement. "I had thought you capable of anything!"

"Very funny. Will you teach me?"

For answer, he handed over the reins. She took them, suddenly nervous.

"No." His deep chuckle sounded as the off horse jerked its head in objection to the unfamiliar touch. "Hold them this way." Richard took her hands between his and repositioned the ribbons so that they just rested on her fingers, then passed through her hands for a firm hold. "There, so you can feel your horses' mouths without being heavy-handed." He slowed the pair of blacks to a stop, then released Andrea. "Give it a try."

Almost recovering from his touch, she allowed the pair to walk, then drew them to a stop with care. When they responded sweetly, she let out her breath in an excited laugh. She started them forward once more, practicing the motions she had observed Richard using. "This is almost as easy as riding!"

"Well, I may be able to turn you into a tolerable whip," he pronounced, "*if* you learn to treat your pair as two separate horses and not as one!"

She apologized, for she had tried to turn them on a

165

curve as if she held a steering wheel and sat in a car. "Are you are a member of the FHC?"

"Of course." Surprise sounded in his voice, as if he wondered why she had even bothered to ask the question when the answer must be obvious.

She spared a glance from her pair to flutter her lashes at him in only partly feigned admiration of his abilities. "Then I suppose you do not waste your time with such foolish pranks as driving unicorn in the park?"

"I have done so." His smile sounded in his voice, making it even more enticing than usual.

"It seems a dangerous and foolhardy thing to do." Her tone held nothing but top-lofty disapproval. She threw him a look brim full of disdain, encountered his amused expression, and was hard-pressed not to giggle.

"I will engage to drive you random-tandem any time you name—and under any conditions!" Devils danced in the depths of his gleaming eyes as he threw the challenge at her. "Do you think I cannot control my cattle?"

"Them, yes" came her candid reply. "It's your cork-brained notions I have my doubts about."

He burst out laughing. "*Where* have you picked up your cant? Don't you know it is not the least bit seemly for a lady to use such expressions?"

"I told you, I'm an Original."

"That you most certainly are! But I still have no desire to be overturned by you." He retrieved the reins from her just in time to prevent the near horse from cropping the straggly weeds at the verge of the road. The wheel beneath him teetered on the icy brink of the shallow ditch. The pair responded at once to his authoritative touch, stopped their meandering, and in a moment they trotted briskly down the snow-slushy lane.

"Does this mean the first lesson is over?" She folded her hands demurely in her lap and peeped up at him as if fearful of disapproval.

166

"I would hardly call that a lesson."

She laughed. "What? Are you crying off? I warn you, I mean to try again. This afternoon?"

"Persistent," he murmured, his shoulders shaking with his enjoyment. "Very well. This afternoon."

They returned to the stables and Andrea jumped down to the cobbled ground. Richard paused to speak with his groom and Andrea, not wanting to bring their delightful morning to an end quite yet, waited for him. It was so beautiful out, so crisp and cold and clean. No smog marred the air. She breathed deeply and sighed in contentment.

Across the drive, the Court stood solid and beautiful, silhouetted against the gray, snow-filled clouds. The East Tower rose tall and stately and the West . . . She shivered.

"Cold?" Richard came up behind her and offered his arm.

She took it, holding it tightly. "Does anyone use the West Tower? It . . . it doesn't look very safe."

"No, it isn't. I believe my father had it boarded up a long time ago. One of these days I'll have it either rebuilt or dismantled."

Her clasp tightened on his sleeve. "Leave it."

His free hand covered hers briefly. "For the moment, I'll have to."

Relief flooded through her. He would not go wandering about the West Tower just yet, inspecting it for damage. There was too little money to spare any on the collapsing structure. Unless, of course, he sold something of value. But what did he have, besides his unique snuff boxes—and the Imperial Star?

"And what would you care to do now?" he asked, reverting to his role of host as they reached the house.

"I would love to see your collection." She looked hopefully up at him. And not just your snuff boxes, she

167

added silently to herself.

But though she raved, and in complete sincerity, over the dazzling array of enameled, chased, and bejeweled boxes he drew out of cabinets to show her, he made no mention of the one art object she desired to see. Momentarily stymied, she accompanied him into luncheon. How, she wondered, did one bring up the subject of Russian icons in a casual manner?

The answer to that vexing question still eluded her when, later that afternoon, Richard took her out for her second driving lesson. To her dismay, this session proved every bit as disconcerting as the first. She might be an apt and eager pupil, but his nearness sadly disrupted her concentration. In spite of severe lectures to herself, nothing could prevent her from trembling when he placed his hands over hers to show her how to guide her horses. There was nothing amatory in his manner. If anything, he regarded her as an entertaining child, but that knowledge didn't help.

The next few days slipped past, divided between disappointing tours of the paintings that hung in odd rooms of the Court and far too enjoyable driving lessons. Though she made no headway in her search for the Imperial Star, she made considerable progress with her handling of the ribbons. By the fifth lesson, much to her delight, Richard showed her how to loop her rein in style with a twist of her wrist. In an attempt to cover her confusion caused by his touch, she begged him to show her how to catch her thong over the leader's ear.

"Perhaps when I get back from Scotland. You should practice your latest lesson until then."

"Scotland?" Her gaze flew to his rugged face.

"Yes." If he detected her dismay, he betrayed no hint of the fact. "A race with Giles. He seems to think that might be more entertaining than my joining him in Melton Mowbray." He sat silent at her side a moment, watching while she negotiated a turn with gratifying precision. "I shouldn't be gone long, certainly no more than a fortnight."

"But it is snowing. A race will be dangerous. Or have you a deep-rooted wish to break you neck?"

"I must, or I wouldn't be teaching you to drive, would I?" came the affable response.

She laughed, taking no offense, for she knew herself to be doing extremely well. To demonstrate this to him, she put them along into a canter and neatly feathered a corner.

He nodded his approval of her technique. "I'd expect nothing less from one of my pupils. But if I hear that you've been hunting the squirrel while I'm away, I'll comb your hair with a joint stool."

She ignored the threat. "'Hunting the squirrel.' Is that trying to graze the wheels of another carriage while I pass? No, you have my word. I haven't the precision of eye—yet—for such a stunt. Nor will I try to see how many times I can drive at speed through a gate without scratching the sides of the carriage."

His deep answering chuckle sent enticing thrills through her.

"Lord, that's a child's prank!"

"But Bella told me you did that only last year!" She threw a challenging glance at him.

"On a bet with Giles, my girl. Only for a bet."

"You gentlemen do the craziest things for a bet. It doesn't seem to be the least bit sensible."

He lounged back against the cushioned seat, watching her with a slight smile just touching his firm lips. "No, it isn't. But one must do something to alleviate the boredom, after all."

"Can you not find anything constructive to do?" She spared him an exasperated glance.

"But I have." He pretended surprise. "I am going to

169

race to Scotland through the snow. And while we're on the subject of foolishness, what about you ladies, thinking of nothing but your ton parties and gowns?"

Andrea drew in her breath and slowed the horses to a walk through a patch of shade where the ground was still covered by ice. "It is a frivolous, selfish world, your beau monde, is it not?"

"Is it different in America?"

To her surprise, she caught the note of sincere interest in his voice. "Perhaps," she said slowly. "Yes, I am sure it is. Life is less secure. You can find any measure of challenge you like, just by journeying farther from the cities."

Richard fell silent, gazing off into space. With a sense of shock, Andrea caught a touch of wistfulness in the depths of his intriguing eyes. He would welcome such an adventure! Yet she had made so great an effort to get back to the England of the Regency era, to a time and style of life that to her had seemed perfect. What a blow if he were to leave it . . .

She broke off that thought. He *would* leave it, but by death, not by choice. She shivered and urged the horses back to a trot, needing desperately to put as much distance between herself and Greythorne Court as possible at that moment.

Giles arrived only two days later, and the period of Andrea's enjoyable intimacy with Richard came to an end. Giles pulled into the stableyard, the chestnuts harnessed to his curricle steaming, just as Richard and Andrea returned from another driving lesson. Richard jumped lightly to the ground and greeted his friend with a warmth that left Andrea feeling very much left out.

Giles swept her a magnificent bow, then turned his laughing countenance to Richard. "Are you ready for our race?"

Andrea did not wait to hear Richard's answer. She left them in the yard and hurried through the softly falling snow to the house where Bella would be awaiting her. She found her in the Gold Saloon, peacefully setting stitches in the hem of a handkerchief.

"Mr. Kendall has arrived." She crossed to the fireplace and held out her chilled hands to the crackling blaze.

Bella looked up, fine lines of displeasure marking her normally smooth brow. "He will take Richard off on this hey-go-mad race of theirs! Oh, how I wish I could prevent it. They will break their necks."

"No." Andrea shook her head. "I am sure they will be all right." She was, after all, in a position to know—though she could hardly explain that to her worried hostess. However tempting it might be at times to reveal it, she must keep her knowledge of the fates of both men secret.

"I suppose you approve of such folly." Bella hunched a petulant shoulder.

"No, but he is bored. They both are. If only we could provide him with something challenging though less hazardous to do." Like maybe revealing the hiding place of the Imperial Star? Andrea stared into the flames, frustrated. She had already looked in the obvious places. Why had the icon been so thoroughly hidden?

Bella sighed. "It is my heart's desire to see Richard settled down, setting up his nursery and devoting himself to the home farms."

Andrea shook her head; she had sensed a spirit in him, kindred with her own. "He will never be satisfied with a peaceful existence," she warned Bella. "He will always need to pit his wits and strength against something."

"Do you really think so?" Bella sighed in dismay, unable to refute this reading of her brother's character.

171

The snow began to fall in earnest once again during the night, and when Andrea rose in the morning the world outside was white—not just the ground and trees, but the air itself, thick with swirling flakes. With the help of the maid Lily, she donned the warmest of her gowns, draped a woolen shawl over her shoulders, and made her way down to the breakfast parlor. She paused at the door as the sound of deep, laughing voices rose in friendly argument within.

"Double the stakes if we make it to the border in our original estimate of three days." Richard's words struck foreboding in her heart as she entered.

Giles glanced out the window. "The same bet if we make it just into Bath in that time."

Richard chuckled. "Faint heart?" No malice lurked in his tone. He glanced up and rose at sight of Andrea, who remained uncertainly just over the threshold.

Giles stood also, but his attention remained on Richard. "Lord, if you really want to set off in this blizzard . . ."

Richard shook his head, a slight smile in his eyes as he looked at Andrea. "Let's postpone it, by all means."

Giles sank back into his chair relieved but brooding. "What shall we do instead?"

"You might teach me to play piquet." Andrea crossed to the sideboard, poured out a cup of tea, and carried it to the table. "It may not be physical activity, but at least it will help pass the time."

A sudden gleam lent a silvery glow to Richard's gray eyes. "Shall we begin after breakfast?"

"Begin what?" Bella entered the parlor and looked from one to the other with undisguised mistrust.

"Piquet. Do you care to join us?" Her brother smiled wickedly at her.

Bella's gaze rested a moment on Giles Kendall's handsome face and her pretty lips tightened. "I have

172

other things to do this morning. But pray, don't let that stop you."

As soon as Andrea finished her light meal, the gentlemen led her to the bookroom and searched out a deck of cards. She seated herself on a comfortable sofa, eager to be initiated into the mysteries of the game that no one seemed to have heard of in her own time but was a staple of every Regency novel. Giles arranged a table before her and Richard produced the pack of cards from a drawer in his desk and began to separate out the lower pips.

"Will you play against the pair of us?" Richard handed the remaining thirty-two cards to Giles to shuffle.

"But you are the better player," Giles protested.

"Once the rules are explained to me, I will play my own hand, thank you." Andrea looked toward Richard, her shy smile doing nothing to disguise her anticipation. "If you will merely make sure that I make no major blunders?"

To this Richard agreed, and the two gentlemen set about explaining the different scoring combinations. Andrea listened intently to talk of points, sequences, and sets, and realized the game would not be mastered in one sitting. Finally, at her suggestion, Richard and Giles played a hand, with Richard explaining his moves and reasonings. She was still trying to comprehend the intricacies and ramifications of capotes and repiquets when Prindle entered, announcing the arrival of the Earl of Malverne.

"What could have brought the old fellow out in this blizzard?" Richard laid down his cards and looked at Giles as if he expected an answer.

A moment later, the butler bowed Malverne into the room. The earl stopped just inside the door and looked in consternation at the threesome gathered about the card table.

Richard stood. "What may I do for you, Malverne?"

The earl ran a finger along his neckcloth, obviously ill at ease. "Came to have a word with you."

He cast another, meaningful, glance at the other two occupants of the room and Andrea stiffened with sudden nerves. She didn't know why, or what it could be, but the conviction filled her that something momentous was about to take place. Tension almost vibrated through the air, but whether it came from her or from Malverne, she couldn't tell.

The earl turned back to Richard. "In private, Grantham."

"In private?" Richard had started forward but paused now, his expression questioning.

Dull color flooded Malverne's rotund countenance and his fingers fidgeted with the riband that held his quizzing glass. His gaze darted about the room, as if expecting some unseen person to be lurking in a corner. When he spoke, his words were muttered, barely audible.

"About the Imperial Star."

Chapter 13

Giles rose from his chair and Andrea reluctantly followed suit. She longed to remain, to find out what the Earl of Malverne had to say about the Imperial Star. He, after all, had been the one to sell it to William Westmont—for the price of Greythorne Court.

The price of the Court. Andrea faltered at the door, then recovered and followed Giles out. Richard—and Isabella—regarded the place as theirs. Which must mean that they did not yet know about the sales document—and Richard's father couldn't have told them of the collateral he used to purchase the priceless icon.

But that made no sense, for she could think of no reason why Malverne should not have come forward to claim the Court as his at the time of William Westmont's death. Andrea's head spun with questions.

Uncertain where else to go, she turned her steps toward the Gold Saloon. Giles accompanied her, blithely unaware of her tension.

"The sequence is really very simple, Miss Wells." He held the door and followed her in, his mind still occupied with piquet. "One point for each card, unless you have five or more. Then you get an extra ten points. What could be easier to comprehend?"

175

Bella, who sat near the crackling fire with a branch of working candles at her elbow, looked up from her embroidery and eyed him coldly. "I suppose next you will be teaching her faro and hazard."

"Unless she already knows?" Giles turned an inquiring glance at Andrea.

"I do not, but it is a wonderful idea." She gave Bella an apologetic smile. "I should like of all things to learn. And all the other games, as well."

"Loo and casino will be far more to the point if you intend to take your part in card games in town." Bella's tone held only reproof.

"Very true." Giles shook his head in sorrow. "They are boring, these ladies' games, but you will be expected to play. Though I promise to rescue you from such a fate if I can."

Bella let out a wistful sigh. "I wish someone might rescue me from silver loo with Lady Winnett."

"I promise, fair lady, if it lies within my power." Giles swept her a magnificent bow.

Bella met his teasing hazel eyes and looked away at once. "You are quite foolish." Soft color stole into her cheeks and she concentrated her attention once more on her needlework.

Andrea looked speculatively from one to the other, but prudently kept her tongue. Instead, she begged Giles to once again explain the scoring of the sequence.

He had barely finished when Richard, his brow creased and his expression closed, strolled into the saloon. Andrea's gaze flew to him, searching. Something had occurred to disturb the good humor that usually lurked just beneath his surface, something that unsettled even his deep-rooted love of a challenge.

And it obviously had to do with Malverne and the Imperial Star.

"Well? What was the urgent matter that brought the

176

old fellow out through the snow?" Giles posed the question that Andrea felt she had no right to ask.

Richard looked at his right hand, making a show of examining his perfect manicure. "He wanted to buy back the Imperial Star."

"The what?" Giles stared at him, his expression blank.

Bella dropped her embroidery and regarded her brother with wide, startled eyes. "He wants to buy it back?" she repeated, dumbfounded. "But does he not . . ."

Richard shook his head, an odd smile twisting his lips. "I thought he had it, too. But it would seem he does not."

Andrea sat down abruptly in the nearest chair. The Imperial Star—surely, it was in Richard's possession. She glanced at his guarded face again and her suspicions rose. Was that why he looked like that? Did he have the icon, but for some reason, some unfathomable, obscure, peculiar reason, he did not want that fact known—not even by his own sister? But why make so great a mystery out of it?

No wonder the icon became so hopelessly lost—and she had assumed it was because of her! Richard's secretiveness was not going to make her task an easy one. If she could not induce him to trust her enough to reveal the hiding place of the Imperial Star—and soon—he would die, and the secret of its whereabouts with him.

"Shall we return to the problem at hand?" Richard's deep voice, very much alive and once again calm and self-possessed, broke into her thoughts. "Miss Wells, I believe we were in the midst of a game of piquet."

She stared at him. He appeared to have completely dismissed the matter from his mind—as if Malverne never had paid that visit. For the next two hours, Richard devoted himself to the entertainment of his guests, and Andrea, try as she might, could detect no sign of uneasiness in him.

Malverne's visit, though, made one fact very clear to her. The Imperial Star would not be lying around in plain sight for her to discover. And as one enjoyable day gave way to the next, with nothing unusual or suspicious happening, she found it all too easy to let the problem of the icon fade to the back of her mind. There was no urgent rush for her to find it, after all. She could bide her time, wait until Richard was ready to reveal its hiding place.

By the third day, Bella at last abandoned her disapproval and joined the card players. In deference to her, they concentrated on such unexceptionable games as loo, whist, and casino. But when she left the room to see to household concerns, Giles and Richard swept these innocuous pastimes aside and turned their attention to initiating Andrea into such unladylike pursuits as hazard and even blind hookey.

The blizzard outside eased up to a light, scattered snowfall and the fifth day dawned clear with the promise of sun. Andrea gazed out her window, thoughtful, then made her way downstairs. Richard and Giles, she supposed, would now be off on their postponed curricle race to Scotland.

But neither of the gentlemen, whom she found lounging over tankards of ale in the breakfast parlor, showed any inclination toward taking advantage of the improved weather. Richard pronounced that the sun would create an icy slick on the road surface while Giles held out that it looked likely for the snow to start up again before the day ended. Recognizing from the meager nature of these excuses that the two men were content to remain at the Court for the present, Andrea made no comment.

Bella greeted the news of the indefinitely postponed race with a sigh of relief and a speculative glance at Andrea. "And this, my love, should at last put a stop to

178

your worries about how welcome your visit is. You may be sure they are sufficiently entertained, or nothing would induce them to remain at the Court for so much as a single day, even in the worst weather."

Much to Andrea's dismay, Bella's obvious speculation continued throughout the morning. She watched her brother closely whenever he came in Andrea's vicinity and looked from one to the other, anxiously searching out any sign of growing regard. Driven to desperation even before nuncheon, Andrea declared her intention of taking a walk and firmly refused all offers to accompany her.

Absenting herself from Bella's company proved a mistake. By the time Andrea returned, much refreshed, her hostess had hit upon a new scheme to throw her brother and their visitor together. The card games, she declared, must be abandoned in the face of far more important lessons for any lady about to make her curtsy to society. Andrea must learn to dance.

"For I am sure the steps will not be identical with those you learned in America." Bella beamed on her in smug satisfaction at the perfection of her scheme.

"No." Andrea shook her head, momentarily stymied. "I am sure they are not." Even to herself, her voice sounded weak. She had learned to waltz in a third grade ballet class, and though she had loved it, she seriously doubted her meager experience would stand her in good stead now.

Giles looked up from his copy of the *London Times*. "An excellent suggestion. I shall even offer my services as her teacher."

Bella frowned. "I am sure that is not necessary. Richard . . ."

Her brother directed a quizzing glance at her and ignored her beseeching expression. "Giles will perform the task to admiration, I make no doubt. Will you play for them, Bella?"

She looked daggers at him. "And what will you do?"

"Oh, keep a critical eye on proceedings. What else?"

"If Mr. Kendall does not mind, I shall be delighted."
Andrea spoke up promptly. She had no desire to analyze
Richard's obvious thwarting of his sister's blatant
attempts to foster an intimacy between them. She had
reasons of her own for not wanting it, for not jumping at
an excuse to be in his arms for even so innocuous a
reason. She liked his company far too well already. With
all her heart, she wished she did not know the fate which
would come upon him all too soon.

They repaired to the Music Room in the early
afternoon. Giles and Richard pulled furniture ruthlessly
out of the center of the apartment and Bella seated
herself at the pianoforte. She struck up the opening
chords of a country dance and Giles bowed before Andrea
in an exaggerated manner.

The basic steps did not prove difficult and, between
Giles's encouragement and Richard's laughing criticism,
she mastered the movements in a very short time.
Putting them together and going through an actual
dance, though, proved to be another thing. After several
attempts, with Giles encouraging her to imagine invisible
members in their nonexistent set, he surrendered.

"We need more people. Mrs. Brixton, if you and
Richard will do us the honor of joining us, I shall hum the
melody."

"Is that a threat?" Richard regarded his friend with no
little amusement.

"Do not be so disobliging. I am sure Mr. Kendall will
provide excellent accompaniment." Bella jumped to her
feet and dragged her reluctant brother onto the cleared
floor.

With the addition of another couple, the session
became much like a folk dancing class Andrea had taken

in high school gym. She had enjoyed that and found the country dance similar in many ways. Giles hummed loudly, off key, and Bella abandoned her disapproving look.

"You cannot concentrate on the melody when you must watch Andrea's steps." Neatly, she took advantage of the situation. "Richard, change with him."

Andrea faltered as she found herself staring up into Grantham's disturbingly rugged countenance. Recovering, she curtsied as required by the dance and took his hand. His clasp was firm, unlike Giles's, and he moved with an athletic grace that drew and held her eyes.

"Relax." He spoke the order softly. An enigmatic smile played about the corners of his mouth as if he were well aware of—and satisfied by—the havoc he wreaked on her senses.

For the next quarter hour, to the combined humming and singing of Giles and Bella, Richard held her hand, spun her gently about, drew her close. Always, his gleaming silvery eyes bored into her as if seeking to know every thought, every sensation she experienced. With Giles as her partner, it had been nothing but a game. With Richard, the whole concept of dance took on a provocative meaning.

When they completed the final step, Richard retained her hand and gazed down into her face with an arrested gleam in the depths of those disturbing eyes. Andrea looked away, glad of the break called by Bella, who found herself breathless from her vocal accompaniment. Andrea suffered with the same complaint, but from a very different cause, and was only too glad when Richard suggested they continue on the morrow.

Andrea awoke to a determined sun forcing its way through threatening clouds. Thrusting her window open, she stuck her head out, welcoming the chill, fresh air after the stuffy smell of stale smoke that permeated her bedchamber. A light snow had fallen during the night, which gave the grounds a fairy tale appearance that beckoned her. She breathed deeply and felt energy suffusing through her, replacing the sluggishness brought on by too many days remaining indoors. She would not do so this morning . . .

She hurried down to the breakfast table a half hour later, gowned in the royal-blue habit and filled with eager anticipation. The others were gathered there before her. She went in, her steps light, and greeted them with a cheery word.

"Will anyone join me for a ride?" She looked about expectantly.

Richard set down his tankard, looked across at Giles, and both burst out laughing. "We had planned one already," Richard assured her.

"Do, by all means, join us!" Giles added. "Mrs. Brixton, will you make us a foursome?"

"I suppose I must. Andrea and I can keep each other company when you gentlemen gallop off on one of your reckless races."

"Stay behind?" Andrea shook her head. "We shall be setting the pace. Now, don't, I beg of you, frown at me. We are not in London where we must keep to a sedate trot. And it is too beautiful a day to just amble along."

"So it is." Richard stood and dropped his napkin beside his plate. "I shall have the horses saddled."

Andrea finished her light meal in minutes and joined the gentlemen in the hall where they awaited Bella, who had gone upstairs to change. As soon as she came down, they went outside into the icy breeze. Andrea drew a deep breath, reveling in the fresh, pungent country smells and the clean, crisp air.

Unbidden, vivid, the image of her parents' farm sprang

182

to her mind—the old red barn with the shutter that refused to be mended and the sprawling house with the paint that continually peeled. There had been many mornings like this, cold and beautiful. She and Cathy had remained abed as long as possible, then dressed in their warmest clothes and raced out to the barn to gather eggs for breakfast. She almost always found one under Olivia, the large barred rock.

Andrea's heart wrenched. She would never see it again! Nor Cathy, nor her parents, nor even her hen. She couldn't pop home for visits, like she had after moving to Minneapolis. She was here, in the past, to stay. Would they miss her—wonder what happened to her? She should have written a letter and had Catherine Kendall send it for her.

Tears of homesickness filled her eyes, blurring her vision—and causing her contacts to slip so that she could see their edges. Glad of this practical matter on which to concentrate, she surreptitiously dabbed at her eyes and restored the lenses to their proper position.

Snow crunched beneath their booted feet. Andrea firmly put aside her memories. Her past wasn't over, it was still to come! It hadn't happened yet. Her family wasn't dead, the people she loved were still to be born.

That thought filled her with the quiet joy of hope. Not death, but life. Winter would soon give way to spring. She had almost forgotten the resurgence of life, the first budding flowers, the bees buzzing industriously, everything that meant rebirth on a farm.

They reached the cobbled stableyard, and two grooms led the horses forward. Richard tossed Andrea lightly up into the saddle of a chestnut. She hooked her knee over the pommel and arranged her skirts in the manner she had copied from Bella. It felt strange, this style of riding, but she would not let its newness worry her this morning. She could not suppress the surge of energy that swept

183

through her.

Nor, as she discovered barely minutes later, could she control the similar surge that set her mare dancing and sidling. In an attempt to run the fidgets out of her mount, Andrea urged her into a canter, leading the others. But it was not enough for the headstrong chestnut. The horse pulled farther ahead, stretching her long-legged stride into an easy gallop, then, with the bit firmly between her teeth, into a heedless flight.

Her shod hooves pounded the icy turf, sending up a shower of muddy snow. Ahead of them lay the lane, and before it the wide ditch. Surely the mare would slow or turn aside! Freezing wind whipped tendrils of escaping hair into Andrea's eyes as her mount covered the last few yards at a dead run. She jerked on the reins, but her mount paid no heed. The only response was a bunching of muscles as the horse took off flying. Andrea, clutching the reins, discovered that jumping in a sidesaddle was a far cry from jumping while sitting astride, but somehow they landed neatly in the lane, rider and mount still together.

She reached down and grasped the reins as near to the bit as she could, but the sidesaddle lacked the balance to which she was accustomed. She slipped, barely regained her seat, and the next moment abandoned all attempts to pull the mare's head about. She ducked low, clinging to her mount's streaming neck as they dodged beneath the low limb of an elm tree.

From behind came the sound of hooves beating the hard ground. Richard's magnificent roan pulled beside her, then in front, and he caught her bridle. With a firm hand, he forced the chestnut to slow, then at last to stop. The mare stood still, trembling. The roan threw his elegant head, snorted, and its warm breath formed clouds that hovered in the freezing air.

Richard's fingers clenched on the rein. Hard lines

marked his unyielding face, revealing his anger more clearly than if he shouted. When he spoke, he held his voice under careful control. Only a slight tremor betrayed his savage feelings.

"How dare you play off such tricks! Have you no more sense than to—" He broke off as his furious gaze came to rest on her white face, her eyes still round from her fright. "Did she take her head?" His tone altered, still filled with anger but no longer aimed at Andrea. "I thought I trained that trick out of her!"

"Well, she remembered it." Once again in control, Andrea recovered quickly. Only embarrassment remained at not being able to handle the animal. "How should I have stopped her?"

"It looked like it was all you could manage to stay on."

She flushed. "That was because I tried to pull her nose around to my knee. This saddle wasn't designed for that."

"Good God, I should say not! Where did you learn that trick? That's only safe astride!"

Under his accusing gaze, her color deepened even more. His eyes widened in sudden humorous enlightenment, banishing the last of his ill humor. "You've ridden astride!"

Andrea looked down, unable to meet the look of unholy enjoyment that lit his face. She nodded. "But, pray, do not tell Bella. She would be scandalized! She merely thinks I had never ridden before, not that I had never sat in a sidesaddle."

Richard's shoulders shook in silent laughter. "My dear Miss Wells, may I say that you are a source of never-ending delight for me?"

She made the mistake of meeting his amused gaze and could not look away. Silvery lights danced in eyes the color of the stormy clouds. They drew her in, mesmerizing, even more compelling than their painted image

185

that had drawn her back across the ages. She felt herself sinking in their depths with no desire to escape.

"Andrea!" Bella's voice penetrated the hypnotic spell, shaking her back to reality. "Are you all right?" Bella rode up with Giles right behind her. "That horrid mare! I never would have let you use her if I thought she still did that!"

Andrea dragged her gaze from Richard's and ordered her unruly senses back into line. "She merely recognized my inexperience and took advantage of it. She will not get the chance again, do not fear."

They turned back toward the Court, and Andrea risked another glance at Richard. A new, mischievous gleam lit his countenance. He would take great delight in discovering in what other ways she did not behave like a simpering miss. She knew a deep foreboding not untinged with anticipation.

Leaving the horses in the charge of the grooms, they returned to the house. Richard went at once to the small table that stood against the wall beneath a huge gilded mirror in the Great Hall. The morning's post lay piled on a silver tray.

He picked up several letters, glanced at the fists, and tossed them aside. The sixth, though, caught his attention, and he looked over his shoulder to where Bella had started up the stairs.

"Here's one that ought to interest you, my dear." He broke the seal on a single folded sheet, scanned it, then nodded in approval. "How does a house on Curzon Street sound?"

"Richard! You're not joking?" Bella clapped her hands in delight. "Oh, it is of all things what I should have liked the most!" She ran across the hall and threw her arms about her brother's neck, giving him an impulsive hug.

Over her head, Richard glanced at Andrea. "After all,

186

this is to be your first Season. I hope it will live up to your dreams."

"It will, I'm—" Her dreams? Andrea broke off, profoundly shaken by the realization that swept over her. "I'm sure it will."

She turned away abruptly and hurried up the stairs, needing to be alone with her thoughts. That's what the time of the Regency had been to her, nothing but a dream, a fantasy. She had no real conception of history, of everyday life in the past. She had built her future on the shifting foundation of daydreams.

And that portrait of Richard. Even more than the Regency era, it had been he who drew her back, he for whom she had moved heaven and earth—possibly literally—to be with. When he looked at her like that, with his piercing eyes holding that teasing, understanding glint, time stood still and lost all meaning. How could she ever live on here—or anywhere—when he was gone?

Chapter 14

Breathless with excitement, Andrea stared out the window of the traveling coach as they passed through the outskirts of London. There had been no sign of Richard for the past hour, not since he whipped up the pair harnessed to his curricle and sped ahead, out of sight. There were so many things she wanted to ask him, like the names of buildings and various districts of the town, the identities of a variety of workers performing innumerable tasks and services.

Even in the icy chill of late February, the streets were filled with people . . . and unappetizing smells. Andrea wrinkled her nose in distaste and drew her head back inside the coach.

"Does it not meet with your expectations?" Bella's sleepy voice sounded from the corner. Apparently the transition from the dirt road to cobbled stones awakened her from the doze into which she had drifted as the miles crept slowly by.

"It's all so different from—" Andrea broke off, catching herself. Bella had no idea she had ever been to London before. And in truth she hadn't yet—not for nearly two hundred years more.

"It's impossible to imagine exactly what anything will

actually be like, isn't it?" Bella put her own interpretation to Andrea's words and was satisfied.

Reflecting that Bella's comment held more truth than that lady realized, Andrea let the subject drop and instead concentrated on the unfamiliar sights. Vendors pushed barrows and loudly hawked their wares while street sweepers brushed accumulated litter from the path of anyone who looked able to give them a coin for this service.

As they continued through the streets, Andrea became absorbed in trying to locate buildings that would still remain in the city in her own time. She was surprised by how much she recognized. But the more she looked, the more the less appealing aspect of London became apparent to her. Everywhere, poverty assailed her eyes in the form of ill-clad children and ragged cripples and elderly men and women.

Andrea swallowed, appalled by the unbearable social conditions. No government should ever ignore the homeless and hungry and favor the few wealthy aristocrats. Disgust swept over her at the realization that she was now one of these. But as soon as she became established in this new world, she would use the money gained from the horse races to champion the cause of the less fortunate.

Helpless at present, she closed her eyes to block out the sight. She was glad of the activity she would find in town. All had been so quiet these last two weeks, with no one glimpsed lurking about the great old house. The only occurrence, aside from the general bustle of packing and her own surreptitious and depressingly futile search for the Imperial Star, had been Giles's departure from the Court to return to Melton Mowbray. Richard had suggested that he join them in London, to entertain him while the ladies indulged in shopping, but to Andrea's dismay, Giles, with a scathing look, declined the offered treat and made good his escape.

The carriage turned off Piccadilly onto Half Moon Street, then a block later turned onto Curzon Street. Their baggage fourgon stood at the side of the road, about halfway along. There was no sign of Richard's curricle. Servants, engaged by his man of affairs, carried trunks inside.

Andrea followed Bella out of the carriage and stared up at the tall house, their home for the next few months. Her earlier depression vanished, to be replaced by an unquenchable excitement at what lay ahead. At last, London, the Season, the Fashionable World, hovered within her grasp.

"Does it meet with your approval?" Richard appeared in the doorway and came down the steps. A half-teasing note lent a lilt to his deep voice and his eyes held a lingering smile.

"The house, yes." Her visions of glamour faded. She behaved exactly like any other selfish member of the beau monde! Out of sight, out of mind. Was that the problem? Another wave of self-disgust washed through her.

Bella ran lightly up the steps, anxious to look about her home for the Season. Andrea followed more slowly with Grantham at her side.

"You do not approve of London?" There was a curious note in his voice.

She glanced at him, surprised that he really seemed interested in her answer. That did not fit with her mental image of a rake. She behaved in exactly the same manner for which she mentally criticized him! He attracted her, physically, but she had avoided discovering what lay behind the magnificent packaging. Once she labeled him "rake," she had expected him to behave in the typically self-centered mode laid down by the novels for such a person. Yet he had proved to her, and more than once, this was not the case.

They stopped in the spacious hall where mounds of bags and trunks were being sorted in various piles according to ultimate destination. Bella stood in earnest conversation with a stout woman of comfortable aspect, apparently the housekeeper hired with the house. In another minute, the two women disappeared up the stairs, bent on arranging bedrooms.

"You don't answer."

Andrea looked up into his eyes. "No, I don't know if I do approve of London. I have never seen such poverty, so many people who desperately need help."

The smile faded from Richard's eyes and his mouth tightened. "That is not a fashionable subject. If you want to be all the rage, you had best pretend you don't see those things."

"Oh, I know enough not to talk about social injustice at a soirée, but this isn't a ton party. I'm just talking to you! Or do you feel the same way as the rest of this so-called Polite World?"

"No, I do not." Richard took her arm and led her along the hall. "But I find very few of my fellow creatures agree with me."

He ushered her into a small but cozy apartment toward the back of the hall. It was furnished in a comfortable style, a gentleman's room. He seated her on a sofa and himself took the chair opposite. "If you do not wish to be shunned this Season, it will be best if you keep any but the most frivolous thoughts to yourself. You would not want to be thought a bluestocking, would you?"

She sighed. "I suppose that is exactly what I must seem. But I can speak to *you* about such things, can I not?"

He leaned back in his chair, folded his hands across his

191

subdued floral waistcoat, and regarded her through narrowed eyes. "You may say anything you wish—to me."

"Then something desperately needs to be done to help these people. Does the government not fear a revolution after the manner of the French? There has already been one rebellion, the poor Luddites trying to protect their jobs."

"The who?" Richard stared at her blankly.

Andrea's eyes widened. "No, I . . . I was thinking of somewhere else. Sorry. But it could happen here." She searched her mind, trying to remember when the Luddite rebellion had taken place. All she knew for certain was that it was before 1817. A new fear washed over her: How many more mistakes would she make of this nature? She had to watch her step, particularly with Richard, who already considered her peculiar.

"But you are right." He drew an enameled snuff box from his pocket and took an infinitesimal pinch. "Something should be done."

"Indeed, it must. The old concept of noblesse oblige seems to be seriously ignored. The gentlemen with the money and power appear to be concerned only with their own pleasures."

"Not all. I have brought a bill before the House of Lords since I became a member, and it has not been ignored."

"You have? Then you *do* care!" she exclaimed in relief.

He laughed outright. "Did you think me such a monster?"

"No, but so many others are blind to injustices that have existed all their lives." She sighed. "They seem to take them as natural."

"My poor Miss Wells, what a low opinion you have of the British."

She shook her head. "No, only of those who can

remain unmoved by the plight of those of 'lesser' birth."

"That would seem to be something you are in no danger of doing." His tone was dry, as if he teased her, but the warmth of approval lurked there also. "Well." He stood. "Shall we see which bedchambers Bella has assigned us?"

Andrea preceded him from the room, her thoughts in a whirl. She was disturbingly glad to have it confirmed that her rake felt just as he ought on this very important subject. Her respect for him soared.

After inspecting the elegantly appointed apartment on the third floor that would be hers, Andrea gathered her courage—along with another pearl necklace and race information. Leaving her unpacking to Lily, who made rapid strides in her acquisition of such essential abilities for a lady's maid, she went once more in search of Richard. As she reached the stairs, he came running down, pulling on his gloves.

"Grantham! May I have a word with you?"

He stopped, eyed her narrowly, and frowned. "I have the oddest sensation you are about to make some outrageous request. Am I right?"

"I'm afraid so. But Bella has been telling me about the numerous purchases I must make, and I fear my funds will not be sufficient."

The corner of his mouth twitched into a derisive smile and he held out his hand. She pulled the pearls from her reticule. "And which race?" he demanded.

She could not tell if he were angry or resigned—or possibly even enjoying her unorthodox behavior in a strange sort of way. "Can you place the bet at Tattersall's at this time of year?"

"For an American who has never been to London, you certainly know a great deal about the ways of the turf."

She flushed. "England is not completely unknown in America. And gentlemen talk about their favorite pursuits no matter how far they travel from home."

He pocketed the pearls and let the subject drop. "Which horse and which race?" he repeated.

She drew the slip of paper from her reticule. "Any of these. Whichever you can get the best odds on."

"Are they all guaranteed winners?"

This time there was no mistaking the sneer in his voice. He couldn't suspect the truth—that was too absurd! But her last win while he lost must still rankle. He must be as curious as all get-out about how she did it—and how she could be so confident she could do it again. The situation amused her.

"Let's say I have my hopes. Is there such a thing as an accumulator here?"

"What, may I ask, is that?"

"Where you place three or four bets, and all the winnings from the first are placed on the second, and all the winnings from that on the third. But it is no matter. Perhaps you could leave instructions for such an arrangement?" She gave him an enigmatic smile and started to retrace her steps down the hall. "Oh!" She turned back. "Could you help me set up a bank account? I have not the least notion how to go about it."

"To be sure, you'll be needing one after your next win, will you not?"

"To be sure, I will." Without giving him a chance to comment again, she hurried away.

The better part of the next four days was devoted to shopping. Andrea found herself busy from early morning until evening, when she and Bella retired to their elegant drawing room and made plans for the following day. Exhausted, Andrea leaned back in her chair and agreed with everything her hostess suggested.

"Your new carriage dress will be delivered on the morrow, so we may go driving in the park. And once we have seen who else is in town, we must start paying

194

morning visits. That reminds me, we shall have to call on a printer and have cards made for you. And for me, as well, now that I think of it, for I shall have to give out this address. Andrea, are you listening?"

Andrea nodded sleepily. "Dress, park, morning visits, cards. That sounds like enough to keep us busy for a while."

"We are only just beginning. We must plan a small rout party so that you may meet a few people."

To this, Andrea agreed, for it was time she enlarged her circle of acquaintances. She would need to be firmly established before—before May. She left it at that.

They departed the following morning to visit a milliner's shop, for Bella, after considering all the previous evening, decided she could not possibly live without a charming little confection of frothy lace and peach-colored ribands with an exorbitant price tag. Andrea let her prattle on about it as they stepped out the front door and down the stairs to the waiting berline.

Glancing up the street, she paused. A man, who stood lounging opposite, turned and walked briskly away. A man she had seen before, and more than once over the past few days, now that she thought about it. Not a gentleman by his dress, nor the sort of lad she had seen who haunted the homes of the wealthy in hopes of holding a horse or performing some other service in exchange for a coin. She had paid him no heed before, but today the oddness of his manner disturbed her. This seemed all too similar to what had been going on at Greythorne Court, except that in London there were no bushes in which to lurk.

Disturbed, she followed Bella into the berline but kept her own counsel. She couldn't decide whether or not to mention this to Richard. There might be nothing in the least bit sinister about the man's being there—but somehow she didn't really believe her assurances to herself.

Three hours later, when the carriage turned the corner into Curzon Street, bringing them home, Andrea looked quickly about, curious whether she would spot the man again.

Several people strolled down the road, but none were near their house. And none bore any resemblance to the man she had noticed that morning.

None, except a dandified gentleman who minced his way toward them. Andrea sat up, watching him intently. He seemed to be about the same size and build, but beyond that she could tell nothing. She hadn't been certain about the coloring of the man she had glimpsed before. Nor could she tell about this one. His high-crowned curly beaver sat low on his head and his collar rose high, covering most of his face and hair.

He sauntered past their house with no more than a casual glance at it. As he came abreast of their carriage, he paused and bent to examine the golden tassel of one Hessian boot. His face was completely obscured. Chance—or design?

She had banished those incidents at the Court from her mind, but now they sprang once more to the surface, unable to be ignored any longer. Someone kept the house under observation. But who—and why? Did it have something to do with the priceless—and possibly missing—Imperial Star? Or was it Richard, perhaps incurring someone's enmity, who was the object of this stealthy surveillance that might end in his death?

She shook her head in a vain attempt to clear her jumbled thoughts. She was indulging in ridiculous flights of fantasy! The simple—and unbearably painful—fact was that Richard would die on May Sixteenth. There didn't need to be anything sinister about it; it was probably nothing more than a tragic accident. But because she knew it would happen, she read treachery and deceit into innocent occurrences.

Nor was Andrea the only one to search for ulterior motives. That same pursuit occupied Richard the entire morning, with doubts and suspicions hanging about him like thunder clouds. Drawing up his horses near Hyde Park Corner, he jumped down before his curricle came fully to a stop. He tossed the reins to his groom Samuel and faced the august establishment before him. Nodding to himself in grim determination, he entered the portals.

It was Monday, and that meant reckoning day at Tattersall's.

He strode back out a little less than an hour later, swearing softly and fluently under his breath. There had to be an explanation. There had to be some simple, logical, plausible explanation. And before the next hour ended, he intended to have it from Miss Andrea Wells if he had to choke it out of her.

A single win—or even two, if he wished to be generous and stretch the point—could be laughed at and dismissed as uncanny luck. But when a female—and one newly arrived in the country, at that!—picked five out of five winners and not so much as one loser, something was badly amiss!

He waited in growing impatience while Samuel, who had been walking the blacks, brought them up. He didn't really believe Andrea to be part of a plot to fix races, but at the moment no other answer presented itself. If it were true, he would not permit her to get away with it! The possibility that she might be dishonest, in league with some nefarious persons, hurt him, made him feel used and manipulated. And that did not please him in the least.

The drive back to Curzon Street did nothing to calm his growing temper. She had no right to make a May game of him! And so she would find out in short order.

He found her sitting in the front saloon, staring broodingly out the window into the street, her untouched embroidery lying in her lap. Probably contemplating her ill-gotten gains, he fumed. She looked up, a smile lighting her huge brown eyes, and the strength of his physical reaction surprised him. A cunning vixen, who knew to perfection how to entrap a man into doing her bidding. Well, he was no lap pug for her to toy with.

Her smile faded and a deep furrow formed in her normally smooth brow. "What has happened? Ri—Grantham, are you all right?"

He drew a small but bulging purse from his pocket and threw it with savage force into her lap. She picked it up and started to open the strings, but his voice, steely even to his own ears, stopped her.

"Just over fifteen thousand pounds. If you invested that, you would earn a small income that would keep you for life."

"Then you bet well for me."

"I followed your instructions for what you called an accumulator." His hands clenched tightly into fists so that his carefully pared nails dug into his palms. He stared down at her, seeing not the very pretty young woman he had thought he was beginning to know, but a mass of contradictions and tormenting questions. He didn't like this sensation of not being in complete control.

"You knew those horses would win." He made the comment an accusation. "You didn't have a single doubt. You *knew*."

She met his penetrating gaze, wavered under his blazing anger, and looked quickly down at the bulging leather pouch she clasped between her hands. "How could I?"

"I don't know, but you're going to tell me."

Bella's voice sounded in the hall and he looked up,

swearing softly under his breath. He didn't want to be interrupted. Until he knew precisely what game this young woman played, he did not want to involve his tender-hearted and easily deluded sister. They would continue this in private. He came to a rapid decision.

"Put on your bonnet and pelisse. You are coming for a drive with me in the park."

"Is this an invitation?" Andrea arched a haughty eyebrow.

He was not to be put off. "It's a damned order. You and I are going to have a talk!"

Andrea bit her lip, then set aside her untouched handkerchief and hurried out of the room. He watched her go with a certain measure of satisfaction. She was hiding something, that was obvious. Perhaps he shouldn't have given her time to think.

But, unreasonably, he found he looked forward with interest to whatever story she would concoct for his edification. She was an amusing minx, he'd give her that. And a damnably attractive one. She appealed to the irreverent, adventurous side of him that rose to challenges with soaring spirit. Too few opportunities existed in his orderly world to give in to his humorous impulses. He found himself hoping she could explain the seemingly unexplainable.

She rejoined him in a very short time and he escorted her out to the curricle that waited at the door. Not wanting any audience for this interview, he dismissed Samuel with a curt word, climbed into the seat, and gave his horses the office. They drove in stony silence through the cart-filled streets, for he wanted no distractions.

They reached the Stanhope Gate into Hyde Park, and he turned the blacks onto the Carriage Drive. Free of surrounding traffic, he spared her a glance. She gave every appearance of outward calm, but he sensed nervousness radiating from her. Good! He wanted her just a little bit afraid.

"You are now going to tell me precisely what you are up to."

She seemed torn, and lowered her face to stare at her hands. His irritation swelled. Damn her, she wasn't going to make him feel sorry for her! She was involved in something and he was going to find out what.

"And don't give me that nonsense about being a relative from America come for the Season." He snapped the words at her, angry with himself for falling under her intriguing spell. "I don't think I ever believed it for a moment."

She rallied. "Then why did you not denounce me at once?"

His hands clenched on the ribbons. "You admit I'm right."

Hadn't he wanted her to do just that? Her admission of that lie tore at him. He didn't want her proved guilty, he realized in self-contempt. He wanted to believe her lies, not only the verbal ones but also the ones she told with those laughing, delightful eyes and the smiles to which he had come to look forward.

She looked down at the whitened knuckles in her lap. "I am an American and I do know your ... your relations. And I have come to live here. It's been the dream of my life."

He gazed at her for a very long moment, disturbed by her aura of sincerity. He wanted to believe her, and that clouded his judgment. There were too many mysteries about her for him to accept her at face value any longer, yet still ...

"I don't know why," he said at last, more to himself than to her, "but I'm willing to believe you are neither a thief nor a fortune hunter. But ..." he fixed her with a piercing gaze that brooked no misunderstanding. "To use the cant you have no business knowing so well, what is

200

your lay?"

"If I told you, you would never believe me" came her honest reply. She shivered. "I don't think I believe it myself. It . . . it is a story too incredible to be possible. Can we not leave it at that? The strangest quirk of fate has brought me here, and here I must now stay."

His lip curled in a sneer that faded at once. "You expect me to take you on trust?"

She placed an urgent hand on his elbow. "I do not mean you—or Bella—harm. You must believe that."

He drew a deep breath and let it out slowly. "As ridiculous as it is, I do." He shook his head. "Are you an adventuress or a witch?"

"Neither. I'm just—me." She looked up, helpless, as though afraid she had alienated him.

"How did you know those horses would win?" He had to know, to remove that last niggling doubt of her dishonesty.

"Do you believe in ESP?"

He stared at her blankly. "In what?" What the devil did she talk about now?

"Extra sensory perception. Premonitions?"

"Is this some new American religion?" The idea appalled his Church of England soul.

"No! But sometimes I just know things will happen. I've always been like that. I . . . I don't get those feelings often, but when I do, I'm invariably right."

She was lying again! He knew it, felt it in his soul. Yet he also knew as a certainty that no dishonesty or evil lay hidden within her. Just how he could be so sure, he didn't know. It was almost as if they were so finely attuned to each other that pretenses simply could not exist between them.

Her uncanny ability at picking race winners must be a trick and nothing more. Relief flooded through him, surprising in its strength. He hadn't realized how very much he wanted to vindicate her, to prove to himself that his instinctive liking for her had not been misplaced.

His shoulders began to shake and his deep, rich chuckle escaped him incongruously. "By God, you're a mystery! I'm going to enjoy solving the riddles you pose!"

Chapter 15

The near horse tugged at its bit and sidled into its restless partner. For the next several minutes, Richard occupied himself with settling his pair. Andrea grasped the chance to steady her racing pulse. He would not press her for answers! And even more important, he would not throw her out.

She stole a glance at him and thought she understood his remarkable forbearance. She sensed a kindred spirit in him, one that needed a good healthy dose of challenge. And now that he had sold out of the Army, his comfortable, hedonistic life in Regency London did not provide it.

Andrea relaxed against the back of the curricle's seat and allowed the tension of the past half hour to seep away. She was luckier than she deserved. It had been a foolish risk to have the same person place her bets—and to have risked an accumulator. She should have waited, tried to find another way, learned a little more about the betting process. But it seemed firmly closed to females.

She turned to look at the other vehicles that made their stately rounds. Hyde Park was thin of company so early in the year. Only a few gentlemen rode along Rotten Row, exercising their mounts within the strict rules of the park. A few fashionably dressed people strolled along the paths, but the chill weather was not conducive to the luring out of more of the notables who had so far come to London.

The curricle before them slowed, then lurched, as the pair harnessed to it played off their tricks. With an excess of spirits, the near horse reared and set his companion dancing sideways. Theirs were not the only horses to be fresh and unready for town traffic. Richard drew up his blacks to wait.

Andrea's gaze strayed down a side path and suddenly she sat up straight. That was Giles Kendall! He was supposed to be in Melton Mowbray, not standing half hidden behind some bushes, talking to two men who could only be described as odd. They weren't gentlemen, nor were they from the lower orders of society. Their dress, she realized with a sense of shock, was similar to that of the man she had glimpsed that morning lounging outside the house on Curzon Street. Nondescript, and in an age when dress was distinguished either by elegance or flamboyance. There was not a single thing about these men she could exactly identify, almost as if they sought to be inconspicuous.

Possibilities flooded her mind, only to be dismissed as ridiculous. What could Giles Kendall have to do with her watcher? He was a good guy, not the villain in this piece! He was to marry Bella.

Unless . . . A horrible idea occurred to her, and she forced herself to consider it. Just because he was Richard's friend did not preclude his playing an underhanded game, as well. There was something furtive about this meeting that made her very uneasy. She really knew very little about him except that he was a younger son with little money—and that he would eventually marry, if not a fortune, then at least tenancy of a sizable, elegant estate. He might well be a villain. The thought left her chilled.

"Is something the matter?" Richard's deep voice startled her.

"Is that not Mr. Kendall?"

Richard looked, just as Giles handed something to the two men. They took their leave of him with a brief nod, as if to an equal, and Giles turned to continue his stroll along the path. He glanced up toward the carriage drive, stopped as he saw the curricle, then waved and strode up to them.

"Strange company you're keeping." Richard kept his tone bland, but Andrea detected the suspicious note that underlay it.

Giles laughed, though to Andrea's apprehensive mind it sounded a trifle forced. "Have you never employed someone to do a little errand for you?"

"Usually I send a footman."

Giles shook his head with mock sorrow. "I lack your servants, my dear fellow. But this is not the subject to discuss in the presence of ladies." He finished this comment with a broad wink.

Richard nodded, enlightened, and turned to address Andrea. "We are to assume this errand concerns a female of questionable morals." He watched her narrowly, as if to judge her reaction to his indelicate comment.

"Shocking," she said calmly. Both men laughed, and the mood lightened.

A carriage maneuvered to pass them. Richard glanced at it and his expression changed, taking on a gleam of devilish enjoyment. "I have always wanted to foist an impostor onto society." He murmured the words, too soft for Giles to hear. Without further explanation, he hailed the two haughty ladies who sat in the passing landaulet.

The elder smiled a warm greeting. "Grantham. I hardly expected to see you in town when you might be hunting.

How is dear Isabella?"

"In fine fettle, I promise you. Permit me to introduce her protégée for the season, a cousin of ours from America, Miss Andrea Wells." His mocking gaze touched Andrea. "Mrs. Drummond-Burrell and Countess Lieven."

Andrea's eyes widened and she stared in awe at the two patronesses of Almack's who so frequently appeared in Regency novels. She had always known they were real people, but to actually meet them . . . ! It helped bridge the disconcerting gap between fantasy and reality.

Gathering herself together, she stammered an almost incoherent greeting. Mrs. Drummond-Burrell gave her the briefest of nods in acknowledgment. Countess Lieven unbent so far as to invite her, in tepid terms, to pay a morning visit with Bella.

The ladies drove on, leaving Andrea with a sinking sensation in the pit of her stomach. The great condescension was for Bella's sake, not her own. They were not in the least impressed by her American accent. A strong pang of disappointment swept over her. She was not exactly making a rousing start at taking the ton by storm as a genuine Original.

Richard watched them drive off with a speculative gleam in his eyes. "Well, you've taken your first steps at storming the Holiest of Holies. Satisfied?" He took his leave of Giles and headed his horses out of the park. "Not bad for a blatant impostor."

"Oh, it helps to have friends." She threw him a look of supreme confidence which she was far from feeling. He might do nothing to hinder her in society, he might even go so far as to help—but not for a moment did she believe he would forget the mystery she presented. She would have to be very much on her guard with him or he would start demanding ticklish answers and refuse to be fobbed off as he had been, surprisingly, today.

They drove in a strained silence that neither seemed willing to break. When he drew up before the house in Curzon Street, Andrea jumped lightly to the pavement. Richard drove off to the mews, and Andrea, relieved at escaping his penetrating eye, hurried up the steps.

Bella stood in the hall, just taking off her muff and pelisse. "Back so soon? Did you enjoy the park?"

"Very much so," Andrea lied. "And you must know that we have been invited by Countess Lieven to pay a morning visit."

Bella clasped her hands. "How fortunate that you should have met her! We must call as soon as possible."

Andrea burst her bubble. "She and Mrs. Drummond-Burrell were no more than coolly polite, I should warn you."

Bella's mobile face fell. "Never mind. They feel obliged to be odiously rude to people they don't know. After all, they have their reputations to maintain. They have never heard of you, you must remember, but they will soon find you are not a . . . a social-climbing mushroom."

That was exactly what she was, Andrea thought in dismay. And in this world, it mattered more *who* one was than *what* one was. If Richard ever told Bella that she was in fact not related to them, would this sweetly warm and impulsive creature shun her at once?

But her host chose to hold his tongue. After an evening of nervous agitation, Andrea accepted the fact that he meant to keep his word. She would have breathed more easily, except that every time she looked up, she found his gaze resting on her, calculating, a disconcerting intelligence in his brooding gray eyes. She shivered and sought her couch at an unreasonably early hour.

Sleep, though, did not come easily, for her quest lay heavily on her mind. The odds of Richard's ever revealing the whereabouts of the Imperial Star to her had been considerably lengthened this day. That thought depressed her. Here in London, in a hired house, her only hope toward making any progress on her search would be to win his trust. She wasn't exactly going about it the right way.

Her visiting cards arrived from the printer two days later and, at Bella's insistence, they set forth upon the instant to visit Countess Lieven. As they stepped out of the landaulet before her house barely a half hour later, Andrea experienced the most ridiculous wave of disappointment. That great lady's residence looked no different from any of the others on the street. She had expected something distinctive.

But it wasn't. Countess Lieven was just a regular person living in a regular home. There was nothing magical or otherworldly about any of it. The fact that almost two hundred years later the woman would be a character appearing in numerous novels made no difference whatsoever now.

A sense of letdown, followed by nostalgia, swept over Andrea. The Regency era was just like her own time, not a story-book world at all.

Bella plied the knocker on the door, and Andrea fought down another pang of homesickness. Her sense of loss was every bit as poignant as ever, despite the passage of time. The phrase stabbed through her mind like the blade of a sharp knife. The passage of—or through—time.

The door opened and she found herself staring up into the formidable countenance of a portly butler. Andrea blinked, glad when Bella stepped into the breach and asked if Countess Lieven were in.

"Her ladyship is from home." The man inclined his head in a combination of apology and dismissal.

"Then we will leave our cards." Bella, the veteran of eight seasons, was not to be intimidated. She drew a gold case from her reticule and extracted a small piece of cardboard, which she handed over. Andrea followed suit.

Andrea remained silent and thoughtful on the drive home, listening with only half an ear to Bella's cheerful prattle of the toilette she meant to order for the first ball.

They had almost pulled abreast of their house when Bella stiffened. She stopped talking in the middle of a description of a flounce, then said, "That man is here."

Andrea started and looked frantically about. But the only man in sight was Giles Kendall, who stood on their doorstep. It took a second for her to realize that it was he, and not some mysterious watcher, to whom Bella referred in that scathing tone.

Unaware of her hostility, that gentleman strode down the steps to hand them out of the landaulet. He greeted them warmly, bowing over each of their hands, and retained Bella's longer than was strictly necessary.

She pulled her fingers free. "I fear you have come at a bad time. We are just off shopping and Richard is not home. You should look for him at either Jackson's or White's." With a curt nod, she dismissed him. Linking her arm through Andrea's, she pulled her resolutely inside the sanctuary of the house.

"Has he angered you?" Andrea regarded her in no little concern. "I thought you had become reconciled to him during his stay at the Court."

Soft color crept into Bella's cheeks. "I had to make the best of things there. Here I do not have to suffer his company—and I can only abhor his influence on Richard. Now we must change. I wish to visit Bond Street."

She hurried up the stairs, leaving Andrea to stare after her in dismay. It was going to be no easy task, getting these two together.

They returned from their shopping expedition considerably lighter of pocket. Bella was not content to purchase merely the several new pairs of long gloves and

209

stockings that she needed. In an almost reckless mood, she added to her wardrobe at random, thus coming home with two wholly unneeded shawls, a new reticule, a shockingly dear lace cap trimmed in ribands and ruffles, and a frivolous morning gown she decided she could not live without for the simple reason that Andrea had expressed disapproval.

By midafternoon, the dark, threatening clouds of the past few days blew off, leaving the day sunny with the promise of spring. Andrea, anxious to bring her hostess out of her odd humor, suggested a drive in the park, for it was almost four o'clock. Bella agreed and, after they partook of a light but much needed refreshment, ordered out the carriage once more.

Andrea went upstairs and put on the new rose muslin carriage dress that had arrived only the day before. She topped it with a matching pelisse and silk-lined bonnet, and hurried back down to await her hostess. Aside from that one ride with Grantham, when her thoughts were far from her surroundings, she had not visited Hyde Park. That was what she needed to pull her out of her growing depression, to see the Regency era of the novels. Then she might feel more at home.

Traffic filled the cobbled streets as they wended their way toward the afternoon mecca of the fashionable world. As soon as they entered through the gate, Andrea saw the change wrought by the passage of only a few days and her heart leapt with elation. A comfortable throng of vehicles paraded along the carriageway. The ton came to London, slowly but surely, just as her novels promised.

Her sense of delight, which had deserted her earlier, in front of Countess Lieven's house, flooded back. This was the London of her dreams. And how very different from that drive she had taken in the hired carriage in her own time! That seemed eons ago now—or was that the fantasy and this the reality?

She shook off the fey sensation. This was what the Promenade should be, with the elite of society nodding to each other from their carriages and gentlemen on horseback stopping to converse with ladies either walking or riding in vehicles. Emotion welled in her throat, forcing tears to her eyes, at being part of all this.

She looked eagerly about, not wanting to miss anything. As she glanced down a footpath along which buds just appeared on the shrubs, a tenor voice hailed them. She looked up and, to her dismay, saw her elderly, rakish acquaintance from Bath pulling abreast of them in his tilbury. Lord Brompton maneuvered into a position that forced their driver to stop.

"Oh, dear," Bella murmured with great inadequacy.

"Spring has indeed come to London." Lord Brompton leaned across, to the imminent danger of his protesting corset, and took their hands in greeting.

"Do your horses pine?" Andrea managed a polite smile.

He stared at her blankly. "My horses?"

Andrea sighed. Apparently, quickness of wit did not characterize him. "I seem to remember your saying that they like the snow."

Lord Brompton blinked. "Oh, yes, to be sure." He beamed at her. "But you shall find my horses perform to perfection in the spring, as well."

"You never let them try out their taste for winter weather," she pointed out.

He laughed in a knowing manner. "Is that an invitation?" There could be no mistaking the look of predatory interest that lit his eyes.

Andrea drew back, revolted. What on earth gave him his supreme confidence? The man was horrid! Yet he seemed certain that not only would she not rebuff him, but that ultimately he would succeed with her, and very well indeed.

"There is Wilfred, with Lettie!" Bella sat up in relief, unconsciously stepping in before Andrea could deliver the snub she had tried to formulate. "I had no idea they were in town."

Wilfred saw them and drew his curricle up on the other side of the landaulet. Andrea exchanged greetings with them and, to her surprise, noted that Lettie sat stiffly, her vivacious little face pale, her expression one of defeat. Her huge, expressive eyes lacked the dancing lights Andrea had noticed before. She hunched a shoulder and turned away as Wilfred leaned over to kiss Bella's fingers.

"When did you arrive?" Bella withdrew her gloved hand at once.

"Just two days ago. A tedious journey—endless, it always seems—but we spent the night on the road, of course. So early in the Season, but we simply had to let Lettie do some shopping. Ah, and that reminds me, my dear. I do wish you would take her about a bit. I cannot, simply cannot, permit the Dragoness to be in charge of dressing her. She hasn't the least notion of fashion, and I won't have the little puss here not looking all the crack. Such a dreadful way to make her debut."

Lettie raised her sad eyes to Wilfred's face and lowered them again. "You have been wonderful, standing up to her that way over the dreadful gowns she wanted me to purchase." Her voice held just a hint of a tremble.

"Never you mind, Lettie." Bella smiled warmly at her. "I shall be delighted to take you under my wing. Wilfred, have you walked down Bond Street? There is the most shocking quiz of a hat on display. I made sure you would laugh yourself into stitches when you saw it."

"Miss Moreland." Lord Brompton, who had remained silent during the exchange, spoke loudly from the far side of the landaulet in an attempt to make himself heard. When Lettie looked up, startled, he doffed his tall, curly beaver in a sweeping gesture. "The sun indeed shines brightly over London this day."

Lettie shrank back, her expression so pathetic that Andrea longed to shake her. Weak and helpless, the girl was exactly the sort of prey that roués of Brompton's stamp thrived on. If she would but stir herself and give him a stinging set-down, he would quickly withdraw and seek his amusement elsewhere.

With relief, Andrea saw Giles and Richard, deep in conversation, ride toward them. Richard glanced up and saw Andrea, but his dawning smile faded at sight of Brompton. Giles, though, felt no constraint and drew in his horse beside them.

"How do your plans for the ball progress?" Giles did not appear to notice the sudden tension that seemed to grip Bella, nor the abrupt formality of the bow she awarded him. "I beg of you, do not let it be an insipid affair," he continued. "I have heard little but plans for entertainments since I came to town, and they all sound so exactly alike."

"Indeed, I hope ours will not disappoint you." Bella turned back to Wilfred, her manner marked.

Andrea glanced at the dandy, so very different from the Corinthian precision of Giles and Grantham. What, she wondered, could Bella possibly see in this epitome of a Tulip? They had nothing in common except a sense of ton. When it came right down to it, Wilfred was little more than a fashionable fribble who would bore Bella in the long run. She needed a real man, one more like her brother. Someone like Giles Kendall.

Richard shifted in his saddle. "Well, Brompton, I hadn't expected to see you in town so early."

"Nor I, you." Brompton turned with reluctance from Lettie's enchanting profile.

Richard's lip curled. "I am sure I shall see you at White's sometime." With a curt nod, he dismissed the man.

Brompton glanced at Andrea, but, not receiving any

encouragement from her to remain, he accepted the situation. With a bow, punctuated by a groan from his corset, that encompassed them all, he took his leave, backed his horses and eased his tilbury into the parade of vehicles.

"It is a pity that fortune makes anyone acceptable." Richard's brooding eyes rested on Brompton's retreating back. "Shall I tell him you have your own unique resources and have no interest in his wealth?" His words were for Andrea alone.

She could not but be pleased at his irritation and the ease with which he removed Brompton from her side. She did like a man to be in control. But Richard wasn't her man. In only a few short months . . .

With an effort, she forced the thought from her mind. "Do you feel up to the explanations that might entail?" Her tone matched his, mercifully free of sorrow and regret, and she met his amused glance with one of challenge.

"One of these days—and soon!—*you* had better be!" But no malice colored his tone.

Andrea bestowed a gracious smile on him to hide her flutter of nerves. He seemed prepared to let her have her head—for the time being, at least. She could only be relieved. And not only because she had no desire to tell him more lies, she realized with a pang of dismay. She enjoyed their verbal sparring and found it far more intriguing than a mere flirtation could ever be.

"It's true, I assure you!" Wilfred's voice startled her. "'M' father has actually induced the Dragoness to hostess a rout party at the end of the week, to let Lettie try her wings."

"You will come, will you not, Miss Wells?" Lettie ventured the question. "I should so much like it if you would bear me company."

So much yearning lurked in that sweet, forlorn

expression that Andrea agreed at once. Wilfred then drove off, and Giles and Richard turned their mounts to ride along side the landaulet. As they completed another circuit, Richard suddenly hailed a passing carriage.

"Sally! You're in luck," he added in an undertone. "Sally Jersey."

Andrea leaned forward, staring in delight. Auburn! Her hair was auburn. She had always wondered about that. And she was so very lovely, so vivacious and animated as she looked up from her lively conversation with her companion in the barouche. No wonder she earned the nickname of Silence.

Lady Jersey greeted Bella warmly and appeared amused by Andrea's American accent. "You must not be put off by those who disapprove of cousins from the Colonies, my dear. Isabella, remind me to send you both vouchers for Almack's." She ordered her carriage forward, gave them a merry wave of farewell, and moved off.

Her social life was well on the way to becoming established, Andrea reflected with satisfaction as she dressed for Malverne's rout party several nights later. The promised vouchers arrived only that morning, and this night would be her first introduction to Regency-era entertaining. Excitement filled her, almost bubbling over. The one shadow that hung over her she forced into the background, refusing to think about it. She would enjoy Grantham's company for as long as she could.

She gave her reflection a final check and approved the way Lily had pulled her hair up into a knot on the top of her head. Thick golden ringlets fell to well below her bare shoulders. No, she could find no fault in her appearance—except that her lashes were too pale, and her eyes could look a lot larger with a touch of pearl shadow.

215

She descended the stairs, further reassured by the gentle rustle of her gown. The half-robe of celestial blue crepe opened at the front to reveal a white silk underdress embroidered with tiny silver rosebuds. With her height, she knew the effect would be striking.

Yet she was nervous. She had always thought Regency dress would suit her, that she would feel at home in it. It was lovely—and very flattering to a tall, willowy figure— but the stays pinched about her rib cage and her breasts were forced up so that they filled the low bodice to an alarming degree. At this moment, she would give anything for one of her own, comfortable bras—or, at the very least, a lace fichu.

It could be worse, of course, she consoled herself. She might have gone back about fifty or seventy-five years earlier and had to put up with lacings about the waist that made it impossible for a lady to breathe. And while she was at it, she couldn't forget the goose fat that the ladies then had worked into their hair so that it would hold the elaborate, powder-drenched coiffures.

As she neared the bottom of the stairs, Richard came out of the drawing room, paused in the hall, and stared up at her. An arrested gleam lit his eyes, and it easily proved enough to make her forget her discomfort—or at least make her think it might all be worthwhile. He strolled forward, his unwavering gaze roving over her slender but rounded figure in blatant admiration.

It didn't take lacings to make it difficult to breathe, she realized. And it wasn't only the glowing appreciation in his expression. For one moment, it seemed as if she saw him again for the first time, as if he stepped down from that portrait, the epitome of her fantasies come to life. His dress was impeccable, from the coat of mulberry velvet to the black breeches and silken stockings. Only a single fob chain crossed his flowered brocade waistcoat and the quizzing glass hung, almost unnoticed, from a black riband. His neckcloth boasted neat, clean folds, nearly military in their precision, and his hair curled with a natural unruliness rather than the artless crimping affected by the town bucks. Andrea met his smoky gray eyes and felt herself sinking beneath a spell that she had no desire to break.

Bella swept down the steps behind her, jolting Andrea out of her disastrous train of thought and sensation. Shaken, she hurried down the last step and away from Richard to don her evening wrap. Behind her, she could hear Bella's laughing approval of her brother's promptness and appearance.

The sounds of a carriage pulling up in the street reached them, and the butler opened the front door. Richard picked up his cape, adjusted his sister's ermine-trimmed cloak, and ushered the ladies outside to the waiting landaulet for the short drive to Malverne House on Mount Street.

Only a few carriages stood in the road, and Bella sighed. "The town is still somewhat thin of company, though perhaps that is best for Lettie's first party. She is the shyest little creature."

It would be best for her, too, Andrea reflected. This would be nothing like the parties she had gone to back in Minneapolis.

Nor was it. As soon as they entered the hall, the gentle strains of a small string quartet drifted out to greet them. A liveried footman took their wraps, then bowed them toward the staircase. The butler, who stood at the top, took their names and announced them in sonorous accents. Through an open doorway of a front saloon, Andrea glimpsed tables piled high with cakes, tartlets, canapés, and a variety of elaborate hors d'oeuvres at which her modern mind boggled. Another table contained chased silver bowls of punch and lemonade.

Gentlemen, playing cards, occupied the room across

the hall. The cardroom, she thought in delight. Decanters, undoubtedly containing brandy, sherry, and madeira, stood within easy reach of the guests. She supposed Richard would shortly retire here to pass a pleasant evening with his cronies.

Following Bella, Andrea entered the suite of connecting withdrawing rooms that had been thrown open for the evening. She looked about, avidly curious. Apparently, she had been right in her guesses gleaned from the novels—rout parties did not include either dancing or formal entertainment of any kind. At least this one didn't, as far as she could discover. Guests appeared to have come for the conversation—and to be seen in their elaborate toilettes.

"Oh, Miss Wells!" Lettie rushed forward, greeting her like a long-lost friend. "I am so glad you are here."

She clasped Andrea's hands and drew her into the second drawing room to join a group of young ladies. Andrea looked them over and felt suddenly ancient. They could be no more than seventeen or eighteen, a good ten years younger than she! "Barely emerged from the schoolroom," that was the phrase.

Busily, the girls discussed the shopping in which they indulged, their orgies of spending, the gowns they planned for their presentations. And, of course, a couple of gentlemen whose names caused blushes and giggles. Andrea experienced the sinking sensation of being transported into any teen-age party, where the topics of conversation would always be boys and clothes. Apparently, some things were universal and surpassed the boundaries of time and place.

Keeping half an ear tuned to this conversation, Andrea let the rest of her attention wander among the other groups of people who stood about in small knots, talking. As far as she could tell, gossip appeared to be the order of the day. These must be *on dits*, she decided in glee—

unless they were *crim. con.* stories. She never had discovered what the latter meant.

An almost irresistible urge to giggle herself welled within her. In nearly two hundred years, people hadn't changed at all. She felt completely at home, and her only regret was that she didn't know who Mrs. Fairfax-Martin was, or why her driving in the park with Lady Palmerston should draw shocked and scandalized exclamations.

She moved away, admiring the gowns and elaborate headdresses of the ladies. If she had wanted glamour and glitter, she certainly found it here. Nobility, aristocracy, gems, silks—everything betokening wealth and position. This was the Regency era, exactly as she imagined it.

Or was it? She closed her eyes and listened to the bevy of voices. The accents sounded odd to her American ears, and occasionally a gentleman used a cant phrase. But on the whole, this could be any gathering of the wealthy in any time period. Another pang of homesickness swept over her, and suddenly she felt disoriented, lost, as if the ground had been knocked away from beneath her feet.

She wanted Richard! He formed the link between her two worlds; perhaps seeing him would help settle her again, restore her equilibrium. With this purpose in mind, she went in search of him. At the fourth door into which she peeped, she was rewarded with the sound of his voice.

"And what is it that you suggest?" she heard. Richard's tone dripped scorn. "Or don't I have to guess? I suppose all this nonsense has to do with the Imperial Star?"

Chapter 16

Andrea opened the door a bit further, knowing full well she should not eavesdrop. But this was a topic that concerned her deeply.

The room into which she looked was obviously a library, for shelves filled with leather-bound volumes lined the wall she could see. She barely spared them a glance. Richard leaned negligently against the mantel beside a crackling fire, a glass of wine clasped casually in one hand. Wilfred stood before him, shifting back and forth, uneasy.

"Well, my . . . I mean I . . . thought you might like to give Bella the Imperial Star as a wedding present."

Richard raised his eyebrows in mild surprise. "Now, whatever would make you think anything like that?"

Wilfred shrugged. "I don't suppose I did, really. But it was worth a try, my dear fellow, definitely worth a try."

"Was it?" Richard's voice almost purred, but his smile held nothing but contempt. "Your father would do better to speak to me in person, you know."

He straightened up and Andrea slipped away, not wanting to be caught listening. But why was Wilfred—or rather Malverne—so anxious to regain possession of the icon? He had received a very pretty price for it.

Or had he? William Westmont supposedly offered the Court as collateral, but so far it seemed that Malverne had said nothing about that arrangement. Andrea could not help but wonder just what had passed between the two men. And why did Richard now hide the Imperial Star?

An overly loud laugh recalled her to a sense of her surroundings. Thrusting her confusion momentarily aside, she strolled back into the drawing room in what she hoped was a nonchalant manner. In a few moments, she located Bella and went to her side.

"Insipid evening," Bella whispered.

Andrea nodded, though, in fact, she had found it far otherwise. But a rout party was no place to try to sort out a mystery. "Do you think we can leave?" she whispered back.

"I shall say I have the headache." On this promise, Bella went in search of Miss Moreland to make their excuses.

In less than a quarter hour, their coachman brought the carriage around and Grantham escorted them out. Bella sank back against the squabs and let out a deep sigh of relief.

"What a deadly evening! Andrea, my love, we must discover the name of the firm of caterers they used so that we may avoid them!"

"Letitia told me it was all handled by their own cook."

"Well!" Bella let that one scathing syllable sum up her feelings. "You may be very sure we won't behave in so scaly a fashion. For the ball, we shall hire the entire dinner, not to mention the pastries and everything else we shall need! And when we hold our rout parties and the Venetian breakfast, we must have something more interesting than a string quartet. Pandean pipes, perhaps? Richard, what do you think?"

"It may be bagpipes, for all I care."

"Do not be so disobliging. We must plan any number of entertainments to launch Andrea into Society."

Richard groaned. Lowering the window, he shouted to the driver to pull up. As soon as the landaulet came to a stop, he opened the door and jumped lightly to the paved street.

"But where are you going?" Bella stared after her brother in dismay.

"You ladies may discuss your parties to your hearts' content. I am off to White's."

"Like a fox going to ground," Andrea called after his disappearing back. "There," she sighed. "He didn't hear. A perfectly good crack gone to waste."

The topic of parties absorbed Bella for much of the next few days, until Andrea began to wonder if her hostess would think of anything else ever again. It was no wonder Grantham had neatly absented himself when the discussion began. Any sane person must. His determined sister ruthlessly hauled her out for shopping expeditions until it occurred to Andrea's preoccupied mind that Bella's actions were not quite as frivolous as they seemed. A touch of sadness lurked in her eyes and she attacked each day's outing with an intensity born of desperation to hide a growing unhappiness. Andrea watched, but, try as she might, she could not determine the cause.

Nor could Andrea be content any longer with so pointless an existence. With each successive shopping expedition, she became increasingly familiar with the frivolous London of the novels. But there had to be more than this! Intellectually, she acknowledged that the start of the Season necessitated a great deal of preparation, but the endless talk of nothing but impending entertainments and pleasures bored her. She was accustomed to an eight-to-five job, to solving difficult problems, and daily dealing with her clients' crises.

222

That was it! She lacked the satisfaction of accomplishment. She needed work, something to occupy her mind, to make her feel useful. And barring making progress on her hunt for the Imperial Star, she knew what she wanted to do.

On impulse as they left a catering firm and started for home, Andrea asked the coachman to instead take them into some of the districts she had not yet glimpsed. They turned down an unfamiliar street, and within minutes the elegance of the fashionable quarter faded. Now they traversed a neighborhood that Bella slightingly spoke of as being populated by "cits," the wealthy but underbred hangers-on of society who made their ungenteel fortunes in the City.

Andrea peered down dark side streets, then suddenly hailed the coachman. "John!"

He turned on his seat. "Yes, miss?"

"Drive down that alley." She could just glimpse a dingy passage, barely wide enough for their landaulet, filled with ragged urchins playing a game of tag.

"No, miss." The coachman shook his head. "Begging your pardon, but that's not the place for the likes of you."

Bella shivered. "I should say not! We would encounter only nasty, dirty people."

"People who need help," Andrea corrected.

"It is not your concern, my dear." Bella patted her hand gently. "What do you think of wearing the white lace—acceptable in a debutante of your age, you know—over the blue sarcenet underslip to Almack's the first time you go?"

Andrea shrugged, not really interested. Almack's had lost its Nirvana image. For that matter, the whole damned Regency era no longer shined for her. "Tarnished," that was the term she wanted. As if the layer of silver plating were too thin to stand up to close inspection and showed the dullness and rust of the base metal beneath.

It seemed impossible that the beau monde really could have insulated itself so thoroughly against the stark reality of the poverty that existed just around corners, barely out of sight. Her companions tried to shield her from it, but still it remained, and that knowledge disturbed her. If only she could make the wealthy members of society share the guilt she experienced for not helping. Then perhaps something would be done.

The terrible living and health conditions of the poor still occupied her mind when they pulled up in their isolated little world on Curzon Street. She hurried into the hall, her packages forgotten, and almost collided with Grantham.

Grasping her shoulders, he steadied her, and his laughing eyes stared down into her sobered face. His expression altered to concern—and something more—and he took her arm and led her into his bookroom.

"What has happened?" His tone demanded the truth.

She shook her head as she took the seat beside his desk. "Nothing. It . . . it was just very distressing. I knew such poverty and misery existed, of course, but to actually see it so close to the most elite of residences—but well out of the sight—and interest—of the beau monde."

Richard sat on the corner of his desk and regarded her through cloudy eyes for once devoid of any traces of merriment. "It will take much to make the upper classes conscious of the need to help." He reached over and poured some brandy from a decanter into two glasses and handed her one.

She took it and sipped the amber liquid. Was this Napoleon brandy? she wondered fleetingly, and the whimsical humor eased her mood.

"It is rare to find one so much concerned." Richard swirled his glass.

MORE PASSION AND ADVENTURE AWAIT... YOUR TRIP TO A BIG ADVENTUROUS WORLD BEGINS WHEN YOU ACCEPT YOUR FIRST 4 NOVELS ABSOLUTELY *FREE*
(AN $18.00 VALUE)

Accept your Free gift and start to experience more of the passion and adventure you like in a historical romance novel. Each Zebra novel is filled with proud men, spirited women and tempestuous love that you'll remember long after you turn the last page.

Zebra Historical Romances are the finest novels of their kind. They are written by authors who really know how to weave tales of romance and adventure in the historical settings you love. You'll feel like you've actually gone back in time with the thrilling stories that each Zebra novel offers.

GET YOUR FREE GIFT WITH THE START OF YOUR HOME SUBSCRIPTION

Our readers tell us that these books sell out very fast in book stores and often they miss the newest titles. So Zebra has made arrangements for you to receive the four newest novels published each month.

You'll be guaranteed that you'll never miss a title, and home delivery is so convenient. And to show you just how easy it is to get Zebra Historical Romances, we'll send you your first 4 books absolutely FREE! Our gift to you just for trying our home subscription service.

BIG SAVINGS AND FREE HOME DELIVERY

Each month, you'll receive the four newest titles as soon as they are published. You'll probably receive them even before the bookstores do. What's more, you may preview these exciting novels free for 10 days. If you like them as much as we think you will, just pay the low preferred subscriber's price of just $3.75 each. *You'll save $3.00 each month off the publisher's price.* AND, your savings are even greater because there are never any shipping, handling or other hidden charges—FREE Home Delivery. Of course you can return any shipment within 10 days for full credit, no questions asked. There is no minimum number of books you must buy.

4 FREE BOOKS

TO GET YOUR 4 FREE BOOKS WORTH $18.00 — MAIL IN THE FREE BOOK CERTIFICATE T O D A Y

Fill in the Free Book Certificate below, and we'll send your FREE BOOKS to you as soon as we receive it.

If the certificate is missing below, write to: Zebra Home Subscription Service, Inc., P.O. Box 5214, 120 Brighton Road, Clifton, New Jersey 07015-5214.

FREE BOOK CERTIFICATE

4 FREE BOOKS

ZEBRA HOME SUBSCRIPTION SERVICE, INC.

YES! Please start my subscription to Zebra Historical Romances and send me my first 4 books absolutely FREE. I understand that each month I may preview four new Zebra Historical Romances free for 10 days. If I'm not satisfied with them, I may return the four books within 10 days and owe nothing. Otherwise, I will pay the low preferred subscriber's price of just $3.75 each; a total of $15.00, *a savings off the publisher's price of $3.00.* I may return any shipment and I may cancel this subscription at any time. There is no obligation to buy any shipment and there are no shipping, handling or other hidden charges. Regardless of what I decide, the four free books are mine to keep.

NAME

ADDRESS   APT

CITY   STATE   ZIP

(   )
TELEPHONE

SIGNATURE   (if under 18, parent or guardian must sign)

Terms, offer and prices subject to change without notice. Subscription subject to acceptance by Zebra Books. Zebra Books reserves the right to reject any order or cancel any subscription.   039002

She threw him a challenging glance. "You say you look for amusement. Could you not find it in championing the needs of climbing boys or orphans or war-wounded?"

"We are not all completely heartless, you know. Things have been done. After the Battle of Trafalgar, for instance, a ball was held in Brighton to raise money for the dependents of those who died."

"Was it? I . . . I didn't know. I'm glad, but that's only the tip of the iceberg, you know."

"The . . . what?" His eyes widened in sudden enjoyment.

Warm color flooded her cheeks. "I mean it barely touches the surface, when the problem goes so very deep. Like the first two feet of a mile-long race."

"I thought we'd get back to the turf," he murmured, but a gentleness softened his tone. "But you are right. We must all do more."

His gaze continued to rest on her, and his expression altered slowly as a slight crease formed in his high brow. A bond seemed to forge between them, so real it was almost tangible, and Andrea caught her breath at its strength. He cared, as deeply as she, but lacked her modern, liberal upbringing that made acting on social issues seem natural. For his time, he must be an advanced thinker.

He reached across and just touched her cheek. Stillness engulfed them as his finger traced the line of her jaw. Her heart stopped, then beat hard and rapid. A new light sparked in the luminous depths of his eyes and glowed like a smoldering ember. Time stood suspended as his gentle touch moved slowly to her throat.

He drew back abruptly and rose, moving away from her as if he needed to put some distance between them, and not only physically. "If you will excuse me, I have a few things to take care of." He exited the bookroom, leaving her staring after him from amidst the shattered

225

fragments of the emotions that had encompassed them the moment before.

She drew a deep, steadying breath and came to her feet. To her relief, her legs remained strong enough to support her. She followed him into the hall, but he was nowhere in sight.

Shaken, she made her way up to her own room to put off her bonnet. For nearly twenty minutes, she sat at her dressing table, staring at her reflection in the mirror and wondering what he saw when he looked at her. She didn't seem to be anything out of the ordinary. Her features were pleasant, but without her makeup she felt plain.

Yet their mutual attraction went deeper than the merely physical. With Richard, she experienced the oddest sense of a kindred spirit, something she had never before encountered. There was far more to him than the surface frivolity he showed the fashionable world. Beneath it lay a caring side that drew her, that touched a chord deep within. Perhaps that was what brought her back through time, this unity she felt with him. But if that were so, why did she have to come so late in his life, when she could only share so very few months with him?

Suddenly she needed to see him again and at once, to reassure herself that he was still there. Jumping up from the table, she hurried back down the stairs. As she neared the second landing, the firm thud that signaled the closing of the front door reached her. She ran down the last flight.

Bella looked up from the hall as Andrea reached the bottom steps. "Men," that lady said with undisguised loathing. "Richard has gone to a mill, and I make no doubt it is that Giles Kendall who has suggested it."

"A mill? He . . . he did not mention it." The bottom seemed to fall out of Andrea's world, leaving her floundering for firm footing. "Where does he go?"

"Near Bristol, so he will stay at the Court. He

226

shouldn't be gone above three or four days, but, oh, I could kill Mr. Kendall! To drag Richard away, just when things were going so well between—" She broke off, flustered.

Andrea's throat felt dry. It hadn't been Giles who caused Richard's precipitate departure. It was she who had driven him away. He, too, must sense that inexplicable bond that linked them together, and he rejected it, wanting nothing to do with a mysterious impostor.

In her estimation of the situation, Andrea was absolutely correct. Richard had stormed out of the house on Curzon Street bent on putting as much distance between himself and the deceiving Miss Andrea Wells as possible. That only twenty minutes before he had wanted to kiss her, he thrust from his mind. He was no green youth to fall for the blatant lures of an adventuress!

He drove first to Giles's lodgings on Clarges Street, only to be informed by the proprietor of the house that Mr. Kendall had departed earlier in the day. This should have neither surprised nor irritated Richard, since he had already turned down Giles's suggestion that they attend this mill together; still, it did both. His mood was far from reasonable.

Well, he would catch him up at Greythorne Court, where Richard had suggested his friend put up. Rooms any closer to the millsite would be impossible to obtain at this late date, and he knew Giles had not written ahead for accommodation. Scowling, he headed his pair toward the Bath road and sprang them as soon as they cleared the heavy city traffic.

He could have used some companionship on this journey. Almost a hundred miles lay ahead, with no one to divert his mind from dwelling on the disturbing Miss

Wells. That he lacked a passenger was his own fault, and that knowledge did nothing to improve his stormy temper. He should have agreed to attend the fight in the first place. But he hadn't. He had preferred to remain in London, watching and enjoying his false cousin's exploration of the city and tentative forays into the ton.

Damn her! Every instinct told him to trust her, but how could he? She admitted she lied. She admitted they were not related. She explained nothing, not even her impossible wins on the track! The bank account he had opened for her only days before contained more money than did his.

He didn't believe in the supernatural—except, of course, for the ghost of the monk that haunted the ruins of the Norman Abbey near the Court—but the thought crossed his mind that she might be a witch. He dismissed it the next moment. Did he think she read the names of racehorses in her tea leaves? He had never seen her performing incantations or making mysterious, symbolic gestures.

Yet he had fallen under a spell of her weaving, whether conscious or not. That fact disturbed him.

The cattle to be obtained at posting houses were less than the best, so even with frequent changes, he could not cover much more than twelve miles an hour during daylight. As the dark of night made the uneven roads hazardous, he was forced to slow his pace almost by half. Still, he determined to reach the Court before midnight.

Five miles beyond Swindon, though, luck turned against him. The off horse stumbled in a deep wheel rut and pulled a tendon. Nursing the animal carefully, Richard drove on to the next village, no more than a collection of cottages and boasting only one ale house. A fresh horse was not available, but the landlord, recognizing a member of the Quality, promised to obtain a suitable animal by morning. With an outward cordiality he was far from feeling, Richard accepted the man's offer of dinner and the use, for the night, of his one cramped and mildewed guest room.

When Richard came down the rickety stairs to the common room the following morning, the landlord's wife prepared a meager breakfast of watery porridge and a tankard of questionable home brewed. His curricle, he discovered, waited only for the arrival of the promised horse.

More than an hour passed in impatient pacing before the tap boy returned with a half-broken colt in tow. An additional twenty minutes were wasted while the recalcitrant animal was harnessed to the shafts. It promptly lunged at its partner, teeth barred and ears back. Gritting his own teeth, Richard took firm hold of the ribbons and gave them the office.

The turnoff to the Bristol road lay only two miles beyond the village, but long before they reached it, Richard had set up a steady swearing under his breath. Even if he did reach the millsite in time to get an adequate vantage point, the odds were that his obstreperous colt would refuse to stand.

The animal's first reaction to the heavy traffic in the village streets was enough to give Richard deep forebodings. Although the colt by this time had reached a tentative truce with his partner, it did not, Richard discovered quickly, extend to any other horse on the road. With every ounce of his concentration focused on the vicious animal, he maneuvered his carriage through the crowd to the outskirts of the village where the ring had been laid out.

Every vehicle and contraption that could be driven appeared to have been requisitioned for the occasion, and the front circle of carriages boasted everything from curricles to pony and dog carts. Richard positioned himself in the second line, between a farm wagon that still smelled of fertilizer and a crane-necked phaeton that swayed alarmingly. He had two hours to wait, and occupied himself with convincing the colt to remain where they had stopped and not to bite or cow-kick at his neighbors.

The only thing that would make the day bearable, Richard decided, would be to locate Giles and have a good laugh over his frustrating morning. But that outlet was denied him. Though he searched through the arriving throngs, he did not catch so much as a glimpse of the sandy brown head he sought.

He should have just gone with his friend in the first place. But no, he had let a misplaced fascination with a mysterious woman cloud his judgment. His temper, already sadly mangled that morning, inched nearer the breaking point. Only a rousing good mill would make all the difficulties seem worthwhile.

He was not to have it. Both combatants were young, though the advertisements had touted them as promising challengers. Richard watched the first round with interest when he could spare his attention from his horses. But while the fighters displayed to advantage, neither possessed stamina. By the second round, cross and jostle work proved to be the order of the day with little science remaining and the footwork all heavy and laborious. The third ended abruptly with a punch that would have made Gentleman Jackson groan had he been forced to watch.

Disgusted with the mill, with the horse, and with himself for allowing a mere female to disturb his normally rational thinking, he waited in seething impatience to join the unending line of carriages leaving the field. He would probably find Giles at the Court, they would put away a bottle or two of madeira and talk over better fights they had witnessed.

But even this pleasure was to be denied him. When he

at last persuaded the colt, to whom he had given a rather impolite name, to complete the eighteen-mile journey to the Court, he found that Giles had not spent the night there, nor was he expected. Fuming, Richard turned his carriage over to Samuel's care and stormed up to the house. A long, boring evening dragged ahead.

The consumption of an excellent dinner did little to soothe his frustrated spirits. In desperation, he set off for a rapid walk. The chill, clear night beckoned, and he followed the path drenched in moonlight through the rose garden toward the hawthorn hedge that bordered the drive. Near the gate, he turned back to stare up at the myriad stars that winked and glittered in the black sky.

Another light winked, not above him but near the East Tower. Richard stiffened. The light blinked again, as if a shutter slipped on a lantern.

The last shred of his carefully held temper snapped. He had put up with enough this day, he would not have some poacher or sneak-thief poking about his home! He broke into a run, avoiding the gravel path. He had no intention of making any noise that might warn the intruder he had been bubbled.

He crept the last dozen yards, keeping low behind a row of hedges. A slight man in a voluminous frieze coat, clearly visible by the light of the half moon, stood on tiptoe at a window of the tower, peering inside. His lantern, cloaked in black cloth, stood at his side. On the ground lay a sack from which something long and narrow protruded. Tools, Richard realized, with which to break in.

A murderous fury swept caution to the winds. No one would get away with invading his home! He rushed the man, ending with a lunging tackle that took the intruder about the knees. They went down hard together.

The little man struggled, but Richard had the advantage of both bulk and science. He landed his

231

opponent a facer, drawing his cork, then dug his fingers into the man's neck.

"Just what the devil do you think you're doing?"

Fear shone in the sharp-featured face. He made a gurgling, strangled noise, and Richard relaxed his grip. He wouldn't mind throttling him, but he wanted some answers first.

A whisper of dislodged pebbles was his only warning. Richard straightened, alert, but too late. He caught a glimpse of movement before a blinding pain shot across his skull and he fell forward into oblivion.

Chapter 17

After Richard's departure to the mill, Andrea returned to her room, dismayed more by her reactions than by his actual absence. A sense of loss and emptiness overwhelmed her. She was besotted with the man! And that was something she could not allow.

She sank down on her bed and slammed her clenched fists against the feather mattress. She was becoming involved with him, inch by insidious inch! All right, so what if he was the epitome of a Regency hero? She'd read about any number of them and never once lost her heart.

But this one was real. That knowledge frightened her. This hero was very human, with foibles and vulnerability, a streak of stubborn pigheadedness and the most gloriously dancing lights in his intriguing eyes she had ever seen. Warmth raced through her at just the touch of his hand, and a tantalizing hint of bay rum teased her nostrils whenever he was near.

She closed her eyes and let out a groaning sigh. She had journeyed across the ages to be with him, even knowing their time together would be short. And she wouldn't change her decision for anything.

Oh, Lud! She was becoming maudlin! With an effort, she managed a smile for her ladylike oath, one of the few she knew. Her own taste ran to something stronger. At any rate, it helped her shake off the depressingly mawkish mood. Rather than sitting about acting like some silly heroine, mooning over her unattainable hero, she might as well turn her mind onto some productive channel.

Richard was not the only reason she had gone back to another time. Her primary purpose, if she would choose to remember, was that she loved the Regency era! And secondly, she intended to help Catherine Kendall. With a sense of shock, she realized it had been some days since she had last thought of the yet unborn woman.

And at the rate things were going, Catherine might never be born! Andrea had two tasks ahead of her—to get Bella safely married to Giles and to find the Imperial Star. But the latter was like to prove every bit as formidable as the first. Since Richard bristled at the very mention of the icon, she didn't dare ask about it.

For the next two days, she went through the motions of shopping with Bella, of paying morning visits and attending a small card party. But London was empty without Grantham's deep laugh and quick, firm footsteps.

To her further consternation, the excitement of living in the Regency era had faded completely. She no longer looked about with the wide eyes of innocent anticipation. She was distressed by the poverty she saw, sometimes side by side with luxury. But much as she would like to try, she could not hasten social reform. She could not try to change history.

It was late in the second day of Grantham's absence before she realized she had not noticed anyone loitering in the streets or hanging about in a suspicious manner. A thrill of fear raced along her spine. The man might have followed Richard, and if so, he might well be in danger. Why? She could guess the answer. The Imperial Star was

234

worth a very great deal of money, well over a hundred thousand pounds. Someone who knew of its existence could be trying to steal it. Not for the first time, she wished she knew where Richard had hidden the icon.

Preparations for the ball continued, and Andrea tried to appear enthusiastic for the sake of her hostess. Cards were ordered, caterers interviewed, musicians hired. Andrea threw herself into the activity with a fervency that surprised and gratified Bella. Andrea smiled with false brightness and turned her attention to anything that might help to drive Richard and her roiling thoughts from her mind.

On the afternoon of the fourth day, a commotion arose in the hall and Richard's deep voice, answering his sister, carried back to where Andrea sat addressing cards of invitation in a back saloon. The joy that flooded through her startled her by its intensity. She jumped up and hurried out to greet him—and stopped short at sight of his face. A gasp of horror escaped her. An ugly, large bruise covered Richard's left temple and part of one eye, and deep scratches sliced through to the bone above his cheek.

"It is nothing," Richard said shortly. "The crowd took exception to a few of the calls and started a mill of their own." His tone was one of forced cheerfulness.

"Let me get something to put on it. I am sure Cook must have some salve or ointment." Bella strode away, distraught, paying no heed to Richard's curt command not to subject him to any unneeded and unwanted remedies.

Andrea regarded him solemnly, waiting until he allowed his gaze to meet hers. He looked away at once, but not before she detected the veiled guard in the depths of his eyes. He hid something, and she had a shrewd idea what it was. The shadowy figure near Greythorne Court and the man who no longer haunted Curzon Street had

235

never been far from her mind. But he did not speak of it and she forebore to force the issue.

Over the course of the next week, the cuts healed and the bruise faded from Richard's face and became more a fearful memory on Andrea's part than anything else. Grantham pretended it did not exist, unless he wished to use it as his excuse to absent himself from the boring parties to which Bella demanded his escort. In his present somewhat colorful state, he preferred to visit his clubs and eschew the society of females whom he claimed might be shocked by his unorthodox appearance.

Not to be thwarted, Bella declared that dancing lessons for Andrea must once again be of top priority. Giles, paying them a morning visit the following day, was instantly pressed into service. Bella dashed off a note, summoning Letitia Moreland and Wilfred to make up sufficient numbers to form a set.

Richard took the opportunity to drag Giles aside under the pretense of pouring them both wine. "You didn't attend the mill." He made it a casual comment.

"No, something came up and I had to leave town for a few days. Did you go after all?"

"You didn't miss anything." Richard tossed off the contents of his glass. "I've seen better among street urchins."

Giles leaned back in his chair and regarded his friend. "It looks like you took part in one."

"No, I disturbed an unexpected visitor at the Court."

Their gazes met and Giles frowned. "Did you, indeed? Now, I wonder . . ." He fell silent and Richard, his eyes narrowed as they rested on his friend, let the subject drop.

Their guests arrived within the half hour. Wilfred obviously looked forward to the "impromptu hop," as he phrased it, but Lettie did not appear to share his enthusiasm. Her lively spirits seemed subdued, as if a great care rested on her frail shoulders. Miss Moreland, much to everyone's consternation, accompanied her charge with the fixed intention of playing for them.

"It's enough to weigh down anyone's spirits," Bella confided to Andrea in a too-loud aside as the Dragoness pounded her way through a desultory country dance. "At least it is better than Mr. Kendall's dreadful humming, though."

"I doubt you can talk her into playing a waltz," Andrea whispered back before the movements of the set separated them.

Bella rolled her eyes heavenward but kept her tongue.

The piece drew to its painstaking end and the Dragoness stood. "Letitia, you may bring me a cup of tea."

Lettie scurried from the cleared floor to the tray that rested on an occasional table and the others, recognizing that an interval had been called, followed. While Bella poured out for the ladies, Richard served the gentlemen with sherry.

"Well, I don't think we're doing that badly." Giles emptied half the tiny glass at one swallow. "What do you think, Grantham, shall we set up as caper merchants?"

"Oh, you've definitely found your calling in life." Richard poured more of the wine. He smiled more easily than he had for several days.

"You do an excellent job, my dear Grantham, quite excellent," Wilfred assured him. "But I never thought this was quite in your line."

"A host must do his duty." A sudden, teasing light sparkled in Richard's eyes, and the look he threw Andrea was as eloquent as if he threw down a gauntlet to her.

"A far better pursuit than visiting Jackson's Saloon." Wilfred nodded his approval. "One hears you are putting in even more practice there than usual. Really, this love of violence you seem to cherish!"

Richard directed a quelling glance at him, but it was too late. Andrea stood and moved to join them.

"What do you mean?" Her anxious gaze rested not on Wilfred but on Richard.

Giles shrugged. "Just keeping ourselves in shape. Nothing to interest a female."

"And in practice at the art of self-defense." Andrea could only be glad, though she knew it would ultimately prove to no avail.

Richard strolled over, murmured something to Miss Moreland, and she resumed her playing. He turned to Andrea, took her hand, and led her back to the floor. Wilfred partnered Bella, and Lettie, shyly, accompanied Giles. A quadrille, Andrea realized with a sinking heart, and threw a fulminating glare at Richard. He had done this to her on purpose! Her whole reliance must lie on him and his ability to perform the moves.

Her whole reliance . . . She needed him, and that knowledge distressed her. She could have him for only such a short time longer.

She looked up into his mischievous face and a wave of dizziness, akin to nausea, swept over her. She couldn't bear the thought of his death. Unshed tears burned in her eyes and she averted her face, not wanting the others to see. Strong fingers pressed hers, comforting, and she blinked rapidly before looking back up into Richard's teasing eyes.

"Tired? You will have to dance much longer than that to get through a ball."

The charm of his smile enthralled her. As she gazed up into his face, that odd sense of awareness, of being tied to him, flickered through her once more. Not just her mind, but her very being seemed bound to him. In a moment, the sensation faded, but an overpowering physical awareness remained in its wake.

Unable to stop herself, she swayed toward him, losing

her sense of self in the depths of his mesmerizing eyes. The door to the drawing room opened, but she paid it no heed. Nothing mattered but Richard, his nearness, the compelling eyes that held hers in a spell that spanned the ages.

"Excuse me, my lord." The butler's voice penetrated her absorption. "The Earl of Malverne has called."

The Dragoness stopped playing and Richard dropped Andrea's hand. Malverne hesitated on the threshold, startled to see so many members of his household present. He flushed deeply and his gaze sought out Grantham.

"I want a word with you."

One glance at Malverne's nervous, fear-filled face proved enough to set Andrea's pulse racing in anticipation of she knew not what. Richard excused himself and went out with his guest. Andrea, murmuring an excuse, followed them down the hall. At the open door to the bookroom, she paused and waited.

Malverne strode up to a wing-back chair but did not sit down. His fingers gripped the back for support as he noted the greenish-yellow remains of the bruise on Richard's face. He winced.

"How much do you want for it?" He made the question, almost a demand, point-blank.

Grantham drew his snuff box from his pocket and offered it to the earl. Malverne waved it aside with a clumsy, impatient gesture. Grantham helped himself to a pinch.

"It is not for sale—for any price." Richard raised his gaze and held Malverne's. "I am sorry if this inconveniences you, but there is nothing you can do to change my mind."

Malverne blanched visibly. "Twice what your father paid." His voice came out hoarse, almost rasping from a tight throat.

Richard's mobile eyebrows rose. "Indeed? I had not thought it worth even the shocking price my deluded parent offered. How very odd. I wonder what makes it worth so much more now?"

"Sentimental value." Malverne looked down, unable to meet the compelling regard of those stormy eyes. "I should never have sold it."

"Sentimental value?" Grantham pocketed the snuff box and fingered the riband of his quizzing glass. "It was my understanding that you purchased it in Italy only months before you offered it to my father."

Malverne ran his tongue across his dry lips. "Three times as much. I know you're strapped. You can't tell me the money wouldn't be welcome."

"Whether it would or not makes no difference. The Imperial Star is not for sale."

"Richard!" Bella, unnoticed, had come up behind Andrea. She stared at her brother, shocked, but he silenced her simply by raising his hand.

"I am sorry you have come on a useless errand. But my answer must be no."

Malverne appeared to crumple. Grantham poured him a glass of sherry, which he gulped down. Casting his host one last pleading, almost helpless, look, he took his leave.

"What on earth was that all about, Grantham?" Giles came out into the hall from the saloon as the front door closed behind the earl.

"Why does he want the icon so badly?" Bella shook her head in confusion. "It cannot be worth a fraction of what he offers! But what a . . . a godsend it would be if we *could* sell it! Why did you not just tell him it is not in our possession?"

Richard strolled back into the bookroom and poured himself another sherry. His gaze rested on the amber liquid as he swirled it in his glass. "Simply because it is *not* worth a fraction of what he offers, my dear.

240

Therefore, we must assume that it is something else he wants."

"Then why does he not ask for whatever it is?" Bella regarded her brother in exasperation.

"That, my dear, can only remain a subject for speculation until he chooses to admit us into his confidence." Richard drained the glass and turned to Andrea. "There is hardly any need to look so concerned, Miss Wells. It is a simple matter of business that need not concern you in the least. Unlike the steps to the quadrille. Shall we return to the drawing room? The others will be wondering what has happened to us."

Andrea allowed him to lead her back into the dance, but a chill which she could not banish took possession of her heart. She might have had fears before, but now she felt certain. Richard's death, which crept inexorably closer, would be no simple tragic accident.

241

Chapter 18

After the party from Malverne House took their leave, Richard and Giles departed for White's—or more likely for Jackson's Saloon, though they denied it when Andrea asked point-blank. She did not see Grantham again until late that evening, long after Bella had gone up to bed.

Andrea remained below stairs, sipping a glass of sherry she had appropriated from Richard's bookroom, and waited. At last, she heard the front door open, the low murmur of his deep voice, and his firm, even footsteps crossing the hall. She came out of the drawing room as he paused at the foot of the stairs to light his candle.

"Please, Grantham, I want to have a word with you."

"Just one?" He inclined his head, his smile urbane. Without speaking, he led the way to the bookroom. She stood in the doorway while he lit one of the candelabra, then took her accustomed seat beside the desk.

"And what may I do for you this evening?" His tone held only polite curiosity.

"Cut line." She stared at her hands, then looked directly up into the calm mask of his face. "I want to know what is going on. I'm not a child, you know. What really happened to your face? Was it another intruder at the Court?"

242

He drew a deep breath and studied her earnest expression. Something like surprise flickered across his own and he nodded slowly as if he came to a decision. "There were two men hovering about the East Tower. I thought it was only one and tackled him. They left before I got any answers." Only a trace of chagrin at his failure colored his voice.

Andrea extended a hand to him. He took it, and she found the gentle pressure of his fingers reassuring. "I thought it must be that. There was someone watching the house, here, but after you left I didn't see him again."

"Are you sure?" His eyes narrowed.

"Yes . . . no. It was no more than an unsettling suspicion, really. If I had been positive, I must have told you." She drew an unsteady breath. "And what is Malverne afraid of?"

"I wish I knew." Richard stared off into space, as if searching for an answer, then shook his head. "I wish I knew," he repeated. He looked down at their joined hands and his grip tightened. Gently, his thumb brushed across her fingers, caressing. He raised his solemn eyes to meet hers. "But I'll find out. About all of this."

Richard said no more on the subject, and the next several days passed in a whirl of shopping, visiting, parties, and preparations for the ball. A new, almost tingling awareness hung in the air between them, manifesting itself in an electric shock when their hands touched, in his brooding, penetrating gaze that rested on her more and more frequently, and in the longing that filled her whenever she glimpsed him across a room.

Rapidly, it became more than she could bear. Never had she wanted a man so badly, so completely. And it was far more than in any mere physical sense. Richard was a part of her, and she a part of him. Inseparable, drawn to each other across time—only to be parted irrevocably, all too soon, by death.

The day of the ball arrived at last, and, frantic from her thoughts of Richard, she lost herself with a grim determination in the last-minute details. Gratefully, Bella turned over innumerable tasks, such as making sure the flowers arrived and were arranged, that the refreshments ordered from the caterers were delivered to the kitchens, that the chandeliers glistened from their baths. Not for one moment did Andrea feel that her nerves arose from the prospect of making her formal curtsy to Polite Society. The only question in her mind was what Richard would think of her in the ballgown she had ordered especially for the occasion.

In the midst of this chaos, Letitia Moreland called, bursting in on them over the protests of the butler. An angry red flush colored her complexion.

"It is unforgivable of him!" Her usually gentle eyes blazed with her fury as she faced Andrea in the middle of the cluttered ballroom.

Bella, very much aware of the interested stares of the footmen who raised the chandelier once more to the ceiling, drew her from the room and into the front saloon. She rang the bell in an abstracted manner and sent the butler to bring ratafia to calm their guest.

Andrea took Letitia's white-knuckled hands between her own and gave them a comforting squeeze. "Tell us what has occurred."

"It is my guardian! He . . . he has arranged the vilest marriage for me, and with the most revolting old man! Oh, I am so angry, I could kill Malverne!"

"Lettie!" cried Bella, shocked.

"Why should he arrange such a marriage?" Andrea fixed her with a penetrating regard.

"Because he is rich. I promise you, there could be no other reason for *anyone* to consider marrying him. And there is not a single thing I can do to save myself!" Exhausted by her unaccustomed rage, she sought refuge in tears, which welled up and slipped unheeded down her cheeks.

"But . . . but are you not an heiress?" Bella blinked, confused.

Lettie nodded and sniffed, her manner now pathetic. All fight had gone out of her. "It is the most dreadful thing. My fortune is very large, you must know," she said naively. "Yet here is Malverne, positively forcing me to accept that horrid Lord Brompton."

"Lord Brompton!" Bella stared at her in dismay. "Why he . . ." She broke off, realizing the impropriety of what she had been about to say, under the circumstances.

"You cannot be serious." Andrea raised her gaze from Lettie's shredding of a fine lawn handkerchief. "But then I don't know him very well. Perhaps he is—"

"He is terrible! He ogles all the young females in the most disgusting manner, and he is dreadfully fat and all of fifty if he's a day." Lettie sniffed again, saw the mess she had made of the delicate square of fabric, and groped in her reticule for another.

Andrea offered her one. "But why should his wealth matter, if you have a fortune of your own?"

"Oh, this is absurd." Bella shook her head. "Malverne would not force you. Why, he is the most indulgent of parents."

"Well, he is not my parent, he is my guardian. And I am wholly in his power!" Lettie's voice broke on a sob.

Andrea recognized high melodrama when she saw it. This must be "enacting a Cheltenham tragedy." But in this instance, it seemed that Lettie might in some measure be justified. A girl of seventeen had no say whatsoever about her future and would be expected to do her guardian's bidding, even in marriage. But still . . .

"Are there not trustees for your inheritance? Surely one of them would protest this alliance!"

"He is the only trustee! Oh, what am I to do?" She

collapsed into noisy sobs.

"An arranged marriage is not so bad." Bella made a vain attempt to comfort her. "Many work out very well, indeed. You must know that my . . . mine to Mr. Brixton was arranged."

"But he was not a . . . a vile man with . . . with cold hands forever pawing at you!" The girl's voice took on a note of rising hysteria.

"No, but surely—"

"Brompton is dreadful!" Lettie buried her piquant face in the borrowed handkerchief.

The butler entered silently with the tray, cast an apprehensive look at the weeping visitor, and hastily took his leave. Andrea poured a glass of the ratafia and pressed it on Lettie. The girl took a long, revivifying sip, and shuddered as the mildly alcoholic beverage burned in her throat.

"Do you not think you could come to care for him if you tried?" Bella regarded her in concern.

Lettie shook her head and raised large, soulful eyes to Andrea. "Not when—" She broke off, cast a frightened glance at Bella, then turned back to Andrea. "Not when my heart is already given to Another," she finished in a whisper.

At a loss for words, Andrea again squeezed the little hand that lay trembling in her own. She had few doubts as to who this Other might be. She had seen the way Lettie looked at Wilfred. And a perfect arrangement that would be! Far better than Bella's engagement to him. Her ever-fertile brain went to work on sorting out the couples.

"I . . . we'll think of something," she murmured.

Lettie blinked back her tears at this sign of hope. "Do you really think you can? I . . . I am so very desperate."

Andrea poured herself a glass and took a sip, all the while wondering to what dire straits she might be committing herself. "You may be sure we will not let you be married off in this dreadful way. Now, dry your eyes and don't, whatever you do, take any silly notions into your head. Do you think for one moment Wilfred would back his father in this odious scheme?"

Lettie's color rose, setting flaming spots in her pale cheeks. "He . . ." She averted her face. "What could he do?"

"Speak to his father, you may be sure," Bella replied staunchly. "Why, he regards you in the light of a sister! You may be sure this plan has not his approval."

Andrea glared daggers at Bella. Certainly Wilfred looked on Lettie with a brotherly regard. They had been raised as siblings. But she had seen the warmth of his affections. Properly stirred, it easily could turn to something more. And Andrea intended to stir like crazy.

After further assuring Lettie of their support, they managed to coax a half-smile from her, dried her eyes, and sent her home to rest before the ball. Lord Brompton, they promised, had not been on the invitation list, so she might look forward to the evening with untrammeled pleasure.

Andrea saw her to the door, then mounted the steps slowly, lost in thought. She could use a rest herself; it would be a very late night. She had trouble adjusting to this partying until dawn. She missed curling up in bed with the ten o'clock news—as depressing as that often was. But she didn't miss her own time! she told herself firmly. She couldn't. It was lost to her forever. Better focus her thoughts on finding the Imperial Star and helping Miss Letitia Moreland.

Now, there was a heroine if she ever saw one, she reflected as she reached the landing. Petite, fragile, vulnerable, an heiress, dreadfully put upon by her evil guardian, forced into marriage with an ogre. What could be better? And how could Wilfred help but go to her rescue once the true state of affairs was made known to him?

So Andrea's job, obviously, would be to make him aware of Lettie's distress. If he were convinced that everyone else regarded her plight with callous unconcern, then surely every chivalrous instinct must be aroused. And from playing the role of knight errant to that of cavalier was only a short step.

In the privacy of her bedchamber, she took out her contacts, removed her dress, and lay down on the bed in her chemise. But she was too nervous to rest. She should be looking forward to the ball. Instead, she realized with a pang, she would rather spend a quiet evening playing piquet with Richard. At least he would dance with her, though. That should make up for a very great deal.

She was disturbed from her reverie an hour later by Lily, who brought her a small package done up in silver paper and string. A folded note, with an elaborate "G" impressed into the wax seal, lay on top. Grantham's signet.

She broke it open and peered farsightedly at the fine copperplate letters. The note, which she held at arm's length to decipher, was simplicity itself: "In honor of tonight, G." She set it aside, knowing as she did so that she would save that brief message to the end of her days.

She unwrapped the parcel quickly, then held up an elegant little fan with an exquisite rendering of Zeus and Leda painted on the chicken skin. Traceries of gold were laid in the pierced ivory sticks. No mere trifle, this! It must have cost him a great deal. A pang of guilt assailed her, not unmixed with awe, for she knew how little he could afford such a present.

"It's beautiful, miss!" Lily held it up to better admire it. "Now, it's time you was getting ready, for the first of the guests will be arriving in an hour."

Lily busied herself at the dressing table and Andrea

248

took the opportunity to fit in her lenses. With her maid's help, she donned the undergown of silvered silk, then the delicate half-robe of white lace. Even to Andrea's critical eye, no fault could be detected in the gown. Lily combed her hair to the top of her head, fastened the heavy golden waves in a becoming knot, then arranged the ends into thick ringlets that fell below her bare shoulders. Clusters of silver ribands were arranged in the thick knot and entwined in the curls. Even without makeup, Andrea decided she looked pretty good.

At last she was ready for her presentation ball, an event for which she had longed ever since reading that first Regency novel.

She picked up her fan, hung it about her wrist, and gathered her courage to go downstairs. Only one person's opinion mattered. She was a fool, and she knew it, but that fact remained. If Richard was not captivated by her appearance, her first ball would be a waste.

As she reached the bottom landing, she saw him in the hall, conferring with the butler. He turned to look up as she came down the last steps and she faltered, then stopped at the base as time stood still. He was magnificent, dressed in a coat of midnight-blue velvet and black satin breeches, his cravat tied to neat perfection. He met her gaze and breathing no longer seemed important. Nothing mattered but Richard West-mont, Viscount Grantham.

Was this love, this breathless, heart-stopping, lurching sensation that rushed through her? No, it must be nothing more than a wild infatuation, which would fade with time. She couldn't let it be anything else! For time was the one thing she and Richard could not share.

Forcing a smile to her suddenly quivering lips, she swept forward to join him. The subtle rustling of her silken skirts gave her a badly needed confidence and poise that evaporated the moment he raised her fingers for a kiss. He retained her hand in his warm hold, and the look he bestowed on her went beyond admiration. He held her immobile, a prisoner of his hypnotic, sparkling eyes.

"You'll outshine them all," he said softly.

"I'll leave that to Wilfred." She had to keep this light, as if they did no more than flirt. Desperately, she searched for a distraction and found it in the fan that dangled at her wrist. "Thank you for this. It's beautiful."

"Then it suits you. I'm glad if it gives you pleasure."

"More than you know. I . . . I'll keep it always." Sudden tears filled her large brown eyes and she blinked rapidly, glad she wasn't wearing mascara that would run.

"Why so solemn? This is an evening to rejoice. Your long-awaited presentation to Society." He took her arm and led her to the drawing room where the dinner guests would shortly gather.

Bella, resplendent in a flounced ballgown of dull gold, joined them. Only moments later, sounds of arrival drifted back and the first carriage pulled up before the house. Bella peeped anxiously into a gilt-edged mirror, patted the gold artificial roses that were sprinkled amongst her raven curls, and threw a look brimful of nervous anticipation toward her brother. The butler sailed forth from the nether regions of the house and opened the door.

The next two hours passed in a daze for Andrea. Everything seemed new to her, and she existed in a state of dread, convinced that at any moment she would commit some shocking breach of etiquette. A succession of elaborate dishes passed before her, unrecognizable and barely tasted. Her glass was replaced for different wines, and she lost count of the times her cups were refilled by an overzealous footman. She felt giddy and light-headed but struggled to maintain a firm hold on herself.

By the end of the third course and at least her fourth

full glass of wine, her worries began to evaporate. The other guests enjoyed themselves, and there seemed no reason why she should not do the same. Her glance strayed to the head of the table where Richard sat in splendid state. He raised his head, caught her watching him, and the secret, special smile they shared intoxicated her every bit as much as did the unaccustomed alcohol.

Through the pleasant, almost singing, haze that seeped over her, she became aware of one discordant note. Letitia Moreland, lovely in a gown of celestial-blue crepe, sat huddled in her chair, casting meaningful, angry glances at Malverne, who sat across the table and up several places.

Something about the set of the girl's chin startled Andrea. With an effort, she shook off a portion of her growing lassitude. Something she couldn't quite place— resolution! That was it. A new and uncharacteristic determination altered Lettie from the fragile child who had wept in despair only that afternoon.

Andrea directed an appraising glance up the table at Malverne, and her suspicions solidified that something was amiss. The earl appeared patently nervous and threw frequent, uneasy glances toward the long window at the far end of the room, as if he expected to see someone there peering in at him. Lord Brompton, perhaps? But while she could understand Letitia's being revolted by the man, she could think of no reason why he should frighten Malverne into a quivering heap.

She sat back in her chair and sipped her newly refilled glass of wine. She did not know Malverne all that well, but she would never have suspected him of being the sort to force his ward into a distasteful marriage. Unless Brompton had some hold over him, of course. Malverne might make a sacrifice of his ward to protect himself. That sort of thing happened in novels.

Andrea glanced at the earl again and almost giggled at

the absurdity of the whole situation. Not in her wildest imagination could she envision the plump, normally jovial Malverne doing anything even remotely dishonest or disreputable. Nothing, certainly, that could be used against him in any way.

She'd dismiss the whole as nothing but an alcohol-induced fantasy if the facts, as she knew them, did not definitely indicate that something was very much wrong. There was Letitia, frightened and grimly determined, and there was Malverne, jumpy and uneasy. And making preposterous offers to buy back the Imperial Star.

Isabella came to her feet, and Andrea realized with a start that the meal had ended. The assembled company rose and made its way up the stairs to the ballroom, which took up most of the first floor at the back of the house. Almost as soon as they reached it, the guests who had not come for dinner began to arrive.

For the next hour and more, Andrea stood beside Bella in a receiving line and heard a seemingly endless stream of names. She would never remember who was who! Occasionally, she caught a title she recognized, but none stood out for any Regency-era notoriety. They possessed no historical significance, either past or future. The sensation left her drifting, lost in a sea of time, floundering between her safe if dull world of the future and her present chaotic existence.

The musicians struck up a country dance, Bella introduced her to a fervent young officer whose name she never caught, and Andrea found herself drawn into a set that formed nearby. She cast her partner an uncertain glance, managed an almost convincing smile, and took his hand for the first move. No matter how many times she practiced, performing under the critical eyes of so many people was very different than just dancing with Giles or Richard.

Richard. She looked about, wanting him with a desperation that left her shaken. He was in the next set, dancing with an elderly lady whose hawklike countenance and innumerable jewels clearly stated her importance, if only to herself. Richard looked up, caught her worried glance, and his special smile reassured her. She continued through the steps with only one slight fumble.

As the dance ended, her hand was claimed once more. Wilfred, resplendent in a coat of fuchsia over black satin knee breeches, bowed low before her, then stood back to give her ample opportunity to admire the pains he had taken over his appearance. These were truly remarkable, and she found herself hard put not to burst into laughter. His quest for sartorial notoriety had led him to thread narrow ribands through the larger chains that crisscrossed his elaborate waistcoat. A large ruby stickpin nestled in his enormous cravat and ruffles of lace adorned his shirtfront and just peeped out from beneath his sleeves.

"Still determined to set a fashion?" she could not help but ask.

He appeared aggrieved. "You'd think those self-proclaimed Tulips would have the sense to see how elegant a ruffle can appear." He raised one hand and allowed the delicate lace to fall from his white hand over his fuchsia sleeve. He looked about quickly, caught a budding Pink of the Ton watching him covertly, and smiled in satisfaction. "A matter of time, my dear. Just a matter of time."

Andrea kept her tongue. The ruffles made him look as dated as if he had shown up in bell-bottomed jeans and a Nehru jacket at a party back home.

Back home. The words repeated themselves in her mind. But she had best forget that future. This was home, now, with a new future. The thought ought to provide her with more satisfaction. She had tried so very hard to come back through time!

"Would you care for something to drink?" Wilfred led

her from the floor as the boulanger came to a close.

"Lemonade, please."

"What? I believe Grantham has provided a rather excellent champagne."

She shook her head. "I had more than enough wine at dinner, thank you. Lemonade."

He left her sitting on a settee by the wall and went to brave the crowds about the refreshment tables. Andrea leaned back, looking around with an oddly detached interest as if she merely observed the scene but took no part in it. In a way, that was almost true. Gentlemen did not precisely flock to her, she noted, but that was hardly surprising. She was by far too tall. Several fashionable young bucks of moderate height gazed up at her as if she were a giraffe. It would be easier to blend into the past if she were six inches shorter.

With a sigh, she turned her attention to Lettie and her problem. It shouldn't take much of a comment to make Wilfred take up the cudgels in the girl's defense. And once he had a taste of being a hero in her eyes, he would probably want more. Bella certainly never looked at him with adoration.

But when Wilfred returned with her glass, he took his leave at once to seek out his next partner. Andrea remained where she was, momentarily stymied, and sipped her lemonade while she watched the quadrille that was in progress. More than one young lady, she noted with an almost catty satisfaction, missed a step. She wasn't the only one who had difficulty learning it.

On Bella's daring instructions, the musicians next struck up a waltz. The dance, Andrea had been told, was still not fully accepted. She had no idea how long before it would be introduced at Almack's. More than one debutante withdrew to the chairs set about the room.

Andrea sighed and stayed on her settee. The last thing she wanted was to offend anybody by performing the questionable dance. She was too new to Society, her position tenuous at best. Yet to swirl about the room in Richard's arms would be sheer heaven! And she had so little time left with him. Somehow the days had slipped past, and already March drew to a close. That only left her with April and half of May.

On impulse, she sprang up and hurried over to where Richard stood in conversation with a dowager of imposing mien, and touched his arm. Excusing himself, he drew aside with her.

"Please, won't you come with me to an empty room— and dance?" She bit her lip, looking up at him with mingled hope and nerves.

Amusement lit his sparkling eyes. "Why not here?"

"I don't want to be thought fast!"

"But disappearing with me into an empty room is perfectly acceptable behavior?" Humor lent a delicious quaver to his deep voice.

She met his gaze and an irrepressible giggle escaped her. "Of course not. But will you?"

The amusement faded from his expression to be replaced by an intentness that made it impossible for her to breathe. "Anything to oblige a lady," he said softly, and she knew his meaning went far beyond her simple request.

Together, they slipped out of the ballroom and up the hall to a saloon too small to be thrown open, even for cards.

"We won't have much room." Without waiting for her answer, he drew her gently toward himself. His left hand took her right and his other encircled her waist, not in the proper manner that had characterized their lessons but with a possessiveness that sent a thrill of desire racing through her. The pressure of that hold tightened as they spun about the room, carefully avoiding furniture, in time to the muffled strains of an Austrian

255

waltz that penetrated the closed door.

Heady with the dinner wine and cradled so close in the arms for which she had longed, she banished everything from her mind but him. Raising her face, she looked up into his smoldering eyes and for once did not even try to hide her need of him. His arms tightened about her and they ceased to dance. He still moved, but it was only to draw her closer, to crush her against his powerful chest as his lips found hers.

Her hands crept up to his broad shoulders, then about as much of him as she could hold. His mouth covered hers, enticing, awakening a passion deep within her that she had no strength or will to control. Every part of her being responded to him and she knew, as a certainty, this was only a promise of more wonders still to come.

He released her slowly, as if loath to let her escape. If he asked her to go to his bed at this moment, she had not a single doubt that she would—and without any hesitation. She had no desire to withstand the potency of what passed between them. He possessed himself of her hand, planted a kiss on her gloved palm, and a shiver of pure ecstasy ran through her.

"Thank you for the pleasure of this dance." He bowed and, taking her arm, he led her out of their private sanctuary.

She followed him back to the ballroom, numb, her sense of loss overwhelming. Didn't he know how she felt? It was impossible that she hadn't betrayed herself. Biting her lower lip which trembled with her frustration, she risked a glance into his rugged face and caught his self-satisfied smile.

He knew, all right. And he also knew full well that this postponement heightened not only her desire but also the sweetness of their fulfillment. He was no stranger to the art of exquisite seduction. And damn him for it!

Chapter 19

Andrea directed a measuring glance at Richard's compelling profile and squared her shoulders, determined to play this game as he wanted. She could wait for him—just so that it wasn't for too long. She wanted his lips on hers again, but doubted whether she could control the passion that surged through her if she got her wish. And it had been present in him, too. When next she had the opportunity, she would make him forget any plan of campaign he might have concocted. He might not know it, but they did not have time for such nonsense.

As they passed the stairs, the sounds of a late arrival drifted up to them. Giles Kendall, his expression grim, removed his cloak in the hall below, handed it to the butler, and started up the steps two at a time. As he neared the top, he saw them.

"Sorry I'm late. I was what you might call unavoidably detained." He attempted an urbane smile.

"What happened?" Richard's sharp eyes missed nothing.

Giles might appear his usual elegant self, but a tension hung about him, a hardness that Andrea didn't recognize and that frightened her. He shook his head and directed a significant glance at her. The sounds of merriment reached them from the ballroom, filling the silence.

"You'd best tell me before we get inside." Richard stood his ground.

Giles's mouth tightened into a firm line. "Just watch your step, will you? Don't go out at night alone."

"Why?" Richard demanded.

"I can't tell you yet. I don't know myself, for sure. Just be careful."

"Of what?"

Both men started, then turned to see Bella standing behind them.

"Richard, what is this? Why should you be careful? What's going to happen?"

"Nothing," Richard tried to soothe her, but to no avail.

She rounded on Giles. "What have you gotten him into this time?"

"Nothing, I promise you—"

"You've led him into danger, haven't you? Richard, I beg of you—!"

"Enough, Bella." Richard's firm voice cut her off. "You may ask Miss Wells, nothing has happened. Now, let us go back into the ballroom, and remember you are the hostess. No sullen looks from you, my girl."

"Sullen! As if I would! I know my duties very well, I thank you. And I know you are merely trying to change the subject, so don't look so pleased with yourself. But I realize a ball is hardly the place to discuss such matters." Gathering what little dignity she possessed, she led the way back to their guests.

Richard threw Giles a look of amusement, but that gentleman's gaze rested on Bella's defiant back with an odd, sad expression in the depths of his eyes. Andrea noted this and let out a sigh of relief. Perhaps her task of getting these two together would not be as difficult as she at first thought.

That comfortable conclusion vanished less than five minutes later. Malverne, dragging Wilfred along with him, approached Richard and Bella. Richard nodded, albeit somewhat reluctantly, and together the little group made their way to the musicians. When the dance ended, the players struck up a fanfare and all eyes turned to the far corner where the foursome stood.

With proper ceremony, Richard announced the engagement of Bella to Wilfred. Andrea drew back, allowing the couple to receive the congratulations of their acquaintances. To her satisfaction, one other person was patently not pleased by this. Giles Kendall leaned negligently against the wall, a scowl marring his handsome features. After a minute, he hunched his shoulders and started from the room.

On inspiration, Andrea hurried up to him. "Will you not stay for the next dance with me?"

His surprised expression warned her that ladies of this era did not behave in so forward a fashion, but the circumstances called for drastic measures. She took his arm and almost dragged him onto the floor, where sets were beginning to form for a round dance.

"I hope they will be very happy." Giles stood stiffly, looking about as if he sought an excuse to escape her.

"They won't be." Andrea smiled sweetly up into his startled face and swept him a deep curtsy as the dance began. "They are not in the least suited to one another."

"Then why . . . ?" But the movements separated them, and Giles could only throw her a confused look.

"Because they are old friends." Andrea took his hand and circled primly about him, talking in an urgent undervoice the whole time. "She was pitchforked into one marriage with a man she barely knew, and who was killed on the hunting field little more than six months later. Is it so surprising she should seek a safer marriage, one with someone she knows will not expose himself to danger?"

The dance separated them again, but Giles did not seem interested in making a reply. His eyes narrowed, he watched Bella where she stood quietly beside Wilfred at the edge of the dance floor, a smile fixed firmly to her lips.

"She is afraid to try for love," Andrea pursued at the next opportunity.

"And now it is too late, they are engaged."

The bleakness in his voice pleased Andrea. She made no further attempt to speak to him during the lengthy dance, leaving him to flounder in a sea of regrets. She wanted him in the right state of mind. When the music at last ended, she took him firmly by the arm and led him off to the refreshment table.

"An engagement is hardly a marriage."

"You seem to have a very odd opinion of me." His voice sounded tight. "To approach her now would be to put myself beyond the pale."

Andrea took a deep breath, frustrated by proprieties that now seemed ridiculous to her. "She's entitled to change her mind, isn't she?"

"Whatever may prevail in America," he informed her stiffly, "I assure you that in England it is very different. No lady would wish to be branded a jilt."

"Well, it is not as if she would be turning from a penniless nobody to marry a title and fortune! Then the gossips would indeed have cause for comment. But the case is . . ." She broke off, aghast at what she had been about to say.

"But the case is just the opposite?" Giles obligingly, if somewhat tartly, finished her sentence for her. "Quite true. I'm a younger son with a meager portion. And Wilfred is heir to an earldom and all the treasures of Malverne Castle. And Bella is welcome to them."

She caught a glimpse of his bleak expression as he

turned away, and she called softly after him. "She doesn't want them."

Giles spun back to face her.

"Are you going to let her make such a mistake all for the want of . . . of a little dash?" she asked him.

A lopsided smile twisted his lips. "It doesn't seem to be quite the thing, to be plotting the dissolution of this engagement when it is only minutes old."

"The sooner the better, before she feels it is too late to cry off."

Giles regarded her with a new light glinting in his hazel eyes. "Has anyone ever told you that you are a very unsettling influence?"

Andrea shook her head. "There is the signal to go down for the supper. Will you not stay?"

Giles offered her his arm and they strolled over to where Richard and Bella still stood with Wilfred and Malverne.

"No need to wait," the earl was saying. "Make an early marriage of it!" His joviality sounded forced, and his uneasiness was obvious. "Post the banns and you can do the thing in three weeks. Or better yet, get a special license and it can be taken care of in a trice."

"There is no need for unseemly haste." Richard drew his snuff box from the depths of his pocket and offered it to the other gentlemen. Malverne waved it aside, but Wilfred took too large a pinch and sneezed. Giles took some, then dusted his fingers with care.

"No need to wait, either." Malverne looked from Bella to Wilfred, his expression almost pleading.

Bella, her complexion unusually pale, tried to restore her slipping smile. "Do go down to supper," she urged them. "I must stay and arrange partners." Then she hurried away.

Giles turned to Andrea. "May I escort you?"

She hesitated, seeing the smoldering glow in Richard's

eyes, but he did not intervene. Andrea accepted Giles's offer and together they made their way to the supper room that rapidly filled with the laughing guests. If only life could always be so gay and carefree . . .

"What is wrong?" Giles kept his voice low, but his gaze caught and held hers. "You look as if all the problems of the world had just descended on you. Are you worried about Bella—Mrs. Brixton?"

Andrea finished filling her plate and led the way to a corner of the room where chairs had been placed about a tiny table. "No, it is Richard—Grantham. What is the danger to him?"

Giles managed an almost convincing laugh. "Nothing, I am certain."

"But you warned him!"

He shook his head. "It is nothing that need concern you."

"Because I am a mere female? Don't be so ridiculous."

Giles's eyebrows flew up. "And what do you think you could do?"

"How should I know, if you won't tell me where the danger lies?"

He shook his head maddeningly. "You may not be a 'mere' female, but you are certainly an unconventional one."

"And you are not answering my question. I'm not some pitiful creature who must be sheltered from the realities of life. I prefer to know what I'm up against so I can take precautions and make plans."

A soft laugh, this time quite genuine, escaped Giles, and his eyes narrowed. "Lord, unless I am much mistaken, I would say that Richard has met his fate."

The sparkling defiance died from Andrea's eyes and the blood drained from her face. "His fate," she whispered, then stood, murmured an inarticulate excuse, and hurried from the room, fighting back the tears that tried to slip down her cheeks.

She almost collided with Richard in the hall beyond. She gripped his arm, hanging on as if she were afraid ever to let go. People hovered about them, some going into the supper room, some coming out. This was not the place . . . In a moment, she mastered her composure.

"I . . . I am just going up to see if the musicians are ready to resume."

"What happened?" Richard was not in the least deceived. "The supper has barely begun."

She shook her head, but her heart showed clearly in her eyes. He drew in a slow, unsteady breath, but before he could speak, a friend hailed him and Andrea pulled away and darted up the steps.

As she neared the top, she saw Letitia Moreland emerge from the ballroom, cast a furtive glance up and down the hall, then hurry past without even noticing Andrea on the steps. She went straight to the tiny saloon where Andrea had danced with Richard earlier. The girl looked positively unwell! Or did she need solitude after the announcement of Wilfred's betrothal? In either event, comfort, if she knew Letitia, would not be spurned. Andrea followed her.

Lettie slipped into the small room but didn't close the door completely behind her. Andrea reached it, started to push it open, then stopped dead.

"What is the meaning of this?" Malverne's deep and somewhat shaky words carried clearly. "A pretty thing it is when my ward orders me—*orders* me, for I can think of no other term for it—to meet her in so clandestine a fashion! You will be kind enough to explain the meaning of this infernal piece of impertinence!"

The soft tones of Lettie's answer reached Andrea, but she could not make out the words. Apparently, Malverne had no such difficulty.

"I will have no more of this nonsense from you, my

girl. You will marry Brompton!"

"I will not!" came Letitia's hissed reply. "You . . . you cannot make me, and if you try, I . . . I will go to the authorities and tell them everything!"

Malverne gave an uneasy laugh. "Tell them what? Now, really, Lettie, you know nothing of the matter. Here I am, arranging a very eligible alliance for you, and you are talking nonsense!"

"Am I?" Her quavering voice betrayed both her fear and her determination. "I may not be of age, and I may not have control of my fortune, but I . . . I am not helpless! I will make you regret it if you force me to take Brompton!"

"All nonsense!" Malverne repeated, almost blustering. "In my day, no young lady would dare speak to her guardian in this manner! When I think of all I have done for you!"

"And I would dearly love to know all that you have done *to* me! I'll find the proof!" Letitia shot back at him, then gave an audible gasp.

Malverne spoke sharply, then quieted. Try as she might, Andrea could only hear the murmur of voices, his deep one interrupted occasionally by Lettie's quavering tones that rose to an almost hysterical wail.

"No!" the girl cried suddenly. "No, I . . . I won't! I'll . . ." She broke off. When she spoke again, her tone was deadly cold. "I'll kill you before I let that happen!"

Malverne's deep voice rumbled on for almost three minutes without pause, too low for Andrea to make out. Then he ended audibly. "We have no choice." His words were now gentle, persuasive, and Lettie's muffled cry reached Andrea. "Dry your eyes, now, my dear. Mustn't let on anything's amiss."

"Is . . . is there no other way?" Lettie asked, forlorn.

"None. Believe me, Letitia, I've tried to think of something." He sounded old, discouraged—defeated.

"There is no other way. Promise me now, you won't do anything rash."

Silence followed, broken only by Lettie's sniff. "I cannot marry Lord Brompton." But the pathetic voice lacked her earlier conviction. She drew a ragged breath and Andrea slipped away, perturbed.

What was going on? What was Malverne afraid of? And what hold did he have over his ward? Andrea stopped. And what "proof" did Lettie hope to find against her guardian? Why should she go to the authorities? The whole situation made no sense! But somehow it was all tied in with the Imperial Star and Malverne's attempts to repurchase it, of that Andrea was certain.

Chapter 20

No matter what other problems haunted her during the long, sleepless watches of the night, Andrea reached one conclusion. She had only a bare six weeks left in which to be with Richard and she was wasting them. Any other concerns could wait until after . . . well, until later. Right now, she was going to enjoy his company to the fullest and store up memories that would last her through the bleak, empty years that stretched before her.

A ride in the park should help clear the cobwebs that cluttered her head from her late night. She needed fresh air. She rose, donned her royal-blue habit, picked up the close-fitting hat with its curled plume, and went downstairs at an early hour, when the sleepy servants had only just begun to clear up the clutter left from the ball the night before.

Andrea peeped into the breakfast parlor, found that dishes had not yet been laid out, and, with true enterprising spirit, made her way to the kitchens. Encountering a startled and yawning footman, she sent him to the stables with a message that she would like her horse brought round as soon as possible.

She entered the basement kitchens and, much to her surprise and pleasure, she discovered Richard, bent on the same errand as she. He looked up, a tankard of ale in his hand and a large slab of bread piled high with cheese and ham on the plate before him. A humorous light glinted in his eyes and he waved a hand, inviting her to join him.

"And dressed for riding." He looked her over, his approval patent. "Would you care to accompany me?"

When they finished their meal, they made their way back upstairs. Richard's horse arrived shortly, but he had his groom walk the restive animal until Andrea's mount appeared ten minutes later. They went out into the street and Richard helped her into the saddle. In a companionable silence, they made their way through the early-morning traffic that consisted mostly of vendors hawking their wares, carts bringing produce to market, and wagons trundling corded boxes to and from warehouses. The morning was warm, promising heat long before noon.

"And what are your plans for the day?" Richard looked down at her from the lofty height of his massive roan stallion.

Andrea considered. She couldn't just say "whatever yours are," as she would like. "I thought perhaps a visit to the National Gallery. There was some talk last night about the Royal Exhibition, and you know how Bella hates to be thought behind the times."

"I have not seen it yet, myself." Richard regarded her, his smile becoming more pronounced. "Perhaps I shall escort you."

She looked up and met his unsettling gaze with a warm smile. "That would be very nice."

A slightly puzzled frown creased his brow, but it did not appear to be caused by displeasure. She must seem an enigma to him—a lady, yet wholly lacking in coquettishness and subterfuge. She wanted him and felt no constraints about it. Color warmed her cheeks. Her behavior was that of a wanton, though he must know she was no lightskirt.

They entered the park and found they had it almost to themselves. In the distance, a few other riders, mostly grooms, exercised their employers' hacks. As one, Andrea and Richard urged their horses into a trot, then a gentle canter. By degrees, their strides lengthened into a controlled gallop. At last, as they drew near the grooms, they reined in.

Richard's face glowed from the exercise. What was it about being on horseback that made a man appear so very much more masculine? And with Richard, that hardly seemed possible.

"You can have no notion how pleasant it is to find a lady not devastated by a ball." A smile that sent Andrea's heart racing lurked in Richard's eyes. "Bella will stay abed until noon, if I know her."

Andrea shook her head. "I shall get her up as soon as we return. I want to be back from the exhibition before luncheon."

Richard laughed. "Are you sure you are 'reckoning with your host'?"

Andrea's merriment, which never seemed to be far from her when she was with Richard these days, bubbled forth. "Hostess, you mean. But the days are too short to waste in sleep. There are so many things I want to do, and that means an early start."

"And what have you planned for the afternoon?"

"Anything but shopping!" she declared with feeling. "I haven't gone sightseeing this age! Would it be possible to visit Hampton Court? I have always wanted to try my hand at the maze."

"Why don't you make out a list of the things you want to do, and we'll try to cover all of them."

Andrea bit her lip. "*All?*" she asked demurely, but her eyes sparkled with a wicked gleam.

"Minx," he murmured. "What have you in mind?"

She shook her head. "I wouldn't want to shock you."

"I doubt you could, anymore. Out with it. What outrageous scheme have you thought up?"

"It's not so very bad, really. I only wish to visit the Daffy Club and White's."

He stared at her, and his horse sidled in startled surprise as his hands clenched on the reins. "Not so very bad," he repeated as one bemused. His shoulders began to tremble and a deep, reverberating laugh broke from him. "Good God, do you plan to walk right in the front doors?"

"Well, since I don't know where the back ones are located, I see no other way."

"Even if you succeeded in crossing the thresholds, which I doubt, your reputation would never survive!" A note of sternness underlay his words.

Andrea felt as if she had come up against a stone wall. "Not if I went alone, no. And not dressed like this. That would be foolish beyond permission." She cast a sideways glance up at him. He still showed a tendency to be amused, but he had his limits.

"I will not permit you to ruin yourself," he stated flatly.

"But I won't. At least, not the way I have it planned."

"Tell me the worst." He regarded her in a mixture of consternation and resignation.

"Well, as you pointed out, it would never do for a female to visit such places."

An arrested gleam lit his eyes. "Are you trying to tell me that you would be so lost to all sense of propriety as to disguise yourself as a boy?"

"Yes." She had no need to consider her answer.

He seemed to struggle with himself, but his sense of the ridiculous got the better of him. His deep, enticing laugh sounded once more. "My dear Miss Wells, you are

269

the most shocking hoyden it has ever been my dubious honor to encounter!"

"Thank you. But you must see, I cannot do it by myself. Will you help?"

His gaze rested on her, an unfathomable expression in the depths of his stormy eyes. "The challenge is almost irresistible," he murmured.

"Only almost?" She put as much disappointment as she could muster in those two words.

He gave up. "Very well, I will help. If only to see if you really have the audacity to go through with it."

"But I do so want to see the inside of a gentleman's club." She fluttered her long lashes at him and sighed in a wistful manner.

"You will find it vastly disappointing, I fear." He tried to sound stuffy but failed completely.

"Oh, no. Believe me, I wish to see White's of all things. And no one would ever suspect anything so outrageous! Ladies only dress as gentlemen in novels!"

With this, he agreed, though his knowledge of romantic stories he admitted to be sadly lacking. As her experience was primarily confined to books that would not be written for well over a hundred and fifty years, she did not suggest any examples.

"We will have to plan this carefully," he mused. Now that he had committed himself, he seemed intent on making sure that nothing went wrong. "When would you like to go?"

"This evening? No time like the present, and all that." Conversely, an attack of nerves assailed her. What if she made a mull of this? What if the gentlemen guessed her identity? It would not make things pleasant for Bella. And what of herself? She would be shunned by Society. But to see the inside of White's—no, it would be worth the risk. And even more so, no risk was too great if it meant spending time with Richard in one of his hey-go-mad moods.

"I will have to procure suitable clothing." He ran an appraising look over her tall, rounded figure and smiled as a soft flush tinged her cheeks. "You will make a creditable youth, if we take care."

"Thank you." She wasn't certain whether or not to be pleased. "I am somewhat taller than most females, but will the rest of me pass?"

She regretted the words the next moment. His gaze rested on the curve of her breasts in a manner that sent the blood racing hotly through every part of her body.

"Very well, indeed," he said. "But for our purposes tonight you will need some disguising." Amusement at her embarrassment lit his entire countenance.

They returned to the house, and for the next hour, Andrea did not see Richard. When she and Bella were ready to depart for the Royal Exhibition, he strolled down the stairs and calmly joined them, much to his sister's delighted amazement.

His pleasure dimmed somewhat when he learned that Wilfred, along with Letitia and Miss Moreland, meant to meet them within the hall. His manners remained impeccable, though, and aside from directing an accusing glance at Andrea for not mentioning their inclusion in the party, he made no comment.

To Andrea's regret, they did not remain long within the crowded rooms. Bella's sole purpose, it seemed, was to be seen admiring the works and perhaps to memorize an overheard phrase or two to repeat to her acquaintances. Wilfred evinced no interest whatsoever and Lettie, her eyes puffy from recent weeping, barely glanced at the walls lined with paintings. The Dragoness, emerging from her own contemplation of the landscapes, saw her charge's apparent indisposition and pronounced that she could not come down ill when they were to hold a musical evening in three days' time. She bore Lettie off homeward amid threats of subjecting her to various draughts and potions, all of which, the elderly lady swore, would put her back in curl in a trice.

Richard, Andrea noted, paid no heed whatsoever to the numerous works of art. His entire attention remained focused on the crowd. When their party returned to the house on Curzon Street, he saw the ladies to the door, then announced his intention of returning with the landaulet to the stable where he wished to pick up his curricle. Without further explanation, he departed on his unspecified errand.

"I hope he means to return in time to take us to Lady Glasden's tonight," Bella sighed.

"Do we go out?" With reluctance, Andrea looked away from the carriage that disappeared up the street. "I thought to spend the evening at home."

"A card party, my love. You will find it quite amusing, and a chance to try out the games you have learned."

Andrea nodded, but wondered how she would get out of it. Of course, there was always the chance Richard would cry off from their illicit outing at the last moment, but she would at least be prepared. Artistically, she covered her eyes with one hand. "I have quite the most dreadful headache coming on. I think I will lie down for a while."

Bella, at once all sympathy, fell for the ruse. "You should not have ridden out so early, not after so late a night!"

After declining offers of burnt feathers, pastilles, and a variety of other remedies that suggested themselves to Bella's mind, Andrea escaped. There was little for her to do to wile away the hours, though. She was hungry, she decided, and rang for a tray to be brought to her room.

Bella followed hard on the heels of her maid, wanting to send for a doctor. "For you have not been the least bit ill since you arrived in England!"

272

Andrea managed a weak smile. "Then I must be overdue. If you do not mind, I think I would rather not go out tonight."

"Of course not. I shall send our apologies at once."

"There is no need for you to miss the party!" That wasn't what Andrea wanted at all. "I have no intention of going downstairs, you know. I will go to bed and read, and be asleep before you have started your second hand."

Bella reluctantly agreed and took her leave. Andrea flopped back down on the bed, unhappily aware that she had committed herself to an afternoon of acute boredom.

In this, though, she was wrong. Less than an hour later, as she plowed her way through *Adeline Mowbray*, by Mrs. Opie, a soft knock fell on her door. Before she could arrange herself into the image of an invalid, Richard entered, a bandbox under his arm.

"It's as much as your reputation is worth if I'm caught in here," he said, his voice low. As a precaution, he turned the key in the lock. He grinned, enjoyment for their misadventure shining in his bright eyes. "Of all the harebrained, ramshackle females I have ever met, you are the worst!"

"Merci du compliment." Andrea rose and curtsied, accepting the rebuke in the spirit it was given. "What have you brought?"

"Oh, you'll be in the height of fashion, that I promise." He set the bandbox down on the bed and unfastened it.

"You haven't been raiding Wilfred's wardrobe, have you?"

His deep chuckle wrapped about her like a caress. "Not quite that bad. Giles's young brother. And the amazing part is they didn't press me to find out why I needed the things." He drew out a coat of blue superfine and a fine lawn shirt. Stockings, evening pumps, and a pair of knee breeches remained in the box, but he showed no sign of picking the latter up.

Andrea, not raised with his nice scruples, knew no hesitation and subjected them to an interested examination. "Do you think they'll fit?"

"You can have no idea how interested I am to find out" came his provocative response.

She threw him a darkling look. "I suppose I had best try these things in case they need alterations." She went to the door, peeped out, then held it wide. "You may go."

Somewhat to her regret, he did. With a sigh, she turned her attention to the clothes. These fit well enough, she discovered. Since Richard intended to pass her off as a country neighbor, it would not be expected that her appearance be perfect. Better, in fact, if it were not.

She took the things off again, donned a dressing gown, and secreted the bandbox and its contents away in the back of her clothes cupboard. She returned to her novel, but her thoughts were all for the night to come. At home, she had drawn her share of appreciative stares when wearing tight jeans. She hoped Richard would like her in the early nineteenth-century version.

Not until after she had rid herself of the well-meaning Lily, and Bella had come up to bid her good night before leaving for her party, did Andrea again unearth the shocking garments and put them on. At last, she stood up in knee breeches, clocked stockings, pumps, shirt, and waistcoat. Except for her long hair and lack of neckcloth, she was satisfied.

The briefest of knocks sounded before her door opened. Andrea spun about, relieved to see that it was Richard who slipped inside. He stopped just over the threshold, staring in blatant admiration, then turned the key behind him.

"It suits you." He came slowly forward, his gaze sweeping over her in an approval that had nothing to do with fashion or the quality of her disguise. "I'm damn glad no one's going to know you're a girl." His scrutiny settled on her slender hips in their tight breeches. "They'd have to be blind not to guess!"

"What can we do with my hair?" Andrea turned away, afraid yet longing to meet the intensity of his eyes. Heat prickled through her.

He regarded her long golden hair critically. "Cut it, I'm afraid."

Andrea nodded, having expected as much.

"You don't mind?"

She shrugged. "Cropped ringlets are the fashion." And without blowdryers and her familiar clips and curlers, her heavy hair had been nothing but a nuisance in this time period. "Besides, it will grow again. And I may never have another chance to visit White's."

They were forced to resort to embroidery scissors. Andrea sat at the dressing table and Richard stood behind her, running his fingers through the golden strands.

"It's a crime to cut it," he murmured.

"It will grow," she repeated. But he wouldn't be there to see it. Her determination wavered. "Do you like long hair?" She met his eyes in the mirror.

He ran a gentle hand over it, starting at the crown of her head. "It would be more becoming on you cropped and curled about your face," he admitted at last. "But there is something about the length. There is so much of it." He crushed handfuls, then smoothed them out. "You will let it grow again, after this." The words were an order, and she did not question either his desire or right to make it.

"I'll never cut it again." She made it a vow.

With hands that trembled, she braided her hair and fastened it at the bottom with a riband. Richard tied another at shoulder length at her direction. With care, he went to work with the scissors. She supported the bound length until the last strands were snipped through, and at last a loose braid just over two feet long rested in her hands. Richard returned the scissors to her and she went to work shaping what remained.

Free of its own weight, her hair displayed an unfamiliar and highly becoming tendency to curl on its own, but not necessarily in the directions she wanted. Lord, what she wouldn't give for a can of styling mousse or even some old-fashioned hairspray! It took industrious work with both scissors and comb, but when she finished, her honey-blond hair waved back from her forehead, away from her ears, with the ends confined by a black riband at the nape of her neck.

She stood and faced Richard. "Will anyone recognize me?"

Once more, his gaze moved over her and an undisguised desire lit his eyes. "You make an excellent youth. A trifle out of fashion, perhaps, but you'll do. By Gad, you'll do."

Her throat felt suddenly dry and she tried to swallow. He worked magic on her, sent riotous, wanton need through her, controlled her in a way that no one ever had before. And she wanted him so badly she ached with it. The intensity of his gaze held her, drawing her closer and, unable to stop herself, she closed the gap between them.

He reached out and his fingers barely caressed her cheek. "You're beautiful even as a boy," he murmured, and his hand slipped down her neck and around her shoulders as he drew her into his warm embrace.

She grasped his arms and pulled herself even closer as his mouth found hers. His lips brushed her cheek, her eyes, then her mouth once more. Reluctantly, she returned to earth as he released her at last.

"It's more than *my* reputation is worth if I'm found kissing you when you're dressed like this." His voice held a slight quaver, but whether from laughter or emotion she couldn't be certain. "Come. If we don't leave now, we won't at all, and your hair will have been sacrificed for naught."

He took the neckcloth that lay on the table and arranged it for her in the Mathematical. It had all gone beyond the playful game she had envisioned for this outing. She and Richard grew more intimate; he acted a maid—or rather, valet—for her, something no gentleman of his era would do for a lady. Yet it seemed completely natural to be all things to each other.

He gave her appearance his final approval, took her hand as casually as if he had been doing it for years, and led her to the door. She looked out, saw the coast was clear, and together they emerged into the hall. With Richard in the lead, they made their way down the main stair.

In minutes they were out the front door and strolling down the street in search of a hackney to take them to the Daffy Club. Excited laughter bubbled within Andrea until it could no longer be contained. Richard grinned at her, sharing her exultation at their reprehensible, madcap outing.

She might not be able to cling to his arm as she longed to, but she was free to look her fill at the tavern they approached less than half an hour later. Vile-smelling smoke from cigarillos and fumes of cheap gin engulfed her as they entered the dimly lit taproom. Large, rough men, identified by Richard in an undervoice as celebrities of the prize ring, crowded about, mixing freely with Corinthians and young bucks who were eager to rub shoulders with their idols. Men, all men, from every walk of life, most with tankards in their hands, sat hunched together at tables or stood about in groups, discussing the most recent mills or the doings at the Royal Cockpit.

Richard led the way toward a booth in a far corner, pausing occasionally to greet acquaintances, but never staying long nor introducing Andrea. For the most part, she was ignored; she was not of the sporting world, and therefore beneath notice. Andrea found it amusing and adopted an expression of vacuous awe, as befitted a country nobody in the presence of so many Bloods and Goers.

Richard stood back and let her slide along the wooden bench until she was mostly hidden in a corner. "Is it what you expected?"

She shook her head. In a novel, when the hero visited the Daffy Club, it was always so romantic! But this was nothing but a dirty, smelly room filled with equally smelly men who had not bathed since their last sporting encounters. Bluish-gray smoke hazed the air, stinging her eyes until they watered and leaving a vile taste in her mouth.

And the talk might fascinate a hero in the books, but it left her nauseated. To read about a hero drawing someone's cork was one thing. To see the resulting bloodied, broken noses was quite another. And talk of pugilism, with their cryptic references to "cross and jostle work" and "science" was for the most part wholly unintelligible to her.

Richard ordered Blue Ruin for them both, and when it came, he settled back to watch Andrea's reaction with an expression of unholy amusement on his face. She took a tentative sip and recoiled as the harsh gin seared her throat. An unsympathetic chuckle escaped him.

Over the babble of conversation, a man spoke from the booth behind them. "Have you not seen her? The liveliest little opera dancer I've ever beheld!"

"Have you bedded her?" came another voice.

The first laughed. "Oh, she played the shy piece, I promise you, but well worth the winning. Never have I . . ."

But Andrea did not get to hear the rest. Richard rose,

grabbed her by the elbow, and pulled her to her feet. Even in the dim, hazy light, she could see the dull flush that tinged his face.

"Damnable place to take a female," he muttered. He threw a few coins on the table and guided her through the crowds and out to the street.

"I think you're more shocked than I am." She threw a saucy glance up at him.

"If you had any sensibility, you'd be near swooning! I ought to plant that fellow a facer, saying such things in your hearing."

"But he had no notion I was there, and you should be glad I am wholly lacking in sensibility. What would you do if I swooned?"

His deep, rumbling chuckle broke from him again, dispelling his anger. "No, that wouldn't be like you, would it? Come. It's time you went home."

"No! I want to visit Watiers!"

He stiffened. "That's no place for a lady, either."

"But tonight I am not a lady, remember? And I have always wanted to play faro." She touched his arm, her expression part teasing, more than half beseeching, for this experience would never come again.

He scowled. "I suppose you'd be quite capable of trying to force your way inside on your own."

She considered. "Yes, I daresay I would."

A slow smile started in his eyes and lit his entire countenance. "Baggage," he murmured. "But not Watiers. A gaming hell?" He offered her his arm, she linked hers companionably through it, and they set off.

The establishment in Pall Mall to which he took her proved much more to her taste. It boasted an elegant arrangement of rooms, elaborately and fancifully decorated with painted scenes of classical mythology lining the walls. At one gilt-trimmed table, a woman in a shockingly low-cut gown and an elaborate headdress of feathers and lace presided over a dicing box. The company proved far more sedate and select than at the Daffy Club—the sole attractions here were the various games of chance.

Chandeliers, filled with hundreds of flickering candles, reflected in long, gilt-framed mirrors, multiplying the light to a glittering intensity. Richard led Andrea to a crowded table which stood between gold velvet hangings, where they watched a hand of faro in progress. Andrea listened carefully, nodding, as his low voice explained the simple game. No skill whatsoever was involved; this was played for the sake of the gamble. The dealer held the cards in his box and bets were placed. Andrea followed the lead of the others and set a chip worth twenty pounds on the table. Two cards were drawn and Andrea, along with the other players, lost to the bank.

She blinked and stared up at Richard, mouthing, "Is that it?"

He nodded, she shrugged and bet again. This time, she won. Her glance strayed around the table, where several gentlemen watched the dealer with avid, fanatical eyes. Addicts, she decided. She relinquished her chair.

"Would you rather play something else?" He took two glasses of champagne from a tray carried by a passing lackey and handed her one.

"I'm not a gamester, I guess. This isn't . . ." She broke off, unable to explain her feelings.

"Now, why do I take leave to doubt that?" he mused. "Somehow I thought you played a very deep game."

"Only for stakes that don't matter." The moment the words were spoken, she knew they were not true. She had bet her entire life on this venture of going back through time. And what she had won would soon be taken from her.

She looked about, trying to concentrate on her surroundings. Excitement ran high in the room, but it didn't touch her. Or rather, it did. It made her uncomfortable. She had only visited a casino once in her own time, in Las Vegas, and she had enjoyed the floor shows more than the gaming halls. Apparently, it wasn't in her blood.

What had made her think it would be different, just because she traveled back nearly two hundred years? She was still, somewhat to her amazement, the same person with the same tastes. It was more fun, she realized in dismay, to read about these places, dressed up in a writer's imagination, than to actually visit them.

Richard led her to the door and she made no protest. There were several other games she would like to learn, but not at the stakes she saw piling up at the tables. No one in his right mind would wager five hundred pounds on the turn of one card! Yet more than one gentleman obviously did just that.

"Disappointed?" Richard looked down at her as they strolled along the street, headed for St. James's.

"Not really." She regarded with disfavor the pumps that rubbed blisters on her heels. "I don't know what I hoped for."

"You'll prefer White's," he promised.

And he was right. That most famous of gentlemen's clubs lived up to her every expectation. From the moment they mounted the steps—the same ones he had mounted when she saw him in London of her own day— and entered the portals, they were surrounded by a subdued elegance bespeaking refined taste. The rooms, with their conservative wine-colored hangings, comfortable chairs of brown leather, and tastefully arranged furnishings, were not crowded. Richard exchanged greetings with several friends as he led the way across the plush wine-colored carpet to a small table. With a wave of his hand, he sent a waiter for cards and brandy.

Andrea felt curious stares directed at her, but no one

demanded who this intruder might be. It spoke volumes for Grantham's standing that no one bothered to question the identity of one brought to the august club under his auspices. Relaxing, she settled down for a quiet game of piquet with him. A low hum of conversation sounded about them, never loud, never intrusive. Friendly games and conversations were the order here.

"The stakes?" An odd, challenging light gleamed in the misty depths of Richard's eyes.

Her breath seemed to be swept from her throat. Tonight, with him, she dared anything. Reckless, she met that intriguing regard. "Whatever you will."

"The truth, then." His triumph at her response sounded clearly. "If I win, you tell me who you really are and what you are doing."

She swallowed. "Then I had best win, hadn't I?" She kept her tone joking, but she knew, if she lost, she would tell him the whole of her story. There was no room left for pretenses between them. "And it is not so impossible that you might lose, you know. If—when—you do, you will tell me what is going on at the Court."

He shook his head. "That I cannot, for I don't know myself." He held her clouded gaze for a long moment and his expression softened. "Then let us play for penny points."

He dealt the first hand, she declared a point of seven, and, though she took the first few tricks, the advantage went to Richard, the more expert player, and he won. As he collected the cards to reshuffle, his fingers brushed hers and a tingling shock raced up her arm. He hesitated, obviously feeling it, too, then resolutely gathered the deck.

"Perhaps I should name other stakes." The smoldering embers of his eyes burned into her. Awareness pulsated between them, almost unbearable in its strength.

"Whatever you say." Her words were no more than a whisper, but their intensity left her trembling.

"Is it, by Gad! You'd better watch what you agree to, my girl, or you'll find I'll take you up on it." With an unaccustomed savageness, he dealt the cards once more.

Her concentration, she discovered, lay shattered and could not be pieced back together. She gazed at him, unable to look away, unable to think of anything but him and the desire that radiated between them. Why did he hesitate? But he was a gentleman and she a lady, and in this time period different rules applied. He knew she was not Haymarket ware, despite the mass of contradictions she must represent to him.

Richard stood abruptly. "Let's go home." His voice was unsteady.

With Andrea at his side, not daring to look at him, they started across the room. They were stopped near the door by a pair of young bucks set upon throwing the ivories. Declining this treat, Richard led her firmly outside.

They emerged onto the street and he took a deep, steadying breath of the cool night air. Andrea looked up into a velvety sky of midnight blue lit by a mass of twinkling stars, and her spirits soared. A night of such beauty, such a hey-go-mad, crazy adventure, and Richard, so strong, so masculine, so wonderfully near . . . The heady mixture of sensations intoxicated her and she gripped his arm as a soft, sensual laugh escaped her.

He stiffened and she glanced up, perplexed and hurt by his sudden withdrawal. He did not look at her, but down the street. Sobering, she followed the direction of his gaze. Several shadows detached themselves from the walls and bore down on them. And in the hand of the leader, she made out the outline of a sword.

Chapter 21

Richard's grip tightened on Andrea's arm. "Run!" He shoved her away, hard.

Andrea staggered but held her ground. Her eyes widened and the blood drained from her face in growing fear, but she remained, grimly determined. Richard retreated a pace and thrust her in back of himself as their attackers advanced step by cautious step. His wary eyes never left them.

From behind, a door slammed and loud laughter drifted down the street. The four shadowy figures paused, as if uncertain.

"Grantham!" A gentleman, just leaving White's, waved. "Hey, Grantham, a moment, if you will!"

The shadowy shapes drifted back into the darkness and disappeared in different directions. Richard drew a deep breath and straightened up. Turning, he exchanged greetings with the Honorable Mr. Peregrine Knowles and the youthful and somewhat inebriated Viscount Fothingham. As a foursome, they strolled to the corner where Richard hailed a hackney. He almost shoved Andrea up into the carriage and followed her. Their companions waved jovially, linked arms, and meandered off down the street.

Andrea sank back against the squabs, closing her eyes and shivering with reaction. If those two young men had not left White's when they did, she and Richard would have been set upon! And the sword could only mean that their purpose was deadly. And Richard—

Her eyes flew open. "You weren't surprised! Richard, you . . . you were almost expecting it! This isn't the first time you've been attacked like this, is it?"

Richard settled back and watched her through half-closed eyes. "Someone wants something from me." He kept his tone casual, as though it were a matter of the most complete indifference to him.

"The Imperial Star," she breathed. "But who? Surely, Malverne cannot want it that badly, or he never would have sold it in the first place."

"No, I rather imagine someone else must be trying to use him to get it from me."

"Why? Oh, I know it's valuable, but—" She broke off as a thought occurred to her. "Could it be Greythorne Court this person wants? No, that doesn't make any sense! No one really gets it, in the end."

Richard didn't move, but his voice became as smooth as silk. "What do you mean by that?"

She stared at him, aghast, realizing what she had said.

"What the devil do you know about all this? Are you in on it?" Richard's tone took on a grim note.

"You *know* I'm not." Her sincerity rang clearly in her voice.

"Maybe. But I think the time for your games is past, my girl. What do you know of the Imperial Star?"

"Very little. I don't even know where it is."

He gave a short laugh. "That makes two of us."

"But . . ." She stared at him, aghast. Did that mean it disappeared *before* it came into his possession?

"And what did you mean about the Court?" Richard continued, ignoring her interruption. "No more pretenses, my girl. I want the truth."

She averted her face from the steely glint in his eyes. He was right, it had all gone too far. This was no mere search for an object that would make Bella's descendant comfortably well-off. Richard's life—perhaps her own— lay at stake. She had thought she strolled down a garden path only to discover that somehow, inch by inch, she had entered a deadly maze, and now did not see her way out.

"The truth," he repeated, and she could not oppose the strength of his will.

The hackney pulled up on Curzon Street and Richard swore softly under his breath. He jumped to the ground, dragged Andrea out after himself, and paid off the jarvey. Still holding her arm in a tight grip, he led her inside.

A single candle rested on the table at the foot of the stairs. Bella must have returned and gone to bed long ago. Richard noted these signs, nodded to himself, and escorted Andrea to the bookroom.

"You might pour us each a brandy." She took her accustomed seat. "I think we're going to need it."

He complied. He handed her one, then perched on the edge of his desk. Restless, he swung one leg, his own glass clasped in his hand, untasted. His gaze never left her face.

"You may begin."

She took an incautious gulp to steady her nerves and choked. "You're . . . you're not going to believe this, any of it. I don't really, myself. But I swear what I am going to tell you is the truth."

"Go on then." He sounded grim.

She stared at the amber liquid in her cut-crystal glass. She trembled inside, fearing his reaction, fearing the result if she kept her tongue. She had to tell him—but how could she make him believe? So much lay at stake! But even if she alienated him forever, he had to know the truth, if it could in any way help him.

"I'm an accountant from Minneapolis, Minnesota." She dove in, not daring to give herself time to think. "It's in America, but you won't have heard of it. It won't be settled for another thirty years or so."

"Then how—" Impatient, he broke in.

She held up a hand. "Hear me out. I told you, you're not going to believe this. But that doesn't change the fact it really happened." She focused on her glass again, not able to bear the skepticism on his face. Perhaps he would think her an escaped Bedlamite. That might be preferable to having him believe her a liar.

"I . . . I had a good life, but I was bored. I wanted something more, something romantic. I wanted to live inside the pages of the novels I read."

"That's not so very unusual." Again, he broke in.

"No, but you see, I only read Regency novels."

"What the devil are those?"

She took a deep breath, held it, then let it out with a derisive half-laugh. "Books written by modern writers that were set in the period when George III was declared mad and the Prince of Wales was declared Regent. Between 1811 and 1820."

It was Richard's turn to draw a deep breath. "Well, it's not impossible," he said at last. "A regency has been discussed. Speculative novels—is that what they're writing in America these days?"

"Oh, damn!" She took a more careful sip of brandy to recruit her forces. "I'm not explaining this well at all! Not speculative, but historic. The novels started to become really popular during the 1970's."

"The—" He broke off. "1770's?" he suggested.

She shook her head. "1970's."

"But that's almost—"

"Almost two hundred years from now."

He slammed his glass down against the desk, snapping the fragile stem and sending the contents spilling over the papers that rested on the surface. Ignoring it, he rose and loomed over her, furious and threatening. "Damn it, will you stop creating stories?" His hands clenched, and with obvious effort he brought his flaming temper back under control. He started to sit back on the desk, saw the mess, and instead took a chair. A sneer settled over his grim mouth. "Are you trying to tell me I exist only in some rubbishing novel?"

"You know perfectly well you don't. You're very real. So real, you brought me back through time to be with you." That reached him, she saw, for a sudden light flickered in his eyes.

"Then why don't I know about it?" With difficulty, he recovered.

"It was your portrait. I saw a picture of it in a newspaper and then—then I began to see *you*, everywhere I went. I knew I had to learn more about you, so I went to visit the Court. And I met a descendant of Isabella's who lives there in my day. She told me about the Imperial Star, that it had been missing since it came into your possession. And when she spoke about my traveling back through time, as if she knew I really did it . . ." Andrea shook her head. "She begged me to find the icon and hide it where she could use it to . . . because she needs the money desperately."

Richard rose, selected another glass, and poured himself more brandy. This time he drank it in one gulp and restored the glass to safety on the tray. "And how do you claim to have made such an impossible journey?"

She shook her head. "I don't know. I wanted to, more than anything. But it was your portrait—it was as if you pulled me back. It took nearly two weeks, I think. I don't really remember. It was all a blur. I just kept willing myself to be with you." She swallowed the remaining liquor and gasped as it burned down her throat.

He took several pacing steps and came to a stop directly in front of her. "I hope you don't think for even one moment that I believe this farrago of nonsense!"

"What about those horse races and the money I won? I *did* know! I copied the winners from old racing-form books! You can see for yourself, I have several dozen more, for the next few months."

"You have an accomplice, fixing the races."

She shook her head. "I don't know what else I can say to convince you. I could tell you major events, the outcome of the war—so many things, but they won't take place for years." A thought suddenly struck her. "But just in case you're interested, Bella won't marry Wilfred."

That stopped him. "You spoke of her descendant. Who, then?"

"Giles."

A sharp laugh broke from him. "Good God! Poor Giles." He caught himself up. "It's lucky for him this only exists in your fantasies!"

"Well, here's something that doesn't." Goaded by the derision in his voice, she played her sole ace. "Are you aware that your father signed a document, giving Malverne possession of the Court in exchange for the Imperial Star?"

"What the devil are you talking about?" His brow snapped down.

"No, I rather thought you didn't know." She frowned, then shook her head slowly. "And Malverne behaves as if he doesn't, either! It doesn't make sense."

"Of course he doesn't know. The idea is absurd. That ridiculous icon isn't worth a tenth of the value of the Court."

"No, it couldn't be. Which makes the whole thing preposterous."

"Yes, it does." He glowered at her. "And where, may I ask, did you get that bacon-brained piece of information?"

"Because in my time, the current Earl of Malverne owns the Court. But by stipulation in that sales document, Isabella's descendants are permitted to live there for two hundred years."

"Oh, my God! Of all the smokey, trumped-up, bags of moonshine it has ever been my misfortune to hear—"

"Please, Richard, there's something deadly afoot, and—"

"There certainly is!" His hands clenched convulsively as if they longed to settle about her throat. "But luckily for you, I can control my impulses."

Very slowly, very deliberately, he gripped her shoulders. His fingers dug cruelly into her flesh. "Now, enough of this playacting. What are you really up to? I'm going to get the truth out of you if I have to wring your lovely neck!" His fingers caressed her throat in a far from loving gesture. "Are you in league with Malverne—or with someone else?"

"Nobody!" She tried to pull away, but he held her easily. "Please, you're hurting me!"

"I'll do a damned sight more than that if I don't get the truth out of you."

"It *is* the truth!" Tears of frustration started to her eyes. She had gotten nowhere—had made the situation worse, if possible. She had made him angry enough to barge heedless into danger. "No, forget it! All of it. It doesn't matter if you believe me or not. Just please, Richard, be careful. I can't bear your being in danger."

His brow lowered as he studied her desperate face and a haunted, tormented yearning clouded the smoky gray depths of his eyes. He released her abruptly and turned on his heel. At the door, he turned back. "Do not think you have fobbed me off, Miss Wells," he informed her, though the fury had vanished from his voice. "We shall continue this discussion, and in the very near future. You *will* tell me the truth."

She closed her eyes and tried to control her trembling. She had known it wasn't going to be easy, but she hadn't been prepared for this! She couldn't bear his accusing, mistrusting glare. And now . . . There was no way of knowing what he thought of her. Only time would tell. Only time . . .

Suddenly, she was exhausted. She stood and trailed Richard up the stairs, glad the servants were not about. A glance at the mantel clock warned her it was just after three. At least she had every right to feel awful and depressed. She undressed, hid away the youth's clothes, and prepared for bed without the assistance of Lily.

As she bent over the basin to slosh water over her face, she caught sight of her unfamiliar cropped hair. The morning would bring no end of questions. She had better rest while she could.

Lily, bringing her chocolate and rolls at ten o'clock, was the first to comment on the change to her appearance. Drawing back the bed curtains, the maid took one look at her shorn head and squeaked in surprise.

"Lawks, miss! Your hair! Your beautiful hair."

Andrea closed her tired eyes. "It was too much trouble, always needing to be washed and taking forever to dry. I wanted a change."

Bella, when she encountered her later in the drawing room, proved no less startled but much more pleased. "Why, you look all the crack! My love, if I had had the least notion you meant to do this, I would have summoned my own hairdresser for you. But I vow, you look quite delightful."

That left her with only one more hurdle to surmount. She still had to face Richard. But much to her mingled dismay and relief, Bella informed her that her brother had left the house at an early hour and had not said when he expected to return.

"Which is so very vexatious of him, for you must remember that he promised to escort us to Almack's tonight. Your first visit, too. It would be just like him to be disobliging at the last moment."

But in this one respect, at least, he wasn't. Andrea and Bella dined in solitary state, but when they rose to send for the carriage, Richard put in a belated return to the house. Less than half an hour later, much to the surprise of the ladies, he came back down the stairs, dressed in the proper knee breeches, coat, silken hose, and black pumps. He did not so much as glance at Andrea in her carefully selected gown of rose-colored silk. He merely escorted them out to the carriage where he sat on the facing seat in glowering silence. Bella cast one measuring look at his face and refrained from comment or question.

The evening should have been one of unmixed joy for Andrea. Here she was at last, at the Holiest of Holies, the legendary club that no Regency novel failed to mention in terms of awe—or derision, if speaking of the refreshments. But Andrea almost quailed at the door.

She ought to be ecstatic. She possessed an actual voucher! One part of her mind kept repeating that, but it failed to help.

She entered the vestibule, released her wrap into the hands of a waiting footman, and accepted the quadrille-card offered her by another. The great Mr. Willis himself bowed her through into the first of the rooms. But nothing mattered except Richard's unyielding countenance and the irreparable rift she had created between them—by telling him the truth.

The rooms, she noted with an appalling and depressing lack of interest, were not crowded. Small groups of people stood about or sat near the walls. The primary attraction, she realized, was not dancing nor even meeting one's friends, but simply being seen. Gentlemen and ladies alike appeared bent on displaying their finery, of attracting notice. It was aptly nicknamed the Marriage Mart. One only passed through the sacred portals if one possessed the proper breeding and lineage. That meant one could shop for a spouse without the fear that one's fancy might alight on some wholly ineligible outsider.

Except for the stray impostor who stormed the citadel as she did. Andrea could not help but smile at the thought, albeit wistfully. She did not belong here. Her manners, her upbringing, her whole outlook on life separated her from these people with whom she must spend the rest of her days. The thought merely added to her depression.

As soon as they found seats, Richard left them without a word. A few minutes later, he led Lettie Moreland out into a country dance. Wilfred claimed Bella and Andrea sat beside Miss Moreland, knowing that her inches would frighten off any would-be partners.

Tonight, the pageant of color and elegance of the dance movements could not hold her attention. She was heartily bored within minutes and made her way to the refreshment table, where she procured glasses of weak punch for herself and the Dragoness. Listlessly, she sipped the insipid beverage and wondered if walking out would be considered a social solecism.

The music ended and Richard restored Lettie to her chaperone. He did not cast so much as a single glance toward Andrea. Lettie sank into her chair, her whole demeanor bespeaking misery and dejection.

"Richard!" Bella hurried up, minus Wilfred. "Will you not lead out Andrea? I fear she knows so few gentlemen, still."

His gaze strayed toward Andrea and he looked instantly away. His lip showed a tendency to curl. "I fear that honor must be denied me. I am promised to a party of friends in the cardroom." He turned on his heel and left them.

Bella blinked. "I wonder what has happened to put him out of temper? Oh, excuse me, my love. Here is my next partner." Bella went off on the arm of a dashing officer in scarlet regimentals.

Andrea forced back a sigh and paid Bella no heed. At the moment, she could see no way to break down the barriers she had created between Richard and herself. He seemed afraid of her—or at least of the confusion she created in him. Which could only mean that some part of him still cared for her. Incongruously, her heart lifted.

It fell a moment later. Lord Brompton, his round, heavily jowled face wreathed in an unctuous smile, descended upon them. With an awful creaking, he bowed low before Lettie and took her tiny hand between his pudgy ones.

"Delightful, just delightful, my dear." He raised her fingers to his lips for a lingering kiss. "And Miss Moreland." To the accompaniment of another protesting shriek, he made an inelegant leg to the Dragoness.

Andrea recoiled, which proved a mistake, for it brought her to Brompton's attention. His gaze moved across her tall, graceful figure and his eyes lit with a contemplative gleam.

"Miss Wells! I am overwhelmed by beauty." He accompanied the words with a broad, knowing wink, as if he thought she would welcome such fulsome compliments.

Remaining in complete ignorance of Andrea's true feelings, he regained Lettie's hand, which she had drawn away, and fondled it in a manner that left the child close to tears. "You must honor me with this next dance, my dear." He drew her to her feet and led her into the round dance that formed near them, leaving Andrea to frown after them.

There was nothing threatening or evil in Lord Brompton's manner—at least as far as Malverne should be concerned. So why did the earl force Lettie to be the recipient of his disgusting attentions?

Wilfred strolled up and, much to Andrea's relief, voiced the same opinion. "I cannot, simply cannot, understand this. It isn't like my father to arrange such a marriage." He regarded the couple, his expression aggrieved. "I always thought he'd let Lettie make her own choice. She's such a taking little puss and he's always been very fond of her. Never would I have thought he'd force her against her will."

"Is Lord Brompton really that wealthy?" Andrea's frown deepened as she saw Lettie snatch her hand away from Brompton's fawning hold.

"Rich as Croesus." Wilfred noted the little byplay, also. "But that shouldn't matter. Lettie has a tidy fortune of her own." He shook his head. "It's not as if he's trying to save her from some fortune hunter, either," he continued, dropping his affected drawl in his concern. "The silly chit's not one to flirt and don't encourage the advances of anyone."

"And Lettie isn't anxious for a title, either," Andrea stuck in as if musing. "Really, I can see no good coming of this. Someone should make a push to save the poor child."

Wilfred eyed the couple on the floor with disfavor. "Can't say I'd mind sticking a spoke in the wheel, myself. But I don't see what's to be done. The announcement is to be sent to the papers next week." He shook his head and went off to fetch Miss Moreland some unappetizing biscuits.

Andrea's only consolation was the way Wilfred's brooding gaze remained on Lettie. This particular knight errant was going to need a hefty shove to get him onto the field of combat—especially since he had an engagement of his own that must be broken.

Andrea danced the quadrille with Wilfred, but did not enjoy herself despite his capable guidance through the difficult steps. At an early hour, she pleaded a headache, and Bella found Richard and sent for the carriage. They returned to the house in silence, none of them having found the least pleasure in the evening. At the door, Richard changed his mind, bade the ladies good night, and announced his intention to visit his club. Andrea, her heart heavy, watched him ignore Giles's advice to go about with caution as he strode heedlessly off down the street.

Andrea lay awake long, considering her various courses of action. Of one thing she was certain—she could not bear any more of Richard's antagonistic distrust. She would either prove her improbable claims to him or alienate him forever. And in either case, she would emerge from the deal with a tidy fortune.

When she came down the stairs at an early hour, Richard was already at the breakfast table, glowering over a copy of the *Morning Post*. He looked up as she entered, hunched a shoulder, and disappeared behind the pages once more. This wasn't going to be easy, but by now she knew his vulnerable spots.

"I need your help, Grantham." Andrea made a pretty show of hesitating on the threshold. Just a touch of a pathetic plea colored her tone.

The papers rustled as his fingers tensed. Reluctantly, he lowered the *Post* and regarded her through suspicious eyes.

"I need you to sell another necklace for me."

"Go to the devil." He disappeared behind the sheets once more.

"Richard!"

He drew a deep breath and glared at her over the top. "Drawing the bustle with a vengeance?" His voice sounded unnaturally tight.

She shook her head. "Merely planning for my future. I have the names of five winners at one meet. Newmarket, in three days' time. Will you do it?"

A guarded look closed over his features like a mask. He hesitated, as if weighing possible consequences from having any further contact with her.

"You could place money on the same horses," she suggested.

"No, damn it! I won't play your games!"

"But will you help me?"

His jaw clenched, but he held out a hand. She passed over the milky strand and a sheet with the names and races. "An accumulator?"

"If you please."

"You know damned well I don't." But both the necklace and the list disappeared into the depths of his pocket before he again retreated behind his newspaper.

During the ensuing days, she saw very little of him. He avoided her, she knew, and her heart ached with a pain that grew more unbearable with every passing hour. She longed for his companionship but could hit upon no way to break through his defenses.

Nor was she the only one troubled by Richard's sullen withdrawal. Bella watched him with worried eyes but refrained from comment. Instead, she busied herself to an alarming degree and made a show of enjoying her betrothed's company. Determinedly so, Andrea decided while watching her friend's forced vivacity one evening. It might almost seem, to one with a suspicious mind, that Bella regretted her engagement. Faint hope stirred within Andrea, but it was not sufficient to lift her depression over Richard's angry glares.

On the following Monday, as Andrea changed into a carriage dress to drive in the park with Bella and Lettie, a sharp knock sounded on her door. Richard entered on her call, his face an impenetrable mask. Without speaking, he handed her a slip of paper.

She took it and saw that she held a draft on his bank. Her winnings. He must not have wanted to carry the cash on his person, and she could not blame him. Then she swallowed, her throat strangely dry as the meaning of the figures penetrated her bemused brain. The sum was for just over two hundred thousand pounds. She was now, to be blunt, filthy rich.

Without so much as a single word, Richard turned on his heel and left. Andrea's knees gave out and she sank down onto the bed. She would deposit it in her bank on the morrow, then arrange for investments. And she must make a will, leaving her fortune to charitable organizations, just in case . . .

Bella's voice, calling her, at last shook her from her reverie. She put on her bonnet, tucked the draft safely into her reticule, and hurried downstairs.

As she reached the bottom landing, a carriage pulled up before the house and the two started for the door. But it was not their landaulet that waited out front but Richard's curricle. Moments later, he came down the stairs, followed by a footman carrying a valise.

"Richard?" Bella started toward him in surprise.

"I'm going down to the Court." He brushed past and outside without so much as a glance at Andrea. He saw his luggage secured, then swung up into the seat and set his pair going with an angry snap of the ribbons.

Andrea swallowed hard. It was only April. He was safe, at least for a little bit longer. But she would give anything to be with him for what little time remained.

A horseman rode down the street, hailed the curricle, and Richard drew up. Giles, Andrea saw. But apparently his friend made no attempt to stop him. Her heart in her throat, Andrea watched Richard whip up his pair and continue.

But at the corner, he turned the equipage. Giles fell in beside him and together they made their way back to the house. Both jumped down and Richard left the vehicle with his groom. Giles tossed his bridle to a surprised footman and accompanied Richard up the stairs.

"I think your sister had better hear what I have to say. And Miss Wells, too." Giles looked down at the toes of his impossibly polished boots and did not meet their anxious gazes.

Richard, tight-lipped, nodded and led the way to the bookroom. Bella and Andrea exchanged bewildered glances and followed.

As soon as they were all seated, Richard turned to Giles. "What is this about?"

Giles ran a hand through his tousled brown locks. "I'm going to have to rely on your discretion not to repeat what I'm about to say." His gaze rested on Bella's worried face. "For the past year, I've been working for our government in a minor capacity. Keeping an eye on things, you might say. I admit I'd wondered, but—" He broke off and shook his head. "The whole thing seems so preposterous."

"What does?" Richard watched him closely.

"Our people recently have been approached by an emissary from Tsar Alexander. It seems that the tsar is anxious to recover a certain piece of art, an icon known as the Imperial Star."

Bella gasped and Richard sat up straighter. "Go on."

In as few words as possible, Giles related the history of the theft of the icon from the tsar's mother. Andrea, though she had heard the tale from Catherine Kendall, listened in fascination.

"And now the matter becomes more serious." Giles leaned forward in his chair and fixed his intent regard on Richard's face. "The tsar has agreed to an alliance with Napoleon, *if* Bonaparte can recover and return the Imperial Star to him."

"If . . ." Richard got up and poured Madeira for Giles and himself. He drained his in one swallow. "An alliance with Napoleon," he repeated. "Good God, England could never withstand the combined forces of two such powerful enemies." He turned to Giles, his eyes blazing with determination. "That must be prevented, at all costs."

Giles nodded. "There are French agents here now, searching for it. They have traced it to Malverne, and from him, to you."

"Those men lurking about the Court!" Andrea's eyes widened in dawning alarm. "Richard, they weren't thieves, they must have been spies!" She stood, horror filling her, and reached out a shaking hand toward him. "And those men with the swords . . ."

His fingers closed about hers in a sustaining grip. "We guessed they weren't simple ruffians, but spies!"

"Experts, trained in . . . in the means of getting what they want . . ." Andrea's voice trailed off. An icy hand seemed to grip her stomach. French agents. What chance did Richard have against skilled assassins? That was how he would meet his death—and in less than a month.

Chapter 22

"Oh, Richard!" Bella cast a frantic glance a about the room, as if she expected sinister French spies to converge on them.

Richard poured his sister some wine and she took it with trembling hands. When he spoke, he forced a note of calm into his voice. "You said an emissary has come from the tsar?"

Giles nodded. "Alexander would rather not form an alliance with Napoleon. If *we* can find the Imperial Star first, he promises to send his troops against the French." He regarded his friend through narrowed eyes. "Where is it, Grantham? The fate of England rests in your hands."

Andrea blinked at the melodrama of the statement but experienced no desire to laugh.

Richard raised his troubled gaze to look squarely at Giles. "I don't know where the icon is."

"You . . ." Giles opened his mouth, then shut it, his expression comical in its dismay.

Richard shook his head. "My father hid the Imperial Star shortly before his death. And I have no idea where."

"You've got to find it!" Giles stood and took several agitated steps about the room. "Think man! Consider what is at stake! If the French locate it first, England is lost! But if we can hand that blasted icon over to the tsar, Napoleon won't stand a chance. The war would be over in a matter of months!"

Andrea swallowed. What would that do to history? This was only 1810. If the war ended, there would be no Peninsular campaign. Wellington was still Arthur Wellesley, not even a viscount yet. There would be no Iron Duke, no Waterloo, no removal of the Portuguese government to Brazil, no . . . no suffering, no countless deaths.

And what would the ramifications be of close ties between Russia and England? Alexander already showed liberal tendencies. Would the serfs, under the democratic influence of the British, be freed? Her mind reeled with the possibilities. What if there were never a Russian Revolution? What if—

But she was getting beyond herself, beyond the current situation. For any of this to happen, the Imperial Star must be found—and by the British, not the French. And as far as history—as she knew it—was concerned, neither side possessed it. Therefore, to keep history unchanged, *she* must be the one to find it—and conceal it for Catherine Kendall to find almost two hundred years in the future.

"The war over." Richard's deep voice cut across her frantic speculations. He gazed off into space, lost in thought. "No wonder Malverne has been near the end of his tether if he's been hounded by French agents. Somehow, we must find it."

"Be careful," Giles cautioned. "Both sides are now aware it was in your possession."

"My father's," Richard corrected. But all knew that didn't matter.

Isabella regarded Giles with a fear not unmixed with awe. "Can you keep Richard safe?"

302

Richard gave a short laugh. "I don't want any attention drawn to anything I do."

Giles nodded agreement. "He's right. No one knows for certain where the Imperial Star is. But you may be sure we won't let any harm come to him."

The bottom dropped out of Andrea's stomach. That was the one thing no one could guarantee. And in fact, they were like to fail miserably at it.

"And the first thing will be for me to continue as I had planned." There was a touch of smoothness in Richard's voice, as though he expected argument and hoped to forestall it.

"Richard, you cannot . . ." Bella turned to him, distraught.

"On the contrary, I can and I will go to the Court. Exactly as planned. Alone." He threw one defiant glance at Andrea and strode out of the room. Moments later, the front door slammed, proclaiming his departure.

Bella drew a deep, ragged breath. "Will . . . will he be all right?" She looked to Giles, her blue eyes clouded with worry.

"You may be certain he will not be there alone, no matter what he might think. There is too much at stake."

His manner exuded confidence, and that had its effect on Bella. She managed a tremulous smile. "Thank you."

"Bella." Andrea drew her frowning contemplation away from the door and the now-empty hall beyond. "Is it true? Does he really not know where the Imperial Star is?"

"Yes." With difficulty, Bella looked away from the fascinating smile on Giles Kendall's face. "We have no idea, either of us. And you may be very sure we talked about it at great length after Father died. The money it would have fetched had we sold it would not have come amiss."

"So your father hid it somewhere?" Giles leaned

303

forward, intent. "I wonder why?"

"More like he gambled it away." Bella sighed and shook her pretty head.

Andrea went to the table and poured herself a glass of Madeira, ignoring the startled glances from both Giles and Bella. Maybe Regency-era women didn't need stiff drinks occasionally, but Andrea did. No wonder they were forever swooning, between the tight corsets about the rib cage and the lack of medicinal spirits.

What if history could be changed? What would happen to the world she knew if the Imperial Star were uncovered? It was not so preposterous to consider that she might never have been born. And if that were the case, would she simply cease to exist? But what about her presence for the past few months? The thought of the ramifications left her with a severe headache, a dislike for all philosophers, and a strong desire to swear off speculative thinking herself.

She drained her glass in one gulp, choked, and poured another. Was this one of those moments of crisis she had read about in novels? Where the heroine suddenly realized she had to take destiny in her own hands? Only this wasn't one of the books she devoured. This was reality. She couldn't close her story and put it back on the shelf. She had to go right on living it.

And she *had* to find that icon, no matter the cost to . . . to anyone. Since she couldn't save Richard, she would at least save the Court for Catherine Kendall—and history, as she knew it—in spite of the British, the French, and the Russians!

They were scheduled to attend a card party that evening under the escort of Wilfred, but Bella sent a message crying off, claiming the headache as her excuse. Andrea made no objection. The thought of going out into society, of having to adopt artificial manners when her heart cried out within her for Richard was unbearable.

As she drove in the park the following afternoon with an unusually subdued Bella at her side, she considered the disturbing truth. For some weeks now, the Regency era had lost its glittering, romantic appeal and London was nothing more than a dirty city filled with social injustice. Richard, imperfect and aggravating as he might be, was far more important to her than any silly dream or any novel. He was her life, and without him she was lost and the world was meaningless.

Somewhere in the back of her mind lingered the hope he would return to her. But as another day crept by, empty of his deep laughter sounding in the hall below, she realized she would have to take matters into her own hands. It was not an easy thing to do, to so openly flaunt the society she had moved heaven and earth to join. But at whatever the cost to herself and her reputation, she would go down to the Court to be with Richard.

There were a couple of matters to which she must tend before she would be free to abandon the world and follow her reckless heart. First thing the following morning, she went to her bank and, through one of the officers there, found a solicitor who drew up her will on the spot. Satisfied with both this and her investments, and secure in the knowledge that her future would be settled no matter what, she turned her attention to the all-consuming matter of Richard.

Her next stop was one that would have shocked even Bella. Ordering the carriage to take her to a *modiste* who had not previously enjoyed her patronage, Andrea settled back to consider the purchases she would make. These, to the wide-eyed wonder of the seamstress, included a truly elegant, wispy negligee that would put even Bella to the blush. It was a pity there was as yet no Frederick's of Hollywood, but the garment—to use the term lightly— she found would do very well.

She set about packing at once. No Regency miss, she

did not need the help of her maid. The fact that her gowns would be sadly crushed did not concern her. She had to go, not only to find the Imperial Star, but to be with Richard—whether he wanted her or not.

Lily, not unnaturally, discovered what she was about when she went to help her mistress dress for a dinner party that night. Andrea swore her to secrecy and the maid, all agog, set about repacking her things with care. Andrea watched, grateful for both the help and the silence. She had no desire for Bella to accompany her on this trip. The need for a chaperone was not instilled with her as it would be with a lady raised in this period. In fact she very much did *not* want one.

She was on the verge, in true heroinelike style, of sending Lily to the mail coach office to buy her a ticket when it dawned on her there was no need. She was well able to hire a post chaise—in fact, if she wanted, she could buy one for the journey. She was not beset by the normal monetary problems of the average heroine. But the thought proved to be no more than momentarily diverting.

Andrea went to the dinner party, which was held by Malverne, without comment, for she did not want Bella to guess her intentions to slip quietly out of town on the morrow. She needed time alone with Richard, time to settle his distrust, time to build a few memories to last her through the empty years ahead.

Bella, she noted early in the evening, seemed unusually pale and quiet. She cast frequent, unhappy glances in the direction of her betrothed, who seemed preoccupied with coaxing Letitia Moreland into a more cheerful frame of mind. The situation satisfied Andrea. There would be time enough to settle all of their affairs after—after May sixteenth.

They did not get back to the house on Curzon Street until just before midnight. The butler met them in the

306

hall with the information that his lordship had returned barely an hour before. A surge of elation swept through Andrea, and she started forward toward the bookroom where she knew instinctively he would be. Before she had gone three steps, he emerged and stopped in the hall, staring at her, his brow haggard and drawn.

"Richard! I am so glad to see you!" Bella hurried over and planted a sisterly kiss on his cheek.

Andrea gazed up at him and her world both tumbled and soared. He was here, unharmed, and she could even ignore the confusion and anger in his stormy eyes as they rested on her.

"I want to have a few words with you." His tone came out as stiff as his manner.

"Can it not wait until morning? You must be tired, and I assure you Andrea and I are." Bella hugged his arm.

He set her firmly aside. "It is only Miss Wells with whom I wish to speak. And speak with her I shall." Taking Andrea's arm in an uncompromising clasp, he marched her into the room.

She settled on the chair across from his desk. She seemed to have spent a great deal of time doing that of late. Thrusting the irrelevant thought from her mind, she faced Richard with an outward calm. She could only hope it hid the flutter of sensations she experienced from just looking at him.

He poured himself a brandy, and it was obvious this was not his first glass since his return. "You are now going to tell me exactly what you know of the Imperial Star. And don't try to fob me off with that nonsense you gave me earlier. I *must* know the truth."

A deep sigh escaped her. "You might give me a glass of that." He handed her one, but she didn't take a drink. "I did tell you the truth," she said at last. "But I can't think of a single way to prove it."

"My God!" He gave a short, mirthless laugh. "Why

307

does that make your story sound less of a lie?" He shook his head, torn. "I'd give a great deal to be able to believe you, but it's too preposterous!" He took several restless, pacing strides about the room.

"I know it is. I could tell you of inventions, of books, even the future of England, but since none of it will happen in the next few days, none of it is proof." She sank her head into her hands. He would never trust her. The mystery of her would always stand between them. Always, until May sixteenth . . .

He came to a stop before her. "What about another horse?" He sounded almost desperate. "That seems to be the one trick you do well. Can you name a winner for tomorrow?"

"I . . . I don't know. I can check."

His eyes narrowed. "You don't just pull them out of your head?"

She tried to smile, but it was a pathetic attempt. "Now, that *would* be ridiculous. I can't foretell the future. I just *come* from it."

"Show me that list." The words came out tight.

"It's in my room."

"Bring it."

She did. He took the tightly written pages when she returned and subjected them to a careful examination.

"They only begin after you arrived," he accused.

"I threw out the earlier ones. There was no need to keep them."

He read it over again. "You didn't bet on all of these. Why not?"

"I didn't have to—or you weren't available to make the arrangements for me."

"Here's the next." He nodded slowly. "Catch-Me-Who-Dares, running at the York meet tomorrow. We'll just see how he does."

"You might put something on him, then." Andrea

took a much-needed sip of her drink.

He met her gaze with one that left her chilled. "I just might."

The following day he set off on the errand which was his ostensible reason for returning to London. He visited his father's bank to see if the icon had been left there in safe-keeping, but drew a blank. After reporting this failure to his anxious sister—and informing Andrea through clenched teeth that he had placed her bet—he took himself off to his club. He would not hear the results of the race for another three days, but perhaps then he would be in a more open frame of mind about her. The success of Catch-Me-Who-Dares might convince him she was not some sinister spy.

Andrea went about her routine, trying to maintain the pretenses of normalcy. Bella did the same, with a noticeable lack of her usual spontaneity and impulsive laughter. Not mugh longer, Andrea kept telling herself. Not much longer.

And it wasn't. The following morning, Richard entered the saloon where she sat staring unseeingly at a novel. She looked up and her heart rose, filling her throat so that its frantic pounding threatened to choke her.

"What are you, a witch?" He breathed the words, his expression confused, tormented. "Catch-Me-Who-Dares was only added to the race at the last moment. You *couldn't* have known!"

Relief flooded through her. Here, at last, was something tangible! "I know it's hard to accept that I'm from the future. But please, just consider it as a possibility! Isn't my being a witch equally absurd?"

He strode forward and sank down on the settee at her side. Gripping her shoulders, he stared down into her eyes as if he sought to read the truth there. "I want to believe in you."

"Then do." She covered his hands with hers and gazed

up earnestly into his eyes with every ounce of love she possessed showing in hers.

"My God," he breathed. "Whatever you are, I've fallen under your spell."

The biting grip of his fingers shifted, becoming no more gentle but infinitely more enticing. He pulled her against himself and his mouth covered hers in a kiss that held all their pent-up emotions.

Abruptly, he pushed her away and stood, controlling himself with a conscious effort. "I can't resist you when you're near."

"Please, I don't want you to." Andrea rose, trembling, to face him. All that mattered most was that he was here, that she could see him—and that she was deeply in love with him.

He slid his hand about the nape of her neck, his fingers caressing. "Well, my witch? Is that an invitation?"

"Will you be going back to the Court in the morning?" She tried to keep her voice calm.

He shook his head. "I'll be leaving within the hour."

She closed her eyes for a moment to gather her courage. "I'm going with you."

Surprise flashed across his face, to be replaced in a moment with skepticism. He stepped away from her as if retreating back into himself. "I'll not have a pack of females hampering my search. This is like to prove very dangerous."

"Not a pack. Just me. I'm not letting you go alone." She met his gaze steadily.

There was no mistaking the expression that crept into his cloudy eyes. The smoldering glow that she had missed so terribly flickered and ignited once more. "Without a chaperone?" The unspoken meaning behind his seemingly casual question hovered in the air between them, almost tangible.

She drew a deep breath, knowing it was what she

wanted more than anything. But she had to keep it light—at least for now. "If necessary."

But then she made the mistake of meeting his searching gaze and she was lost. Slowly, he held out his hands. She knew not so much as a single moment's hesitation. She walked straight into his open arms and raised her face to his, so desperate for his kiss it was a physical ache.

Chapter 23

Bella returned from her modiste's in the midafternoon to be met by her distraught butler. Not only had her brother departed the house unexpectedly, that haughty individual informed her, but Miss had accompanied him, with her baggage strapped to the back of his lordship's curricle. His manner conveyed in no uncertain terms that while the disagreeable duty of relating this shocking occurrence might fall to him, he washed his hands of so unsavory an affair.

His censorious manner was completely lost on Bella. She stared at him in dismay. "What ever occurred to send them off in such a manner?" she demanded.

"I could not say, madam." He regarded her in no little disappointment. In his experience, ladies of quality tended to go off into strong hysterics when they discovered they'd been sheltering lightskirts beneath their roofs. "His lordship left you a mesage." Philosophically accepting the vagaries of the Nobs, he proffered a salver, on which rested a folded and sealed note bearing Grantham's crest.

Bella tore it open and read the few words. Richard had decided to return to the Court, it said, and Miss Wells had accompanied him to help with the search for the Imperial

Star. Bella let out a sigh of relief.

"Oh, thank heavens!" she exclaimed, thus drawing a profoundly shocked stare from the butler.

But she could gain no clue as to what had precipitated their departure. Lacking solid evidence, it did not take her long to invent any number of wholly imaginary disasters. In less than no time, she managed to work herself into a state of advanced nerves.

Richard and Andrea were sensible people. They would not have just left like that, leaving themselves open to the vilest gossip, unless the matter were urgent. She could only be grateful that her unconventional friend had not allowed her lack of a chaperone to stand in her way. Well, she would not fail her. She would set forth herself at once, thus preventing the inevitable tongue-wagging. Andrea must not suffer for her kind-hearted determination to be of assistance!

Her first move was to summon Wilfred. While she awaited his arrival, she ordered her portmanteaux packed. Leaving this to three maids, she went downstairs and set to work writing notes of apology to the hostesses of the various entertainments to which they were pledged for the next week.

Wilfred, somewhat alarmed by the tone of her message, put in an appearance almost at once. She told him what had taken place and ended on a pleading note.

"You see how it is. I must go to poor Andrea at once."

Wilfred shook his head. "Really, my dear, I don't see that at all! It is not, simply not, the thing for you to go haring off about the country like that. No, not the thing at all."

"Do you mean you will not take me?" Her eyes glittered with indignation.

He looked revolted. "I should say not! A fine thing it would be for me to do. You may depend on it, if your brother had wanted you, he would have waited for you or

313

himself arranged for you to travel down."

"But Andrea is with him! And if we are to talk of improprieties . . . !"

But Wilfred held his ground. "That's their concern."

"Wilfred!"

"Look here, Bella." He colored to the roots of his reddish-brown hair. "If she wants to go off with him, let her! You're not her keeper. Nor your brother's, for that matter. She probably wouldn't thank you for interfering —or me, either," he added with feeling.

She fixed him with a withering look. "You're afraid of Richard!"

Wilfred's flush deepened. "No, now, really, Bella. I'm not afraid of him, precisely. But he does have a punishing right, you know."

In high dudgeon, she sent him about his business. He seemed relieved, which angered her even further. But when her temper settled, she realized she was still without a much-needed escort for her journey. At last coming to the conclusion that it couldn't be helped, Bella sent a groom to order out the traveling carriage. She would leave as soon as it arrived, she decided, and spend the night on the road. No one need know she had been unable to join Andrea until the following day.

She was roused from her nervous pacing barely ten minutes later. The butler bowed a tall gentleman of decidedly foreign appearance into the drawing room. She stopped and looked him over with no little curiosity.

"Madame Brixton?" He bowed over her hand. "Forgive me for disturbing you. It is Lord Grantham I seek."

"He is . . . away from home, at the moment. Might I be of assistance?" His accent—he was Russian! Bella stared at him in consternation.

The gentleman frowned. "Would you tell him that I have called? The name is Palitov, Polkovnik Palitov."

314

"Pol—"

"Colonel," he translated, smiling. "Colonel Palitov."

"Colonel. He . . . he may be gone more than one day."

"*Proklyatye!*" He swore softly. "Forgive me, madame. It is most urgent that I speak with him. Will you convey to him the message as soon as he returns? He may reach me here." He handed her a card on which an address had been scribbled at the bottom.

Bella accepted it, promised to give it to her brother the moment he should enter the house, and saw her disturbing visitor to the door.

By the time her carriage pulled up before the house, an even better idea had occurred to Bella. If Wilfred would not oblige her, she would invite Lettie to bear her company, thus making a delightful house party their excuse for bolting to the country at the height of the Season. That should properly fool anyone who watched their activities with avid interest.

After her bags were carried downstairs and secured to the vehicle, Bella requested her coachman to take her to Malverne House. But it was the hour of the Promenade, as Malverne's toplofty butler informed her. Miss Moreland and Miss Letitia Moreland would be found strolling in the park.

Not to be daunted, Bella ordered the vehicle there, then at the gate stepped down to walk the paths in search of her quarry. Nothing would be more like to cause unwanted comment than a traveling carriage traversing the drive.

She lost nearly half an hour in fruitless search. Then, on the verge of giving up and returning to Malverne House to wait, Bella spotted Lettie on the arm of her elderly swain with the Dragoness bringing up a decorous rear guard.

"Lettie!" Bella hailed her and hurried forward, relief flooding through her. "Lettie!"

315

The girl looked up, pale, miserable, and frightened.

"My love." Bella took her hands, thus forcing Lord Brompton to release the one he clasped. "Pray, say you will not disappoint me! Andrea and I have grown weary from so many late nights and thought to take what dear Wilfred would call a 'repairing lease' in the country. Do promise you will come and bear us company."

Real hope shone in the girl's face. "Oh, I should love it above all things! When do you mean to set forth?"

"Letitia!" Miss Moreland spoke sharply. "You know very well we have plans for the immediate future."

Lettie cast a terrified glance at the Dragoness's stern frown and the momentary vivacity died from her expression. "Could I not—"

"It is out of the question." Miss Moreland sniffed and directed a dismissive nod toward Bella. "Come along, now. We must not so monopolize Mrs. Brixton."

Tears filled Lettie's lovely, sad eyes. "Thank you, Bella. I . . . I only wish it were possible."

Bella opened her mouth to protest, met Miss Moreland's steely eye, and faltered. "I . . . it was not important. We just thought . . . But never mind. Perhaps another time." Bella turned away. What was she to do now? She would have to go alone, for she could not fail Andrea.

"Mrs. Brixton?"

A deep voice called her name and she looked up, surprised to see Giles Kendall astride his black gelding come trotting toward her along Rotten Row.

"Alone? And on foot?" He swung to the ground. "Allow me to be your escort."

She stared at him, her expression arrested. "Yes. Oh, would you, Mr. Kendall? I . . . I don't mean here, in the park. But to Greythorne Court?"

He checked, then continued walking beside her. "Is something amiss? I would have thought Grantham or Miss Wells more suitable companions on such a journey."

"But they have already left!"

"Have they, by gad!" He spun to face her. "And without a word to me! When did they go?"

"Earlier today, while I was out. I have no notion what took them off like that. But you must see I have to follow, and as quickly as possible!"

"Someone must, certainly, but it might not be wise for it to be you."

"It is not that dreadful icon I am worried about, it is Andrea. She has not even the vestige of a chaperone. I can only admire her for being so selfless as to accompany my brother, and I will not permit her to suffer for her kindness."

Giles's eyes gleamed, but mercifully he refrained from comment. "When could you be ready to leave?"

"I am, now. My traveling carriage is outside the gate."

He grinned. "Grantham always said you were a wonder of efficiency. Allow me fifteen minutes to pack a valise and I'll be with you." He swung up onto his horse, pulled it about, and took off at an indecorous canter toward the exit.

Bella stared after him, bemused. Now, *there* was a man of action. He no sooner knew she needed help than he sprang to her assistance. Her heart filled. A dependable man, so like her own dear Richard . . . Color flooded her cheeks. She was engaged, she had not the right to think in such a manner. Wilfred might be wanting in dash and daring, but he would make her a comfortable husband, his ton was excellent, and he would never cause her anxiety or pain. That such a life would be beyond anything dull, she tried to ignore.

Nor was Bella the only one to experience certain regrets concerning the current circumstances. Richard drove his pair hard, wanting to cover as much ground as possible in the shortest amount of time. It was imperative

317

that they not spend a night on the road. He wanted Andrea, more than he had ever wanted any female in his life, but whatever else she might be, she was no bit o' muslin to be treated casually. Until he had her sorted out in his mind, he had no desire to compromise her nor to damage her reputation.

The more miles they covered, the more he thought about Andrea and the more withdrawn he became. She was an enigma, she fit no rules that he understood. She threw out blatant lures to him, yet she was so completely lacking in subterfuge or coquettishness he wondered if he could have mistaken her meaning. He knew himself a master of the art of elegant seduction, yet Andrea did not behave either as an experienced Paphian or a missish virgin. The situation left him perplexed and uncertain how to proceed.

She was an admitted impostor, he reminded himself. But if he took her to his bed, as he wanted, he had no idea what the outcome would be. Or rather, he did! Blood pounded through his veins at the imagined prospect. But what about afterward? He shied away from considering what role he wanted her to play in his life. He had enough problems at the moment.

In an attempt to divert his mind from the intriguing paths presented by his companion, he stopped at the next posting inn and called for a change. With fresh horses harnessed to the curricle, they set off at a spanking pace.

"There are so many unanswered questions." Andrea spoke quietly from beside him out of deference to the groom who perched up behind.

Richard frowned down at her, then immediately forced his attention back to his mismatched pair. "Of which are you thinking in particular?" These were the first words they had spoken since leaving London.

"Lettie. What difference can her marriage to Lord Brompton make? What could Malverne gain by that?"

"Do you think it's tied to the search for the Imperial Star?" He kept his voice steady, his gaze focused three inches above the horses' ears.

She shook her head. "It doesn't seem reasonable, does it? Unless Brompton possesses some influence that he could bring to bear on—on someone?"

"Who?" He spared her a humorous glance.

"Well, it was just a thought. Have you any better suggestions?"

"I'm afraid I don't. Brompton is wealthy, but with the military power of Imperial Russia at stake, I don't think mere money would influence many of the players in our little game."

"Perhaps underlings might be bought or . . . or slowed down."

His hands tightened on the reins, checking the pair, then released and once again allowed the horses their heads. "I wonder just what role Malverne plays. Perhaps we should consult with him."

"Do you think he knows more than we?"

Richard considered, then slowly shook his head. "No, I think he's been threatened, and probably by the French."

They continued in silence for some time. He could think of no way that Malverne could help them. Until he placed his hands on that damnable icon, there was little he could do about anything. Find it he must, if it meant dismantling the Court—brick by stone by timber.

Beside him, Andrea shivered. He leaned down and pulled a lap robe from beneath the seat and shook it out as best he could with one hand. She helped, and in a moment he draped it over her lap. The afternoon wore on and soon the evening chill engulfed them.

"I'm afraid." Andrea's soft voice held a tremor.

He covered the hands which lay clasped in her lap. "No one will hurt you."

319

"That's not—" She broke off, biting her lip. "It . . . it's you I'm worried about."

An unfamiliar, warm glow crept through him and his fingers tightened about hers. "I'll be all right. I'm an old hand at looking after myself."

She nodded, but he found her silence oddly disturbing. Did she doubt him? The idea rankled. He was not some green, callow youth, but a seasoned campaigner. He was more than capable of taking care of both himself and her. And so she would learn.

"Where could your father have hidden the Imperial Star?" Andrea looked up at him, her brow creased in her concern. "Do you realize, I don't even know how big it is!"

"Not very. The icon itself is about twelve inches high and not as wide, perhaps eight inches or so. Then it has a frame, made out of gold and set solid with jewels. That adds about three inches all around. Deep, too, as I remember. I've only seen it a couple of times." He chewed on his lower lip, thinking. "It's too large to slip between books."

"Where is the last place you'd think to look for it?"

He smiled. "Somewhere in the open, I suppose, staring at us. But I can't think of any reason why he should have hidden it in the first place. I'll swear he didn't know its potential significance. When he showed it to me, he was like a child with a new toy."

"A new toy," Andrea repeated. "I wonder if—"

"What?"

"I'm not sure. Was he a collector?"

"Not in the sense I am. No, it fascinated him. It was the piece itself that mattered."

"Then he probably hid it where he could get at it easily, to look at it," Andrea decided.

"His room? His study? I've gone through them both."

"Did he have a retreat? Somewhere he went to be

320

alone? The folly near the lake, perhaps?"

"No." Richard slowed the horses for a curve, than whipped them up again. "He hated that place, said it was always damp or drafty."

Andrea sighed. "Well, we'll just have to go over the Court, room by room. Shall we start in the attics or the basement?"

That drew an appreciative chuckle from him. "If we do it that way, the war will end of its own accord by the time we're done. The Court is a regular rabbit warren!"

He glanced down at her, suddenly feeling ready for anything. She stimulated his mind, brought excitement and enjoyment to a potentially boring and exacting task. "We'll find it—together," he said, then wondered if he meant more than the Imperial Star.

She looked up and met his gaze. Her own held an infinite sadness that made him want to pull her into his arms and kiss it away. He touched her cheek and the thought occurred to him that a man could become lost in her huge brown eyes and never want to find his way free.

She tensed; then he, too, heard the eerie creaking sound.

"M'lord!" The groom shouted from behind, but it was too late.

Richard hauled in on the pair as the curricle's shaft snapped cleanly in two. The near horse reared, pulling his companion sideways, but the carriage shot straight until the harness leathers snapped it about. It teetered on the off wheel, then crashed on its side.

Richard was thrown hard to the side of the road and landed sprawled against the trunk of a tree with Andrea beneath him. A blinding, piercing pain shot through his head and he lost consciousness.

Chapter 24

Andrea groaned. Every part of her ached. The last thing she wanted to do was open her eyes, but something touched her forehead, stroking . . . She lay on something sharp—a rock? It didn't seem reasonable. The curricle—there had been an accident! Her lids fluttered open and she groaned again with the pain this simple action caused.

"Lie still." Richard's deep, gentle voice sounded only inches from her ear.

Everything about her blurred, but a few things, at least, began to make sense. She lay on the ground, her head cushioned in Richard's lap. The large blob of dark near them must be the overturned curricle, the bleary movement was the groom unharnessing the horses, and the problem with her vision was all too familiar.

"I've lost my contacts."

"Your what?"

Andrea sighed. "Little pices of plas—glass that fit over my eyes. They work like glasses—spectacles. I'm blind as a bat without them." She dragged herself up into a sitting position and looked around, wishing she could see anything, at any range, clearly. "They've got to be here somewhere!"

"Little pieces of glass," Richard repeated. "Good God, you don't really put anything like that in your eyes, do you?"

"I have to. Otherwise everything's a blur."

"That's hardly surprising, under the circumstances. Why don't you lie down until your head clears? You'll feel better shortly."

She shook her head, wincing at a pain at the base of her neck. "I only wish that would do it. Are you going to help or not?"

He regarded her skeptically. "What do these things look like? Are they colored or clear?"

"Brown, but so faint it's hardly worth counting. Damn it! Of all things to lose!"

A short, uncertain laugh escaped him. "We have just come through a pretty bad accident and that's all you can think about?"

"Well, how would you feel if you couldn't see a blasted thing?"

The groom approached and Richard stood and brushed off his buckskins. "I fear I must leave you to search alone for a moment."

Andrea closed her eyes, then winced. Yes, there was one! It had slid sideways but thankfully had not been knocked out. She adjusted it, blinked, and it stayed put. If she used only the one eye, she could make some sense of the world.

She began with a careful examination of her clothes which, from experience, she knew to be her best bet to recover the flimsy lenses. Convinced at last this was not going to be her lucky day, she transferred stiffly to hands and knees and began a painstaking search of the immediate vicinity.

"Any luck?" Richard came up.

"Stay back! You might step on it." She looked up through one eye. "It could be anywhere."

He sighed. "A little piece of glass?" He joined her on the ground.

"It's very thin and tiny. And sort of dish-shaped."

They were silent for several minutes while they searched. The sounds of a carriage approaching reached them and Richard looked up, then stood and strode over to his groom. The vehicle, a post chaise, rounded a corner into sight then slowed as it neared.

The passenger, a middle-aged gentleman of comfortable aspect, let down the window as the vehicle came abreast. "Accident? Can we help?"

"The shaft is broken, but if you could send someone back from the next village, I'd be grateful."

The coachman cleared his throat. "Begging your pardon, sir, but there's a town less than three miles ahead."

The gentleman beamed. "Then could we offer you a lift? Perhaps your good lady—" He broke off as he eyed Andrea, who still groped around in the dirt beside the road.

With creditable effort, Richard kept his amusement at the man's expression under control. "That won't be necessary, thank you. But if they have a posting house, could you warn them we'll be coming?"

The gentleman nodded, still staring in a bemused manner at Andrea. The driver started forward.

"I suppose he'll tell them you're an escaped Bedlamite," Richard informed Andrea in a purely conversational manner. "Do you suppose you could give that up, or would you care to continue your search while I take one of the horses and ride ahead?" He offered his hand.

She took it and came unsteadily to her feet. "I hurt all over," she sighed. "And being able to see with only one eye is going to give me the most awful headaches. How does someone go about getting spectacles around here?"

His shoulders shook with repressed laughter. "I'm

sure we'll be able to find you something in Bath. Is your sight really that bad?"

"Worse. I can make things out approximately three feet from my face. Anything either closer or farther is—" She broke off. His shoulders still shook, and something sparkled in the westering sunlight that shone on the breast of his olive-green riding coat. With a cry of delight, she pounced on him. "You've got it!"

Fascinated, he watched as she extricated the tiny piece of brownish plastic from the fibers of his coat.

Lacking any other method of cleaning it, she licked it, then carefully placed it back in her eye. She blinked, then sighed in relief. "Thank heavens! Remind me to get an emergency pair of glasses made up. I don't think I could bear going through this again."

The lurking amusement had died from his expression as he watched these proceedings, and the look he directed at her held a wealth of speculative misgivings. Abruptly, he strode over to the groom, who Andrea could now see had been freeing one of the horses from the harness.

"He seems a might mettlesome, m'lord." The groom tossed the long reins over the animal's back and it sidled uneasily.

"Can't be helped, Samuel. No, I'll go. Keep an eye on Miss Wells, please. I'll send a carriage back for her."

With an athleticism that drew Andrea's admiration, he grabbed fistfuls of mane and swung himself up onto the back of the rangy bay. It spun, rolling its eyes at this unaccustomed assault, but quieted under the steady hold. Taking the ribbons in his hand, Richard looped up the long ends that dangled down to the ground and urged the recalcitrant animal forward. In another moment, they trotted down the road with only an occasional crow hop to mar their progress.

Samuel tied the other horse to a tree, then set about righting the curricle. Since the verge sloped down toward the road and the carriage was light, designed for racing, he soon had it swaying. Andrea dusted herself off and went to his aid, and shortly they had it back on its wheels.

"Thank 'e, miss." Samuel eyed her in uncertainty. In his experience, ladies of quality did not help with such work.

Andrea ignored the censorious look. "Do you think it's damaged?"

He subjected the undercarriage to a thorough examination. When he crawled out at last, he seemed satisfied. "It'll do," was all he said.

Andrea climbed into the vehicle to wait in comparative comfort.

In a surprisingly short time, a post chaise came down the road toward them, followed by a cart driven by a man whose rough garb and sinewy muscles gave him every appearance of a blacksmith. Both vehicles passed them, but only far enough to find room to turn about. They drew to a stop just behind the curricle. Samuel transferred the luggage to the chaise and saw Andrea safely into this vehicle. As she was driven off, she turned to see the groom and the blacksmith examining the broken shaft.

At the second fork of the road, the carriage took the branch to the left. In less than half a mile, they reached the outskirts of a sizable village. The post chaise pulled into the wide yard of a peaceful inn and an ostler hurried forward to let down the steps for Andrea. Richard came out, followed by a beaming, elderly man she took to be the owner.

"They will put you up for the night."

"And you?" She took Richard's arm and allowed him to lead her into the dark, cool interior.

"There is another hostelry, just up the road. I'll stay there."

A wave of disappointment swept over her. "It—"

"It is very necessary," he informed her in an undervoice. "There is no private parlor here, so you will have dinner in your room. Is that understood?"

She stuck her tongue out at him.

He appeared to struggle with his amusement, but his frown won out. "You may not take it seriously, but I must. Now, for once, do as you're told. I am going to see about the curricle."

There was little Andrea could do. She followed the innkeeper's wife up the stairs to a cozy little bedchamber. Giving this a cursory once-over, she caught sight of herself in a mirror, and at once set to work smoothing her ruffled curls and removing stray twigs and leaves from her hair and clothing.

The evening stretched before her, long and boring with nothing to do. Richard might at least have come to dine with her, she fumed. But, of course, he would not. His instinctive chivalry was as deep-rooted as it was, in her opinion, misplaced. She finished her meal in solitary state but could not bear the prospect of remaining indoors without so much as a book or a deck of cards with which to play solitaire.

She unpacked her shawl, donned her walking boots, and set forth to explore the surrounding area. Her rambling not unnaturally followed the lane, and after a while she emerged onto the main road. She turned and strolled back the way they had come. It was only seven-thirty; it would stay light for well over an hour and she needed the exercise to stretch out her bruised muscles.

A carriage approached, the horses held to a sedate trot. Through the window she caught a glimpse of a lady dozing peacefully to the gentle bouncing of the well-sprung body. Rapid hoofbeats came from behind and she turned to watch a stagecoach bearing down on the first vehicle. It passed without so much as a check, but a gentleman seated on the roof waved cheekily to her.

327

Andrea sighed and turned around. Apparently, a lady did not walk by herself along a post road. Another lesson she would rather not learn.

Had a female no freedoms? she wondered. The restrictions of this society became increasingly irksome. She would give a great deal to exchange her shawl for a Pendleton wool shirt and a backpack, and her dainty walking boots for a pair of Reeboks. And instead of that stuffy inn, perhaps she could stay at a hiker's hostel where the conversation would be in at least five different languages, and if couples paired off to seek diversion within their sleeping bags, no one would even blink. And while she was at it, what she wouldn't give for a Bartles and James Premium Berry! And a hot dog, with lots of mustard and onions and potato salad. And a huge dill slice!

She checked the thought. She couldn't miss such ridiculous things! She had wanted to live in this elegant time, attend elegant parties, wear elegant gowns, and be courted by elegant gentlemen. But the truth was, she was elegant ed out.

The sounds of more hoofbeats approaching from behind sent her hurrying off the road to partial concealment in the shrubbery. A large traveling chariot barreled past, bouncing with alarming force to the team's brisk canter. A crest, emblazoned on the panel, proclaimed the passenger's nobility.

Andrea stared in disbelief. She knew the crest, and the passenger she glimpsed through the window was none other than the Earl of Malverne. She straightened up. But why had he left town, and in such obvious haste? Because she and Richard were en route to the Court? He could have been ordered to follow them! Malverne Castle was located near enough to provide the perfect place for someone wishing to keep a surreptitious eye on doings at Greythorne. Richard, she decided, should be told of this at once.

By the time she neared the village once more, she had reached the conclusion that Regency bootmakers did not understand the mechanics of the foot and arch. Her feet were killing her, and blisters formed over the toes of her left foot. She was intimately acquainted with every stitch of the top seam.

Limping slightly, she made her way past the sparse selection of shops and buildings until she saw the other inn. The curricle lay in the yard, the shaft removed. Richard stood with his groom and two men she didn't recognize as they fitted a new piece of wood into place.

"Cut through?" Richard knelt to examine the broken piece that lay on the ground. A deep frown marred his brow.

"What do you mean?" Andrea strode up to him, forgetting her hurting feet.

He looked up, displeased. "What are you doing here?"

"What a delightful greeting. I've been for a walk. But never mind that. What do you mean 'cut through'?"

He took a deep breath as she sank down at his side. "You're like to ruin your gown."

She threw him a scathing look. "Don't try to fob me off. What happened?"

He pointed to unmistakable saw marks that sliced more than halfway into the shaft. The only miracle was that it had not broken the rest of the way sooner.

Andrea stood slowly. "It was done on purpose," she whispered. Her gaze flew to his steady expression. "But why?"

He took her arm. "Come, I'm going to walk you back to your inn." He led her out of the yard.

"Someone tried to kill you!" She hung back, staring at him in horror. But it was too soon . . .

"Oh, no, I shouldn't think so. Too chancy. As you see, we're all right except for a few bruises."

329

"Then slow you down? Keep you from reaching the Court?"

"Possibly."

He urged her forward and she realized she had come to a halt. She resumed walking. "We're not the the only ones going that way."

It was his turn to stop. "What do you mean?" She told him about Malverne's carriage and his lips tightened. "Did he see you?"

"No. I . . . I kept out of sight." She covered his hand with her own. "You should be safe enough for tonight, but—do be careful. Whoever it was might very well have meant murder."

A warm glow lit the depths of his troubled eyes. "I'll be all right. Now, go inside and stay there." He remained where he was, watching, until the door closed behind her.

It took the better part of the morning for a wheelwright to repair several cracked spokes which had escaped the groom's examination of the night before. They at last set forth for the Court just after luncheon. Richard whipped up the rested pair and they made excellent progress, yet it was not until early evening that they finally turned onto the drive leading to Greythorne.

Richard reined to a stop before the house and turned to Andrea. Before he could speak, the front door was thrown wide and the butler hurried forth.

"My lord!"

Andrea drew closer to Richard, aware only of the usually calm butler's agitation.

Richard muttered something under his breath. "What is it, Prindle?"

"My lord, I was on the verge of sending for you! Housebreakers!"

Richard met Andrea's startled glance with a slight shake of his head. "When?" He jumped to the ground and tossed his reins to Samuel.

330

"Last night, my lord." Prindle almost wrung his hands in his distress. "They don't seem to have taken anything, but the undergroom is certain he saw someone in the bushes again today."

Richard came around and held up a hand to assist Andrea down. "Have you contacted the sheriff?"

"Of course, my lord." With a visible effort, Prindle pulled himself back together. "I sent the undergroom at once."

Richard nodded. "Very well, then. Have Miss Wells's room prepared."

Andrea joined him and they started for the house. "Could it have been—?"

"No." He cut her off. "Malverne could not have reached the Castle until the early hours of the morning. Most likely, he spent the night on the road."

"It would be interesting to find out," Andrea murmured, not wanting to give up on such a likely prospect.

They went inside.

"The first thing to do is start a systematic search." Richard headed straight for his bookroom and Andrea followed. She sank into a chair beside the long windows. Prindle entered a moment later, bearing a tray on which two decanters and glasses rested. Richard, familiar with Andrea's unconventional ways by now, rejected the lemonade out of hand and poured sherry for her.

"We might as well begin in here," she suggested.

"Why not? Dinner won't be ready for some time yet." He drained his glass and went to work.

After an hour of thorough and fruitless search, Andrea sat back on her heels and ran a dusty hand through the unruly curls that kept creeping into her eyes. "I don't think he put it in this bookcase," she announced judiciously. Every volume had been taken out and lay in haphazard and wobbly stacks on the floor. Every inch of paneling had been tested for hollow compartments and every carving pressed, pulled, and twisted to discover possible hidden-door mechanisms.

Richard eyed the mess with disfavor. "I suppose we had better put it all back." His voice lacked enthusiasm.

"But of course. We'll need places to put everything from the next shelves." Andrea rose and brushed off her hands. "Do you think we should—"

She broke off, for the unmistakable sounds of arrival reached them from the hall beyond. Richard held up his hand, then crept up to the heavy door and pressed his ear against it. Andrea, from experience, could have told him how pointless such an undertaking could be, but she let it pass. Nervous, she crept up beside him and gripped his arm. He abandoned his attempt to hear in a moment and simply opened the door a crack and looked out.

"Oh, my God!" He threw it wide. "Bella, what the devil are you doing here?"

"Richard! I came as soon as I could. You can have no notion how disobliging some people can be, I promise you! But Prindle tells me you only just arrived yourselves. Tell me, how can that be?"

He sighed, threw a speaking, half-comic glance at Andrea, and ushered his sister into the room. As he started to close the door once more, Giles entered the hall from outside. Richard groaned. "You, too?"

Giles grinned and strode down the hall to join them. "Did you really think you could leave me out of this?" He looked about the bookroom, which still bore eloquent testimony to their search. "Good, you're not wasting any time. Any progress yet?"

"We removed a spider." Andrea returned to her seat and tried not to look daggers at her unwanted chaperone.

"But you have not told me what happened," Bella protested.

"Curricle accident." Richard caught Andrea's eye.

"What? Don't tell me you overturned it?" Giles accepted the wine Richard offered and strolled over to pick up one of the stacked books to leaf through it.

"I'll tell you about it later." He turned to his sister. "You may be very sure I took every precaution possible to protect Miss Wells from any breath of scandal."

Bella hugged his arm. "Of course you did. And that is why I came so quickly. I knew you would have need of me. Though it was so very brave of you, dear Andrea, not to let him come down here on his own like that. I cannot tell you how grateful I am to you."

Andrea managed a brilliant, artificial smile. "I knew it was what you would want me to do."

Bella beamed at her. "My dearest friend! I—" She broke off and glanced at Richard, who had snorted and seemed to be having difficulty pouring wine.

He met her inquisitive glance with a bland stare and handed her a glass. "There was really no need to rush down here, you know."

"But, Richard, there was every reason! A Russian colonel called, wanting to speak to you!" She nodded, triumphant to have startled her brother. "He said it was most urgent."

Richard met Giles's arrested look. "I think, perhaps we had better take steps to secure the house tonight. Even more than usual. Andrea, Bella, why do you not go upstairs and change for dinner? It cannot now be long delayed."

Andrea nodded, took Bella by the arm, and led her inexorably out. She would find out later what Richard had in mind. That he didn't want to frighten his sister was obvious.

Back in the Rose Room, she was relieved to discover that Bella's sense of propriety had involved bringing their abigails. Lily stood beside the valises, shaking out a gown. Others already hung in the cupboard. With her maid's help, Andrea scrambled into an evening dress, then ran down the stairs.

Richard and Giles were no longer in the bookroom; they must have gone upstairs to change, as well. But on the desk lay two pistols and a wooden box containing balls and powder. Andrea slipped out and closed the door firmly behind her. In a way, she almost wished there was a third gun. It would make her feel a lot safer if she could hold one. But since she had never so much as picked one up before, it might not be as safe as she hoped.

She was not to have the questionable joy of finding out. Dinner passed peacefully enough, though several times during the meal the elderly Prindle stopped serving, posed in a dramatic fashion with one hand cupping his ear, and tilted his head to listen. On each occasion, the younger footman set down his tray and ran to the window to peer out into the darkness where Prindle had set the groom and his assistant to patroling the grounds. Several comments sprang to Andrea's mind about being a castle under siege, but her ready smile faded and they remained unspoken. That was exactly the case.

They were not, in fact, invaded until well after dinner, and then in a manner that vastly disappointed the undergroom, who had armed himself with a fowling piece. Richard had called a halt for the night to their exhausting search and the party had returned to the Gold Saloon where the tea tray awaited them. As Bella poured out a cup for Giles, the unmistakable sounds reached them of a carriage pulling up on the gravel drive before the house.

Richard sat up, alert, his gaze meeting Giles's over Andrea's head. Giles reached suggestively for his bulging pocket and Richard nodded.

"If you will excuse us a moment?" He rose and Giles followed. A loud knock sounded on the door and Richard raised surprised eyebrows. "Whoever it is, they are taking the direct approach."

"That doesn't make them any less dangerous." Giles murmured the words, but Andrea overheard.

Richard waited as the sound of Prindle's stately tread approached. The door opened and the butler announced: "The Earl of Malverne." He stepped back to allow the visitor to enter.

Richard relaxed and withdrew his hand from his coat pocket. It sagged outward from the weight of the pistol that remained within. "I did not expect to see you down here." Richard kept his tone purely conversational.

Malverne, unusually pale, darted an uneasy glance about the room and did not even bother to acknowledge the presence of the ladies. His frightened gaze returned to Richard and he looked him over as if seeking some sign of injury.

"You're all right," he breathed in relief. With an obvious effort, he mastered his voice. "I beg of you, sell me the Imperial Star. For both our sakes."

Richard shook his head. "I am not so craven. I intend to see this thing through."

Malverne appeared to sag. He drew out his handkerchief and mopped his brow. From an inner pocket of his coat, he pulled a folded document. He hesitated, as if debating within himself, then handed it to Richard. "I . . . I think you had better read this."

Richard looked at him through narrowed eyes, then opened the three crisp sheets. Giles, unashamedly, peered over his shoulder. Andrea glanced at Bella, who sat stiffly, the teapot still clasped in her hand. Andrea's throat constricted. She already knew what those pages would say.

Richard lowered them at last and stared directly at Andrea. "I don't believe it."

Malverne turned away and his complexion darkened

335

alarmingly. "That . . . that's your father's signature. You can't deny that."

Andrea went to Richard and took his arm. "I had nothing to do with it!" she whispered. "I just knew."

Richard's fingers crushed the pages in his angry grip. "I don't believe it," Richard repeated, but it was Malverne at whom he stared, hard.

"What is it?" Bella's voice trembled. "Richard, what is the matter?"

"In effect, this is a sales document, purportedly signed by our father. It exchanges Greythorne Court for the Imperial Star."

"What?" The pot dropped from her shaking hand and broke into several large pieces. Tea ran out over the Aubusson carpet, unheeded. "Richard!" She looked at her capable brother, expecting him to do something on the instant.

"Ring for a maid," he advised, deliberately misinterpreting her plea. "Why haven't you brought this out before? I know damned well my father practically beggared himself to buy that blasted icon, but he never said a word about this!"

Malverne shrank back a step under his host's anger. "He . . . he never paid the full price. As it says, if he didn't come up with the rest of the money within two years, the Court stood as collateral. But—" He broke off, retreating another step from the savageness of Richard's expression. His hands trembled where they rested now on the back of a chair. "But he . . . he provided for you. It says—you can see it, there, at the end—that his heirs should be permitted to live at the Court for two hundred years at a very low rent."

"This has been forged, damn it, and you know it! My father would never have made up any such document."

Malverne ran his tongue over his dry lips. "You . . . you would never be able to prove it. Grantham, for God's

336

sake," he begged, and there was no trace of irreverence in his voice. "Just give me the Imperial Star and let us be done with it. It's the only way!"

The blood drained from Andrea's face, leaving her chilled. This was all happening, exactly as history said it would. She couldn't change a thing! They were trapped, all of them, with no way out. They had no choice, they had to play this deadly game to its tragic end—at the cost of Richard's life.

Chapter 25

Richard gained no more information from Malverne. Abandoning the attempt at last, he escorted the shaken earl to the front door. Andrea followed them into the hall and waited while Malverne made one last, desperate plea for the Imperial Star. Then she strode quickly up to Richard as he turned back. He looked up and his solemn gaze came to rest on her.

"I had nothing to do with that sales document, Richard. Please believe me." She took a tentative step toward him, holding out her hand, afraid of his angry rejection.

He went to her and folded her gently into his arms. The embrace lacked any passion, but she found it reassuring.

"I do believe you. You couldn't do anything to hurt us. It simply isn't in you." He kissed the top of her curls. "You just have fey spells where knowledge comes to you. I've heard about it. I've just never known anyone before who experienced them."

"Richard, it's—"

"No!" With unusual vehemence, he stopped her explanation. "You have fey spells. I can accept that. Let's leave it that way."

She leaned her head against his broad chest and closed

338

her eyes. It was enough. He didn't spurn her, and that was all that mattered.

The search for the Imperial Star began in earnest the following morning. Giles, Bella, Richard, and Andrea all started in the attics, but each took a different room. They searched every trunk, every inch of wall, every possible hiding place the chambers might have to offer. Not until one o'clock did they take a rest, when they met in the breakfast parlor for a light nuncheon.

"It is hopeless!" Bella sank her head into hands newly cleansed from dust. "The Court is too big, we will never find that horrid icon."

"Not hopeless, just a challenge." Giles attempted a smile, but exhaustion wore on him also.

"We're not giving up." Richard fixed a compelling eye on his companions. "We are not handing over either the Court or the Imperial Star to Malverne! We are going to find it and settle this business ourselves. Now, let's get back to it. Would you rather work in pairs? It might be less depressing to have company." He rose and looked at Andrea. "Coming?" He gave her an encouraging smile. "The search will seem to go twice as fast this way."

Andrea stood and followed him from the room. She would search, but in her heart she was certain they would not find the icon. Still, Richard's company would make the drudgery of their work worthwhile.

They were not disturbed until late that afternoon. Andrea, kneeling on the floor in an attic at the front of the house, heard the crunch of gravel below through the open windows. Richard peered out, then turned on his heel and strode from the tiny room. Andrea scrambled up and hurried after.

"Richard!" Bella emerged from the next door. "It is that Colonel Palitov, the one who visited me in London!"

Richard slowed down and drew a deep breath. His fingers unclenched. "Not an invasion at all, then. Relief forces?" He threw a reassuring glance at Andrea and went down the stairs two at a time.

Andrea followed, but to her fury, Richard closeted himself in his bookroom with his visitor and firmly excluded the others. Andrea, Giles, and Bella stood in the hall, just outside.

"I could go in there, as a representative of the government." Giles eyed the door with undisguised longing.

"That might be the last thing the colonel wants." Andrea sighed. "If he can settle this, with just Richard, it would make everything so much easier for him."

"He can't stop us from listening at the keyhole." Bella suited action to words. A moment later she straightened up, a look of disgust on her pretty face. "They have left the key in the lock!"

"We will do more good if we continue the search." Andrea started back toward the stairs and the other two reluctantly followed her.

It was almost three quarters of an hour later when Andrea, half submerged in the last cupboard the attics boasted, heard Richard's steady footfall coming up the steps. She jumped, banged her head on the low ceiling, and muttered an indelicate word as she emerged.

"Well?" She turned to face him. With one hand, she probed the bruise and winced as she found it.

"Palitov wanted to buy the icon, too. But at least he believes that I don't know where it is." He looked grim and sounded tired.

Andrea's heart went out to him. Dear God, this really was going to be the death of him. She held out her arms, and he wrapped her in his solid embrace. Leaning his cheek against the top of her head, he held her tight. She ordered herself not to cry, but the tears welled up in her eyes and her shoulders trembled, betraying her.

"No, Andrea, it's not hopeless." He whispered the

soothing words against her curls. "We'll come out of this all right, you'll see. Everything will be all right."

She swallowed in an attempt to force back a sob. "Tell . . . tell me the truth. What did he say? What is going to happen now?"

His fingers caressed her waist. "You are not to mention this to Bella. Palitov fears that since Malverne has failed, we may have the French agents on our doorstep at any time. No." One arm wrapped tighter about her shoulders and he kissed her forehead. "We've had them here already. I don't think we need worry until after we find the Imperial Star. Everyone must know by now that we have no idea where it is. They'll wait. We're safe." He did not add "for now," but the unspoken words hung in the air between them.

"Did . . . did he say anything about the tsar's forming that alliance with France?" She felt his cheek, roughened by afternoon stubble, move against her forehead as he nodded.

"The tsar is none too friendly with Napoleon, but it seems that icon is of more importance to him. He will ally himself with anyone to get it back. Have you finished here?"

Reluctantly, Andrea returned to the task at hand. They completed the cupboard in minutes, then went down the steps—searching every inch as they went—and began at the back of the house on the next floor. Holland covers shrouded every piece of furniture and dust filled the air as they pulled these free. Andrea went off in a fit of sneezing and Richard threw the windows wide.

"I'll have to have the unused rooms cleaned more often."

"At least once a century." She looked around, let out a heartfelt sigh, and went to work on a huge old trunk that had probably not been opened since the time of the Pretender.

"What an awful fuss to be made over one icon, even if it is jewel-encrusted and belonged to Catherine the Great." She pulled out a selection of moth-eaten shawls and placed them in a pile on the floor at her side. "It couldn't possibly be worth so much trouble. Nothing could."

"And don't forget that the tsar hates Napoleon," Richard told her, grinning at her disgusted expression. "He refused permission for him to marry his young sister only months ago."

"And Napoleon has just married Marie Louise. Why would the tsar ally Russia with France now?"

Richard shook his head, but made no other answer. He dragged a chest away from the wall and proceeded to sound it for secret panels.

Andrea frowned. "What can be so important about the Imperial Star? Unless, of course, it holds the key to something even more important, like the location of a priceless fortune."

"Now, *that* we could use." Richard abandoned his methodical tapping and turned his attention to an ancient bureau.

Something tugged at the fringes of her memory. Something about a fortune. The Imperial Star—but not the icon. Only it had nothing to do with this period of history. Or had it?

She sat up, dropping an armload of brocaded gowns that dated back to Queen Anne. "Richard. Have you ever heard of the Imperial Star?"

He turned to regard her in exasperation. "No, of course not. I'm looking through these moldy old relics for my health. What did you think?"

"No, not the icon. The *other* Imperial Star. The diamond necklace."

"Yes." He said the word slowly, drawing the syllable out. "What about it?"

342

"Has anyone actually seen it in the past few years?"

"What are you suggesting? It's not missing, is it? Colonel Palitov never mentioned it."

"But don't you see?" She sank down before him where he sat on the edge of a rickety chair while he went through a drawer. "I don't think it's the icon the tsar wants, but the necklace. Have you ever heard the legends about it? About the luck it brings?"

He regarded her with patent amusement. "It hasn't brought *us* luck, if you're implying that *we* have it."

She felt chilled. "No. It . . . it hasn't. But that could still be the answer." She closed her eyes, trying to remember details. "You said the frame on the icon was unusual, didn't you? That it was very thick? Would it have been thick enough to hide a diamond necklace inside?"

"It might. But that necklace is in the possession of the Empress Mother of Russia."

"As far as you know. And until it was stolen, so was the icon. And fifty years from now, the necklace will be reported missing."

"Damn it, Andrea, not now!" He clasped her hands between his own. "No more of these premonitions of yours! I need you, sane and normal." He folded her into his arms, holding her close, almost suffocating her with a grip too tight to let her lungs expand.

"Damn you," he said softly, this time without rancor. His arms slacked enough for her to gasp a breath. "Very well. Catherine had the frame built for the icon, and she named that necklace after it." He looked down at her, his brow deeply furrowed. "What can you remember about the diamonds?"

Andrea wracked her mind. "Not much. Catherine Kendall—sorry, a friend—told me a little. It was given to Catherine the Great by one of her lovers, who paid a king's ransom for it. It had the reputation of bringing

343

luck and love to anyone who possessed it—unlike other diamonds, which bring catastrophes. I don't think there was ever a single murder or curse associated with it. Just happiness."

Richard's lips brushed her forehead. "I've found that, at least. Maybe we do have it stowed away in the icon, after all. But we'll never know until we find it." He released her. An odd light lingered in his eyes, but he returned to the bureau without another word.

Reluctantly, Andrea went back to the trunk. She removed another brocaded gown, but her brain still whirled, far from the search. She barely noticed when the door to the room opened.

Prindle entered and gave a respectful cough that drew the attention of both occupants. "Excuse me, Miss Wells. Miss Letitia Moreland has called and desires to speak with you. I have shown her into the Gold Saloon."

"Oh, dear. Richard . . . ?" Andrea looked at him in consternation.

"So she followed Malverne. Well, well," he mused. "Go ahead. This should prove interesting."

"Is Bella—Mrs. Brixton . . . ?" Andrea looked hopefully at Prindle.

"Miss Letitia asked to speak with only you, miss. Alone."

Puzzled, Andrea made her way down the stairs and found her visitor pacing about the room, a haunted expression on her lovely face. She clutched a long, thick wooden box between her hands. Tears of relief sprang to the girl's eyes as she saw Andrea.

"Oh, I am so glad you could spare me a moment! I must speak to you!"

"Of course." Andrea looked back into the hall, saw Prindle, who had followed her down the stairs, and sent him for refreshment. Taking Lettie by the arm, she found the girl trembled. She led her to a couch and obliged her

344

to take a seat. "What has happened to distress you?" She kept her voice calm only with serious effort.

Lettie let out a ragged sigh. "You . . . you are so sensible, dear Andrea. I do wish I had your spirit! But I do not, and I am so a-afraid!" Her voice broke on a sob and she buried her face in a scented handkerchief.

Andrea sat quietly at her side while the girl wept, and wished she was possessed of half the sangfroid with which she was credited. "Now, take a deep breath," she advised as the storm abated somewhat. "And tell me. What may I do for you?"

Large tear-filled blue eyes rose to meet hers. "I . . . I have come to you because you are the only person I can trust!" she exclaimed in high drama. "I cannot stay long, for I have left without telling the Dragoness, and you know how angry she will be if I do not return soon. But you must keep this for me!" She thrust the box over.

Andrea accepted it into reluctant hands. At first glance, it closely resembled a case for a set of dueling pistols. Exquisitely wrought in cherrywood, the corners were protected with pierced metal clips. She ran a hand over it, noting that it was locked and the key not attached. Could it . . . But no, it was not big enough to hold the icon as Richard had described it.

"Do not let any harm come to it, I beg of you!" Lettie pleaded.

"What is in it? No, do not cry, Lettie, of course I will keep it. But is it valuable? Should I lock it away somewhere or—or place it in a safe?" Were there such things at this time? Andrea realized she had no idea.

"It is only papers, but they mean my very life!" Lettie broke down into sobs once more.

"Lettie," Andrea began sternly, then broke off, staring at the box in dawning horror. Lettie was Malverne's ward. Could she have found information regarding the Court or the Imperial Star? If so, her life could very

345

well be in danger!

"Lettie," she repeated, though this time she spoke in anxiety. "Does . . . does anyone know what you have here?"

She shook her head firmly. "I stole them when my guardian was not there. They are the proof that will protect me! Please, Andrea, keep them for me!"

"But . . . should we not take them to Richard? If this can stop a war—" She broke off, seeing the shock and confusion in the pansylike face across from her. She was wrong. It had nothing to do with the Imperial Star. Then what, she wondered, was in the box?

"No! Oh, no, it is nothing like that. It concerns no one but me. Oh, pray, do not ask questions I dare not answer!"

"Of . . . of course not." Andrea agreed weakly. For a moment, she had been sure that she held at least part of the solution to their troubles in her hand, but it transpired that all she held was another mystery.

"Dear Andrea, will you hold these safe for me until I need them?" Lettie looked up at her, fluttering damp eyelashes in a beseeching look.

"Yes." Andrea still felt dazed. How safe could anything be in this house, though, with all the strange goings on? She did not voice this thought aloud and Lettie, considerably relieved to have discharged her errand, made a hurried departure, leaving Andrea staring helplessly at the wooden box.

It defied speculation. Absolutely any sort of paper at all might rest within. Or was it just papers? She gave the box a speculative shake but could hear nothing that might indicate the rattling of a diamond necklace. No, just papers. Only the key would release its secrets, and that she did not possess. She went to her room to lock the box away in her dresser drawer.

This task completed, she went out into the corridor

and paused. There was one place she wanted to search—and very badly. She felt drawn there, wanting to see it again so much she could barely withstand the temptation. And why not? Everyone was still on the floor above, and it was, really, the most logical choice.

She hurried down the hall and into the next wing, where the master's bedchamber lay. Before it had been Richard's, it had been his father's. What more likely hiding place? She slipped inside, looked to make sure his valet did not lurk in the dressing room, then gazed slowly about the room that was so hauntingly familiar. It had been many months since she last stood in here. Many eventful months. And this time her purpose was not a journey through time, but to find the Imperial Star—possibly *both* Imperial Stars.

Any dresser or cupboard might contain a secret compartment, though she knew Richard had already subjected these to a thorough search. Her attention centered on the bed. It had been her idea to hide it somewhere in the massive frame for Catherine Kendall to find. Perhaps Richard's father had thought of the same place, where it would constantly be under his eye.

The door opened behind her and she spun about, guilty.

Richard stopped, startled, then crossed the great chamber to join her. "I see we had the same idea. There is so much wood around the base and supporting canopy. It's the one place I haven't tried yet."

"Then shall we?" She dragged her gaze from his face with reluctance and instead regarded the great four-poster, considering. "Where do we start, the top or the base?"

They began on the carpeted steps that led up to the dais. While they worked, Andrea told him of Lettie's odd visit and the wooden box. Richard sat back, frowning, his eyes staring past Andrea without seeing her.

"Papers. In a box." He shook his head. "Now, what

347

the deuce could she have found that would be of such importance?"

"She wouldn't tell me."

"Well, perhaps if we find the icon, it won't matter. I have this feeling that everything strange that has happened of late is tied up with it, in one way or another."

They continued to search the steps. Hiding places abounded, but no one had taken advantage of a single one of them. Satisfied at last that the icon did not lie concealed there, Richard began on the footboard while Andrea kicked off her slippers and crawled to the top of the bed to examine the carved headboard.

This completed, she sat back with a sigh. "Not here. I'm running out of ideas."

"Are you?" A strange, husky note colored Richard's voice. "I'm not." He strolled around and sat on the edge near her.

Andrea settled amid the pillows. "The canopy?"

He nodded and started to pull off his boots. They wouldn't budge. He muttered, and Andrea jumped to her feet, grinning.

"Here, let me." She accepted his handkerchief, covered her hands with it, and pulled. The boots slid free. "There. Now, do you mind if I walk on your bed?"

His lips twisted into a wry smile. "I can only think of one thing I should like more."

Her lips parted and she forgot to breathe. She took a hesitant step toward him but he abruptly turned about, climbed up onto the mattress and began to examine the posts that supported the heavy canopy frame. So tall was it that the velvet cloth just brushed the top of Richard's dark curls. Andrea swallowed, forced her desires under a semblance of control, and followed suit.

They fell silent, working on opposite ends, studiously concentrating on the job at hand. Slowly, they worked their way around the edges and at last met in the center.

"Nothing." She whispered the word. He was so close, there seemed no point in speaking louder. Hot and cold flashed alternately through her and she tried to force her thoughts away from the breadth of his shoulders and the squareness of the chin that was at eye level for her. "I . . . I don't know what to try next." Her voice, even to herself, sounded throaty.

"Don't you?"

She looked up into eyes where desire no longer merely smoldered. It had fanned into full flame and now burned with a passion that sent heat coursing through her. He pulled her against himself and held her tightly as his mouth found hers. She clung to him, not thinking, not breathing, only reveling in her nearness, in the strength of his hands that roamed over her back. His lips brushed across her cheek, her eyes, back to her mouth, and his hands crept to her sides, where they remained, much to her dismay. She broke their kiss, nipped gently at his chin, then pressed her lips to his throat.

He groaned and pushed her away. "My God, Andrea, you don't know what you're doing to me." He drew her back into his arms, just holding her.

She could feel his inner trembling as he tried to control himself. She pushed back so that she could look up into his face. "I do know. The same thing you're doing to me. I want you, Richard. More than anything."

He tensed, then took her hands in his, using them as a wedge between them. "You don't fully understand. You couldn't."

She disengaged herself, found one end of his neckcloth and gave it a tug. It came loose in her fingers and she unwound it. "I do understand. I was raised very differently from you. Where I come from, a woman is as free as a man to express her . . . her love."

She dropped the cravat onto the coverlet at their feet

349

and went to work on his shirt. He stood stock-still, staring at her. A slight smile played about the corners of her mouth. "Does your door have a key?"

Without a word, he jumped down from the bed, retrieved the needed item from the top of his bureau, and thrust it firmly in the lock. He turned to stare at her, his expression a mixture of wonder and disbelief.

He walked slowly toward her.

She held out her hands and he helped her down from the bed. Once on the floor, she turned around.

"I can't reach the buttons. Will you?" She felt his fingers on the back of her neck, nothing clumsy about it. He must be experienced in such matters, and the thought filled her with jealousy. She would make him forget any lover he had ever taken before.

The soft cambric gown dropped to the floor with a whisper of fabric, and in moments her shift followed. He pulled at the ties to her stays and that restrictive garment, also, fell away. She faced him.

"What now, indeed, my love?" She still whispered, for the simple reason she could not control her voice.

He scooped her up into his arms and sat down with her on the bed, cradling her close. "Now we do a bit of exploring of our own."

Chapter 26

Andrea stood at the window, staring out over the parkland toward the ornamental lake in the distance. The sun rode low in the sky. It must be growing late—at least two hours since she had gone to Richard's chamber to search for the Imperial Star. Warmth rushed through her. It didn't seem possible that the intervening time could have been so perfect.

Richard came up behind her, brushed her curls aside, and kissed the nape of her neck. With deft fingers, he fastened the buttons of her gown, then turned her to face him. Lingering embers of passion shone in his eyes.

"Very nearly respectable, my dearest Andy. No one would ever know." He kissed her, slowly and thoroughly, then held up the comb he had just used to restore his own disheveled hair to order and coaxed her ringlets back into place. "Delightful." He grinned his approval as he looked her over. "And now you may take it all off again to dress for dinner."

This time, when his mouth found hers, he allowed his hands to roam freely over the now familiar contours of her body. Abruptly, he stepped back. "If you don't go now, Bailey will be coming and we'll have a scandal on our hands. And I'd find it very hard to care."

She kissed his chin. "Me, too. But whatever would your poor valet say?"

He grinned. "I'll see you at dinner, my love. And mind you behave yourself. If you look at me like that, I won't answer for the consequences."

Andrea hurried along the halls to her room, rang for Lily, and removed her shoes and stockings once more. When the abigail arrived, she made no comment other than that her mistress was like to be late if she didn't make haste. Andrea did, and went down to the Gold Saloon barely five minutes after the arrival of the others.

Richard looked up as she entered, and the glow in his eyes sent her pulse shooting skyward. Dear God, it seemed impossible that they should *not* give themselves away. If she followed her instincts, she would be in his arms right this second, and damn the consequences.

Fortunately, neither Bella nor Giles was in any mood to notice her flushed cheeks or Richard's constant hovering about her.

"We have accomplished nothing!" Bella accepted a glass of sherry from Giles and glowered at it in disgust. "The whole day has been wasted."

"Oh, I don't know about that." Giles strolled over and settled on the sofa at her side. "You found that trunk filled with your nursery toys that you thought had been lost."

"True." Bella brightened. "What about you two? What great treasures did you discover?"

Andrea choked over her wine and looked down at her glass, fighting a losing battle against the color that surged to her cheeks. If Richard looked at her with that special smile, they would be lost.

He carried his drink over to the fireplace and leaned against the mantel. "Oh, we're no closer to finding the icon, but we did explore some fascinating places."

Andrea's color burned even hotter. "Think of it this

352

way." She rushed into speech. "There are fewer rooms we will have to search tomorrow."

Prindle entered to announce dinner, but as they crossed the hall, the sounds of a carriage pulling up on the gravel drive could be heard. Giles reached for his pocket, which bulged with his pistol. Richard did the same.

"Take Bella to the dining room." Richard just brushed Andrea's cheek with his fingers.

With an effort, she kept herself from kissing them. The ladies left the hall and Prindle opened the front door.

"I wish to speak with Mrs. Brixton! Grantham, what the deuce is going on here?" The aggrieved tenor voice reached them. "I think someone should have told me, really I do."

Bella let out a sigh of relief. "It is only Wilfred." She hurried out to greet her betrothed, and pulled up short just through the door.

Andrea did the same. Wilfred had outdone himself. He took off a driving cloak that boasted upward of a dozen capes to reveal a coat of delicate lavender velvet over a waistcoat that boasted inch-wide stripes of purple, lavender, and white, embroidered overall with silver thread. His pantaloons matched his coat to a shade, as did the clocking in his white stockings. A gleaming amethyst punctuated the pristine ruffles at his throat.

Bella regarded him in disapproval. "For heaven's sake, Wilfred, wherever did you get that waistcoat?"

He spun to face her with all the grace of an opera dancer performing a pirouette. "Bella! I have never, but never, been more upset in my life!"

"Well, I can't say I blame you." Bella shook her head. "It makes you look a positive figure of fun."

Wilfred bristled. "Not my waistcoat, dash it. You!"

"Me? Why, whatever for?"

"You have made me a positive laughingstock!"

"Oh, come now, my dear fellow, I'm sure you didn't need any help from her." Giles propped his shoulder against the wall and regarded Wilfred with open enjoyment.

Wilfred blinked, then raised his quizzing glass, which hung from a purple velvet riband, and regarded Giles through it for a moment. He allowed it to drop and turned back to Bella.

"That," Giles explained in an overly loud aside to Andrea, "is an exquisite example of depressing pretension. I doubt even Grantham himself could do it with greater flourish."

"I shouldn't try," Richard informed him.

Wilfred stiffened but gave no other sign of having heard. "Why did you leave town without telling me?" he demanded of his betrothed.

"But I did. I even asked you to accompany me, and if you will remember, you refused!"

"Well, really, Bella. That's no reason, no reason at all, to go haring off with a man whose reputation with the ladies is less than savory!"

"Do you mean Giles?" Bella demanded, dumbfounded.

Giles straightened up. "I do believe he is jealous. But unsavory? Grantham, do I really have a reputation of being a loose fish? I ask you as a friend."

Richard grinned, a look of unholy amusement lighting his eyes.

"You . . . you are being offensive, Wilfred!" Bella's expressive countenance flushed with her anger.

"I don't think he can help it," Giles stuck in.

Bella ignored him. "I will thank you to apologize to both Mr. Kendall and myself. How absurd, to think it improper that my brother's friend should escort me to my own home!"

"Well, think of me!" Wilfred positively glowered. "I don't enjoy being made to look foolish."

354

"Then why do you persist in wearing your coats with their waists nipped in like that?"

"Isabella!" His tone was that of one deeply shocked. Then his brow cleared, and he nodded. "I see what it is. I've come at a bad time. You're knocked up from the journey, that's what it is. It's put you out of curl. I can't say I'm at all surprised, though, not at all. I told you not to come down here like that. The Dragoness always gives Lettie some evil-smelling potion to drink and it puts her back in twig in a trice. I'll send you over some."

"Can you not join us for dinner?" Richard strolled forward. "I believe it has been waiting these past ten minutes and more."

Wilfred shook his head, missing the sarcasm. "No, I thank you. I must be getting back. My father has gone out somewhere and Lettie is in a taking, poor little thing. I promised I'd play at jack straws with her and keep her company. I'll call on you tomorrow when you're feeling more the thing." He possessed himself of Bella's hand, kissed it, and took his leave.

The front door closed and Bella drew a shaky breath. "Mr.—Giles, I am sorry. The idea that your escorting me could have been the least bit improper is absurd, as . . . as are his accusations against your reputation."

Giles's eyes sparkled in amusement. "I did not take offense, I promise you. And yes, it is absurd. I may be an accomplished flirt, but I am by no means a rake nor loose in the haft." He offered her his arm and led her into the dining room.

Richard's eyes met Andrea's and both grinned. She went to him, and barely stopped in time to prevent herself from walking into his embrace.

"Poor Wilfred." Richard took her arm as if he had been doing it for years.

"Not really." Andrea looked up into his smiling face and felt her heart wrench. "He can go home and let the adoring Lettie smooth his ruffled feathers." Richard's deep, enticing chuckle sent a shiver through her.

"Perfect. I see the end to all our problems."

Andrea checked, then tried to cover her lapse. "Except the Imperial Star."

He squeezed her fingers. "Never fear, we'll find it." He escorted her to her seat, held her chair, then took his own at the head of the table.

When the meal ended, they elected to remain where they were and subject the dining room to a thorough search. Andrea would rather have split up once more, for she wanted desperately to be alone with Richard, not under the eyes of anyone else. They began on opposite sides of the long apartment, first searching the sideboards and beneath the table, then testing for secret panels and possible priest holes. Finally, exhausted, Bella called a halt to their labors for the night and announced her intention to seek her couch.

Andrea followed suit. But when she climbed into her lonely bed and blew out her candle, memories of the afternoon filled her. In exquisite detail, she recalled Richard's caresses, his lips, his body pressing against hers. She ached for him once more. Rolling over, she forced her thoughts from him, from the dizzying sensations he created in her. If she concentrated very hard on her own heartbeat, she could still it, calm her desires, perhaps slip off to sleep.

She had almost succeeded when a slight click announced that someone turned her doorknob. She stiffened and terror flooded through her. Who . . . ? The door opened silently and a dark, shadowy shape inched slowly inside. Andrea froze, afraid to move, to betray she was awake. She had no idea whether the person searched for the Imperial Star or intended her harm. She didn't look forward to finding out.

The figure stopped near her bed and Andrea held her

breath. It moved, and the slippery, whispering sound of brocaded satin reached her ears.

"Andrea?" Richard laid his dressing gown across a chair. He lifted the covers only enough to slide in beside her.

"You scared me!" She turned in the bed to nestle against him. "I thought . . ." She shivered and he held her close.

"No." His lips brushed her forehead. "Unless you thought it was someone come to ravish you. For that is exactly my intention, you know."

And he did, with such tender yet enticing completeness that she clung to him in almost unbearable pleasure.

She did not stir again until the sun streamed into her room through the curtain she left open. She reached across, wanting Richard once more, but her questing hand found only the empty coolness of her pillow. Her eyes flew open and her blurry gaze searched the room. He was gone.

She sat up, holding the coverlet to her, filled with a sense of loss. He must have left early, before he could be detected in her room. A slight smile played about her lips. He had a touching but badly misplaced concern for the proprieties. They had barely two weeks left together.

She shuddered. They didn't have time for such nonsense. Stifling that thought, she groped about on the bed until she found her muslin nightdress and pulled it on.

Bella, all unknowingly, thwarted Andrea's intention to go to Richard's chamber as soon as she was dressed. Her hostess came into her room and sat on the edge of her bed while Lily still did up the buttons on her morning gown.

"I suppose we should search the lower portions of the house this morning." She did not sound enthusiastic.

"Why don't we just continue where we left off yesterday? I don't fancy going down to the chill cellars at the moment." Andrea patted a curl. Though why she should worry about her hair, when she would shortly be covered in cobwebs, she had no idea. Or rather, she did. She wanted Richard to see her at her best, which wasn't easy without makeup.

Accompanied by Bella, she made her way down to the breakfast table. The gentlemen were there before them, most of the way through impressive plates of beefsteak and tankards of ale. Richard looked up, caught Andrea's half-smile, and the light in his eyes could have illuminated the entire room. Andrea looked hastily away and went to the sideboard. At random, she heaped food on her plate.

As soon as the meal ended, they made their way to the Long Gallery, where portraits lined the walls. Unable to stop herself, Andrea paused before the likeness of Richard. She had only seen it twice since going back in time, as her room lay in a different wing. The likeness was magnificent—but as nothing compared to the real man.

"Seems a good place to hide a painting," Richard commented.

Andrea glanced toward him. Yes, the real man was infinitely superior—in every way. Except he would die and the portrait would remain, all that she would have left of him ... But she mustn't let him see the unhappiness that flooded through her at the thought, mustn't ruin the little time they had left together. She summoned up a forced brightness. "À la *The Purloined Letter*?"

"The what?" Richard looked up from where he had knelt on the carpet to examine the paneling.

"Just a principle," she explained. "The best way to hide something is out in the open, where it's too obvious."

He laughed. "Then this is exactly the right place.

Unless—" He broke off, his expression arrested, and stared across at his sister. "The chapel! Come on."

"But of course!" Bella ran after him.

Andrea and Giles exchanged blank looks. She gave an expressive shrug and they followed the other two. Richard led the way down the stairs, through the halls, and into the east wing. They passed through the tower, then emerged into a chamber that made Andrea gasp.

Colored light flooded the chapel from a multitude of stained-glass panels. At one end, light from a rose window shone down on the altar. Andrea entered slowly, awed by the atmosphere of reverence and beauty. A musty smell, as of disuse, filled her nostrils.

"Well?" Richard looked about. "Does anyone see an icon?" They went to work, exploring every inch of paneling.

Bella, from her position on a back pew, peered up at a carved cherub near the ceiling. "Richard! I see something. It's . . ." She cried out as her foot slipped. She teetered, then fell into Giles's arms.

He sat down abruptly on the bench, still holding her safe. For a moment, she stayed where she was, staring into Giles's laughing face with an expression of shock on her own. Soft color flooded her cheeks and she pushed him away.

The smile faded from Giles's lips to be replaced by consternation. Gently, he set her aside and stood, visibly shaken. "I . . . perhaps you had better let me have a look." He took her place and reached along the ledge, probing.

"It seems that your prediction about them might well be coming true." Richard murmured the words in Andrea's ear.

She nodded, risked a look at him, and the joy of their shared love filled her, momentarily crowding out the painful knowledge of his impending death.

Giles found nothing but a cracked rafter board making the protrusion that Bella spotted, and they all returned to their search. Three hours later, disgusted, tired, and very dirty, they trooped back to the main portion of the house.

"Not even a priest hole!" Giles complained. He shook his head. "Well, at least we know the icon wasn't hidden there. Shall we return to the Long Gallery?"

They reached the hall and Prindle hurried toward them. "My lord." He bowed and presented a silver salver on which a sealed note rested.

Richard took it. "Miss Moreland. I wonder what she wants?" He broke it open, scanned the brief message, and handed it to Bella.

She read the contents. "We are all invited to dinner tonight." She looked up at Richard. "A truce?"

"No." Richard shook his head. "Probably just an entertainment for Lettie and Wilfred's sakes."

"How delightful." Bella's tone lacked enthusiasm.

"We could do with the rest," Giles commented.

"An excellent idea. I think you should go." Richard regarded his sister with a mischievous gleam in his eyes.

"Me?" She returned his look with one of suspicion.

He drew his snuff box from his pocket and offered it to Giles. "Certainly. I shall stay and guard the house—and continue the search. It is, after all, of considerable importance. But I see no reason why you should not go."

"But not alone!"

"Certainly not. Giles will escort you to keep you safe on the dangerous journey."

"Andrea?" Bella threw her a speculative look. "Do you know, I think someone should stay here and bear Richard company."

Andrea nodded, ignoring Richard's frown. She felt no need whatsoever to keep their relationship secret.

Thus the problem was settled. They continued their hunt until it was time for Giles and Bella to change for their party. After they departed, Richard and Andrea turned back from the door. His hand closed about hers and he led her to the bookroom and poured her a glass of wine.

"To the evening." He raised his glass, drained it in one swallow, and set it aside. He took hers from her hand and placed it out of his way and drew her, unprotesting, into his arms.

They dined in the breakfast parlor, though she barely tasted the food the butler placed before her. Nothing mattered but Richard, how much she loved him, that he was here, with her, loving her. Life, literally, could hold no more. But there was so little time . . .

"Shall we patrol the grounds before retiring?" He leaned even closer and murmured the words against the hair behind her ear.

He stood, drawing her with him. Arm in arm, they strolled out through the French windows onto the terrace. Moonlight flooded the area, casting deep shadows from the tall shrubs and illuminating the roses. Their gentle aroma filled the air.

Andrea hugged his elbow, storing up one more memory. "It's beautiful out here. Timeless. It's like nothing will ever change."

He kissed her forehead and slipped an arm about her. "I hope it won't. I could get very used to walking through gardens with you."

"Or doing anything else," she agreed.

He grinned. "Now, there's one thing I wouldn't mind—" He broke off and stared hard into the darkness behind her.

"What?" She turned to look.

"Over there. Near the West Tower." He took off at

a run.

"Richard!" His name tore from her throat. "No!"

Without thinking, she followed, her heart pounding in fear. He must not go near that tower! She reached it, but he was no longer in sight. The moon hovered overhead, casting an eerie glow over the decaying structure that only part of her mind recognized as a purely normal effect of the brilliant night sky. She shivered, filled with a deep sense of foreboding. In that tottering, boarded-up building lay Richard's fate. Would it, she wondered, contain her own death as well?

"Andrea?" Richard emerged from the shrubbery off to the left and came up beside her.

She turned and threw herself into his arms, trembling. Tears slipped unheeded down her cheeks.

"Andy?" He stroked her hair, soothing, gentle, and cradled her close. "It's all right, my love. Whoever it was is gone. You're all right."

She shook her head, barely able to command her voice. "It . . . it's the Tower."

He craned his neck to get a look at it. "It's only the moonlight and the fact that it's falling apart that makes it look so sinister."

"No, it's—Richard, promise me you won't ever go in there!"

He managed a reassuring chuckle. "Premonitions again, darling?"

"No, it's more than that." She pulled away and clung to his upper arms. "Richard, I *know!* It . . . it's dangerous. Promise me! Now! Promise!"

"All right, of course. But why? Can't you tell me that?"

She shook her head. "Believe me, Richard. I *am* from the future. You *must* not go in there."

"For your sake, then." His lips brushed hers, soft and teasing, more an enticement than a real kiss. "Come, let's go to bed. You're shivering, and I want you too much to wait a minute longer."

He didn't believe her warning, she knew, but he would humor her. With that she had to be content. And his last words held a promise too urgent and too compelling to ignore.

Chapter 27

The warm sunshine of the May morning flooded Great Pultney Street as Richard emerged from the home of William Waltham, painter, a newly acknowledged talent specializing in miniatures. Satisfied with the results of his visit, Richard swung up into his curricle. Mr. Waltham would come out to Greythorne Court on the following morning and begin to immortalize his beautiful Andrea.

Richard turned his pair at the corner and proceeded a short distance down the next street before it occurred to him that he behaved like a lovesick swain. Lord, six nights—and one very memorable afternoon—in the woman's arms, and he was making a fool of himself for her. But he had to have this portrait, something to carry with him always, so that he could see her beauty and vivacity even when she was not at his side. But it couldn't capture her soul, or that intriguing aura of mystery that hung about her.

His brow lowered. Somehow, in her bed, he had thought that all pretenses between them must vanish. But still she remained a disturbing maze of contradictions. A lady, yet as free and open with her favors as a courtesan. No, not open, exactly. Loving. That was it.

She knew no constraints, but gave freely of her love. It wrapped about him, filling every part of him, making him forget her uncanny, eerie tricks with those racing bets, her premonition of that damnable sales document and her fey spell by the West Tower.

A sense of unease crept over him. She had been right about the other things. Could she be right about the danger for him in the Tower, as well? He gave himself a mental shake. He was a man, not some pitiful creature to be bound by a woman's freakish starts.

He turned into the London Road and headed out of Bath. He had enough on his mind with the Imperial Star. Once he settled that, he would concentrate on the mysteries Andrea presented. That could prove a very agreeable, if somewhat frustrating, occupation.

He was roused from his reverie some half hour later, after turning down a quiet lane near the Court. Ahead of him, an ancient farming wagon stood crosswise, blocking the road. An overturned curricle lay at an awkward angle on the verge, and the horses stood nearby, peacefully cropping grass. Two gentlemen and a farmer appeared to be engaged in a heated argument. They looked up as Richard approached, and the farmer, a large, burly man, hailed him.

Richard pulled in. "Can I help you?"

"Aye, thank 'e, that you can." He strode up to the curricle. One of the two gentlemen came to its other side.

"Samuel." Richard signaled his groom to go to their assistance. "Do you need a wheelwright?" He secured the ribbons and started to jump down himself.

The farmer caught him halfway with a blow to the chin that knocked him back against the seat. Richard regained his balance, but the gentleman grabbed his arm from the other side and dragged him backward, free of the curricle and the sidling horses. With a tremendous heave, Richard, an experienced boxer and no lightweight, threw off his attacker and swung back at the farmer who came around to join them.

The man ducked, taking the punch glancingly off his jaw, and closed with a telling blow to Richard's stomach. The gentleman threw himself against Richard's legs, knocking him to the ground, and the farmer landed him a facer that left him stunned and groggy, but still game. Richard struggled to a sitting position, only to have his arms firmly pinioned behind him by the two men.

The second gentleman, who had dealt with the groom Samuel, strolled over, dusting off his hands in a fastidious manner. "*Pardon,* my lord Grantham, for our method of waylaying you."

"It was certainly crude." Blood dripped down Richard's face from near his right eye, which he could feel swelling. His mouth seemed to be filled with gritty dirt and tasted salty.

"*Mais oui, m'sieur,* but we wish you to understand that we are very serious in what we say. You may have twenty-four hours. No more. If you do not hand over the Imperial Star to us at the end of that time, the so very lovely Madame Isabella Brixton will die." He smiled in a deprecating manner, as if apologizing for so distasteful a disclosure. "And if you still do not give us the icon, then I greatly fear that your guest, Mademoiselle Andrea Wells, will most regrettably have to be killed as well."

Richard gave vent to his feelings, covering the range of everything from the man's dubious ancestry to his eventual consignment to perdition, missing nothing in between.

The man listened in an admiring silence. "You English, such a range of vocabulary. It is *merveilleux!*"

"*Chameau.*" Richard spoke the one word, softly, then added, "*Voyou repugnant.*"

The phrase wiped the smile from the man's face. "Twenty-four hours." He jerked his head toward the carriages. Richard sensed movement behind him, felt the briefest of agonizing pains, and he slumped forward, unconscious.

He awoke to a headache that made him long to slip back into peaceful oblivion. When he tried to open his eyes, sky and ground tilted in an unmannerly fashion, leaving him dizzy and sick. He seemed to be lying in the dirt on his face. Gathering his strength, he pulled himself onto hands and knees and waited until the world settled.

His tentative groping encountered a large lump on the back of his head, moist and warm. His fingers came away sticky with clotted blood. He took a deep breath, found somewhat to his amazement he was still conscious, and came unsteadily to his feet.

The curricle stood where he had left it, his horses standing sleepily, swishing flies with their tails. His groom lay on the grass verge, bound hand and foot with a short length of rope. The dirty ends of a handkerchief protruded from the diminutive man's mouth, but his open, blazing eyes screamed his outrage as clearly as if he spoke.

Richard staggered over and dropped to one knee at his side, unearthed his knife from the depths of his coat pocket, and went to work. In a few minutes, Samuel sat up and jerked the cloth from his mouth. His vocabulary, which he demonstrated for three minutes without stopping or repeating himself, commanded even Richard's respect.

"Taken for a couple o' green 'uns, we was." Samuel stood, shaking his head in disgust, and regarded his master with the familiarity bred of many years of campaigning together on the Continent. "'Ere, now, milord. Let me drive. That was a whisty castor you took."

"I'm all right. But let's by all means get back to the Court as quickly as possible." Staggering a bit, he made it to the curricle and climbed up onto the seat.

Samuel sat beside him, rubbing a wrist bloodied by his struggles against the coarse rope. "Couple o' right green 'uns," he repeated.

Richard urged the horses to a trot and winced at the jarring his battered head took. They had threatened Bella—and Andrea. He cracked the whip, and the curricle careened forward at a dangerous pace. Samuel gripped the side of the vehicle, his face grim, but made no comment.

By the time they reached the drive to the Court, it was all Richard could do to slow his pair, make the turn, and head up the gravel toward the house. They came to a stop before the front door. Samuel took one look at his master and jumped down to take charge.

Richard sank back in the seat, his head whirling. Andrea. He had to get to Andrea, make sure she was all right. He stood, climbed out of the curricle, and fell forward into dark oblivion.

He awoke once more to the steady throbbing of his head. Only this time it wasn't so bad. He still lay on his stomach, though it was no longer the rocky dirt road beneath him. He was on something soft and comfortable, and a cool, damp cloth rested on his head. The scent of violets, sweet and familiar, surrounded him.

"Andrea!" Memory flooded back and he tried to turn over. The effort left him groaning in pain.

"I'm here, Richard." Her gentle fingers stroked his cheek and wiped the hair back from his bleary eyes. "You're all right. You're in your room, love, and we've sent for the doctor."

He drew a deep, quavering breath. "You're not hurt," he murmured.

"No, only you, my dear."

"Come where I can see you."

Fabric rustled, and he felt the shift on the mattress as she rose. In a moment, she came into his view on the other side of the bed, her golden curls framing her worried face. She wore a low-cut morning gown of peach gauze that suited her to perfection.

"God, you're beautiful," he breathed.

She sat down beside him and he took her hand, feeling the smooth, soft skin and the fine bones of her fingers. He couldn't let anything happen to her, she was by far too precious. The mere prospect proved as painful as the blow to his head. Somehow, he had to protect her.

"Send for Giles." His voice came out hoarse.

Andrea shook her head. "Later, love. When the doctor has seen you. You undoubtedly have a concussion, but don't worry, I won't let them bleed you." She bent forward and kissed his forehead. "I'm here."

"That's . . . that's the problem." He tried to shake his head, but quickly abandoned the attempt. "Got to keep you safe. And Bella. Threats."

Her fingers tightened on his. "Who was it?"

"Get Giles. Only want to explain it once." He closed his eyes, and his grip slackened on her hand as his consciousness faded once more.

He did not stir until Prindle ushered the doctor into his room. He endured the examination with gritted teeth and refused to give in to the dizziness that threatened to overcome him. He rallied enough to give a derisive snort at the verdict of "concussion."

"Damned tooth drawer," he muttered as Bella and Andrea returned to the room.

Both ladies smiled at the doctor's outraged countenance. While Bella escorted him down to the front door, Andrea crossed to the bed.

"I should have thought 'concussion' was obvious." Richard regarded her from beneath his fresh bandages.

"It is, of course." Andrea perched beside him and ran loving fingers over the portion of his hair that remained unwrapped by white lint. "As is the fact this was not

369

caused by any accident. Are you ready to tell me what happened?"

He nodded, with care. "Send for Giles."

"I'm here, dear fellow." Giles leaned negligently against the door jamb, but his worried scrutiny rested on his friend's battered face. "Good Lord, did you take on the entire population of Bath?"

Richard forced a smile. "Only three, in a carefully laid trap. And somehow I doubt they were from Bath. Their spokesman was most definitely French."

Giles's brow snapped down. "Was he, by gad! So they've stopped using go-betweens! This gives us something tangible at last. What did he say?"

"That I have twenty-four hours in which to hand over the Imperial Star." He kept his voice smooth and free of any trace of emotion.

Giles's mobile eyebrows flew up. "And if you do not?"

Richard grasped Andrea's wrist, holding her tight. "Bella is to be killed."

"What!" Giles straightened up, his complexion darkening alarmingly. "That damned—" He bit off his intended description out of deference to Andrea's presence, much to her disappointment. "He had the nerve to threaten her?"

"Andrea also." His hand stroked her arm.

"I'd better take them to safety," Giles decided.

"Bella, definitely." Andrea took Richard's hand between both of hers. "I'm not leaving him."

Giles met her defiant gaze squarely. "For his sake, you must. As long as you're here, they have us shackled, and they know it."

"I want her to stay here, where I can keep watch over her," Richard objected. "I won't risk anything happening to her."

Tears filled her eyes. "He's right. I won't go. But you

370

must persuade Bella."

"Persuade me of what?"

Richard focused on his sister standing in the doorway just behind Giles.

That gentleman spun about to face her, his expression grim. "To leave the Court. Right now. Have your abigail pack for you, we're departing within the hour."

"Are we?" Her uncertain gaze came to rest on her brother. "But is it wise for you to move just now?"

"I'd rather they were both here," Richard muttered, his words slurring as the doctor's potions took effect.

Giles took a deep breath. "I'd better tell her the whole. She can decide for herself." Richard managed to nod and Giles led her, protesting, from the chamber.

The upshot was exactly what Andrea anticipated. Bella, like herself, refused to be intimidated. Her complexion might be unusually pale and the hands she kept clasped in her lap might tremble as she sat by Richard's bedside after nuncheon, but she would not be budged. Scowling, Giles hovered over her like a dog whose only bone might be whisked away from him at any moment.

As the day wore on, Giles induced Bella to abandon her bedside vigil and accompany him upstairs to resume the search. Andrea remained in Richard's room, unwilling to be separated from him for even a moment. To her, the Imperial Star mattered very little in comparison with Richard. She had the rest of her life in which to find the icon. She had barely over one week to be with the man she loved.

Toward early evening, a lone horseman rode up the drive. Andrea rose from the edge of the bed where she had been reading to Richard and looked out over the driveway below.

"Wilfred!" she exclaimed.

"Now, what the devil does he want here?" Richard eased himself into a sitting position. "I had better go down to him."

"That you most definitely will not! You are not to move until tomorrow, at the earliest." Andrea put a firm hand against his robed chest and pushed.

"Then have him brought up here."

She hesitated, then nodded. It would be best not to thwart him, and Wilfred, of all people, could pose no danger to Richard even in his weakened condition.

She found their visitor in the Gold Saloon, sprawled in a comfortable chair, a drained glass in his hand. Giles poured more brandy as Andrea entered, and Wilfred roused himself enough to drink it.

"Horrible!" He breathed the word in accents that would have made Kean jealous.

Andrea, who had little belief in Wilfred's stamina, regarded him with a critical eye. In truth, he was abnormally pale, his costume in considerable disarray, and the wild state of his normally combed and pomaded locks gave him more than a passing resemblance to Shakespeare's fretful porpentine, quills and all. He might very well have a soul-harrowing tale to unfold.

"I think Richard should hear what he has to say," she suggested.

Bella, who knelt on the floor beside her betrothed, looked up, her eyes wide with fear, and nodded.

"Come along, then, old fellow." Giles hoisted him to his feet and guided his tottering steps to the door. He did not release his grip until they arrived in Richard's room. Wilfred promptly collapsed in a chair and buried his face in his hands.

"Good God, what's toward?" Richard straightened up, concerned. "Pull together, man, and tell us!"

Wilfred raised haunted eyes. "My father." He drew a quavering breath and had recourse to the brandy glass he still clutched. "Found him in the woods. Been beaten and . . . and shot."

Bella gasped and threw a frightened glance at Giles.

He touched her hand in a comforting gesture. "Is he—?"

Wilfred nodded and gasped the awful word. "Dead!"

Chapter 28

"He's dead!" Wilfred's voice cracked as he repeated the dire tidings. "But how it could have—" He broke off. For the first time, his stunned gaze took in Richard's bruised and swollen face. He blinked, then his eyes widened in increasing horror. "You've been fighting! My God, Grantham, things couldn't have become so bad between you and my father! Why didn't you just sell him the damned thing? He offered you more than ten times its value!"

"Richard?" Bella stared from one to the other in shock. "Wilfred, you cannot think Richard—Richard, of all people!—had anything to do with your father's death!" Her bosom heaved with her indignation. "How dare you!"

Giles placed a restraining hand on her shoulder. "Easy, Bella. He's suffered a nasty shock. Doesn't mean it the way it sounds."

Bella rounded on her betrothed. "Do you think my brother killed your father?"

"No, no, of course no! That is—I mean . . . well, he *has* been fighting, you see." He quailed as anger gleamed in Bella's sparkling eyes. "Really, if Richard had only sold that icon back to him, as he begged him to, my father would still be alive!"

"How dare you blame Richard!" Bella's voice rose on a hysterical note. "How . . . how could you, when he's been through so much! You may consider our engagement at an end!"

"Bella." Giles took her hand, an odd light in his blue eyes. "Easy, Bella, you're overwrought."

"Is it any wonder?" She pulled free. "This is all your fault! If you're with the government, why don't you do something, like arrange for some protection for us all? But no, Richard is beaten up, Malverne is dead, and the rest of us are being threatened! How can you be so . . . so *useless!*" Tears overflowed her eyes and, convulsed by frenetic sobs, she ran from the room.

Andrea didn't waste time. She hurried after her hostess, caught a housemaid in the hall, and sent her for Bella's abigail and a selection of remedies from hartshorn to laudanum, then turned her attention to Bella's rising hysteria. By the time the abigail joined them, Andrea had managed to get her charge undressed. The maid took one look at her weeping mistress and measured out a judicious dose of the opiate. Between them, they tucked Bella into bed. Andrea sat with her while the maid went for a hot brick, and in relief, saw the high, feverish color fade.

When Andrea at last slipped out of the room, Bella's breathing and pulse rate had slowed to normal. She stopped on the threshold and let out a deep sigh of exhaustion both physical and emotional. Bella would be all right now. But there was one more person she had to face—and the sooner the better. There were a few answers they could use, and now that Malverne could not supply them, she could think of only one person who might be able to.

She went to her chamber, rang for her abigail, and took Letitia's locked wooden box out of her bureau drawer. It

375

was very possible they would find some clues in here. Sweet Lettie might be, but Andrea had formed no great opinion of her understanding. The only thing of which she was certain was that the girl had been afraid. And if Malverne had been desperate to lay his hands on these papers, as Lettie's hiding them seemed to indicate, could they not contain a clue to the whereabouts of the Imperial Star?

When Lily arrived, Andrea put on her riding habit and hurried out to the stable. The undergroom saddled not one but two horses and showed every intention of accompanying her. She didn't protest. For possibly the first time since she arrived in the past, she welcomed the attendance of a chaperone.

She had never ridden to the Castle before, so the groom served as her guide. They followed the well-traveled path through high shrubs and thickets until the old, ivy-covered stone facade of Malverne Castle came into sight. Something fluttered from the top of the door—black ribands, hanging from the funereal hatchment, she realized. When they reached the drive, she saw that the knocker already had been done up in black crepe.

This confirmation of the death of the Earl of Malverne was almost Andrea's undoing. She hesitated, fighting the impulse to turn craven and run. Before she could change her mind she tucked the box more securely under her arm, jumped to the ground, and handed her reins to the undergroom. She went up the steps and applied the decorated knocker with a firm hand.

The door opened a minute later, and Andrea found herself bowed into a vast, drafty hall in which her amazed gaze detected no less than three suits of armor, two cavernous fireplaces, an assortment of oversize chests, and tapestries hanging the length of stone walls. The irrelevant thought drifted through her mind that she would have given a great deal to play hide-and-seek here when she was a girl.

She turned to the butler, a tall, skeletally thin man with a wisp of gray hair bordering his bald, bony head. Andrea shivered. If he had lived in the future, he could have found employment in any Vincent Price or Bela Lugosi movie.

He regarded her with a morose eye. "Yes, miss?"

Even his slow, deep voice carried out the illusion of a horror film. The dark, vast interior of the castle served as an exquisite backdrop for him. In the future, the impoverished earl must be convinced to hire the place out for vampire movies!

Andrea managed a false smile to cover her ridiculous nerves. "Are Miss Moreland and Miss Letitia at home? I am Miss Andrea Wells."

He bowed. "I will ascertain."

So strong was the illusion of Hollywood that she felt startled when he did not limp as he moved off. Andrea stood where she was, uneasily returning the stares of five stuffed deer heads. If the eyes moved, she decided, she would scream.

They didn't, so neither did she. In minutes, the butler returned and escorted her up a wide, curving staircase to a parlor on the first floor. There she found both ladies garbed in the deepest black, Miss Moreland's sense of propriety even prompting her to wear a heavy veil. She clutched a black wisp of lace handkerchief in one hand, but it did not appear to have been used.

Lettie sat stiffly erect upon the sofa, her fingers twisting her own handkerchief in her lap, her gaze downcast. As Andrea entered the room, the girl looked up. With a startled uneasiness Andrea detected the glittering in the depths of the child's eyes. Something animated the girl, giving her nervous energy that she strove to hide. Fear? Or was it relief?

This last idea took firm possession of Andrea's

thoughts. Again, in her mind, she heard Lettie's voice, soft but furious, telling Malverne that she would kill him. But she could not have! The man had been beaten as well as shot.

"Andrea!" Lettie sprang to her feet and came forward, holding out her hands to her visitor. "How very good of you to call!" Her voice was strained, but not with grief. She led Andrea to a chair, then returned to her seat, all the while casting swift, darting glances at the box Andrea carried. Her chaperone received her share, as well.

"This . . . this has been a terrible tragedy." Andrea addressed herself to the Dragoness. "Bella is prostrated, or she would have accompanied me."

"One must carry on." Miss Moreland pronounced the decree from within the recesses of her veil, and Lettie giggled in a manner that verged on the hysterical.

Repressed excitement, Andrea realized. With difficulty, she maintained her countenance, hiding her own disturbed feelings. An unnatural liveliness marked the girl's every move. Andrea directed a searching gaze of inquiry at her which Lettie met briefly before looking away. What was the silly chit up to? she wondered.

The door opened and Wilfred paused on the threshold. He had recovered considerably since Andrea last saw him a little over an hour before, but he was still far from his usual poised self.

In an instant, Lettie flew across the room and threw herself into his arms. "Wilfred, you have been an age! Oh, I still cannot believe I no longer must wed that horrible Lord Brompton!"

Wilfred hesitated, then allowed his fingers to just brush across the top of her shining curls. Almost at once, he set her firmly aside. "Everything will be fine, Lettie."

"Of course it will! Oh, I am so happy to be free of my hateful guardian."

Miss Moreland gasped, but Wilfred straightened, the

378

weight of his new responsibilities already leaving their mark. He spoke immediate, reproving words. "You don't know what you're saying, my dear."

"I know exactly what I am saying! Even if he was your papa, he was not at all kind to me, and I am glad he is dead. And now *you* are the Earl of Malverne and my guardian, and you will not force me into a dreadful marriage."

Wilfred was much struck by the thought. "I should say not!"

Andrea directed a measuring glance over the girl's head at the veiled Dragoness. "Poor Lettie is naturally quite unstrung by all this. Perhaps Wilfred and I can calm her. And dear Miss Moreland, I do so need your help, for Bella has succumbed to a nervous fit and developed the most dreadful headache. Wilfred once mentioned a remedy of yours that he said worked wonders. Unless you would consider it an imposition at such a time . . . ?"

"Do you desire some of it?" Miss Moreland took the bait. She stood and shook out the silk folds of her skirt. "It is good to have something positive to do at such a time as this, when one feels so very helpless and mortal. I believe I have a small bottle of that particular concoction in the still room. An excellent infusion. I prepare it myself, you must know." She swept out of the room.

Andrea let out a deep sigh of relief. "We only have a few minutes," she said briskly, turning back to Lettie. "What hold did Brompton have over Malverne?"

"Malverne is—was—deeply in debt to him." Lettie's eyes filled with ready tears. "Lord Brompton is so very rich, you see."

"But is—was—not Malverne?"

Lettie shook her head and threw a pleading glance at Wilfred.

"The fortune's gone." He joined Lettie on the sofa.

"It's been dwindling for generations, but he liked to keep up the pretenses, you know. Very set on that sort of thing." He sat in silence for a moment and then, with a visible effort, pulled himself together. "I don't know where he came by the money to purchase that icon, but he must have realized almost at once he couldn't afford to keep it. So he sold it to Grantham's father for a pretty penny, and that's kept us from winding up at fiddlestick's end, I can tell you. Then all this damnable business started and he tried to raise the wind to buy it back, and has been touching everyone he knows."

"Brompton?" Andrea asked.

Lettie nodded. "Brompton pressed him for . . . for repayment." She sniffed and sought her handkerchief. "He . . . he said he would forgive the debt if I married him. Oh, you have no idea how *good* it is to be able to speak openly about it! I have been so very frightened, and Malverne has threatened me so dreadfully!"

"What about?" Andrea demanded, then could have screamed in vexation as Lettie hesitated. "Please, you must tell me. What is in this box?"

Lettie grabbed it from her and hugged it close. "A-about a month ago I came across some banker's statements and realized that he was embezzling my inheritance. He was my guardian, and . . . and had control over my fortune. He was supposed to be investing it for me, but it has dwindled by over half."

Wilfred gasped, startled out of his withdrawn silence. "Oh, my God! I . . . I didn't know." He shook his head. "By half, you say? I thought your father cut up to quite a bit."

Lettie nodded, her eyes glittering once more. "More than a hundred and fifty thousand pounds, according to the first statements I found. It is now down to below eighty thousand. I am only glad the trust was tied so he could draw no more."

So Malverne had been pulling funds from everywhere, trying to raise enough to make his offer irresistible. Andrea could only pity him.

"He . . . he told me about the French agents and what they would do to me—to all of us—if we couldn't raise several hundred thousand pounds. And I couldn't touch my money, either, because I am not of age. Then Lord Brompton offered to settle nearly one hundred thousand on me as part of the marriage agreement. It . . . it seemed like our only hope. And I tried to like him, but I just couldn't bear the thought! He's so horrid." She ended on a wail.

Wilfred patted her hand. "Don't worry, you won't have to do any such thing."

"Poor Malverne." Andrea stared down at her hands. "He must have been terrified at not being able to repurchase the Imperial Star from Richard. When I think how much he offered . . ." She shook her head.

"Why wouldn't Grantham go along with it? Damn it, I *know* he needs the money!" Wilfred returned to his main grievance.

"Because he doesn't have it. His father either hid it or disposed of it without telling anyone."

Wilfred's eyes grew wide with horror once more. "Good God, and now they'll be coming after *me* for it!"

"Why? I mean, why did the French pressure your father and not Richard in the first place?" Andrea regarded him in confusion.

Wilfred stared at her blankly. "They can't harm Grantham. He's the only one who knows where the icon is."

Andrea nodded, though a more likely explanation occurred to her. Richard would not be easily intimidated, as Malverne obviously had been. This way, the French brought pressure to bear on Richard without showing themselves. Had they thought the ties between the families closer than they actually were? But their use of Malverne had not succeeded—or possibly the earl rebelled—and so they killed him as a warning to Richard that they meant business. They must be growing desperate.

Andrea looked up at Wilfred's pallid, fear-filled countenance. The French would no longer use go-betweens but deal with Richard directly. And they had proved they were willing to kill to recover the Imperial Star. The thought left her sick. It had been no idle threat made against Bella and herself. Unless something happened, they would be the next to die.

Chapter 29

Upon her return to the Court, Andrea went at once to Richard's room where Giles sat with him, deep in discussion. Both listened intently as she related what had passed at Malverne Castle.

By the time she finished, Richard's frown had deepened and he sat erect in bed. Andrea prevented him from rising only with a firm hand. He glowered at her, but did not try again.

Giles nodded. "That settles it. I'm taking Bella and Andrea to Bath."

"Shouldn't we stay together?" Andrea looked at Richard for support.

He glanced at Giles, then shook his head. "We've been thinking it over. If we send you and Bella off, under armed guard, it will convince the French we took their warning seriously."

"Do you mean we didn't?"

Richard smiled at her tone. "I'm not all that certain. I can't understand their tactics, but I can't afford to take any chances, either. This should make them believe we're afraid."

"You mean we aren't?" Andrea murmured. She shook her head. "None of this makes any sense."

"I'd noticed," Richard agreed dryly. "All we can do is guess."

"I'll be happier with Bella and Andrea under armed guard," Giles asserted.

"Bella, maybe. But I'm staying." Andrea met his frowning eyes squarely. "Someone has to run errands for Richard."

"Bella won't go willingly, especially if you stay," Giles objected.

"Are you so sure you can keep her safe away from here?" Andrea looked to Richard. "I don't like it."

Giles answered. "I've already summoned three of the men assigned to us. And there is a house in Bath, kept for government needs. No one will be able to reach her there. She'll be all right. And there's a possibility this may buy us time before the French make another move."

"Why?" Andrea looked from him to Richard.

"Because it's an obvious show of defiance," Richard explained. "They seem to prefer weakness in the people with whom they deal. Hence their using Malverne to approach me. But I'm not going to let those—"

He broke off, but Andrea's imagination filled in any number of ripe, descriptive terms, none of which, she was sure, could meet the standards of Richard's choice.

"If you're both sure this is for the best . . ." Andrea considered. "Take Bella now, then. While she's sedated. I'll have her maid get everything ready."

She and Giles went out together to make the arrangements. Bella, groggy but protesting, journeyed with Giles in the large traveling carriage. His three armed men rode with them, near enough for protection yet far enough away to foil ambushes and traps.

Andrea watched the departure from the window in Richard's room. At last, she turned back and let the curtain fall. "Do you think they'll be all right?"

Richard nodded. "But I intended for you to go, too."

She sat down on the bed and curled up into his arms. "I won't leave you. Ever."

He kissed her hair and cradled her close. "Damn this aching head," he murmured against her ear. "I won't be able to come to you tonight."

"Of course not. I'll come here."

"Rather optimistic of you. I don't think I'll be good for much." He sounded chagrined.

"There's more to sharing a bed than what you have in mind." She snuggled down so that her head rested against his shoulder. "I just want to sleep beside you tonight—and every night."

And she did, holding him while he slept from a potent dose of laudanum.

Giles returned shortly after breakfast the following morning and found Richard much improved and already hard at work searching. Bella he reported, rested safely in the government's house in Bath. She had been frightened sufficiently by the events of the previous day to agree to remain in hiding. And, Giles asserted somewhat smugly, she had been gratified by his promise to visit her every day to report on their progress.

One by one, throughout the forenoon, six men garbed as grooms, gardeners, and footmen arrived at the Court. Giles identified the newcomers as government agents, all personally known to him. Richard declared himself satisfied with this arrangement and permitted them to patrol the grounds while he concentrated on finding the icon. Andrea welcomed their arrival as well, though she secretly knew they would do little good in the long run. Only one single week was left to them . . .

Tension remained high as they awaited the threatened attack to Bella, but the only person who sought to gain entry to the grounds was the miniaturist, come to begin Andrea's portrait. By the time they retired to bed, it seemed apparent that the French were content to bide their time.

"I don't like it," Andrea told Richard when she went to his room late that night. "It wasn't an idle threat!"

"No, it wasn't. Damn! I wish I knew what they were planning! Why do they play games with us?"

Andrea settled on her stomach and propped herself up on her elbows so she could watch his face. "They might have wanted to see our reactions to their threat. Perhaps they thought if we had the icon, we would bring it out into the open and turn it over to the government to protect ourselves. Instead, we took elaborate means to protect Bella and then turned the Court into a fortress."

"I wonder if we'll ever know what they think."

Andrea shivered and snuggled close to him, seeking comfort. "I wish it were—" She broke off. She couldn't wish it were all over. For no matter how terrible the situation might be, at least she still had Richard.

Another day passed, and nothing untoward occurred. No daring raids were made on the Court, no evil, sinister figures were caught lurking in the gardens. Not one attempt was made on Andrea's life. Giles, accompanied by one of his men, rode into Bath to visit Bella and returned with a comfortable report.

Still, and in spite of the fact that several guards now patroled the grounds at all times, Richard ordered Andrea to remain indoors. Warmed by his love, she divided her time between sitting for the artist and continuing to turn out every cupboard and drawer she could find. For safety's sake, they did not attend Malverne's funeral, which was held that afternoon.

By the third day, Richard's concussion had cleared and he acted much his old self once more. He and Andrea celebrated the completion of her portrait in the most satisfying manner possible, then remained together in her bed until morning light, when he awakened her with caresses to renew their unrestrained lovemaking once more. With reluctance, she at last released him. There was so little time, she couldn't bear to be parted from him for so much as a moment.

When they made their separate ways downstairs, they found that Giles had gone out into the grounds. Andrea, after only a mild testing of wills with Richard, accompanied him to look for his friend. After a ten-minute search, they found him standing in the center of the drive, about two hundred yards from the house, studying the stone facade. Arm in arm, Richard and Andrea strolled up to him.

"Any ideas?" Richard turned back to stare at the beautiful old building.

Giles shook his head. "We've covered most of it. All except the cellars and that . . ." He gestured toward the West Tower.

Andrea looked at it and a sense of dread settled over her. It stood slightly apart from the main house, connected by a line of broken rubble that had been the West Wing generations before. As much as she might fear it, it had to be faced. She could not let the search of the Tower remain until last—until the four days passed that separated them from the sixteenth of May.

"Let's go over it now, today!"

Richard and Giles exchanged glances. "Later," Richard suggested.

"I want to search it now." Urgency underlay her words.

"It's not at all a likely place. The ground-floor room hasn't been touched in ages, not since it was sealed up. And the upper floors are simply unsafe."

"Please, Richard." She hugged his arm tight, feeling sick at the thought of entering that ancient portion of the house. But she couldn't let it wait.

Richard shook his head. "It's not safe," he repeated. "Giles and I will look it over if we don't find the icon anywhere else."

"But, Richard! You've got to—" She broke off as a commotion started down the drive toward the gate, just out of their sight.

Giles shot a quick look at his friend and drew the pistol that rested in his pocket.

Richard took her hand. "Get back to the house. At once."

Andrea shook her head. "I . . . I'm staying with you." With difficulty, she controlled her trembling.

A moment later, a curricle rounded the bend and came into view. Wilfred drove, and one of Giles's guards rode beside him. Wilfred drew up near the threesome.

"I came to see Bella." He regarded Richard coldly.

"She's not here. May I help you, instead?"

Wilfred snorted. "She sent her engagement ring back to me!"

Giles nodded. "That's right. She broke off the betrothal, remember?"

Wilfred appeared affronted, though not necessarily displeased.

"Always flighty, Bella," Richard stuck in with a touch of his usual cheerfulness. "If I were you, and didn't want to be made to look ridiculous, I'd announce my engagement to Lettie on the instant."

"No, really, now. I couldn't do that!" Wilfred stared at him, honestly shocked. "We're in mourning, you know! And it would make it look like I jilted Bella," he added conscientiously.

"Don't give it a thought, old fellow." Giles waved an arm, discovered he still held the pistol, and shoved it discreetly out of sight. "Tell you what. I'll send off an announcement of *my* engagement to Bella on the same day. That will give the gossips something else to talk about."

Richard raised dubious eyebrows. "Has she accepted you?"

Giles threw him a rueful grin. "No, not yet. But she will. I can be no end persistent."

Wilfred hesitated, looking from one to the other, his expression torn. "Are you sure . . . ?"

"Devil a bit. You just go back home and settle it with Lettie. But I warn you, I'll be sending my announcement at the end of the week."

A sudden grin transformed Wilfred's harassed features. "The end of the week," he agreed. With more energy than Andrea had ever before seen the dandy display, he whipped up his pair and set them trotting down the drive at a clipping rate.

Richard stared at Giles, and a low chuckle escaped him. "Well, that's one problem settled, at least."

The rest of the day and much of the next passed in fruitless search. No matter how hard Andrea tried, she could not get them to go over the West Tower. It was unsafe, Richard kept repeating, and he wanted her nowhere near it.

"That's my point!" Andrea almost wailed. "Let's do it now, before it becomes any . . . any unsafer!"

Richard regarded her with fond amusement. "Another of your presentiments?"

"Yes! Oh, please, Richard!"

"All right." He leaned forward to where she knelt on the floor of the pantry across from him, and kissed her forehead. "Tomorrow. Don't worry. We'll find it."

Tears of relief filled her eyes, then the next moment changed to ones of despair. The Imperial Star had lost all importance. Tomorrow would be the fourteenth of May.

That thought haunted her from her first stirrings of consciousness in the predawn. She turned over in her bed and reached for Richard, needing the reassurance that he was still there, still alive, if only for two more days.

"Hey!" he protested, half laughing. "You'll strangle me."

"Hold me!" She clung to him and buried her face in the dark, curling hairs of his bare chest. She breathed deeply and tried to memorize his unique scents, that touch of bay rum that always clung to him, his male mustiness, and just that hint of violets from herself.

His arms tightened about her. "No need to get up yet, is there?"

She raised her face to his and blinked back her starting tears. "Love me!" She whispered the words, half begging, half ordering, and drew him even closer.

It was almost two hours later when Richard at last unwrapped her arms from about himself and climbed out of bed. His return to his own chamber was merely a formality, for they had few doubts that the entire staff knew of their sleeping arrangements. Yet neither his valet nor her abigail would put in their morning appearance bearing trays of chocolate and rolls until Richard and Andrea were each where propriety dictated they should be.

Richard knotted the belt of his dressing gown, then stooped to kiss her once more, lingeringly. Andrea could stand it no longer. Here, in this one man doomed to die in only two days, lay her entire life. Philosophy and reason didn't stand a chance. Somehow, at whatever cost to posterity, she must change history.

She caught his hands and pulled him back down to sit beside her on the bed. "Come away with me!"

"Away?" A puzzled frown creased his brow.

"Please, Richard. Let's leave the Court. I . . . I just can't bear being here over the next few days! We can go anywhere you want, do anything you wish."

He pulled one hand free and stroked back the unruly curls that tumbled over her eyes. "All right. On one condition."

"Anything!" Desperation and relief created utter tumult in her stomach.

"We make it a wedding trip."

She stared at him, robbed of speech by the emotion that set her trembling internally.

He reached into the pocket of his dressing gown and drew out a small box. "I've been keeping this handy for the right moment." He sounded somewhat embarrassed. Opening the box, he revealed a golden band set with diamonds and sapphires. He took it out and placed it on Andrea's finger. "It was my mother's. And now it will be my wife's."

"Oh, Richard!" She managed to gasp the words. She threw herself into his arms, crying and laughing at the same time. He would live! They would leave that morning—at once!—and put a hundred miles between themselves and the West Tower. And when they returned, history would be changed, for the Tower would collapse without him and he would be safe.

"I . . . I'll start packing. Shall we go to Scotland?" It was the farthest-away place of which she could think. "Oh! We could go to Gretna Green! Please, I want to go there of all things."

He laughed, a deep, comfortable sound that sent a thrill of renewed desire and hope through her. "No, love, nothing so scandalous." He held her even tighter, to the imminent danger of two of her ribs. "I've got a special license."

She sat back. "You've been planning this?" His grin sent her pulse dancing erratically.

"Do you think I'd risk losing the most wonderful thing that has ever happened to me?" He smoothed his hand along her golden hair and kissed her as if he couldn't help himself. He let her go only with reluctance. "No need to pack quite yet, though. We'll leave as soon as we've found the Imperial Star."

Her glorious, sunlit world crashed down about her to be replaced by black horror. "Richard! No, we can't wait!"

He laughed. "We've already stretched the proprieties.

They can go a little—" He broke off and stared at her with an expression of mingled wonder and consternation. "Do you mean you're—?"

"No!" Hot color flooded her cheeks. "That is—I mean, I don't think so." She couldn't tell if he was disappointed or relieved.

"Well, a couple of days won't make any difference." He stood. "I'd better be going. Your maid must be getting impatient."

Frustrated and afraid, she threw caution to the winds. "Richard, we must leave *now*. Today. This minute!"

"Andy, love, it's not safe. We'd be easy targets for the French."

She paled. "I . . . I'll take that chance. It's a better one than staying here."

His frown returned and he resumed his seat. "Why?"

She could sense a hint of steel behind the gentle question. She faced it squarely. "Because you'll die if you stay. No, Richard, listen to me! I know you don't believe I'm from the future, but God help me, you must listen! It's documented in history! The West Tower will collapse on the sixteenth—in two days—and you will be inside at the time. Unless you leave with me now, get away from here so it can't happen that way!" Tears once more filled her eyes and streamed unheeded down her cheeks. She held his gaze, pleading.

"Andrea, I—" He broke off, shaking his head. With a low groan, he dragged her once more into his arms and cradled her there. "God, I love you, even as crazy as you are. All right, darling. We'll go. Today. Just to humor you. Satisfied?" He tilted her chin up so that he could look down into her tear-streaked face. "We'll take two of Giles's men as escorts and go to Bath. Bella can be your attendant for our wedding." He kissed her eyes, then set her firmly aside. "We'll leave Giles and the rest of his entourage to guard the place."

Five minutes after he left her, a discreet knock sounded on the door and Lily entered, bearing a tray. Andrea stood at the clothes cupboard, her dressing gown on, staring at her impressive array of garments.

"Lily, I must pack. I . . . I'm going away for a few days."

Lily nodded. "Just as well, miss, with all the strange goings-on there have been. Now, what will you be needing?"

Together, they set about selecting what Andrea realized, with a sense of unreality, would be her trousseau. Several times as they packed, she paused to stare at the ring that shone on her left hand. Love filled her heart, along with a thrill of fear at her defiance of fate. But for Richard, she would dare anything. If he died—well, she might as well die with him.

In spite of their hurrying, there were any number of last-minute details to which Richard had to attend, and they were not ready to depart until late that afternoon. But the time didn't matter to Andrea. Only the leaving. And leave they would. At last, the footmen strapped their trunks to the back of the curricle.

"We ought to be setting off on our wedding trip in the traveling carriage," Richard complained.

"But we're only going into Bath." Andrea hugged his arm, afraid he would delay their departure another twenty minutes by summoning a more suitable vehicle.

Richard smiled. "This is not at all the thing, you know."

"Fustian." She grinned back at him. "When have I ever been 'the thing'? We shall always do just as we please, you and I." The warmth of his expression sent a wave of happiness washing over her.

"I'll hold you to that, tonight." He helped her up into the vehicle, then turned to Giles and took his hand. "We'll be gone for no more than three days. Take care."

"You, too." Giles stepped back as Richard swung up into the curricle. "If it isn't just like you to decide to get married in such a hey-go-mad way. Bella will never forgive you for forgoing all the pomp and ceremony."

Richard chuckled. "You two can do the honors at St. George's. I prefer something a little more intimate." He gave his pair the office and they moved off down the gravel drive with their escort trotting behind. As they neared the gate, he reined in and looked back toward the Court, his gaze sweeping the ivy-covered stone walls and mullioned windows.

"What a wonderful place to come home to." Andrea twisted around in her seat to look. "It's so very welcoming. I thought that the first time I saw it, as if it wanted me to live in it. I—" She broke off.

A light flickered in the shadowed window of the crumbling West Tower. One that should have been boarded over. Richard saw it, too, and swore. He whipped up the pair, drove them through the gate, then made the difficult turn in the lane. They started back up the drive and Andrea's heart turned to ice.

"Richard, you can't! You promised!"

He shook his head, his expression grim. "Damn it, Andrea, it's broad daylight, there are guards patroling the grounds, yet someone has broken into a tower that was sealed closed! Giles can't handle this alone. I'm not leaving my home to be ransacked for that blasted Imperial Star."

"Richard!" She clutched his arm, knowing there would be no dragging him away now. "Whatever you do, *don't go into that tower.* Let the others!"

He covered her hand fleetingly, and his expression softened. "I can't promise that." He pulled up the horses as close to the tower as he could get. Tossing the ribbons to her, he jumped down and took off at a run for the door of the deadly structure. His two escorts followed.

394

She waited, her heart blocking her throat so that she could barely breathe, until at last he came back out alone. He looked up, met her frantic gaze, and shook his head.

"No one there. They're still checking, but we couldn't even find any signs of where they were searching. Damn!" He strode up to the curricle, clutched the side, and glared at his whitened knuckles. "I can't leave."

"You have to!"

He glanced up at that, his expression a mixture of apology and anger. "I can't allow the French to find it. England could never withstand a combined assault by Russia and France. You must understand that."

"It will cost you your life. Please, Richard."

"You really believe I'm going to be killed." He took her trembling hands in his. "You must see I can't let that stop me. I have to try."

"And so do I." She might feel pride in his sense of honor, but not when misery would be the only result. "Damn it, Richard, you're being pigheaded!"

"Possibly. But I won't run away."

"You're fooling yourself. We're just biding time, waiting for you to die, like some . . . some damned death vigil." Furious, she dragged his ring from her finger and almost threw it at him. "This is meaningless! Our whole engagement is nothing but a sham. You'll be dead in two days because you won't listen to me."

"You're wrong, and so you'll see. I have you to live for now." He took the band and slid it onto the tip of his little finger. "I'll give it back to you, personally, on the morning of the seventeenth. I swear it."

With a strangled cry of frustration and despair, she jumped down from the curricle and ran into the house.

Chapter 30

Andrea slammed cupboard doors in the still-room, almost ill with dread, too anxious to accomplish anything useful. Visions of Richard, lying lifeless beneath a pile of rubble, haunted her. But it was only the fifteenth. He was still alive—at least until the morrow.

Tears filled her eyes. She was becoming a watering pot, as the parlance of her adopted time put it. And it was her time, now and forevermore, as little as that thought might now appeal to her. There was nothing in the past for her any longer. Only Richard. And after tomorrow, even he would be gone.

She grabbed a jar of preserves from a shelf and sent it smashing to the floor, but it did nothing to relieve her frustration. She hadn't been able to change history. It was impossible; their fates were already cast. Everything would continue exactly as she had learned it in history books because her presence here, in the past, would already have been taken into account. She had accomplished nothing except to behave in an impulsive, unreasoned manner.

She picked up another jar, but stopped herself before she sent it crashing after the first. Richard, Giles, and several of their guards had spent most of the day searching the West Tower, with no results.

But, of course, she hadn't expected any. Everything progressed exactly as it—as it had. The French would not find the Imperial Star because her history books said there was no alliance between France and Russia. Isabella would marry Giles, just as Catherine Kendall told her. And tomorrow, a fire would break out in that horrible tower and it would collapse on Richard, killing him. Because that was the way it happened. There could be no changing history.

She retired to her room at an early hour that night. When Richard joined her, she clung to him as if she would never let go. At last, exhausted from her emotions, she drifted into sleep.

She awoke the following morning, the sixteenth, filled with a new determination. What a pathetic, helpless, missish idiot she had been the day before! All right, she knew that as far as his family was concerned, Richard was buried beneath that damnable tower. *But they did not have his body to prove it!*

What if she spirited him away, took him somewhere to start a new life? She could still cheat his fate! She would not let him die. She made it a vow. She would not let him die, for she could not live without him.

"Richard!" She sat up in bed and shook his arm. "Richard!"

He opened one sleepy eye and smiled. "Good morning, beautiful." He reached for her.

"No, Richard, listen!" She pulled slightly away. "I know how we can do the trick. Sometime today there will be a fire in the Tower. No, there really will be! And when it happens, you and I will slip away. Then you won't have to die and history will stay the same!"

He chuckled softly. "What a way to wake a man up. All right. I promise. If there really is a fire today, if everything happens just as you say, I'll leave with you, and without telling anyone. Satisfied?"

She nodded, and knew real hope.

"Good." He started to take the ring off his finger.

She shook her head. "On the seventeenth. Remember?"

He slipped it back on and ruffled her curls. "My very own Bedlamite," he murmured, and grinned at her. When he pulled her down beside him again, she went willingly.

They began their search that morning in the rambling cellars beneath the vast old house. Only one more day to endure, Andrea kept reminding herself. If she could keep Richard safe through this last night, everything would be all right.

After several hours of determined ransacking of the damp stone rooms, Richard stopped and turned to Giles. "It must be in the West Tower, after all. We just missed it."

"You're not to go back in there!" Andrea looked up from the massive wine rack she had been probing for secret springs. "Not today!"

"We searched it rather thoroughly," Giles reminded him.

"But we're not fiding it here, either!" Richard looked about the torch-lit cavernous chamber with the eerie shadows that danced on the walls. "I'd swear my father would have told me if he gambled it away."

Giles shook his head. "If he had, we'd have learned something about it. There would have been no reason for someone to keep silent about winning it. No, he kept it, and it's here, secreted somewhere."

"But where?" Frustration filled Richard's voice.

They resumed their hunt. The only treasure to be unearthed proved to be a keg of brandy, which Giles insisted they tap—just to be sure it held no icons. With this suggestion Richard agreed, for the cellars were on

398

the whole a most uncongenial locale. Giles fetched glasses from abovestairs while Richard opened the keg, and all three sampled the well-aged liquor.

Andrea closed her eyes. Not even the brandy helped to untie the knots in her stomach. Richard went nowhere near the Tower, but the day wasn't over yet, either. The hours crept by slowly, as if in no hurry to put her out of her misery. The threat hung over her head like the sword of Damocles.

Toward early evening, it fell, and with a resounding crash. A cry arose abovestairs and Richard, instantly alert, led the way as they raced to see what had occurred. The youngest footman, scarcely more than a lad, stood in the hall, facing the butler who held the ancient fowling piece.

Prindle looked up at their arrival, his lined face pale. "In the West Tower, my lord. Young Henry here spotted two men creeping about."

Richard nodded. "Get your friends, Giles, we'll settle this at last."

"Richard!" Andrea grasped his hand. "Please, you promised!"

He shook his head and put her firmly aside. "We'll be safe once we catch them. Stay here."

Flanked by the butler and two footmen, Richard led the way outside. Giles disappeared down the drive to summon reinforcements. Andrea hesitated, terrified of what was about to happen yet loath to remain behind. But as yet there was no fire . . . Unable to stay away, she followed.

Silently, Richard and his men surrounded the Tower, with Giles's four completing the circle. Each was armed. Andrea stood a short distance back. Nothing could go wrong, she told herself, over and over. They had every advantage. Nothing could possibly go wrong. And at the first sign of flames, *somehow* she would make Richard leave with her.

She looked up at the tall, twenty-foot-square structure with its narrow windows and turreted, semicollapsed roof. It wouldn't take much to bring the whole thing tumbling down. She shuddered, the image of the grass-covered mound it would make clear in her mind. Richard might not even have to be inside! If it toppled . . . Richard left his place and approached the door that had been forced open.

"Richard!"

Her scream was a plea, but he paid her no heed. With a purposeful set to his shoulders and a pistol clasped in his hand, he went inside. After a moment, Giles joined him, his own gun drawn.

Andrea closed her eyes, unable to watch. Would it fall now? Or would her agony drag out for another few minutes? She sank to her knees, half in prayer, half because her legs were too weak to hold her. From within that ancient building, she heard a muffled shout, then the sound of a struggle.

She couldn't just stand by and let Richard die! She was on her feet and running before she even realized she moved. The men about the Tower seemed undecided whether to help or remain in their circle to cut off escape. A splintering crash settled the matter, and Andrea beat a man garbed as a footman to the door by a mere second.

It opened, and Richard, his face grim, emerged, dragging a roughly dressed man with him. Richard's face showed a new bruise, but that was as nothing compared to his opponent. Giles followed a moment later with another man in tow. They handed their captives over to Giles's men, and Andrea ran to Richard's side and held him tightly.

"I told you," he said softly. "I'm safe. Everything will be all right."

"Richard!" Giles interrupted them. "I'm going with

my men into Bath. I'll be back in the morning."

Richard nodded and kept his arm firmly about Andrea's waist. They returned to the house so that she could bathe his scraped face. This finished, she knelt on the floor at his side and laid her head in his lap. He stroked her hair gently.

"All that worry for nothing. Do you have any more dire predictions we can prove false?"

She sighed. "I hope you're right. But I can't believe those are the only men the French have searching."

"No, I'm sure they aren't. But Giles will return with more reinforcements—and stonemasons. We'll dismantle that tower if we have to—and do it in a safe manner. Don't worry, Andy. The danger is over."

"I . . . I just can't really believe it yet. Richard, I've seen that tower fallen, covered in grass. And I've heard the story of how you were inside."

"Then obviously they got it wrong." He seemed willing to humor her. "The stonemasons are bound to leave a pile of rubble that will be buried over time. And you know how stories are exaggerated for drama in the retelling. I probably actually disappear in some completely harmless way. Perhaps after we find the Imperial Star and everything returns to normal, I will get fed up with my boring life and we will emigrate to America. Now, that would be a challenge. What do you say to playing frontiersmen? After the excitement we've had, returning to a predictable life of clubs and parties just doesn't appeal to me."

She caught his hand. "Let's go!"

He laughed and kissed her. "My impetuous love. We'll see how we feel when the little matter of the Imperial Star is settled."

Still, hope filled her, growing with every passing hour. Evening drew near, and still he was safe, beside her, the teasing light once more in his eyes. Her spirits soared and she laughed, intoxicated by the hovering aura of victory. Over dinner, she told him everything she could remember having read about life in America around 1810.

It was not until after she retired to her room to prepare for bed that her fears began to reemerge. Richard might be alive and with her, but did that mean she had altered history in other ways? The possible consequences were enough to give her nightmares! What might she have done? Would Napoleon invade Russia now, as he was supposed to? If he didn't, his forces would remain strong, able to conquer the Peninsula. And if Napoleon were victorious, what might the future hold for France and Russia?

The potential consequences of her love for Richard haunted her. But he was more important to her than anything—even the state of the world.

When he at last came to her bed, she forgot her worries. Here, in his arms, her happiness was complete. She had saved him, and that was all that mattered. The rest of the world could go away and do whatever it wanted. She had her life, here, in this one man. At last, loved and boundlessly happy, she settled into the welcoming curve of his warm body to sleep.

As she drifted off, a pounding sounded on her door. The voice of Bailey, Richard's valet, rose on a note of terror.

"Fire, my lord! The West Tower is on fire!"

Chapter 31

Richard sprang from Andrea's bed and reached for his dressing gown.

"No! Richard, don't go!" Andrea grasped at his hand.

He shook free, ignored her cry of anguish, and ran out the door, securing his belt as he went.

Andrea pulled on her own gown and raced after him. Already, he disappeared down the hall, his valet at his heels. She followed, stumbling over her confining skirts, barely able to see without her contacts, which she hadn't stopped to put in.

She reached the Great Hall and felt the chill night air from the front door that was thrown wide. She couldn't hear Richard and Bailey, let alone see them. She ran out into the darkness, oblivious to the fact she had not pulled on slippers. The gravel brought it home to her, forcing her to slow, but she kept doggedly on.

Off to her right, the West Tower flickered with eerie flames dancing in the narrow, slitted windows. As she neared, she could make out a dark, bleary shape through one of these, silhouetted against the blazing interior. And there was Richard, disappearing through the door.

Ignoring the pain in her feet, she dashed after him. She couldn't let him go inside! But it was too late. His dark figure vanished within the crumbling building. Consigning the consequences to the devil, Andrea pushed past the wavering valet and followed Richard.

The ground-floor room was huge, with a circular stone stair curving about the far end. Vaguely she made out signs of one-time habitation: a bed, chairs, a table. It was these that burned now, lit by a lantern that lay fallen on the carpeted portion of floor. Flames leapt up the tapestries that lined the wall, reaching ever closer to the wooden beams that formed the support to the next story.

Against the opposite side, two men struggled with something heavy, trying to pull it away from the wall as Richard closed on them. Three large stones lay piled on the ground beside them. By the rising, flickering light, Andrea could make out a dark crevice—a hiding place. And there seemed to be something inside, something at which the men tugged in vain.

Richard reached them, dragged one of the men back, and landed him a facer. The other launched himself onto Richard, letting fly with wild fists. All three went down, struggling.

A crackling, snapping hiss sounded from above as the fire licked across the ancient wooden shorings and set them ablaze. A wave of heat washed over Andrea. Desperate, she searched for a weapon she could lift that was not already burning. Grabbing up the smoldering leg of a wooden chair, she went in swinging, and more by luck than design, connected with the head of the man who held Richard in a hammerlock.

He crumpled to the ground. Andrea drew back, only to be pushed aside by a man coming from behind her. She screamed, but it was just one of the footmen, his nightshirt stuffed sketchily into breeches.

"Get him out of here!" Richard shouted. He kept his concentration on his other opponent, who swung wildly with more will and power than science.

A protesting creak from above cut off the footman's reply. Grabbing the prostrate man by the arms, he dragged him toward the door.

Andrea hefted her makeshift club once more. Richard and the other man struggled, locked together, oblivious of the fire that raged about them, burning ever closer. She had to help, get him outside before it was too late . . .

The ceiling supports groaned as if in agony, and one, charred beyond endurance, gave way. Burning splinters and debris showered down over their heads. The acrid, suffocating smell of smoke enveloped Andrea, and her lungs ached and her eyes stung.

"Richard!" She couldn't make him hear.

The men broke apart. Andrea, blinded by the billowing smoke, rushed forward with her club raised high, but Richard didn't need her. He struck, his fist connected with the man's jaw, and his opponent fell, unconscious. Richard stood over him, breathing hard.

"Richard!" Andrea tried again, screaming the words. "Get out of here!"

"The Imperial Star!" He shouted back, trying to make himself heard above the roaring blaze.

"Let it burn! Get out, now!" She pulled at his arm, desperate.

But he ignored her and concentrated on the hole where the stones had been removed.

"My lord!" Prindle and Bailey hovered in the doorway and cast frightened glances toward the flaming roof.

Andrea turned, relieved at this unexpected help. "Get him out! *Make* him leave."

The two servants advanced cautiously into the room. They saw the man on the floor and stooped to pick him up between them.

"Not him, Richard!" Andrea cried, but they paid her no heed. They dragged the unconscious man outside.

Sparks ignited the decaying fabric of the tapestry

nearest and it went up like a torch. Andrea grasped Richard's arm again, frantic, and tugged.

"Help me!" he ordered. "It's wedged!"

There was no other way. Until he had the Imperial Star, he wouldn't leave. Desperate, Andrea reached in. Her hand encountered velvet cloth and the solid corners of something within—the icon. They pulled, but it remained firmly in place.

"Leave it! Richard, it's too late."

A creaking, protesting groan sounded above them. With a shudder, another beam gave way, raining flaming sparks over them. Andrea turned, horrified, to see a wall of fire rising between them and the door.

"There!" Richard's note of triumph penetrated her panic. He dragged the icon free and the cloth fell away. Andrea caught a glimpse of a time-darkened picture of the Madonna with her Child in her arms. A star, held by the infant Jesus, bathed the pair in light.

And the wide frame of dull gold, in which no stones glittered . . .

Above them, another great beam sundered with a splintering shriek. Richard thrust the icon at Andrea and grabbed her hand.

"Come on! What are you waiting for?" His eyes gleamed in the blazing, dancing light. He dragged her toward the open door.

Part of the ceiling crashed down, sending flames shooting high in the air. The heavy debris landed on the trailing hem of Andrea's dressing gown, stopping her. With every ounce of her strength, she thrust Richard toward the door, her one thought to save him. As he stumbled out into the night lit by fire, she fell to the stone floor. The flimsy muslin of her gown sparked and caught.

Richard, free of the tower, turned and saw her trapped within the smoke- and flame-engulfed room. He cried out, but the roar of the fire drowned his words. Another beam fell between her and the door and the wall waved with shimmering heat—then tumbled, crashing as its support gave way.

A scream of pure terror tore from Andrea's throat. A dark figure came toward her, through the sheet of flames. Richard. He heaved the burning rubble aside, freeing her, and pulled her to her feet. Pushing her ahead of himself, he got her to the threshold.

Prindle grabbed her and dragged her away as the doorway trembled and collapsed. The remainder of the tower swayed precariously, then crashed down in a shower of falling stones and timber.

Richard . . . With a moan, Andrea collapsed on the grass.

Chapter 32

The ground swayed and heaved beneath Andrea. Or was it she who was unsteady? Her head reeled. Disoriented, she tried to focus her thoughts. What had happened? The question formed in her mind, only to be replaced a moment later by unbearable loss. Richard. Richard was gone.

She opened her eyes to an eerie dawn. She lay half crouched on grass. Before her, through a weed-covered mound, protruded broken stones. Only hours ago—or was it ages?—those blocks had formed the West Tower.

With a sick sense of shock, the realization hit her. She was back in the future—in her own time. She pulled herself to a sitting position and stared at the mound as horror filled her. Richard, her beloved Richard, lay buried beneath that heap. He was gone, torn from her forever.

Agony swept through her. She had failed to save him. Failed . . . Tears blurred her eyes and she made no attempt to wipe them away.

A sharp pain, physical rather than emotional, finally penetrated her stunned consciousness and she looked down at her throbbing hand. She clutched the icon, the Imperial Star, and a sharp corner dug into her palm. She had brought it with her!

In a mixture of disbelief and despair, she ran a finger along the edge as she stared blearily at it. Tarnished gold bezels studded the frame, bent and misshapen by the tools that had ripped the precious gems from their settings. Not so much as a single stone remained. Richard's father had gambled, all right—not with the icon, but with the jewels that once had made it worth a king's ransom.

A hollow laugh shook her, which turned into a soul-rending cry. It was worthless to them now! It would never fetch the almost one million pounds needed to purchase Greythorne Court. She had accomplished nothing!

She hurled it from her, as hard as she could. She hated it! It had caused Richard's death . . . He might as well have saved himself and left the icon to be buried beneath the falling tower, for neither the Russians nor the French could have ever unearthed it. He had died for nothing.

A groan sounded somewhere across from her, behind the rocky mound. She tensed, surprised she still reacted to anything. Slowly, on guard, she came to her feet. The singed, filthy remains of her dressing gown fell about her bruised legs.

From behind the protruding stones, a bleary shape emerged. A wavering figure with dark, curly hair . . . Shock swept over her, leaving her numb and weak.

"Richard?" She couldn't believe her blurred sight.

Taking one shaky step after another, he came toward her around the grass-covered rubble. He clasped one hand to his bloodied head and shook it slowly, as if he sought to clear his befuddled mind.

Disbelief, joy, relief, all struggled within her. Without realizing she moved, she was beside him, hugging him, laughing and crying at the same time.

He held her tight, as if afraid to let go of his one anchor

to reality. "Andrea?" He made a question of her whispered name. "Oh, my God, Andrea! How . . . how did I get out of there?"

"I don't know. I don't care! You did, that's all that matters!"

He pulled slightly away, but still looked only at her. He shook his head again, with care. "You really are a witch! The fire, the way the Tower collapsed with me inside—" He broke off, unable to assimilate all that had taken place.

A tremulous laugh shook her. "It did happen, just the way I told you. All of it! As far as your family knows, you're dead."

That stopped him. "What do you mean?"

"Look around." She clung to his hand, tightly.

He did look, and his jaw dropped. "It . . . it's the same, yet different. And the Tower—my God, it looks like it's been down for ages!" He drew a deep, ragged breath. "What's happened?"

"It's time for your first lesson in modern living. Suspension of disbelief, 1-A." She knew she must sound hysterical, but that was the way she felt.

"What do you mean?" He didn't seem able to take it in.

"Do you remember I told you I was from the future?"

"Yes, I—" He broke off. "You're not trying to tell me . . ."

She nodded. "Welcome to the future."

He shook his head. "Andy, I've had a rather trying night. If you don't mind, I'm not in the mood for your games."

A teasing smile touched her lips. "Aren't you?" She reached up and trailed her fingers along the back of his bare neck. "That's not what you said last night."

He caught her hand in a firm grip and brought it down.

410

"What's going on? Did someone take those men into custody?"

"I suppose so. But, my love, it really happened such a very long time ago, we may have trouble finding out exactly what occurred that night."

"What the devil!" Exasperation threatened to overcome him.

She smiled. He really had been through a lot, and more than he realized. Almost two hundred years more. It was no wonder he felt disoriented.

"Last night happened a very long time ago, Richard."

He released her and covered his face with his grimy hands. When he spoke, it was through clenched teeth. "Andy, you don't really expect me to believe I was thrown into the future when the Tower collapsed, do you?"

"Not at first, no. But you'll catch on pretty quickly, once you start seeing things. It's going to be a lot easier to prove than my going back through time was."

He dropped his hands and stared at her. *"Can* you prove it?"

"Easily. Look around. Anything you don't recognize?"

He fell silent a moment, gazing at the grass-covered tower. He looked quickly away and scanned the surrounding garden. Suddenly, a frown knit his brow and he strode over to where a recently constructed shed stood. He opened the door and looked inside.

"What's that?" He pointed at a lawn mower.

"It cuts the grass—and a darned sight faster than a scythe, believe me. Here, press that soft button down there about five or six times. That pumps gas into the motor."

"The what?"

She grinned. "Just do it. Now, push that switch. Hard."

411

He did, and the motor coughed, then sprang to life, vibrating the whole machine. Richard jumped back, releasing the handle, and it quieted at once. Silence engulfed them.

"That . . . that's impossible!" He stared at Andrea as if ordering her to come up with a sensible explanation that he could accept.

"That's only one of the things you're going to discover. There have been so many inventions since your time. This same sort of arrangement can propel carriages without using horses."

Fascinated, he burrowed deeper into the garden shed. A moment later he emerged with an electric weed cutter, an edger, and a sprayer. Then he spotted a folded newspaper beneath a stack of clay flower pots. He pulled it out and found the date.

Very slowly, he set the paper back down on the potting bench. He turned to Andrea and a slow, incredulous smile twisted his lips. "I don't believe it! This is the future. This really is the future!"

His expression one of wonder, his gaze lowered to his hand where the sapphire-and-diamond ring sparkled through the soot and dirt on his fingers. "When that roof collapsed, all I could think of was you. Never in my life have I wanted anything as much. It was almost as if I willed myself to be with you."

"You . . . you succeeded."

"You brought me forward through time."

She nodded. "Just as you brought me back, before."

They stared at each other for a long moment, lost in the wonder of the fullness of the bond that brought them together, uniting them even across the ages.

"My love." It was no more than a whisper. He held out his arms and drew Andrea into an embrace that seemed to encompass her soul.

At long last he released her, only to take her hand.

"And what now, my dear?"

"I suppose we should go inside and get cleaned up."

He turned back to look at the grass-covered mound that only the night before, for them, had been the West Tower. Beside it lay the icon. His hesitant smile turned into a broad grin. "The Imperial Star!"

"Richard, the jewels were removed!"

"Were they, by Jove! So that's what my father was up to!" Drawing Andrea with him, he went back out to where the boxlike picture lay on the grass. "And to think this is what caused all that trouble. If only everyone had known—" He broke off as he picked it up.

A panel, secreted in the pattern of the frame's bottom, slid open, apparently jarred by Andrea's mistreatment of it. Before their incredulous eyes, a magnificent diamond necklace fell to the ground. Andrea gasped as she picked it up.

"This is what Tsar Alexander wanted," she breathed. "The legendary good fortune of the Imperial Star." She met Richard's glowing eyes. "It has certainly brought *us* luck."

Richard took it from her. The chain consisted of five-carat diamonds, each set in circlets of pearls. From the bottom hung a blue pear-shaped diamond of well over a hundred carats.

He let out a low whistle. "That is the largest stone I've ever seen."

"Yet it was the stories about it, not its size, that caused so much trouble." She retrieved it and put it back inside its hiding place. "For safe keeping." Suddenly, she burst out laughing. "Richard, we won! We kept the icon from the French, and we have the necklace so Catherine can buy the Court!"

"Who?"

"Come on, let's go up to the house. I'll explain everything while we get cleaned up."

"I could use a bath," he agreed.

Her irrepressible laughter bubbled over. "Just wait until you see a shower! You're going to love this!"

"A what?"

"Oh, Richard!" She hugged him, ecstatic, her fears of the last few weeks at last dropping away. "There's so much for you to learn about! Let's hurry, there are so many conveniences I've missed!"

Together, with Richard looking around, marveling at the subtle but unmistakable changes, they started for the main part of the house. As they neared the front door, it opened, and a frail but erect white-haired lady peered out.

"Who . . ." Catherine Kendall emerged slowly, staring at them in disbelief. "Andrea? Is it really you? My poor child!" She hurried over to clasp Andrea's trembling hands. "Oh, my dear, whatever has happened? It's been months since—" She broke off, staring at Richard in wonder.

"Catherine, how very good it is to see you again! I never thought I'd be so glad to get home." She caught the woman's hand and started to giggle uncontrollably. "And you know perfectly well what happened. The West Tower has just collapsed on us, and we're filthy!"

"On . . ." Catherine's shocked gaze rested on Richard, garbed in his charred, filthy dressing gown, and her eyes widened in mingled horror and awe. "You . . . you're—"

Richard swept her a magnificent leg. "Richard Westmont, Viscount Grantham, at your service, madam. And you?"

With difficulty, Andrea managed to control her convulsive merriment. "Allow me to introduce your great-great-great-whatever niece, Catherine Kendall."

Richard blinked, then broke out in a deep laugh of devilish enjoyment. "Good God, they really did it? Bella and Giles? I can't wait . . ." His face clouded abruptly.

"Lord, they must be—it's odd to think of them as dead."

"For nearly a hundred and fifty years." Andrea hugged his arm tight. "You'll have my family now, and they'll love you. I can hardly wait for you to meet them— especially my sister." And Jim? For one evil and highly enjoyable moment, she considered taking Richard to her old office when they went to Minneapolis to sell her condominium. But no, now was a time to look forward, not back.

"My dear boy, welcome home." Catherine took his hand and gave it a motherly squeeze. Her gaze shifted to the bulky gold box that he held, and her eyes widened in amazement. "You found it! Oh, Andrea, my dear, you've saved the Court! The auction is to be in just over a week, and now I can buy Greythorne!"

"That's right! Malverne's sales document. So the current earl owns my home, does he?" Richard looked at Andrea.

She nodded. "And he is about to sell it because he is in straitened circumstances. That was one of the reasons I went back in time, to bring the icon forward so it could be sold, to repurchase the estate."

Richard looked at the Imperial Star and a slight smile played about his firm lips. He glanced at Andrea with the old mischievous gleam back in his eyes. "Am I now here in the future for good?"

"I guess so. You are certainly dead as far as history is concerned."

He nodded, coming to a decision. "Then I am very sorry, my dear great-niece, but this was my home, first. And I want it back. I shall buy it myself."

"But . . ." Catherine blinked.

"You will live with us," Andrea assured her.

"Yes, but you . . . you'll have to establish a new identity for yourself! No one would believe you are you. It's too preposterous!"

415

Andrea hugged his arm in delight at the prospect.

Richard grinned broadly. "Now, here is the ultimate challenge. God, I was so bored until all this happened. I don't think I ever realized how much so. I'm going to enjoy this!"

"You've lost your title," Andrea reminded him.

He shrugged, his eyes still dancing. "I earned it once. I can always do it again. Do you wish to be a viscountess, or will a knighthood do for us?"

"You can do anything you set out to do, and you know it." Andrea laughed up into the bruised but handsome face above her and knew her fate complete. "We aren't in the past where our destinies have already been cast, we're in the present, where they're ours to form. Oh, Richard, it'll be a world of fun, your adjusting to this different time!"

"That reminds me." Richard turned to Catherine. "Is today the seventeenth?"

She nodded, for the moment speechless.

He grinned at Andrea. "Then it seems to me I promised to return something to you today." He drew the ring from his little finger and replaced it on hers, then kissed her hand. "I fear we'll have to get a new marriage license. Ours must be a trifle out of date." He slipped an arm about her and hugged her close. "Well, there's a reason to set about getting my new identity at once. Where shall we begin?"

THE BEST OF REGENCY ROMANCES

AN IMPROPER COMPANION (2691, $3.95)
by Karla Hocker

At the closing of Miss Venable's Seminary for Young Ladies school, mistress Kate Elliott welcomed the invitation to be Liza Ashcroft's chaperone for the Season at Bath. Little did she know that Miss Ashcroft's father, the handsome widower Damien Ashcroft would also enter her life. And not as a passive bystander or dutiful dad.

WAGER ON LOVE (2693, $2.95)
by Prudence Martin

Only a rogue like Nicholas Ruxart would choose a bride on the basis of a careless wager. And only a rakehell like Nicholas would then fall in love with his betrothed's grey-eyed sister! The cynical viscount had always thought one blushing miss would suit as well as another, but the unattainable Jane Sommers soon proved him wrong.

LOVE AND FOLLY (2715, $3.95)
by Sheila Simonson

To the dismay of her more sensible twin Margaret, Lady Jean proceeded to fall hopelessly in love with the silver-tongued, seditious poet, Owen Davies—and catapult her entire family into social ruin . . . Margaret was used to gentlemen falling in love with vivacious Jean rather than with her—even the handsome Johnny Dyott whom she secretly adored. And when Jean's foolishness led her into the arms of the notorious Owen Davies, Margaret knew she could count on Dyott to avert scandal. What she didn't know, however was that her sweet sensibility was exerting a charm all its own.

Available wherever paperbacks are sold, or order direct from the Publisher. Send cover price plus 50¢ per copy for mailing and handling to Zebra Books, Dept. 2930, 475 Park Avenue South, New York, N.Y. 10016. Residents of New York, New Jersey and Pennsylvania must include sales tax. DO NOT SEND CASH.

The new Zebra Regency Romance logo that you see on the cover is a photograph of an actual regency "tuzzy-muzzy." The fashionable regency lady often wore a tuzzy-muzzy tied with a satin or velvet riband around her wrist to carry a fragrant nosegay. Usually made of gold or silver, tuzzy-muzzies varied in design from the elegantly simple to the exquisitely ornate. The Zebra Regency Romance tuzzy-muzzy is made of alabaster with a silver filigree edging.

THE HOUR OF PASSION

She looked up into eyes where desire no longer merely smoldered. It had fanned into full flame and now burned with a passion that sent heat coursing through her. He pulled her against himself and held her tightly as his mouth found hers.

He groaned and pushed her away. "My God, Andrea, you don't know what you're doing to me."

"I do know. The same thing you're doing to me. I want you, Richard."

"You don't fully understand. You couldn't."

She found one end of his neckcloth and gave it a tug. It came loose in her fingers and she unwound it. "I do understand. I was raised very differently from you. Where I come from, a woman is as free as a man to express her—her love."

She dropped the cravat and went to work on his shirt. He stood stock-still, staring at her. A slight smile played about the corners of her mouth. "Doesn't your door have a key?" she asked.

Without a word, he went to lock the door.

Then he walked slowly toward her.